The Spring

Kerstin Ekman

Forthcoming titles from Norvik Press

Kerstin Ekman: *The Angel House* (translated by Sarah Death) (spring 2002)
Kerstin Ekman: *City of Light* (translated by Linda Schenck) (spring 2003)

Some other books from Norvik Press

Kerstin Ekman: *Witches' Rings* (translated by Linda Schenck)
Silvester Mazzarella (ed. and trans.): *The Poet who Created Herself. Selected Letters of Edith Södergran*
Victoria Benedictsson: *Money* (translated by Sarah Death)
Fredrika Bremer: *The Colonel's Family* (translated by Sarah Death)
Selma Lagerlöf: *The Löwensköld Ring* (translated by Linda Schenck)
P. C. Jersild: *A Living Soul* (translated by Rika Lesser)
Hjalmar Söderberg: *Short Stories* (translated by Carl Lofmark)
Robin Fulton (ed. and trans.): *Five Swedish Poets*
Gunnar Ekelöf: *Modus Vivendi* (edited and translated by Erik Thygesen)
Gunilla Anderman (ed.): *New Swedish Plays*
Christopher Moseley (ed.): *From Baltic Shores*
Jens Bjørneboe: *Moment of Freedom* (translated by Esther Greenleaf Mürer)
Jens Bjørneboe: *Powderhouse* (translated by Esther Greenleaf Mürer)
Jens Bjørneboe: *The Silence* (translated by Esther Greenleaf Mürer)
Suzanne Brøgger: *A Fighting Pig's Too Tough to Eat* (translated by Marina Allemano)
Janet Garton (ed.): *Contemporary Norwegian Women's Writing*
Svend Åge Madsen: *Days with Diam* (translated by W. Glyn Jones)
Kjell Askildsen: *A Sudden Liberating Thought* (translated by Sverre Lyngstad)
Jørgen-Frantz Jacobsen: *Barbara* (translated by George Johnston)
Johan Borgen: *The Scapegoat* (translated by Elizabeth Rokkan)
Jens Bjørneboe: *The Sharks* (translated by Esther Greenleaf Mürer)
Camilla Collett: *The District Governor's Daughters* (translated by Kirsten Seaver)
Annegret Heitmann (ed.): *No Man's Land. An Anthology of Modern Danish Women's Literature*

Aspects of Modern Swedish Literature (revised edition, ed. Irene Scobbie)
A Century of Swedish Narrative (ed. Sarah Death and Helena Forsås-Scott)
Michael Robinson: *Studies in Strindberg*
Anglo-Scandinavian Cross-Currents (ed. Inga-Stina Ewbank, Olav Lausand and Bjørn Tysdahl)
Nordic Letters 1870-1910 (ed. Michael Robinson and Janet Garton)

The Spring

Kerstin Ekman

Translated from the Swedish
by
Linda Schenck

Norvik Press
2001

Originally published in Swedish under the title of *Springkällan* (1976)
© Kerstin Ekman.

This translation © 2001 Linda Schenck.

The Translator asserts her moral right to be identified as the Translator of the work in relation to all such rights as are granted by the Translator to the publisher under the terms and conditions of their Agreement.

A catalogue record for this book is available from the British Library.
ISBN 1 870041 47 X
First published 2001

Norvik Press gratefully acknowledges the financial assistance given by
The Swedish Institute for the translation of this book.

Norvik Press was established in 1984 with financial support from the University of East Anglia, the Danish Ministry for Cultural Affairs, the Norwegian Cultural Department and the Swedish Institute.

Managing Editors: Janet Garton and Michael Robinson.

Printed in Great Britain by Page Bros. (Norwich) Ltd, Norwich, UK.

B elow the ridge is an ancient spring that never runs dry. In the old days it formed a beautiful arc when it rose up in the damp, wooded park where the Salvation Army band played, and people called it Heavenside Spring. Now it's been filled with stones.

In the old days there were dances at Heavenside Spring. The banks of the spring were bedecked with birch sprigs at midsummer and trimmed with ribbons for other festivities. Superstitions clung to the place. People would drink the water on Trinity Eve to be cured of some ill. They'd tie their complaints to coins and buttons and toss them into the spring: the aching joints that had bent them double and the gnarled fingertips, swollen and yellow with pus, the rashes that broke out like licking flames and hurt them all over, the coughs, the earaches that woke them up in tears at night, galloping consumption, rickets that left them with bowed backs, inflammations and bunions, sores on old, slow-healing limbs, infected from not being cared for, shameful, thick excretions and scrofula that only got worse in their dusty, dirty homes and made the children's eyes go bleary and their throats sore.

The spring wasn't defiled by having to absorb all this. It remained clean and uncontaminated and never dried up. They fetched their water there when the wells in the yards went dry or when they began to reek late in summer and were sealed shut because they spread epidemics.

Even so, in the end, Heavenside Spring was covered with a boulder and no one knows why.

One night in January 1910 two women were having coffee in the basement of the building at number 60 Hovlunda Road. They were sitting in front of a bread oven, the fire roaring behind the iron grating. Rye bread dough was rising on the table, where the ceiling lamp had been pulled down low. All the corners of the room were dark and the only visible parts of Frida Eriksson were her shawl and her old canvas shoes, the ones she wore when she went out washing.

Both women needed that coffee. Tora Otter was going to be up baking until dawn and needed it to stay awake. Frida needed it to fall asleep. Her body was all aches and pains from a week in laundry rooms; she often had trouble falling asleep on Friday nights. Usually the coffee they drank was made from old grounds, diluted and reheated time after time, pale brown and acidic. Tonight's coffee, though, was strong and fresh. They blew on it and mumbled over it, their fingers shifting under the hot saucers they drank from. They inhaled the coffee through sugar cubes that dissolved slowly between their lips.

When Tora was done she went upstairs to get some sweet butter. The boys were asleep and she tucked the knitted covers under their chins, and checked the tiled stove. By the time she got back down and raised the lamp, Frida had fallen asleep in her chair. Her hands were folded under her apron, she was pale and she didn't have her teeth in. Her eyelids were large and translucent. When they were closed you could barely tell who she was. Tora touched her shoulder gently.

'I've got the butter,' she said.

Frida awoke. She buttered her index finger and then used it to grease her other hand, extending her thumb to stretch the skin between her thumb and index finger. Her skin was dried out from all the water. It was ashen and cracked, the cracks running so deep in her thin skin they looked like knife slashes, shiny and bright red. She buttered that spot on both hands, as well as the cracks by the bottom knuckle of her index fingers. Then she removed a ball of wool from her apron pocket and wrapped her hands in yarn. Tora helped her to tie the ends.

'It eases the pain,' said Frida.

Tora opened the hot grate with a stick and fuelled the fire. She opened the damper a little. Then she washed her hands in a basin she had set on a wooden box under the window, drying them thoroughly so they wouldn't get sticky when she punched down the warm dough. The oven roared and Frida was warm as toast in her corner.

'My, that baking oven is nice and hot,' she said. 'I'd sit here all night if I could.'

'Oh do, please. I could use the company.'

'Don't think I'd be much company, actually. I'm falling asleep as it is.'

'Stay 'til I've kneaded the dough at least, and we'll have another cup. I've got some cake from the café.'

This time they reheated the coffee and drank it from cups, dunking slices of yesterday's buns from the Cosmopolitan Café. Frida just barely managed to set the cup down before falling asleep again.

'Best you go on up to bed,' said Tora. 'I'll walk you up, I need to look in on the boys anyway.'

She took Frida by her bony elbow and they walked the long,

dark, familiar basement corridor without a lamp. When they got to the basement door they could hear clattering on the stairs, male voices and heavy footsteps. They stood still in the dark behind the door until they heard the last man leave and the door shut behind him.

'They're gone,' said Tora. 'You get up to bed now.'

A thick iron pipe, clamped down at intervals, extended from the laundry room wall and ran all the way to the cement trough with the brass tap. All she had to do was turn it on. In the old days, she had to make ten trips to the well with buckets hanging from a shoulder yoke just to fill the soaking tubs. Now all she had to do was turn the water on. But she had no idea where it came from.

Frida had been doing other people's laundry all her married life. Now she was forty-five. To begin with she had worked along the scrubbing jetty by the lake. They had dragged the carts full of laundry all the way out there. The washerwomen lined up along the jetty on their knees and scrubbed the clothes clean. Frida remembered how the sheets would slap her right in the face before she had mastered the technique of wringing them out. Ladies who sent their laundry out were fussy, and returned it to be done again if they weren't satisfied. You learned to fold the sheets just so, and to wring them out just hard enough and fast enough, one end in each direction. The washerwomen would cuss and swear to keep warm and cheerful. The hot, soaked sheets steamed when they hit the water, and the cold air steamed, too, when their hot breath struck it. It was cold in December and still cold in March. Frida had been intimidated by the others. But today no one was the least bit afraid of her. Everything was different. The scents, the curses, the water rushing clear and clean out of the brass tap.

It was drinking water, of course. She had heard they had a water closet up at the merchant's, and that it, too, used pure drinking

9

water. And still nobody could tell her where it came from.

Later, and for many years, she had washed at the laundry near the market square. A railwayman named Dahlgren had built a washing shed over the stream known as Trash Moat that ran through his property, dammed up the water and then charged for the use of his building. She remembered when Trash Moat really was a stream and the old men sat down there fishing for perch. In those days it ran smoothly and steadily through town, taken for granted. Now it smelled foul and had been covered over in some places. The water was brown. It absorbed impurities and was polluted. In the end, no one could use Dahlgren's laundry shed. The water discoloured the washing and the housewives complained.

That was the last straw, said the people in the know on community issues, and began a campaign for a waterworks and a waste water system. It took four years to wage. Frida didn't understand: one side wanted the waste water to run into Lake Vallmaren, the other into Moth Lake. Their arguments were published in the papers. Sterkell, the former railway engineer, resigned from the town council. He had been for Lake Vallmaren, but the Moth Lake proposal had won the day and there was a vote of no confidence against him. The water tower was constructed, designed to resemble the famed campanile in Venice. It was located right out at Louse Point, where Frida grew up. Wärnström, the factory owner, sold the town the land for the waterworks, the reservoir was built on land sold by Lindh, the merchant. There was a ceremony in the market square when the water system was inaugurated, and the fire department tested the hoses. Sterkell refused to attend. Railway Director J.A. Ström spoke from the rostrum, expressing the community's gratitude both to merchant Lindh for his zealous efforts to resolve the water issue, so vital to the community, and to Wärnström the factory owner for his donation of one thousand kronor to provide granite ornaments for the water tower. The railwaymen's brass octet played, and the fire chief demonstrated water gushing out of a hose. Still, Frida didn't know who to ask. Normally, she paid no attention to community issues, but she had carried so much water in her day that she couldn't help wondering. She had stood over enough dried up wells and contaminated and reeking wells, that she wanted to know: where did this water come from?

Walking home from the merchant's, where she had been soaking laundry that day, she realized she could ask Konrad. The little ones were still playing in the courtyard despite the late hour, and Dagmar, who was nearly grown up, had already gone downstairs to look after the Otter boys, as she always did on the nights Tora was baking. Konrad was the only one at home and he was sitting as she always found him, wasting her good lamp oil at the kitchen table with a book under his nose. Frida walked over and tilted the cover until she could see the title: *Woman.*

'What's that?'

'Bebel's *Woman*,' said Konrad. Although he didn't look up, his voice had a sharp edge. 'It's not what the name sounds like, don't worry. Ebon Johansson lent me it.'

'Then it must be socialism,' said Frida.

He was silent, making a note in the black binder in front of him. Sometimes she would look through what he had been writing down from his books, but it was mostly things she didn't understand, and he probably didn't either. He was just sixteen and had been allowed to come back to his apprenticeship at the Cosmopolitan Café after Tora had beseeched the owner on his behalf. In August, when the general strike had been on, he had written STRICKE in meringue on the café window and walked out.

11

He told his employer, the widow Göhlin, he was joining the strike. Now Frida was afraid he would lose the job once and for all. He started at six in the morning but never went to bed until late.

The water was simmering on the stove and she started to mix in the rye meal.

'At the merchant's they have running water,' she said. 'All you have to do is turn the tap.'

'Lucky them,' said Konrad, without looking up from his book.

'Do you know where it comes from?' she asked.

'The water?'

'Mm hmm.'

He shut *Woman*.

'Don't you know? They pump it up out by Moth Shack.They built a pumping station out there.'

'So it'll run dry one day, then?'

'It's groundwater,' said Konrad.

She didn't know what that meant. Konrad paced the length of the rag runner between the hall door and the door to the front room, telling her about the water running below them all over the world and Frida, who was stirring the porridge with her back to him, didn't know what to think. He said it filled every crack and cranny on earth. It ran through the loose layers of earth and through the sand and gravel and forced its way into whatever it could trickle through.

'Sounds like you know just what it looks like down under the ground, son,' she smiled. But he paid no attention and just went on and on telling her about the water that would not be stopped either by diabase or gabbro, about how it flowed in underground streams and how it rushed and clucked into the hollows of the mountains when it rained. The underground water landscape was an image, an inverted mirror image of the above-ground landscape with its hills and dales and deep recesses. The groundwater, like all other things, strove to achieve equilibrium, Konrad told her, and when the balance between the pressure of the water and the pressure of the above-ground air had been reached, the water table stabilized. In fissures and basins it was near the surface of the land, and sometimes even exposed. That was what made virgin springs.

'In the park below the ridge,' thought Frida. 'Where the Salvation Army band plays.' The porridge had thickened now and just needed to simmer. She would call David and Anna in. Konrad was still going on about hydrostatic and artesian pressure. She had stopped listening a while back.

'Do you know why they blocked up Heavenside Spring?' she asked. But he'd never even heard of it.

The next Monday she went to the Lindh manor to wash. There were bits of dirt floating around in the soaking water, and it smelled foul when she lifted out the clothes. That didn't usually bother her, although it had when she first started, and every time she was in the family way. The odour was fouler in the old days, too, when people only sent their washing out twice a year. Ruth was standing by the boiler, fishing out merchant Lindh's undergarments with a laundry rod. They floated atop the filmy water like big white bubbles.

'Pick them up with your hands,' Frida said. 'You'll just drop them otherwise.'

She didn't consider Ruth much help. Only sixteen, she was the youngest staff member in the Lindh kitchen. She talked a blue streak every time Frida came to do the washing, because up in the kitchen she never got a word in edgewise.

'Can you believe Lindh's worn fourteen different sets of underwear since we washed last?' she babbled. 'That doesn't seem healthy. More than a dozen since September. Wonder if he has another dozen in his closet? Just look at these! They barely look used! Oh, well, here's one little tiny brown spot anyway. He doesn't wipe himself properly. Here Frida, catch!'

But Ruth dropped them and her rod went flying along the floor. It wasn't too heavy but it landed on Frida's feet and that hurt. She had her canvas shoes on. She only wore them for washing and had made holes in the cloth to accommodate her bunions. Unless something like this happened she could stand all day on the wooden slats of a laundry room floor with almost no discomfort at all.

They had the latest scrubbing boards, lined with corrugated zinc, and they scrubbed the dirty clothes in soapy water. They began with merchant Lindh's underclothes and nightshirts, which were sometimes spotted with chocolate.

'He likes his cocoa at bedtime,' said Ruth. 'Mixes it with a sleeping potion. Lillibeth is always saying she never sleeps at all, though I s'pose she must.'

She called Alexander Lindh 'the merchant' even down here in the basement, but she called his married daughter 'Lillibeth' and she just referred to the housekeeper as 'the witch'.

'Watch your mouth,' Frida warned her.

'Aw, nobody ever comes down here. You know why there are so many monthly towels this time? Doctor Hubendick had to operate on the witch. Know what he found? A bottle of violet scented Dralle's *Illusion*. The one she always wears when she goes out.'

'Shush,' said Frida. 'Whereabouts?'

'Down *there*, of course. She had stuck it up, you know, and it went too far in and just vanished.'

'You spread so much dirty gossip you'll be sorry one fine day,' said Frida. 'Just think if anybody heard you. People've always told tales about spinsters. You just hush now.'

'Have it your way,' said Ruth. 'But I know it's true cos the housemaid told Margit.'

That quieted her for long enough to get the serving aprons scrubbed. At nine the kitchen maid called down the stairs that they should come up for coffee, and Frida took her burlap apron off and let down her skirt; she'd pinned it up out of her way. She changed her shoes and retied her head scarf. Still, she was embarrassed to be sitting up there in an old, patched dress that was wet around the middle, with no teeth and worn-down shoes. The others had already had their coffee, of course. Frida dunked a slice of coffee cake in hers and mostly stared down into her cup. Ruth, too, was quiet as a mouse up here. The housemaid ran here and there, the ties of the long cleaning apron she was wearing over her black uniform flying behind her. She filled carafes with water and washed dirty glasses. The housekeeper was sitting at the fall-front chiffonier in the room behind the kitchen doing the accounts. The merchant's kitchen smelled of pickling vinegar and spices because the cook was marinating herring, and the marinade was cooling by the open window.

When they got back down the fire had died under the heating pot and Frida rekindled it while Ruth used the big tin scoop to transfer the still hot water to the wooden tubs. They started scrubbing the kitchen towels, which were very stained. Ruth's tongue was running away with her again. She said Lillibeth Iversen-Lindh never wore anything but white blouses.

'They can get all kinds of ideas into their heads,' she said. 'There's no stopping them. She wants a clean one every single day and the housemaid stands there ironing them in the service passage. You should just see the cuffs. Can't be washed in anything but lukewarm water with soap flakes. I'll tell you Frida, you'll never see diviner. They don't put that kind of thing in with the laundry. Not to mention her underwear. Almost nothing but lace. And her nightgowns. She could wear them to balls if she wanted. She never lets *him* in, though, so I don't really see what good they do her. I mean it, not one single night.'

'What do you know about that?'

'Well, everybody in the house knows all about it even though they pretend not to. Not one single night since they got married. And her so much in love the merchant had to give them his blessing, even though Iversen didn't have a penny to his name.'

'But he's an engineer,' said Frida.

'Engineer! Not likely. He just calls himself that. He's no more engineer than Lame Lasse. He comes from Kristiania, and that's in Norway, and his mother sold fish at the market there.'

'Now there's another lie. You don't know what you're talking about. She had a shop.'

'A fishmonger's.'

Ruth was scrubbing towels the cook had wrapped meat in to pound it. The splotches of blood were persistent, even when the towels had been soaked for a long time.

'Anyway,' said Ruth, 'he went to her room the night they got married, but not one single time since then. And that was more than ten years ago.'

They were working at a ledge in front of the window facing the street. Sometimes feet would pass by. If the windows weren't too steamy from the kettles, they could see people crossing the station yard.

'There goes Ebon Johansson,' said Ruth. 'Didn't know he was back. Well, he can't possibly expect to get a job here after organizing that strike. The witch said he could have been arrested for incitement to riot and ended up in Svartsjö Prison. Did you know Tora Otter, who bakes for Göhlin's, went walking out with him before she got married?'

'She's your aunt, too,' Frida said sharply.

'Is not. Not a blood aunt anyway. My aunt Stella is married to her brother Rickard, but they say he's not her real brother, either. She waited tables at the Railway Hotel and had a purple walking suit and a hat with a feather. And then she had two out of wedlock kids. In the end she married a fellow from Gothenburg and he died and she borrowed money from Mademoiselle Winlöf, the one who used to own the Railway Hotel. And she was just the same herself when she was young. Though she never had any kids because the lying-in woman took care of it. And nowadays Tora Otter doesn't even have any Sunday clothes.'

'Rubbish,' said Frida. But it was true. She knew Tora didn't own a change of clothes.

'Your talk is just about as foolish as you are,' she said. 'Put some elbow grease into it now. We've still got all the sheets to do.'

Tuesday they becked, with lye baths. Lame Lasse, the merchant's handyman, lit the fire under the pot about five in the morning to heat the water. When Frida arrived just after six it wasn't quite boiling yet. Together they hoisted the big washtub onto its stand, Lame Lasse on one side and she and Ruth on the other. That was getting difficult, too. There were lots of things she used not to give a thought to that felt hard to do now. She looked at Ruth who had big muscles on her rough, red upper arms and realized that twenty or thirty years earlier she had looked that way herself. Now there

17

were mainly gnarls and ligaments under her skin. Sometimes she didn't like herself. Not only when she was out in public and embarrassed about her clothes and having no teeth. She could feel it sometimes when she was alone. That was new. Before, she hadn't thought that way at all.

The water was boiling. The housekeeper had given Ruth three tins of lye powder, saying they should dissolve it in the water and then scoop the water over the clothes.

'In the old days we'd put in a bag of birch wood ash,' Frida said. 'It worked pretty well.' The strong lye scared her a little. I'm losing my nerve, she thought. Frightened of lifting heavy things, afraid of getting lye in my eyes. And being seen in public. For washing, she got her meals and one krona a day, so she had no choice but to eat in the merchant's kitchen. On Tuesdays there was meat soup with dumplings for dinner. It was made from stock with parsnips and onions in it, and thin slanted slices of carrot, but the vegetables were cooked so soft she could mash them between her gums. The meat posed a bigger problem. The cook had made the dumplings heavy, and spiced with bitter almond. In the upstairs dining room all they got was consommé, and Frida wondered how they got full. But they had cold boiled tongue and vegetables in aspic as well, baby veal chops with peas and sautéed rice, and crème caramel for afters. The cook had made rice pudding with fruit sauce for downstairs. Frida remembered once when she'd been given a whole tray of pudding to take home, yellow with egg and spotted with soft raisins. Not this time though. They ate it all. Lame Lasse ate like a horse, and Ruth did quite well herself.

When they got down after dinner they set another washtub under the drain on the big tub, and Frida withdrew the wooden plug she had wrapped in a rag to keep it from leaking. The cooled lye ran out, yellow and thick. They scooped it back into the heating pot, and when it ran faster than they could scoop Frida put the plug back in so no lye would be lost. Ruth was silent now. She ran, her clogs clattering, between tub and hearth, pouring scoop after scoop. She'd wrapped the handle of the scoop in a towel so she wouldn't burn herself. Her lower arms were already blotchy from the lye.

'You should be more careful,' Frida warned her. At the same time, she remembered what she had been like. When you were young you thought your body was indestructible. You weren't afraid of anything. Not of work, at any rate. She tried to keep pace with Ruth when they scooped the water back into the heating pot, but she couldn't. The soles of her feet were aching from having stood so long and walked so much. But her bunions weren't bothering her thanks to the holes she had cut in her canvas shoes.

Lame Lasse came down and tried to get them gossiping, but they hardly answered. Frida had to sit down on the laundry ledge while they waited for the lye water to boil again. There were still two tubs of soaked washing to be becked separately, at the end. One contained monthly towels, and Ruth was scrubbing at them. The other one was the handkerchiefs.

'Is it your back?'

'No.'

Her feet hurt most, but she could probably have put up with that. The thing was that she couldn't make herself start on the handkerchiefs. The dried mucus had gone all slimy from soaking and came away between your fingers when you were scrubbing. She just couldn't. What on earth was wrong with her? She only had to peek in the direction of Ruth's tub where the blackened blood in the towels dissolved in the water, colouring it rusty brown, and she gagged.

She went over and lifted the wooden top on the heating pot. The water was nearly boiling.

19

'I'll start scooping,' she said. 'You can do the handkerchiefs.'
That was the first time she tried to get out of something.

By the twelfth and final time they scooped the lye bath back into the tubs it was six in the evening. The laundry room was all steamy. Sometimes they couldn't even see one another from the other side of the washing tub as they scooped the hot lye, now slippery and brown as it oozed through the clothing. At last Frida pulled the plug and let it run out, gurgling down the drain, and they both stood there watching it go. Ruth said: 'Well, that's that,' and Frida had to smile because she hadn't been talkative at all that afternoon.

'I think it took a whole batch of washing to quiet you down,' she said. They put on one last tub of water to heat while they went upstairs for supper, and poured it over the clothes before they packed it in for the night. They'd do the rinsing in the lake out at Gertrudsborg, where the merchant's elderly wife lived, and hang the washing there as well. Frida hadn't given a thought all day to whether it would be good drying weather, but when she walked home the evening was still, and the air bitterly cold.

On the Tuesday morning she wrung out the washing and she and Ruth loaded it into baskets and started carrying them upstairs to put them in the trap that had been sent from Gertrudsborg. The farm hand who had driven it went straight over to the third class dining room of the railway hotel for a couple of beers or a glass of calabria; whatever it was, he was bow-legged when he came back.

'Make sure those baskets get out there soon,' said Frida. 'We've got a lot of rinsing to do today.'

'Why are washerwomen always so crabby?' asked the hand. 'Every single one.'

He pinched Ruth's backside when she had to go up the steps in front of him, dragging a basket of laundry. She grabbed a wet pillowcase and swung it at him, laughing and shouting so loud Frida had to tell her off. She was relieved when they had finally finished loading the trap and it bumped away up the steep hill towards the water tower and the school.

The water was cold. They were on their knees on the sagging jetty behind Gertrudsborg, beating the laundry on corrugated boards. Sometimes the jetty sagged so low their knees were submerged.

'Seems to me they could have sent Gunhild out,' said Ruth. 'She's not all that busy. Her only job is to do a little cooking for the merchant's wife, and that woman barely eats a bite; she lives on port wine. She hardly ever comes into town, either. She won't spend the night in Lindh's town house. Not for anything.'

Ruth was a novice, which was obvious when she got to folding the sheets. The little packets kept coming undone when she tried to turn them over to beat the other side, and she'd have to refold. But she certainly talked ten to the dozen. Frida let her ramble on; at least it took her mind off things.

'She was lucky to get taken on out here. Gunhild, I mean. She was in the family way and would've been out of a job altogether, except nothing came of it. Even so, they'll never have her as a housemaid again. Not in town.'

'Nothing came of it?' asked Frida.

'Nope, God only knows how some people fix it. Same thing happened to Ebba Julin, though they said she strangled it. Don't ask me.'

'You mean Ebba Karlsson, don't you? Who married the brewer?'

'That's right. He spent every single evening at the Railway

21

Hotel where she waited tables. He was crazy about her. And in the end she promised to marry him if she got a two-bedroom flat and a housemaid. Julin would have promised her the earth, you know, he was head over heels in love with her, though he was over sixty. Well, Ebba's no spring chicken herself, she's at least thirty but she doesn't look it since she's never had kids. Still, she was always loose, always had some man around before she married the brewer. You wouldn't know it now, though, the way she goes down to the shop with her hair curled and a brooch on her blouse, so high and mighty she has to inspect every single item, and sends back the milk, complaining it tastes of paraffin oil, and the butter, 'cause she says it smells funny. And Fru Björk doesn't say a word because they're steady customers. Mind you everything from there *does* smell of paraffin oil, Ebba's not the only one who thinks so. Fru Björk doesn't manage a very tidy shop, but they do keep the prices down. And Björk himself never lifts a finger. He had to quit Wilhelmsson's after his broken leg that never mended. Doctor Hubendick operated because the bone was sticking out all funny, and the poor man whinged and moaned and finally fainted dead away when they carried him in. But the incision got full of pus and never healed up right and now he has gangrene and sits there in the shop, winding and unwinding his bandages. Personally, I wouldn't buy milk there if you paid me. Oh, Frida, look how swollen your hands are getting! You're not allergic to water all of a sudden, are you? Maybe it's too cold, after all.'

'I don't know about that,' said Frida. 'I think it's my joints.'

'Well, I wish she'd call us in for coffee now, myself,' said Ruth. 'It would do me the world of good, even though she makes it so weak.'

She was banging the board so hard she was splashing. Suddenly Frida was so tired she told her to shush.

'I don't know how you can go on like that. Give me some peace.'

Actually, she was remembering something from long ago, although only vaguely, and strangely enough it was the water splashing against her arms that brought the memory to the surface. She recalled the scent of a lake, the glitter of water, a much stronger smell than this one, and blue water, not these black icy cold patches of open water between crusted chunks of ice. They'd been working in a line along the jetty, scrubbing and exchanging gossip and memories and looking forward to the aroma of coffee. Everything about those days was different. Girls of Ruth's age kept quiet, and knew to do so without being told. Everyone was always cheerful. Even in the winter, as she remembered it anyway. In those days they did the washing in kettles over an open fire nearby and lifted the hot clothes right from the kettles into the open water between iced-over parts, so heat from the things they were washing made the freezing water bearable. Your body, that indestructible strong body you never gave so much as a thought — it never got tired. At least not before evening. 'It was as if work didn't wear you out,' she thought, 'not in those days.'

Later, you found yourself getting tired and wondering how long you'd last. She couldn't say when it had begun. She simply didn't remember.

'If you didn't talk so much,' she said to Ruth, 'just did your job and kept your mouth shut, you might get to stay on at the merchant's. There's lots to learn in a kitchen like theirs. You've been a lucky girl. Don't take your situation for granted. Just look at my Eriksson who's out of a job now for joining that strike. And nobody knows what's going to happen.'

Instantly, though, she regretted telling her troubles to Ruth, knowing she'd spread it around.

They walked into town when they were done for the day. All the rinsing was finished but for a basket of towels, and on Thursday they'd start hanging it out to dry.

They stretched the clothesline across the field behind the kitchen garden at Gertrudsborg. The ground was frozen hard and there was only a little snow, so it was very difficult getting the poles to stay up. It was already eight o'clock by the time they started bringing out the baskets of washing. They began with the sheets which they hung folded double. They looked nice and white, but the winter sun couldn't be counted on to bleach them much more. The sheets flapped heavily when the wind picked up. In the upstairs bedroom window they glimpsed a face peeping out between the curtains, but pretended not to notice, hanging up the towels with the clothes pegs from the bags around their waists. Old Fru Lindh didn't often get to see any life from her window. Next they started on the underwear, and it didn't take long before fourteen pairs of the merchant's underpants were flapping in an unbroken row. The cold got to them, though, and they were soon frozen, and hung stiff and rigid on the line.

This was better than Wednesday's monotonous scrubbing. All they had left was that one last basket of towels, and then they'd be done sticking their hands down into that cold water. Frida felt her strength return and her anxiety diminish. When they were having their eleven o'clock coffee they looked out the kitchen window at the leafless apple tree with redpolls jumping from branch to branch. There was a thin layer of ice, shiny deep black over what had been the open water. She tried to think about sun and splashing water and loud, cheerful voices along a laundry jetty. But now it had slipped so far away she couldn't find it. Some memories were fragile and dissipated if you touched them too much. Shame and pain, on the other hand, just burned deeper and deeper scars in your memory. She couldn't understand why it had to be that way.

On Friday they used the mangle in the mangling shed behind the railway barracks. It was an old wooden shed with thin walls, and passers-by on the street could readily hear the slamming of the wooden roller against the sides, and the slow squeal of the marble slab. The shed smelt musty and slightly unpleasant, so it was nice to stand and work with the big sheets, with their scent of sun and fresh air. But Ruth was impossible. She was so busy talking she'd forget she was supposed to be stretching and pulling the sheets, and once she let go so suddenly Frida stumbled back against the wall and almost fell down. She was frightened to death of hurting herself, and shouted at Ruth.

She kept noticing how much more anxious than usual she was. Scared she'd fall down and hurt herself, scared her hand would get caught between the mangle and the rollers. And she had no patience at all with that girl. When she rolled a sheet sloppily or too loosely so the sheet creased and was mangled full of hard folds and impossible wrinkles, Frida screamed at her again, although it was no use. When she slammed the rollers down hard on the slab, Ruth finally realized that she was in a foul temper and actually shut up while she worked the pedal of the clanking mangle.

Working when you're exhausted and irritable, unable to think of anything but how to get finished, tends to turn out to be a waste of time, as Frida discovered when at last they got down to the big linen tablecloths. They went on the rollers crooked and came out of the mangle all wrong. Two of the biggest cloths with the *fleur de lis* pattern came out creased instead of shiny, and the creases were so deep Frida had no alternative but to soak them again and leave them to dry overnight.

'I'll come back up early tomorrow morning,' she said to Ruth. 'There's nothing else for it.'

They folded the table napkins and mangled them last, laying them in alternate rows along the mangling slab and running the roller over them. Then they were done, except that they had to make three trips with the baskets between them up to the Lindh manor. The housekeeper counted each piece, and naturally noticed the two missing tablecloths.

'I've got to soak them and hang them out to dry again.'

'Not here, you don't.'

The Lindhs' house had a garden behind it, done up like a miniature of the park behind the estate. It would be inconceivable to put up a clothesline between the cypresses and the plaster goddesses, there was no question about it.

'I'll hang them at home,' said Frida, 'and go over and mangle them in the morning.'

'And they'll be on your responsibility,' the housekeeper responded. Frida gave Ruth a look.

When she got home to number 60 Hovlunda Road that evening she ran a line from the hook on the woodshed to the elm in the courtyard. She soaked the merchant's tablecloths under the pump in the yard, and hung them out to dry. She knew they'd still be there when she came downstairs the next morning.

Upstairs in the flat, the younger children had already fallen asleep in the pulled-out kitchen settee. She hadn't seen them all day and didn't know if they'd had supper. Dagmar had promised to keep an eye on them and give them a meal, but she had her hands full with the extra sewing they'd taken on and Frida didn't know how much she actually looked after them. Now she was already down in Tora Otter's flat watching her boys while Tora was in the basement, baking the loaves she sold at the market.

She could see right away that Eriksson wasn't home, and Konrad was reading the newspaper at the kitchen table.

'Where's Father, then?' she said.

Konrad gave her a strange look. She had to ask him again.

'He's gone to Norrköping,' he said.

'Gone?'

'Yeah, to find work. He's not going to get any here.'

'But the rent,' she said. 'We'll be evicted.'

Konrad sat silently, ostensibly reading the paper but she could see that his eyes were fixed on one spot.

'We've got to have twelve kronor for this month's rent.'

'He said he'd send money from Norrköping as soon as he got work. Down at the docks or something. At least he thought he'd be able to get a job there.'

She sat down on the chair across from Konrad and began to think. Dagmar was paid in loaves of bread for the four nights a week she looked after Tora's boys. Konrad didn't get much at the Cosmopolitan, as he was just an apprentice. She usually paid the rent with his wages. But now they had been without Eriksson's money for so long. Until last summer he used to get twenty kronor in his pay packet. Two went to the health service and his union dues. She would usually get at least fifteen from him to feed the family. She earned one krona a day, sometimes one fifty, doing washing and cleaning in town. That would go to paraffin oil for the lamps and clothes and shoe repairs. And they had to have wood. Fuel money and rent money.

Her kids still scavenged the streets for bones and scrap metal. She didn't have the heart to tell them how little it meant — so little that there was almost no point at all when the rent wasn't paid. Not to mention the wood.

'He can't do this to us.'

'He's doing it to get a job and send you money,' said Konrad. 'Don't you see?'

But it was as if she just couldn't take it in. He was gone. He'd left.

'There's no guaranteeing he'll get a job there, either. Maybe blacklisted means everywhere. You see what happens.'

'You were against the strike,' said Konrad, pulling the newspaper closer. 'That's it. And you're in a foul temper from doing other people's washing. As usual.'

She sat back down at the kitchen table and looked at her hands. Her knuckles were swollen and the skin covering them was taut and shiny. The skin on her palms, however, was wrinkled and grey from all the water and because she'd spent the day in the mangling shed they were all dried out and cracked, and the cracks were bright red again.

'Have you eaten?' she asked.

'Dagmar fixed our supper.'

She wasn't hungry herself, more like queasy. 'I'm not myself,' she thought. 'Konrad was right about that.' She got up and took a little skein of wool out of the top dresser drawer. She tried to look at her face in the mirror. But it was dark in the corner where the dresser was, and the mirror was old and blue-grey. She saw a dark oval. Her eyes and mouth were fuzzy. Just hollows and shadows. The face in the mirror was wreathed in the baby's bliss she'd hung around the frame. She tore it down and stuffed it in the top drawer, feeling how dusty and greasy it had grown.

'What're you doing, Mamma?' asked Konrad, sounding worried.

'Nothing. I'm going downstairs to see if Tora Otter has any sweet butter. I'll be back,' she said.

She was tired. Even when she woke up in the morning the fatigue was there, her body like a huge, heavy egg.

Tora Otter came at her with a comb full of lice and louse eggs and strands of Dagmar's hair. She'd found it on the dresser and Frida was ashamed. She ought to go through Dagmar's and Anna's hair every evening with a comb and a tray. But lately she'd been too tired. Now Tora gave their heads a deep drenching in sabadilla vinegar and then made them sit hooded in towels while it worked. Anna was crying because she'd got vinegar in her eyes. Dagmar was just acutely embarrassed. And Tora rushed around the kitchen grumbling aloud, lit a newspaper in the flue to kill the cockroaches and mopped up the worst of the mess on the kitchen table. She was more than ten years younger, she knew nothing about exhaustion. Not yet, Frida thought.

It was growing inside her, heavier and heavier. She'd just rest her eyes a moment. The instant before it extinguished her thoughts and her head hit the pillow, it was nice. It was the pleasantest inebriation she'd ever felt.

Yet she still couldn't sleep through the night. Before she needed to be, and earlier than anyone else in the whole house, she was wide awake, lying there with a dry mouth and aching eyes, unable to fall back asleep. Eriksson had written from Norrköping to say that he might get to join a longshoremen's collective. For the moment he was only getting odd jobs. But if they let him into the collective he'd be able to move the whole family to Norrköping. He wrote that he was sharing a room down by Salt Flats.

It was impossible to imagine what it would feel like to get on the train and leave town. She'd grown up here, worked here. Raised their first two children out at Louse Point where she, too, was born. Konrad and Dagmar had come into the world in old Hovlunda before the last of the shanties was pulled down, David and Anna were born here at number 60 Hovlunda Road. Her maternal grandmother's grave was at Valmsta and her mother was buried out by Moth Shack. Tora Otter lived here. Frida did laundry for people who knew her, and she knew that Konrad had a decent job. Dagmar, whose back was hunched and who was unable to do much more than turn and finish the collars on the shirts she took in and look after children, was paid by Tora in loaves of bread. Norrköping – who would want Dagmar in Norrköping? And Salt Flats. The very name terrified her. Hooligans and youth gangs. How would she dare send David and Anna to school in such a place?

She'd been lying there for a long time and ought to get up. But she stayed in bed, listening to slippers shuffling down the stairs and to the creaking of the pump. There was the clattering and the echoing of tin pails and buckets. Their old house sighed and wheezed in the wind, and the children's voices down in the courtyard were loud and high-pitched as the screeching of gulls.

But she was accustomed to these sounds and knew that the shuffling feet were usually old Fru Lundin's and the distant hammering was the cobbler in the basement and that when the pump squeaked a lot the children were playing there. The dog that barked for hours, hoarsely and without conviction, was the caretaker's, and she also knew that it was no use asking him to do anything about it.

But she couldn't imagine what it would be like to move to Norrköping.

When she went down for water she stood there peeling flakes of rust off the pump and sucking on them. It was a bad habit she had acquired and was unable to break. In the end she didn't let Konrad go down for the water even when he offered. She couldn't resist those rust flakes, she peeled and peeled and stuffed them into her mouth and found the taste salty like the taste of blood. In the end she had peeled the pump clean. Then she started peeling the coal bucket that stood rusting in a corner in the kitchen, and an iron pipe that ran from the draughty tile stove to the heater. Not even that brought the truth home to her. Not until she found herself standing at the wood-burning stove one morning staring at the jar on the mantelpiece, the one she had covered over with a jam wrapper.

PHOSPHOROUS POWDER
for rat extermination

She undid the string and opened the jar. The powder had absorbed moisture and gone sticky. She hardly ever used it nowadays because Konrad had nailed the tops of anchovy tins over the rat holes. She stuck a finger into the gob and felt the impulse to put it in her mouth. That was when she realized.

Her breasts were swollen and the skin covering them was taut. She had been feeling queasy, with felt a kind of fatigue that drained her of all will power. She hadn't had a monthly all autumn but she had blamed it on her tiredness. There had been times in the past when it had just not come. And she had been irregular for the last year, she had almost thought it was stopping and that once and for all she would be rid of the curse and all that anxiety.

But that wasn't it. She was pregnant. She knew when it had happened, too, and realized she must be more than four months gone. Yet her body showed no other signs beyond the slightly swollen breasts with their protruding veins. She thought that was the only place it could show, because her body had nothing else to give. She didn't like herself, this aching body that had no more nutrition nor pleasure left to give, this foetus that had been fighting with her for life for months now, in a body that had very little life to share.

She had to get rid of it. She didn't have to lie to herself this time and pretend to have a guilty conscience as she had in the past when other shameful ideas had crossed her mind. Conscience was a luxury affordable to those who had milk, bread, meat, potatoes, clothes, wood, paraffin oil and shoes. She, on the other hand, wore hers right down to the inner soles, just like her children, and cut layers of newspaper to put inside to keep the water from soaking through.

She had to get rid of it. No matter how. Her thoughts fixed on that brown tin, and the mantelpiece grew greasy with dust and soot and cooking fat. Her negligence was evident everywhere.

Her first thought was to soak it out. She would fill the zinc tub with hot water and settle into it, pouring hotter and hotter water over herself until she scalded it out like you scald the insects out of an old mattress.

But she was never alone in the kitchen, so that wouldn't work. Moreover, she didn't believe in it. Most of those things were nothing but girlish fantasies: jumping off the kitchen table time and again, or doing really heavy lifting. They didn't help. When she was very young and carrying her first child somebody had advised her to drink water with soft soap in it and then run as fast as she could. But gradually she learned that if it was meant to stay in, it stayed. Her first two children had been brought up by her mother, whom people had called Embankment Britta. They were grown up now.

People said the lying-in woman would sometimes help. But Frida had no idea how to go about it, whether you had to pay her money or if there were other ways to placate her. She knew, though, that the midwife would never see her until it was time for the birthing.

She had heard you could squirt up white spirits. But with what? These weren't plans, just things that came into her head when she lay sleepless in the early mornings. Soft soap, lye white spirits. Her head had barely got that far when her hand opened a drawer and seized something pointed. Slowly, she got used to the thought. At first it had felt so terrifying and loathsome that she had thought it would be impossible to carry out. But many women had done it before her. It could be done. She knew it. Preferably you should have help, but many women had done it by themselves. And it was the only thing that was sure to work. All the other remedies were just the imaginings and wishful dreams of poor girls. Soon she was unable to open any kitchen drawer without being reminded of it. Knitting needles, whisking sticks, larding skewers.

There was nothing worse than the brown glass jar, though. PHOSPHOROUS POWDER —for rat extermination. That would put an end to it all.

Early one Saturday morning not long after Twelfth Night a young man stepped down from a cart at the market square. It was not yet light, and while the horses were trampling down the snow that squeaked under the wagon wheels and axles, the boy wandered amongst the stalls, watching the stallkeepers banging in their poles and stretching their stiff canvases in the cold air. When day broke he walked down to the south end of the square, looking at the women who sold eggs, old hens for stewing and birch root whisks straight out of boxes they set right down in the snow. They stamped their feet and lit coal fires in barrels to keep warm, and they nested the eggs in straw and wool to keep them from freezing. Business was starting to pick up, the butcher opened the flaps on his red van and the fishmonger put a wooden trestle under his cart to keep it steady and started weighing pike.

The young man had been standing there so long the women who sold eggs had begun to remark on it. They saw he had good clothes and thick-soled boots, trousers and a jacket that looked hand made, a high-necked woollen sweater and a new black cap with a shiny brim. He was carrying a rucksack and didn't set it down. In the end he stood looking for a long time at a woman from Vanstorp who was selling home-baked cakes, round white breads and eggs. He tipped his hat as he approached her, asking whether she was Tora Lans.

People's ears perked up when he asked for Tora Otter by her maiden name, and the women began to gossip. Several of the older ones said it wasn't too hard to guess who he might be when he told them he had come on the cart from Stegsjö that morning. They showed him to Tora's stall.

Nowadays, Tora was at the north end of the square under a canvas roof. The potato loaves she had been baking for several years weren't as popular as they had been. People were getting spoiled on white bread and light ryes, and found her loaves dull and reminiscent of hard times. What she sold most of now were the sweets she had started making just for some extra income. She had only made peppermints to begin with, but now she made several kinds: cherry softies, several flavours of wine gums and sugared almonds as well as her peppermints. The whole lot would melt down to one sticky mess if it got rained or snowed on, so she had bought poles and a canvas roof and paid more for a spot further up the square. The price was high — twenty-five kronor a year, but it paid off.

When the women had shown the lad from Stegsjö where her stall was, he stood for a while at the flower stand behind hers, watching without daring to speak with her. It was full daylight now, and cloudy. There were customers buying sweets at Tora Otter's stall, and two women serving them. He stood behind the florist's glassed-in stall, between flickering candle flames and blue hyacinths, watching Tora and Tekla Johansson, who helped her with the weighing. He scrutinized everything, the bags and the brass weights and the bird's beak that closed when the marble slabs on the scales weighed even. He saw two women in black coats and straw shoes. They were dressed identically, in white aprons with the bibs pinned to their coats, white sleeve guards, fingerless gloves, and leather hats tied down with scarves across their ears. It couldn't be easy for him to know which one was Tora.

The snow was collecting on his cap and shoulders and he stamped his feet so often it was obvious he was freezing. When the worst of the morning crowd had dissipated, Tekla went over to Anker's café for her coffee, leaving Tora alone. People watched the young man abandon his place and walk around her stand, waiting at a polite distance while a customer paid. When she was alone she started rubbing her red, swollen fingers and stamping her straw shoes. That must have been when she saw him. The cheese vendor who was cutting a wedge of well-aged Svecia stopped, his wire in mid-slice. His customer, Ebba Lundgren, told him Tora hadn't seen the lad since she gave him up to a cobbler and his wife in Stegsjö fifteen years ago. Anybody could see she had no idea who he was.

The boy took off his cap and stepped forward. The cheese monger, Ebba Lundholm and the florist, who had moved in behind the glass himself, looking out through the frosted pane, heard him ask her whether she was Tora Lans. She acknowledged the name, but told him she was called Tora Otter now.

'I'm Erik Lans,' said the boy.

Tora said nothing.

'From Stegsjö,' he added.

No one could hear her next reply, but they saw her lean across her table and say something to him, brusquely and curtly as she always spoke, and neither of them looked very happy. She took some red wine gums and put them in a bag and gave him one krona from her cash box as well; he put it in his mitten. The boy appeared agitated throughout. Suddenly she had customers. She pointed to Anker's Café across the way and he ran there, his rucksack bouncing.

When Tekla returned everyone expected Tora to go over to Anker's where the boy was, but she didn't. She went on serving her customers and sent Tekla to get her some coffee, which she drank sitting on one of the wooden crates behind her stall. When the other stallholders went to Anker's for their morning coffee they saw the lad sitting there with his cap on the bench beside him. He had had a cup of cocoa and some buns but no one knew whether he was waiting for Tora or just sitting there to warm up. In the end he left and no one saw where he went. Tora didn't abandon her place at the sweet stall all day. At four o'clock she began to pack up along with everyone else and he still didn't come back. She did not walk home when Kalle Bira came and picked up her things, but sat down alongside him on the cart when all the boxes, the poles and the canvas had been loaded, and there she stayed, in plain sight, as the horse-drawn cart headed home to Hovlunda Road.

Owning the ground on which you walk is a special feeling. Alexander Lindh, the merchant, was able to enjoy it nowadays whenever he walked almost anywhere on the north side. He had also bought the Louse Point property south of the Highway Road, with two hundred acres. He shipped horse-drawn harrows and Swedish rib-backed settees, washstands and whole houses, tools of cast iron, bricks, paper pulp, threshers, ploughs, pit props and railway ties out of the freight terminal at the railway station in town. People could afford to buy land now, too.

Permission came from the court for the estate to parcel off some land, including a piece of the Moth Shack property, and Wärnström, the factory owner, bought it. He could now walk on his own property for a long distance south of the cemetery, and after 1907 one piece of land after the other drifted away from the estate and the manor and into the hands of Wärnström or Lindh, thus also falling within the domain of the municipal planners.

Wärnström had come to the village as a blacksmith, a man with no capital. Alexander Lindh had disembarked from the train with very little more than a rucksack with clean, neatly-mended shirts, starched collars and socks. He had had to borrow money to buy cheap and sell dear. But times had been hard, and the village an impoverished, static, hard-line community. The first two decades had tried his patience and at times even his confidence in the future. He had held onto what he had bought, and sold at high prices when he had had no other option.

Now things were different. He began to sell the plots of land near the station to people who had previously been his tenants. He sold his brother Adolf a rocky hillside. Adolf built himself a home with a fast-growing fir hedge and high turrets, which became one of the most stately manifestations of social tedium in town. Adolf walked its long halls blinking nervously, stared down at by elk heads mounted on dark panelling, annoyed with his brother for selling land to the villagers for sixty-five öre a square metre but charging him nearly a full krona for his. He, too, could now experience that special sensation of owning the ground he walked on, and began to think it was fortunate that not more people had tried it. To his horror, however, Alexander continued to sell at low prices.

But, contrary to what Adolf feared, his brother did not believe there was any particular risk that meek railwaymen and carpenters would wish to inherit the earth just because they had begun to buy plots of land to build themselves houses on. Instead, as Alexander knew, people who planted their own gooseberry bushes in their very own soil would become the staunchest defenders of the principle of private ownership. The emotions which, as if through the soles of their feet by osmosis, filled the hearts of men who trod their own ground, were anything but revolutionary. Sixty-five öre was not a bad price, as far as either party to the transaction was concerned.

Carl Wärnström purchased a parcel of the Heavenside estate from Her Ladyship, who was now a widow, for one hundred and ten thousand kronor. It was a large piece of property running south of Hovlunda Road and the ridge. It covered the whole area bounded by the Norrköping train line on the one side and the road to Nyköping on the other. He offered it to the town for eighty thousand kronor on the condition they build a sports grounds over by the ridge and allow him to retain the right to the forest on the

39

land. But Lindh moved that the assembly reject the motion, warning the town against purchases that would put it into debt, and the council followed his advice and refused it.

Then Alexander Lindh granted a lease on a piece of property for a Community Centre. When the association defaulted on the payments he wrote off the debt. In the end he donated the land to them.

Wärnström sold his chapel and donated property for a new, more elegant one. Lindh countered by donating land for a park around the church and a plot for a hospital, places that now bore his name. By that time it was 1909, the year in which, as the successor to Lefvander the merchant put it, the workers revealed that they were predators at heart. Alexander Lindh was unshaken. The trains rolled on, transporting horse-drawn harrows and Swedish rib-backed settees all over the world. He knew that for every two huge predators there are a thousand placidly grazing herbivores, and in his opinion there was a law of nature that prevented the more numerous from clutching at what they could reach and wanting to own more.

Neither was Wärnström upset, because the general strike of 1909 did not hit his factory. Not that his workers were better paid than any others but, as Wärnström put it, there were still some decent, honest Swedes left who valued a sense of community. 'At Wärnström's we're one big family,' he would tell them at Christmas. When it came right down to it, he didn't regard himself as the owner of the factory or its stock. The Almighty possessed all the earth. Human ownership was really only custodial, and some people were more skilful caretakers than others. Alexander Lindh felt exactly the same way about it, as did all the railway workers who had their very own gardens in which they planted gooseberry bushes and flagpoles crowned with turned wooden orbs.

According to Carl Wärnström it was the Almighty (with the stress on the first syllable) or Christ his Son who appointed those who were best equipped to be owners, i.e. to be the custodians and to shoulder the responsibility. Alexander Lindh considered this a kind of law of nature, a principle he referred to as 'natural selection'. Although the Crucifixion in Wärnström's chapel — a Jesus with big pink feet on a blue cloud — may have been somewhat more naively conceived than Lindh's Principle, their underlying spirit and orientation were identical in their resolve, to achieve the best.

Alexander Lindh knew that a railway worker with his own fenced-in garden was no danger. He was far too busy keeping his raspberry patch, his flagpole, his dustbin and his house in order to have time to clutch at more, in addition to which he had his hands full keeping up with his amortizations and interest payments. The dangerous man was the man who owned nothing because he wanted everything. That was why it was a good idea to give him a Community Centre.

Over the last two years, dissenting voices had been raised in the assembly on occasions, and this was a matter of concern to Lindh. 'Raking up a majority' he called their tactics. Motions were passed and coups carried out by people who knew too little about community affairs. What worried him had nothing to do with the bricklayer on the budgets committee or the stock keeper on the school board. Lindh the merchant was always the first to speak out in favour of co-operation with the Social Democrats, and right through to the end of the summer of 1909 he was of the opinion that the leaders of the workers were sensible men, or at least men who could be taught sense.

He proposed the introduction of a town council. His brother Adolf was on his side, as were Wärnström, the head teacher, the railway engineer and the editor of the local newspaper. The members of the council would be elected from amongst those inhabitants who had proven capable of engaging in issues for the public good. Despite the fact that his motion received neither the support of the Social Democrats nor the workers, he was never worried that it might be rejected. Nearly twenty per cent of the votes would be discounted as having been cast by citizens who had not fulfilled their public obligations. The procedure turned out to be a long and complex one, but the assembly finally succeeded in abolishing itself, and Alexander Lindh became chairman of the new council.

It consisted of one merchant, one factory owner, and two company directors. In addition, there was a station master, a chief engineer, a salesman, a senior teacher, an editor, an auditor, an ironmonger and a railway clerk. There were two railway engineers, a tile stove maker, a butcher, an engine yard master, a mechanic, a goods supervisor and a carpenter. There were two masons, a tool and die mould maker, a stock keeper, and a station clerk. Twelve conservatives, five liberals and ten Social Democrats.

Lindh enjoyed walking the streets that criss-crossed the new residential area, admiring the curly green tops crowning the gooseberry branches in spring. Bricklayers and carpenters planted primulas and Star-of-Bethlehem, their wives polished brass doorknobs, and lined their gravel paths with seashells. He would walk there in his plaid, caped overcoat, always wearing his black top hat. He would poke his walking stick at plum trees that had been assaulted by field-mice or frost, giving the owner good advice. He seldom criticised, unless he noticed washing hanging out on a Sunday, or someone working in the garden when they should have been on the way to the morning service. In strictly legal terms, he said to his brother Adolf whom he had made office manager, he no longer owned this land. He would poke the silver-plated foot of his walking stick into the ground to see what the soil was like, and suggest drainage. People tipped their hats to him, and he told his brother he got on with them. Lindh also got on with his office staff. Each man worked according to his ability and there was no fuss about working hours or overtime pay.

People no longer tipped their hats to Lindh when he crossed the town square these days. But when he and Wärnström met, they would always raise their walking sticks and top hats in a reciprocal salute.

One by one, the lights went out at the windows of the co-educational intermediate school on Hovlunda Road. The only remaining light was in the sixth grade room where one girl was still sitting, rewriting the last few lines of a laboratory report. The caretaker was making his rounds, raking the coals in the stoves to hurry the fires out so he could empty the ashes.

Magnhild Lundberg was still there. During her years as head teacher at the school she had always been the last to leave, and she intended to go on that way. She wasn't worried about upsetting the new headmaster, who didn't know about this habit. The hour when the daylight dimmed and the chill came creeping up between the floorboards was hers alone. She would walk from one classroom to the next, checking that the lights had really been turned off. Electricity cost forty öre per kilowatt hour, and her concern about expenses, even the smallest ones, had not deserted her when the school won its state subsidy. They had had electric lighting since September. Before that they were so hard up for good light that she would unscrew her own home desk lamp every morning and carry it to school in a basket so they could use it in the common room.

The school had become a municipal intermediate school a year ago, authorised to issue matriculation certificates. At the same time, a male head teacher had been put in charge. All this was quite according to the rules, and she had worked hard to make it happen. 'I knew how it would be,' she often thought. 'I knew it and strove for it because it was a matter of survival. It would not have been possible for the school to go on much longer unsubsidized.' But at dusk when she made her solitary rounds of the empty classrooms, gathering forgotten notebooks and rolling up maps, she was more honest with herself than she otherwise dared to be, and she knew that deep down inside she had prayed for the rules to be changed, knowing that they would have to be someday, sure of it. But they hadn't been changed yet.

People had expected her to leave town. Several of the women teachers had been dismissed because their qualifications did not satisfy the requirements for a subsidised school. Little Irma Lewin was no longer allowed to have physical education. She had probably never seen a proper physical education class, Magnhild knew but she was ambitious. There was no more playing ball or singing on the gravelled schoolyard. The headmaster himself took over physical education, and he had started a brass band for the boys. Magnhild Lundberg, whose degree was in more subjects than the new headmaster's, went on teaching physics, chemistry, mathematics and biology. It was a peculiar situation, but she had adjusted. Human beings are the most adaptable mammals, as she taught her biology classes.

She did not want to leave the school. She had a more modern chemistry laboratory than in any private school. They had financed it by selling raffle tickets and holding bazaars, putting on plays and organising lotteries, as they had done for all the other teaching equipment that had been purchased. She didn't particularly enjoy making costumes out of crêpe paper or elfin hats, but she had done it. They had played, sung, danced, and been wood anemones, fairies and trolls, King Charles XII's gallant men, angels and elves. They had hand-hemmed the school towels themselves, copied out maps from the school atlas, pinned butterflies into collection boxes, refurbished the physics room when the first equipment had arrived. The student tuition fees had covered the salaries of the teachers and caretaker, heating fuel and lamp oil and classroom cleaning. The four thousand kronor that had served as their initial operating capital was quickly exhausted when they opened the school nine years ago, spent on desks, map frames, rostrums and blackboards. The organ alone, ordered from the J.A. Marnell company, had cost one hundred and eighty kronor. The whole project had been on the verge of collapse more than once, like in 1903 when they were temporarily rescued by a grant of one hundred and seventy-five kronor from the dog license tax fund.

She watered the blue hyacinth on the podium in the auditorium as darkness fell. Suddenly it was too dark to discern the oil painting of the son of the widow from Nain behind the rostrum. Her fingers ran over the organ keys, as she stood there pumping it with one foot.

> Oh may we clearly realize
> That which our Lord requires
> With faithful hearts and open eyes
> As long as we aspire
> Let not our minds be darkened
> By memories of sin
> When eventide us hearkens
> And workday finally ends.

She wasn't musical, but could pick out the melody of the hymn she had listened to most winter mornings of her life. Nor was she religious in the sense of being active in the state church, but she still enjoyed humming the tune. She pulled the Vox celeste stop and changed key. It was a lovely walnut organ with brass candlesticks and ten couplers. She loved it as she loved so many other things at the school, lifeless objects that were not lifeless. She may not actually have loved the two-storey stucco building itself, but she certainly loved the worn-down staircase she ascended every single morning.

There are so many things to love. People said the right thing was to love a man and the offspring you produced together. But she loved twenty-eight young people in black school caps bearing tassels and emblems. She was not head over heels in love with them, but she loved them critically and nurturingly, as a gardener loves his rows of lanky beans. She loved her stuffed viper on its dry tuft of grass, her rat embryos in formaldehyde, the woodcock that had fallen down dead with a broken beak into station clerk Fogel's forcing-frame, and which now stood with varnished legs on a little imitation boulder, the stones from Fårö, the eagle in the cloak room, the valves, the retorts and the fume cupboard, the trilobites, the conch shells and Lundin, the caretaker.

What she did not love about the school was its headmaster, Ossian Jansson, Bachelor of Arts, or his new filing cabinet.

In the icy cold space under the stairwell known as Siberia, where Lundin kept the wood, she had a cardboard carton with flyers and newsletters from the Women's Political Suffrage Society. She thrust a pile of them into her briefcase and was just putting on her coat and galoshes when she saw Gerda Åkerlund's face through the window in the outside door. She was the student who was rewriting her lab report, and Magnhild had told her she was working too hard and it was time to go home. The vestibule was so dark Gerda couldn't see Magnhild from outside. She was occupied with her own reflection in the window. She had one of those berets of Scottish tartan wool known as a tam o'shanter and she was trying to get it to stay at just the right angle over her eye. Her face was that of any adult woman looking herself in the mirror: expressionless, chin up and eyebrows raised. But her hands, pulling her tammy time and again to get it into the position she preferred, were rough and red as a boy's. Magnhild moved closer to the window, and the face Gerda saw in the glass under the beret and the fluffy light-brown hair changed into her older, graver one. Magnhild didn't realize what was happening or why Gerda suddenly looked frightened of her. Her hands dropped, she grabbed her schoolbag and ice skates and began to back down the steps. Magnhild thought she would call to her, but by the time she got outside Gerda had already disappeared down Hovlunda Road.

She walked the same way herself, turning at Warehouse Row where she planned to call in at a couple of buildings to distribute leaflets and flyers. Sallow twilight was the right time of day: the women had had their afternoon coffee and it would still be some time before their husbands could be expected back from work. Many women devoted this time to the sewing or the ironing. She went first to the flat of a tailor called Fällman, one flight up in a new building opposite the printers'. She'd tried there before, but it had been Fällman himself who'd opened the door and when he heard she was there for the suffrage society he said his wife was busy in the kitchen. This was a common reaction. The tailor was a servile man with a tape measure around his neck who chewed aniseed so his clients wouldn't say he had bad breath and whose manner was as fumbling as his hands. At home, however, he could behave like a little Napoleon and no one would be the wiser.

Magnhild had no hope that Fällman's wife would ever become an activist, but she still wanted to give her a couple of leaflets to put into her sewing basket and possibly, though far from certainly, read sometime when she was alone. The woman was so pleased to see her it was embarrassing. Timid, of course, and beside herself with trying to figure out where on earth to put the leaflets. Magnhild had absolutely no idea if she was so happy because she was so lonely otherwise or because she liked her. What went on around here, behind the panes of glass in the doors and the brass nameplates was anybody's guess. From time to time Magnhild would feel quite unnerved on walking into a strange home, and occasionally even frightened for no obvious reason.

When she left, Krantz the watchmaker was waiting for her downstairs. He had noticed her going in. He was the one who stuffed and preserved her various finds and he did an excellent job with most. Her particular favourite was the big female viper she had caught by the tail just after its young hatched. However, he didn't do very good business as a watchmaker, because he was an idealist and a social theorist. To his mind, the question of suffrage was too narrow. Magnhild was impatient to move on, but felt obliged to say yes to a cup of his acrid coffee because he had done her so many favours, just as she had had to accept Britta Fällman's sickly-sweet cherry cordial and to have one of her 'dream' biscuits, sugary and porous and cracked on top. As she went back out onto the street she noticed that the huge clock that marked his shop was wrong again. He had studied Spinoza, but his customers didn't know Spinoza from their elbows, they just made fun of his clock.

She meant to go into the courtyard behind the fire and police stations, where a crooked, two-storey wooden building was tucked in. She had never been there, but knew she would have to figure out a way to get past the smithy. The blacksmith kept a bad-mannered ram. He was unshorn and the long wool hanging down along his sides was black with soot from the forge. You could placate him with snuff or chewing tobacco, but she had no desire to go hunting in the gutters for cigar stubs with the smith standing in his doorway watching. She grabbed a switch of birch twigs from the glass-blower's front steps and strode quickly across the courtyard in full view of the smith and his wife. They watched the schoolmistress and the ram, who lowered his head, at the ready. Her skirt, damp with slush at the hem, hung heavily around her ankles, and when she heard the ram pick up speed she turned on her heel and extended the switch, snapping him hard on the muzzle until he sneezed. She continued backwards, with as much dignity as she could muster, all the while brushing at the ram's nostrils. She didn't dare turn her back on him until she was up on the stoop.

The house was home to policemen's and firemen's families, the midwife, and an unwed seamstress with her sickly son. She made her way systematically from one flat to the next, distributing pamphlets and informing each woman that it cost one krona to join. She wondered if the policemen's wives would use the leaflets as mats under their cats' food bowls.

The seamstress got herself into a tizzy when she opened the door and saw Magnhild Lundberg there.

'I'm here for the WPSS,' Magnhild hurried to say so as not to give the impression that she wanted to have a skirt altered.

'Oh dear,' said the seamstress. 'Just when I've got such a mess in here. Oh, well, do come in. Things get awfully dusty from the sewing, you know, with all these bits of thread. I have to hang a wet curtain in the doorway to keep Albert out of the dust. His asthma's so bad.'

'Fröken Linell, are you interested in women's political suffrage?' Magnhild asked.

'Yes, yes I certainly am. Come in and sit down. Have this chair, I'll just move these pressing cloths. Yes, good grief, suffrage, oh yes. Would you care for some coffee?'

'No, thank you,' said Magnhild. 'I've just had some. Thank you anyway.' She found it difficult to be commonplace. She even hated the word, although it had some lovely relations. 'Community,' she said to herself. But she felt a stranger to the community. She would often enter people's flats with all the authority of a schoolmistress because she was actually afraid. Not exactly afraid they would say

50

something unkind or show her the door, but intimidated by all their bits of thread, their smells and the secrets, their sharp voices through closed doors, their traces of tears.

Things went on here she could never so much as imagine, people managed without Spinoza here, without the proud ideologies of the freethinkers. People lived here using mathematics she could have taught any six-year-old and religion that was no more than a sigh on Sunday and a wipe of the eye with an apron corner when the neighbour was carted away in the hearse. But they had something she couldn't explain to herself and was unable to reach out for. She could note its presence in the very innermost rat-infested nooks and crannies of the community.

Personally, she was more like a viper (and she examined them as a zoologist would, unencumbered by hate and prejudice). Last summer she had stood and watched a huge, pregnant female hatch her young under the pink rose hip bush in the meadow out at Louse Point. They were no longer than pencils when they had freed themselves from their shells and slipped away to live their solitary lives without so much as a look back at their mother or their siblings.

The seamstress insisted on serving coffee. There were some people you just didn't dare to say no to, they would never get over it and would live in the belief that you didn't approve of them or their coffee. But here Magnhild reckoned she could get away with refusing. Her stomach was upset enough as it was. She had to accept some sweets, though, to make up for it. They were damp and sticky and had been traipsed across by flies.

She spoke of suffrage with Fröken Linell the seamstress, who had pins in her collar and who kept claspinging and reclasping her hands that wouldn't stay still and that revealed that she had other things on her mind, such as Magnhild Lundberg's figure and a piece of black georgette she was stuck with because a customer had cancelled an order. It that would be perfect for a dress for Magnhild. Her teeth were too big, looked as if she had probably inherited them from someone. Magnhild realized she might as well be talking to the walls and that the seamstress couldn't think beyond the dress she might ask her about and whether the other teachers would also come and be her clients if she did. But the truth was that she was too badly-off, and both she and Magnhild knew it. The teachers wouldn't be able to stand that smell of poverty in their clothing, wouldn't want to be fitted in front of the damp curtain, wouldn't care for her sweets. This home was inhabited by an alien people.

Magnhild talked to these women about what was necessary and what was just. But not us, they would say, shielding themselves behind their illnesses and their wandering thoughts, their fingers that couldn't keep still and their feet that were constantly shifting along their ice-cold floors. We have nothing to live but our lives.

When she left she knew she had disappointed the seamstress, as well as the smith and his wife and the ram, who didn't even bother to stick his head out the door this time as she re-crossed the courtyard with the birch switch in her hand.

Along Store Street, both opposite and on either side of the town hall, were some of the finer shops. The gentlemen's clothier, the florist, and watchmaker Palmquist's, where the clock outside kept the right time. Magnhild stepped into Erna Wiberg's yarn and knitwear shop, which also stocked ladies' undergarments, and Fröken Wiberg herself welcomed her, whispering discretely that her corset had arrived and she could have a fitting. She and the owner went in the direction of the dim recesses behind the red velvet curtain to the changing room. She began to undress, placing her clothing on a plush stool. It was a cramped space and she wished Fröken Wiberg would leave. But she unpacked the corset from its cardboard box and held it out unlaced to Magnhild, who was now clad only in her underthings. It was pale blue and of shiny jacquard satin. The corset was really far more expensive than she could afford and she didn't know how she had let herself be enticed by it. Laws prevailed at Erna Wiberg's of which Magnhild did not actually approve but the moment the bell rang and the door closed behind her, as she stepped into the cosy, dusky rooms with their fragrance of cloth, she was governed by them all the same.

Fröken Wiberg carried the corset to her as if bearing a sacred chalice, and sent her assistant to get the pins with their multicoloured porcelain heads to mark the necessary alterations. Erna Wiberg began to speak about Magnhild's body as if it were an object they were examining between them and for which they both had intentions. She touched her, not fumblingly and intimately but lightly, with fingertips which occasionally jumped for joy. Magnhild, whom no person otherwise ever touched, stood crowded in between the mirror and the velvet curtain, all her dignity abandoned, all her free will gone.

'This will be excellent,' Fröken Wiberg whispered, signalling to her assistant to tighten it up from behind, and Magnhild agreed as she saw her body lose all its sagging, uncontrolled features. It became subordinated to the shiny satin panels which were the corset, not unlike the dorsal plates of a lizard. Her body was now heavy, hourglass-shaped and smooth. Her breasts were one long, smooth wave leading down to her waistline, which curved seamlessly down towards her back, her hips and the long slope of her bottom.

When she had put her clothes back on she found Fröken Wiberg lurking outside the dressing room with a box of undergarments of the finest Swiss cotton cambric, and by the time Magnhild left the shop she had purchased a corset liner with embroidered edging she had no desire to own. She regretted it the moment she stepped back into the street. But in the shop her actions, sifting through the box of flimsy items, feeling the embroidered edges, letting the ribbons glide between her fingers, even paying and hearing the register ring up the sale, had all filled her with pleasure. For the sake of appearances, she had also given a leaflet and a newsletter to Fröken Wiberg, who accepted them with a conspiratorial wink. Magnhild had no doubt that she would throw them unread into the wood-burning stove which was always kept warm in the back of her shop where women went behind the curtain to undress.

There was nowhere for her to visit on the other side of the street. There were three eating and drinking houses one behind the other, the third of which was known as the Stewpot. It was the place to which the farmers reeled down the rutted road to sober up on pea soup with pork rind. She headed out to the High Street near the town square, stopping in at the dairy to leave a brochure. She couldn't make herself heard in there, however, with the separator whining and the buckets slamming, and the dairymaids in the middle of their work. She crossed the slippery cement floor carefully, afraid of sliding in a puddle of milk foam, holding her breath, as she did not care for the intense smell of milk. It turned her stomach.

She didn't bother with Anker's café, as she had been there on Saturday and left a stack of newsletters. The Christian bookshop was a few houses down. She could see that the only person in the shop was the attendant, but she intended to go upstairs to see the Öhrström sisters and work on them. These were two bleary-eyed, dreamy, coquettish sisters. With a guitar hanging on the wall, they gave the impression of being not in the least religious but extremely sentimental. She stopped in on them because their bookshop made them influential women in the community. It might be useful to convert them to the cause of women's suffrage, so they could sell materials in the shop. Pastor Öhrström, a missionary, allowed his daughters to keep some secular litreature in stock. He was a liberal man, and moreover hardly ever at home.

But this was Magnhild's unlucky day – when she got up to the flat there he was, just back from an evangelical posting. His daughters were on either side of him on the settee, with their abundance of coiffed hair and their scent of verbena soap. They were having tea and she felt obliged to stay, as the Pastor had just been all the way to China and was also something of a genius. It was a highly aromatic blossom tea his daughters boasted, but to Magnhild it tasted of mildewed straw. He enquired as to whether she intended to stay on at the school, said it was being rumoured that she was going back to the College in Stockholm to pursue further studies in chemistry. She denied it.

'Excellent,' said Pastor Öhrström. 'I expected as much. A learned woman is a dinosaur.'

'Pardon me?' Magnhild gasped.

'A species threatened with extinction, soon to be bypassed by evolution.'

Having attempted to persuade Pastor Öhrström that he was wrong and to breathe some courage into his daughters, who stared down at their patterned stockings and their elegant shoes with patent leather toes, she struggled on through the darkening January twilight.

The Öhrström's bookshop was in a new building in the High Street with access to the flats from the back. The courtyard housed a cobbler and a coppersmith. Apprentices carried trays of fresh sweet rolls from the bakery. The smells of newly-baked biscuits and sweetened bread mixed with the odour of blood from the butcher's. No one lived along the courtyard, and all the workers were men.

The slush in front of the wood and coal yard was black with anthracite. She went back out into the High Street. It was dark now and the woman who owned the needlework shop was just lighting a lamp amongst her patterns and half-finished embroideries, as she did not yet have electricity. Magnhild stood in front of her shop window for a few minutes, looking at petit point roses growing out of the needlework canvas in the yellow lamplight. The owner waved to her and smiled encouragingly through the glass, but she didn't go inside. She was getting tired, and was afraid she would come out with a cross-stitch project she didn't at all want.

Turning into Cobbler's Row she thought she had had enough and would continue tomorrow. Then she remembered that she had intended to do the big, grey wooden two-storey house inhabited mostly by workers from Wilhelmsson's. When she got inside she passed the first door and chose the second, instinctively, not realizing that she had done so because this door did not have rows of shoes and things standing outside, but rather a shiny brass name plate that read 'Emil Pettersson'. Before she could knock properly several children came up and were obviously on their way in. Thus she entered the kitchen with them, surprising a woman who was sitting at the table hemming a runner.

Her name was Ärna Pettersson. Magnhild did not know her, and she couldn't understand why she would apologise for having been sewing.

'I started it last Christmas,' said Ärna. 'But I never seem to have time. Do come in,' she said, opening the door to the sitting room, which was quite cold. As Magnhild was about to continue in, a chubby boy blocked her way, saying 'Mind the furniture!'

She was surprised, and Ärna shooed him aside, even more

embarrassed than before. But she was an accommodating woman and Magnhild saw a gleam of interest for women's suffrage in her eye and imagined she could discern a fluttering little flame of enthusiasm after all. So Magnhild said yes to coffee although her stomach was already rumbling and acidic and she was feeling faintly sick.

Ärna Pettersson wasn't, in fact, even remotely interested in women's suffrage, but she listened patiently. She was a kind woman, and accustomed to this kind of thing. The Good Templars had been round and left a leaflet saying that drink was the primary cause of poverty. There was no need to speak with Emil about this, because he only ever took a glass at Christmas. The freethinkers had also been, requesting that they participate in the battle for social reform without class egotism.

Emil Pettersson had his own battles to fight. He turned a deaf ear to religious dogma and political evangelism alike, working ten hours a day plus overtime six days out of seven at Wilhelmsson's Carpentry Shop. He had also married wisely, the daughter and only child of a small farmer from Kedevi. Throughout the strike Ärna's parents had supplied them with food, coming into town to bring them laying hens that were past their prime. Ärna would stew them and serve them with a white sauce, reserving the stock for soup. They also brought geese from Lake Vallmaren and huge covered jam jugs full of blood.

Emil and Ärna were a frugal, decent, right-thinking couple, who owned the Wilhelmsson universal unit, a piece of furniture designed and intended for orderly, improvement-bound working class homes. It was a shagreen sofa that Ärna kept clean with a damp cloth, and it really looked like leather. Under their table they had a rust-red rug, and on the table top there was a velveteen runner with a lamp and books, a gold-trimmed postcard album, photographs of Ärna's parents in mother-of-pearl frames, and a fan over the mirror. Ärna was rightfully proud of all this, and deserved the praise Magnhild heaped on her. Like Emil, she worked virtually non-stop, and it was very rare that she would sit still in the middle of the afternoon sewing. Magnhild had truly caught her out.

She worked as if her task were to recreate a vanished order, the true root of life. Some higher force had calculated that she was to spend a total of forty-eight years of her allotted time on earth — in total if not entirely at one go — wiping surfaces with cloths, although Ärna was not aware of it. She would rub the zinc around the kitchen sink with oxalic acid and powdered limestone and the stove with graphite dissolved in vinegar, and she would wipe the tabletop clean even before they got up from their meal.

Emil and she worked as if they alone had shouldered the burden of proving that a working-class family did not have to be as lice-infested and impoverished as appeared to be the case in the worst houses in their neighbourhood. They refuted the bourgeois thesis that workers were molleycoddled bellyachers and that parsimony and energy were actually upper class virtues. Wilhelmsson, the factory owner, still had rye flour porridge and buttermilk on his breakfast table, and his daughters' stockings were darned at the heels. So did Emil Pettersson's children, and their clothes were made of thick, durable fabric.

This was why they were visited by the Good Templars' and the free church proselytisers, by the representatives of the workers' party who were collecting to build a Community Centre, the freethinkers, the co-operative movement and the suffragettes. Ärna listened attentively and it took some time before Magnhild figured out that this was because she was a good, kind woman. The little flame that fluttered in her eyes was actually anxiety that her visitor would get crumbs on the rug under the table in front of the sofa.

When Magnhild finally realized this, she rose, gathered the crumbs that had fallen onto her skirt in her cupped hand and said:

'Goodness, it's half past five already, I'd better be going. But I'll leave you a flyer, Fru Pettersson, so you can read more for yourself about the suffrage movement.'

'No, no, it's really not much after five,' said Ärna Pettersson in her kindest voice. 'We keep our clock half an hour fast so Emil won't be late for work.'

'I'm sure he never has been,' said Magnhild.

'No, not once,' Ärna replied.

They shook hands and said their good-byes and Magnhild continued down Cobblers' Row, wondering what kind of a man Emil was, never to fall for the temptation of knowing that their clock was half an hour fast.

It had begun to rain, an ice-cold rain that came in with the wind. It tried to pull her hat off, she felt it tugging at her anchors of elastic band and hatpins. Cautiously she put one foot down in front of the other, as it was slippery now. The snow had melted and then frozen to slippery ice on the slope, and now it was raining and melting again. At Carlsborg, where Wärnström lived, the lights were on and she caught a glimpse of the arborvitae bushes in the park. They never ceased to startle her. They looked as if they were sneaking up on her in the dark until she fixed her eyes on them, and then they stopped and stood still.

Her suffrage expeditions always made her reflective, although not entirely discouraged. She knew what she was doing was completely right and necessary, and at the same time she had visions of the women she had been speaking to standing making dinner now, gutting salt herring on the leaflets she had given them. She could find no way to address them so they really understood.

She would have been able to counter their arguments if only they had had any. But if she wanted arguments she would have had to visit them when their husbands were at home. Most women were like Fröken Linell the seamstress and Ärna Pettersson. They would clear her a path, show her to the best armchair mouthing excuses and minor complaints, picking up bits of thread and dusting surfaces as they went, and while she spoke they would eye the hem of her skirt that was coming undone and the yellow leaves that had appeared on the baby's tears.

Now the schoolhouse was pitch dark and in the building where she lived on Hovlunda Road the only lights shining were at the landlady's on the ground floor. Instead of going straight home she went into the villa next to her building. Old Petrus Wilhelmsson lived upstairs. She gave her damp face a wipe with her handkerchief, and stood her boots neatly on the shoe rack and her briefcase on the ledge above it with a sense of relief that she was done.

He was inside, in the sitting room facing the garden with a checked woollen blanket over his legs and no lights on despite the darkness. She rebuked him gently for that, and lit the lamp over the table. She felt the tile stove to see if it was still warm. He was pleased she had come. His life had grown very lonely since he stopped going out. His knees had given out after forty years of running up and down the stairs between his carpentry shop and the office above it. They were swollen and useless. She was afraid he would stop getting out of his chair altogether and be overcome by the cold. The pilot light of his life was being slowly extinguished, and he was doing nothing to prevent it.

This was a house that smelled strict and strange, a house with no woman and no pets and where there had never been any children. A hired woman came to make his meals and do his cleaning. You could smell her furniture wax and polish all the way out in the hallway.

Magnhild walked over to the sideboard and lifted out the cognac decanter. Petrus Wilhelmsson had been a staunch supporter of the temperance movement all his life, but in his old age he took a little cognac morning and evening to stimulate his heart. This was at the advice of his physician and initially he had taken it by the tablespoon. Now, however, they would have their evening drink together, so Magnhild poured two. Neither of them ever mentioned the fact that her own heart was strong and unafflicted.

'How was your night?' she asked.

'Well, my day was better,' he replied.

She was afraid, however, that it had been extremely quiet. He slept so little. His carpentry shop had been sold to an engineer from Stockholm and the sawmill to merchant Lindh's son-in-law. He had plenty of money and really nothing to worry about. But at night he was back down there. Prices were falling, he had trainloads of merchandise just piling up in the stockyards. In his dreams he was bewildered and paralysed, this man who, throughout his professional life, had been so good at making quick, definite decisions. He would dream that a worker was badly injured by the huge lumber saw and would awaken with tears streaming down his cheeks and panic in his heart.

His enterprise was sold and the future impossible for him to gauge. Today he knew as little about the world market as he knew about social democracy or the new methods of collective bargaining. He should have turned his back on it all in indifference or complacency. But in his dreams he was assaulted by all the confusion and fear he no longer had the strength to hold at bay. He was compelled to relive the dark side of his life and to acknowledge it.

Magnhild brought him the local news and gossip, but he had

grown so uninterested she virtually had to force it on him. He preferred to hear her talk about her schoolwork, and he was the only person she told how she really felt about Ossian Jansson.

'He is an extremely insignificant human being,' she said. 'I have studied the matter in great detail and taken my own prejudices into account when judging him. But I reassert: he is an extremely insignificant human being.'

And Petrus Wilhelmsson smiled gently, thinking Jansson was undoubtedly well aware of how Magnhild felt about him, although she thought she concealed it. She was extremely hard on herself as well. They toasted one another and drank in silence, and then Magnhild got up and went to the windows to make sure they weren't draughty. She pulled the heavy green curtains so they overlapped, to keep the cold from coming in.

'Shall I put some wood in the stove?' she asked.

'No thank you. Don't trouble yourself Magnhild,' he said, because he didn't like anyone to fool with his heating. He worked up huge piles of embers shining behind the closed grating and then, with no draught at all to the flue, he could keep the stove hot all night. Even so, he often felt frozen cold to the marrow.

'Time for me to go home and write a quiz on esters. Can I do anything for you before I leave?'

'I have everything I need,' said Petrus Wilhelmsson. 'I enjoyed our conversation, Magnhild, and now I'll just sit here thinking about what we were discussing.'

She took his hand by way of farewell. It was very cold.

The cognac hadn't settled her stomach. She tried to eat when she got home, but all she could get down was a slice of bread with cheese. At ten o'clock she had finished her work and sat down to read. But there was a cold draught from the floor, so she got into bed. Before removing her undergarments she put on her new corset liner and looked at herself in the mirror. Then she put it into a dresser drawer in its box, deciding not to wear it until some time when she was invited out.

When she got up to turn out the light she opened her curtain a crack so that she would be able to see Petrus Wilhelmsson's bedroom window when she woke up at night. They had an agreement that if he ever needed help he would light a lamp in the window. She didn't really think he ever would, though.

The springs in the woods ran even in winter. Every morning the light would strike the live water and it would gleam darkly against the snow. Squirrels' feet pulled down light sprays of snow which melted quickly away after disturbing the surface for a moment.

The nights were bitter and cold. Each night strove to lay a film of ice over the live water. Each morning had less power to melt it than the last, and every night a new concentric circle froze around the spring. The moving water formed wreaths of ice.

This old man's heart was now like an open spring in the early winter woods.

In mid-January Frida turned up in Julin the brewer's flat one morning when Ebba was alone at home. She couldn't even be bothered to look around at Ebba's new life, but collapsed into a kitchen chair right by the door without even taking her mittens off. Her hat was askew and Ebba could see she was unwell. There was a brief exchange of formalities about the brewer and Frida's kids. Then Frida said: 'I'm with child.'

Ebba had already guessed, from the dark lines on her face, but she had no idea what it had to do with her. She said nothing. The Frida burst out, with something like hostility:

'You've got something that'll get rid of it. I know you have.'

'What on earth?' said Ebba. 'You must be dreaming.'

'No, I know you've got something. You have to help me. You just have to, I can't go on like this.'

Anybody could see that, Ebba thought to herself.

'Hasn't Eriksson come back?'

'No.'

'Is he sending money?'

'I expect he will as soon as he gets work. But you have to help me Ebba. I can't cope.'

'I can't imagine where you got that idea,' said Ebba. 'People are the most awful gossips and imaginers. I haven't got anything of the kind. I don't even know what you're talking about.'

'You've got to help me.'

Suddenly they heard Julin coming up. He always came home for coffee at eleven and again at three. People said it was because he was so much in love with Ebba, so jealous by nature and so anxious.

'Come back in a while,' Ebba hissed, and when Frida had gone out the back way, she realized it had sounded like a promise. But as she approached Julin in the front hall, she was glad to be rid of her. Obviously, though, Frida just sat on the woodbin outside the kitchen door, because the minute Julin had had his coffee, his kiss and attempted embrace and had left, Frida was back.

'I don't have anything for you!' Ebba said. 'I did have a miscarriage once — people are such terrible prattlers.'

She heated up a cup of leftover coffee for Frida, after which Frida said she'd have to be going. And she did, but she was back after only a couple of days.

'I've told you it wasn't true,' said Ebba. 'To be perfectly honest with you Frida, I've had two miscarriages. And people will talk, of course. I suppose that old hag of a seamstress started it. She was here once to fit me for a dress and while I was down at the store getting cream for her coffee she snooped all around and went through all my cupboards.'

Frida said nothing, nor did she deny she'd heard it from the seamstress.

'Well all right, I do have something…' said Ebba. 'But it's not mine. It may be what you have in mind, though. Somebody gave me it, I'll never say who. She asked me to hang onto it for safekeeping, to keep it here.'

She was unnerved by Frida's just sitting there in her hat with the loose elastic band and her old black coat that was coming unravelled at the buttonholes. Frida reminded her of all the difficulties she had put behind her by marrying Julin, and that frightened her so much it felt as if Frida and her kind were contagious.

'If you have room for it at home, I don't mind if you take it,' she said. 'Put it in a cupboard at your place, get it out of my way.'

She went into the sitting room and didn't come back for quite a while. She returend with a black oilcloth case.

'Don't you have anything with you to carry it in? Oh, well, I can wrap it in newspaper. But if you let on to so much as one soul that I lent you this ...'

'Oh, I won't,' said Frida. 'What do I do with it?'

'I haven't the slightest idea!' said Ebba. 'Now get out of here. And not a word, do you hear? Not even to Tora Otter.'

But when she was standing at the kitchen door putting on her mittens, with the package under her arm, Ebba took her by both hands.

'Do be careful, now, for heaven's sake,' she said. 'Whatever you do be careful. Somebody really ought to help you.'

'There isn't anybody.'

'There's always someone. But it costs money. You've got to find the right person, you know. There's a little plug inside, almost like the tip of your nose. Have you felt it?'

Frida shook her head and didn't dare look her in the eye.

'That's where you have to go in. But take care so you don't end up in some accursed mess. Good-bye now.'

She got the package at Ebba's on a Monday and she waited until Wednesday when Tora did the baking for Berta Göhlin at the Cosmopolitan and Dagmar spent the night in Tora's flat with her boys. Frida's little ones went to bed early in the trundle bed in the kitchen, but it seemed forever before Konrad fell asleep. She stood there in the kitchen with the door to the front room ajar listening until his breathing grew regular in the dark, and when she was sure he was asleep she shut the door quietly and pushed down the little hasp to lock it. She turned up the lamp to be able to see better, not knowing how else to prepare, feeling all this had happened much too fast. She had already removed the probe from its oilcloth case and set it on a towel. It was sharp and curved.

She had taken down the mirror that served as the lid for a little box of shaving things on the top of the chest of drawers. The mirror itself was no bigger than a page out of the hymnal, and it was dark blue-grey with age. But you could still use it to look at yourself, which was what she planned to do. By the time she was ready to start, the whole thing felt horrid, despite her determination. She had leaned the mirror up against the wall in her settee bed and curled up on the bed with her cotton vest pulled up over her stomach. The table lamp was reflected in the mirror, but when she moved it it cast a shadow across what she wanted to see. She pulled up her knees and scuttled slightly backwards. Then she could see herself, see all that ugliness. Down there where you weren't even supposed to wash. But it looked like she had imagined.

The only thing that surprised her was that it was so little. It felt bigger. Where her light brown hair was thinnest there were two brown lines and inside the lines there were two big tightly closed lips and it was even darker in there, brown verging on deep blue. She had to separate them to get in and when she did she expected to see a hole. But there was only a soft hollow of shiny membranes which met in the middle, shut like a blossom. When she pushed it open she saw two rosy flaps struggling to keep closed. She couldn't get any further in in this position. She was surprised at how she looked inside, surprised to look so young and undamaged, as if nothing had ever happened to her.

She touched the mirror and it slammed shut and she sat there, clammy, listening in the direction of the kitchen in case the sound had woken anyone. But it was perfectly silent. She crouched on the floor, feeling the draught on her backside. Cautiously, she felt inside to see if she could find the way in Ebba had whispered to her about. There were endless moist folds and rises and she was afraid she would hurt herself with the nail on her middle finger. Finally, her fingertip located a soft mound, slightly larger than the tip of one's nose, and she realized this must be it. It was tender.

She didn't know how to do it. The idea of touching herself there with a pointed probe repulsed her. Thinking about it was almost unbearable, not because of the pain but because it was so fragile. She wished she had never felt it with her finger, never looked in the mirror. Maybe I do have to have help, she thought. No one could do this alone. But she knew lots of people had taken care of it themselves, that they had kept the probe inside for hours.

'What if I pass out?' she wondered. 'Or start bleeding and can't get it to stop? What if the kids wake up and find me lying here unconscious?'

It was impossible. She saw that now. She was in a panic, icy cold all the way out to her fingertips. There was nothing to do but to put the probe back into its black oilcloth case and hide it at the bottom of a drawer.

She did nothing for the next two days, except to lie sleepless at night. She knew she'd do it in the end, because she had no choice and was determined to go through with it. But she had to have some kind of help. Late Saturday night she went down and knocked on Tora Otter's door.

Tora had been at the market all day and was tired. When she'd done the cash box and had something to eat, she'd gone to bed. When she opened and saw Frida with her ashen face and a shawl around her shoulders with nothing but her nightdress under, she thought she must be ill. Frida had just as little energy for explanations to Tora as she had to Ebba Julin. She just told it like it was and asked if she could do it down here, at Tora's.

'This thing must be making you strange in the head.'

'Maybe so. But I have to have help.'

'Aren't you the sly one?'

'All I'm asking is for you to let me be here while I do it,' said Frida. 'I daren't be all alone 'cause I might pass out and then the kids would find me.'

'So what about my boys?'

'They're asleep. I can do it behind that curtain you put up when you're going to have a wash. You won't have to know a thing, won't have to see me, I just need you to be here with me.'

They whispered back and forth, both upset and afraid they'd wake the boys in their trundle bed.

'It's my business,' said Frida. 'All I ask is that you be sitting here.'

In the end Tora agreed not to know what was going on and to be sitting at the kitchen table waiting for her. She was at a complete loss after she had put the curtain up for Frida, didn't know whether to make some coffee or just sit there. How long would it take? Frida was quiet as a mouse. Tora tried to hear her breathing but couldn't. Her feet were ice cold but she didn't want to get into bed. The alarm clock was ticking on the chest of drawers and the boys breathed heavily and regularly, fast asleep.

Then she heard some little sounds coming from Frida, she didn't know whether it was moaning or uneasy breathing. She felt nauseous. If only she could think! But everything seemed to be at a standstill, inside and out.

'Frida?'

'Yes, what?'

She could hear that she had frightened her.

'Come out of there.'

She opened the curtain a crack, and Tora had never seen her face so pale.

'Have you done it yet?'

'It's so hard.'

Then Tora grabbed the curtain she had hung between the cupboard and the grating on the tile stove and gave it a tug so it fell to the floor. She gathered it up in great haste.

'Let it be,' she said. 'Forget the whole thing.'

'I can't,' said Frida. 'You know that.'

'All I actually know is that this is worse than anything, no matter how impossible things feel to you. You could wreck yourself. I'm going to make us a cup of coffee and we'll talk it over.'

'It's no use.'

'You won't have the kid until early June,' said Tora. 'And at least you won't need to worry about keeping a summer baby warm. And by then Eriksson will be in work. It's only common sense.'

She was whispering fiercely and holding Frida by the shoulders, trying to shake some expression into her eyes. In the end she set her down on the bed and wound her shawl around her shoulders.

'I promise I'll give you a hand with the kid,' she said. 'Let's shake on it.'

She sought Frida's hand out under the shawl and pressed it time and again.

'Promise me now that you won't do this to yourself! Please? I swear we'll be in this together; we'll work something out. Will you give me your hand on it, Frida?'

And finally she could feel Frida responding to the pressure of her hand and starting to cry. Tora rubbed her bony back under the shawl as if the problem had been that she was cold. She promised her a hot cup of coffee as soon as she got the fire going in the stove and told her to get under the covers and warm up.

So Frida Eriksson's going to have a baby in June and that's all there is to it. If it's meant to stay in, it stays. Once she's into the fifth month the worst of the tiredness has passed, too. She's pretty old, so when her stomach begins to show she's supposed to be embarrassed about it. If you looked at her you'd never imagine that she had any pleasure left to give. Nor did she feel as if she did. Not pleasure, but solace.

She knows exactly when it happened. It was in early September, the last week of the strike. Eriksson had gone down to the carpentry shop to collect his tools. The dispute had been going on for so long he'd begun to worry that he'd never get them back. But the strikers on the picket line hadn't believed him, nor had the crowd outside the shop gates. Thirty Wärnström men had already returned to work.

He came back home with a bruised, swollen upper lip and a bleeding cut above his right eyebrow. He went right in and lay down on the settee in the front room and wouldn't tell Frida what had happened. She didn't find out until her brother Valentin came up and told her. He was the one who had intervened and broken up the crowd at the gate.

Eriksson didn't move. He got up that evening so Frida could put the bedclothes on the settee, but he didn't go out to the kitchen to eat. Frida brought his plate to him.

His lip was swollen and stiff and it was difficult for him to get the spoon in under it without its hurting. He didn't go out again that evening, just peed in the bucket, took off his trousers and got into bed. Frida lay down behind his back.

She couldn't sleep, just lay there thinking about what was going on around them and what was to become of them. Suddenly she heard him breathing strangely and imagined that he was crying, but trying not to be heard. She rubbed his back gently. She seldom touched him because she didn't want him on top of her. Now, however, she stroked his hard back and he slowly turned towards her. She touched his cheeks to see if they were damp, and then he was on top of her anyway.

They lay in a slightly strange position because of his lip; his ear was against her mouth. She felt him less and less although he was thrusting impatiently and obstinately. Finally he slid off her and lay on his back, and when she put her hand on his sex it was little and limp.

'This is what it's like getting old,' he said. 'I'm getting old and soft.'

She was terrified that David and Anna would wake up, as he was hardly keeping his voice down.

'No, that's not the problem,' she whispered. 'It's the strike. You go around worrying.'

'And isn't there a lot to worry about?'

'Forget it now,' she entreated. 'Don't think about the strike. You just rest. We're all right in here. Everything's fine.'

Though she knew it was all lies, for there are no secret rooms for lovers, she put her arm around his neck and helped him with her other hand until he could enter her again.

Now she thinks about that time, wondering why she did it. It had been foolish. But at the time she hadn't hesitated. She felt a couple of quick throbs and a little spurt and then it was over. She got up and went out into the kitchen and wet a rag in the water pail as a compress for his lip, which hurt again.

Everything else is fading, but she remembers what happened that evening. Soon it will be the only thing about the whole strike she remembers.

Konrad remembers everything. Nobody talks to him about it anymore because he's back at Berta Göhlin's and they're supposed to carry on as if nothing had ever happened. For his mother's sake. Tora Otter saw to it.

But on Tuesday evening the third of August he walked out. When he had scraped the baking sheets clean and greased them, he was supposed to mix the meringue batter. That was all he had left to do before going home. Evening had come and it was dark out by the time he was done because he was doing every chore so slowly. Widow Göhlin had already gone up to her apartment and he could hear her footsteps overhead.

He beat the egg whites stiff and white as tooth powder or ground limestone. He turned the bowl upside down over the zinc counter and held it out over the floor; the white peaks didn't so much as quiver. He beat it for another ten minutes with his eye on the ticking clock. He had never done that before though he had been instructed to. He changed hands twice. Never had his meringue stood so stiff. And his wrists ached.

He listened for the widow's footsteps and then went out into the shop. It was pitch dark out now and not a soul on the street, at least he couldn't hear any gravel crunching. Time to try it out. He walked over to the newly-cleaned plate glass window.

When he was done he washed the beater and very quietly put the basket of eggs and the bag of sugar back where they belonged. As he was walking out the back door, the widow shouted: 'Konrad! Is that you leaving?'

'Right,' he answered, 'and I won't be in tomorrow.'

Silence from upstairs.

'The bakers've joined in,' he said. Then he stepped outside and quickly shut the creaking veranda door behind him and pretended he didn't hear her voice ordering him back. As he walked home his heart was pounding. It said 'STRICKE!' on the window of the bakery now. Although he had written it from the inside, every single letter was turned in the right direction.

In the morning neither he nor his father went out. They got up as usual and sat on the kitchen settee waiting for their coffee. Frida said not a word. But when the eight-day clock on the wall chimed six and Konrad hadn't moved an inch Frida turned around, looking first at him and then at the clock. His stomach clutched. It hurt and he felt sick.

Now on winter evenings he lies in his bed under that clock at bedtime and it still hurts in the same spot when he remembers. He gets the same feeling when he remembers his first strike evening out at Starvation Meadows. He was surrounded by the smell of smoke, and cooking fires were glowing all around. He had got hold of an accordion and was skipping around with it. But his mother had turned up there too and caught sight of him. She had on her laundry dress and her cut-toed shoes so he assumed she was on her way home from Gertrudsborg where they had been rinsing in the lake. She grabbed him so hard by the arm he stopped stock still. She asked if he was drunk. But he wasn't - he hadn't touched a single drop.

'Come sit down with us,' said Vera Simonsson who was standing at a fire frying bacon on a tin plate. She had shifted a steaming pot of boiled potatoes onto the grass.

'This is a strike action,' said Konrad. 'We've been here all day!'

'Well, some of us have,' Vera laughed. 'Come and sit down, Frida'.

'They've been playing "The Internationale" all day long!' said Konrad

'You're coming home with me now.'

There was a podium made of empty crates, and a soap box. They'd decorated it with rowan branches, and the under-ripe clusters of berries were bright in the dusk. The men in the brass band had put down their instruments on the crates, and the Workers' Association banner was hanging limp between two poles. It was a hot, windless evening. Accordions, mainly one-rows, droned and people hummed along and conversed. In the end it was impossible to see how many people there were because it kept getting darker and darker. Then Ebon Johansson went up to the soap box and one of the boys in the band jumped up on a crate and blew a fanfare on his cornet. He heard Ebon shout: 'Comrades!' and the accordions went silent.

'Come along now,' said Frida and grabbed him hard by the arm, pulling him across the ditch and up onto the road.

'Comrades! A telegram has arrived from strike headquarters,' Ebon said loudly, and Konrad pulled away, straining to go back. But she held him in an iron grip and they trotted quickly down the gravel road, so Ebon's voice reciting figures was soon out of earshot.

'You're making trouble for yourself,' said Frida.

'You just don't get it, do you?'

'Hush your mouth.'

'The revolution's on!'

'Rubbish!'

'The government's mobilised the army,' said Konrad. 'It's true. Zäta Höglund's declared a republic, and Palm a revolution.'

'Not here, anyhow,' Frida said. 'And we're going home now. Is Eriksson over there, too?'

75

'Haven't you heard that Iversen-Lindh has sold every single share he owned in Wilhelmson's Carpentry shop? And that they've locked themselves in? They say that old Fru Lindh locked herself in at Gertrudsborg and that the merchant's on his way out there.'

'Well, she hasn't,' said Frida. 'I've just been there myself and there was nothing out of the ordinary going on.'

No one was at home but Dagmar and the little ones, and she'd made porridge for them. But they were out of milk and the shop had closed so they had to have it with blueberry syrup. Konrad didn't eat at all, he was too excited. For the hundredth time he tried to persuade Frida that a new era was being born, that soon there would be a time when no woman would spend her days doing other people's washing for one krona per day plus her meals. Soon she'd have boots and teeth and paraffin oil for the lamp, and Eriksson would have work and they would take journeys on the train like Lillibeth Iversen-Lindh and her aunt Malvina did every summer, all the way down to France, speaking Esperanto with the French and wearing hats. Frida couldn't help laughing at him in the end. She was standing there peeling cold boiled potatoes and slicing them onto crispbread spread with margarine. She salted them and gave one to each of the children with their porridge. Finally, though, she did ask him to hush up.

'Tomorrow's another day,' she said. 'Time for bed. The best thing you can do is to go over to Berta Göhlin's tomorrow morning and tell her you're coming back. If you don't you'll have no job when this is all over.' But he didn't go out after coffee Thursday morning either.

'Three hundred thousand workers were on strike one week after the declaration,' he told his mother. Three hundred thousand! They would bring down established society. They were breaking the

76

back of capitalism. They'd struck terror in the hearts of bourgeoisie, who were locking themselves in. Was she listening?

The army was mobilized. The navy had their cannons aimed at the port in Norrköping and at ports and factories all along the coast where a ghostly silence reigned. They were frightened. The shopkeepers had been ordered not to let workers buy on credit.

'Just look around when you go out washing,' he said. 'You'll see things you've never seen before. Something's happening.'

'What's that?'

'Haven't you noticed everything's changing?'

No, she hadn't. Lindh the merchant and Wärnström the factory owner went out again. Housewives lifted their skirts when they crossed the muddy square with their maids in tow carrying their baskets. The water tower with its granite ornamentation was still where it belonged and the trains screeched and whistled in the station yard. It was the same community as before.

'When you say "community" you see a town hall, but you should see a heart.'

'What on earth do you mean by that?'

'That's what Ebon Johansson says,' he replied.

You didn't see so many people on the streets now. The soldiers were still down by the stations, their rifles pointed downwards, and there were donation lists for the benefit of the striking men and their families at the Co-op and the cigar shop. There were guards outside the gates of Wilhelmsson's Carpentry Shop and Eriksson, who had been beaten up when he went round to collect his tools, lay on the settee predicting that the strike was ill-fated now. They'd be starved out like rats, and like rats they would eat one another up and fight with each other. His strike allowance came to five and a quarter kronor a week.

His kids scoured the wet roadside ditches and the ponds for

leeches to sell to the pharmacist. They also collected stag's horn for him, and flayed cats. Konrad couldn't get himself to pick up stray cats and skin them. But he did help the little ones stretch the skins and nail them to the wall of the shed. When they walked around the neighbourhood asking for bones and rags they could sell he was ashamed, because it wasn't very much better than begging. Some people gave them bread and table scraps as well.

He would go out to Hällsjö Lake and fish. He'd lie on the old jetty at Rosenholm Pond with a worm on his hook, hoping to catch a perch. It took a long time, these were big, tranquil perch that would settle in between the algae-covered jetty poles and not be the least bit interested in moving. So he'd lie there with his rod in the water and while the perch considered the worms on the hooks down there in the green darkness he'd dream about being in the capital city or at least in Norrköping. He dreamt of revolutions and riots. Up there in Stockholm the strike-breakers were defended by helmeted policemen with drawn sabres. He would lay his cheek against the warm wood imagining he was being pressed up against the side of a building by mounted policemen on big, restless horses. He felt the flat edge of a sabre, and put his hand to his cheek. He was trampled down. When he finally got away his jacket was torn up the back. Now he was running towards the square up ahead. He heard the rumbling of the canons and the stamping of many feet.

The workers were dangerous. They came rushing down the streets and alleyways. But he had actually never seen real city streets. He'd never seen a paved street. But he knew cities were hazardous places! Their leader tried to placate them. And he, Konrad Eriksson, was running, jumping up onto something — he didn't know what. But he was standing high up at the square, addressing the crowd.

'Comrades!' He thought about his speech all the way home and sometimes he'd swing the perch he had caught and was carrying on a forked branch. 'Comrades!' He could see Ebon Johansson on the empty crate in his mind's eye. 'At last we are at the walls,' he said. 'A crack is opening wide, thanks to our intense perseverance. Our love and our hands will make these walls come tumbling down! Comrades!'

Eyes glazed, he was immobilised under a window, his perch dragging on the ground. Somebody passed by and looked at him but he hardly noticed. A musty smell of bedroom came wafting out of a window because it was still early morning. Slowly Konrad came back to himself and started walking home to number 60 Hovlunda Road, where Eriksson was lying in the front room on the settee saying more and more men were going back to work. 'The ranks are yielding!' said the headline in the hectographed bulletin they got instead of a newspaper now that the typographers were out on strike.

'All you ever read is that pack of lies,' said Konrad, setting *The Answer* in front of him.

On the eighth of September Eriksson's swollen lip had gone down and he went to his local union meeting. He came home, and although he didn't say they'd voted to go back to work, Konrad could tell. Valentin and Ebon sat silently in the empty upholstery shop they'd rented during the strike. They had put away the record books, strike cards, allowance lists and their bundles of *The Answer*. Eriksson placed a hectographed paper on the kitchen table in front of Konrad, not minding that it landed in the margarine. Frida read over Konrad's shoulder.

Those workers who left their jobs on 6 August last are hereby

79

informed that we remain of the view that you committed a breach of contract. That fact is, in our opinion, so indisputable it would be absurd to call for conciliation on the matter. We had also clarified our position before employing you.

We will return to the agreement that applied prior to the strike. However, before we are prepared to do so we demand that you prove yourselves worthy of our confidence and prove your desire for a peaceful labour market for a period of two months.

There will be no reprisals from our side.

We require a response as to whether you desire to continue your employment in accordance with the above-mentioned conditions. Your reply must reach us no later than 9:00 a.m. on Friday the 10th of September.

> On behalf of Wilhelmsson's Carpentry Shop, Ltd.
> Holger Iversen-Lindh

'Is it over now?' his mother asked. Konrad nodded.

'So Pappa will get work.'

Which was also quite necessary. They were living on fish and wild mushrooms, and Tora and she had been out picking berries in their mangling baskets and an old pram. Tora had sold them at the market instead of the loaves she couldn't bake because there was no more flour.

But at work they didn't want Eriksson back. Eight of the men who had gone out on strike back in June were sacked. This wasn't a reprisal, according to Iversen-Lindh. It was a matter of necessary operational cutbacks owing to the interruption in production caused by the strike. The economy of the community was badly damaged and they would all have to bear the consequences. His Norwegian voice rang out cheerful and sing-song when he informed them. The matter was perfectly clear!

Eriksson went to every workplace in the village with his employment certificates. But it did him no good because another kind of testimonial was circulating amongst the employers. Lefvander's was delivering flour again and Tora started to bake bread for Berta Göhlin. But Konrad didn't know if he dared to go back. He hung around outside there in the evenings. The air had grown chilly and harsh and there were tufts of grass under the soles of his shoes. The apples had begun to fall, and the sound frightened him a few times until he realized what it was. He couldn't see much in the dark and when his feet touched the apples he thought they were dead birds.

The evenings were often cloudy. He saw no stars between the branches of the apple trees, and Mars no longer lit up the sky as it had throughout the strike, shining out from beyond the firewall with the words Headstones and Marble on it. It was so quiet in the mornings when the fog was lifting that he could hear the leaves break off their branches before they fell and drifted to the ground or the gentle fingers of the rain on the tarpaper roof over Göhlin's veranda.

People had also gone back to work at Wärnström's and at the foundry, though they were being paid as if they were new hirelings. Valentin was rehired at the foundry, but not Ebon. He would have to go to Norrköping and see if he could get work there, he said.

Nobody took Eriksson on and Konrad was frightened. The two of them were alien to the world order, awake when others were asleep, lying in their beds listening to clogs clacking down the stairs when the men were off to the workshops.

Then Berta Göhlin took pity on him and he had to go back. The first thing she ordered him to do was to wash the display window, although it was already clean and shiny.

Before the strike Tora baked three nights a week for widow Göhlin. While the bakery oven was heating up she baked meringue layers and other cakes to be filled and iced, using batter that had been prepared that afternoon. Then she baked coffee cakes, cinnamon buns and sweet rolls. The last thing she baked was Danish pastries, rolling the buttery dough outside on the back porch where the early morning air was still chilly. She walked home along the empty early morning streets, and twice during that summer of 1909 she had walked without a hat. The doves had begun to coo under the eaves but had not yet flown out. Solitary sparrows sailed from under their gutter nests and down in the direction of Hovlunda Road looking for fresh horse droppings. The finches and willow warblers were already busy around the gooseberry bushes in the upholsterer's garden on the other side of the street.

She saw Konrad's word on the café window that first strike morning and realized right away he was the culprit, but not that it was meringue batter. She had to go in and touch the thick sticky letters. That kid's still wet behind the ears, she thought. But it's nothing to do with me.

Her next thought, though, was that Konrad might lose his job at the bakery. Unless the bakers were also on strike, of course. In which case he'd done the right thing. But if they are, what'll happen to me?

She decided to go and ask Ebon Johansson and Valentin. They were over there in the abandoned upholstery shop on the other side of the street. There was an empty pilsner bottle in the window and she walked over and stood gingerly on tiptoe peeping in alongside the bottle to see whether they were awake.

Valentin was asleep. He was lying on his back with his mouth open and she could hear him snoring through the window. But Ebon was up. He wasn't dressed. On an empty overturned crate in front of him he had a wash basin and he was standing with his back to the window, towelling himself dry. When he was done he walked over to the bed and took down his watch from its nail and began to wind it. He never looked out the window.

He had grown older. He was no longer thin as a wire, but his body still carried no excess weight. Maybe when he sat down on the bed his belly did protrude a little and there was a roll at his waistline that wasn't there before. He had delicate ankles and lovely thin legs she couldn't really imagine being strong enough to carry him around the foundry, where the work was so heavy. He was extremely bow-legged and his whole lower body, his tight bottom, hips and legs appeared weak in comparison with the top half of him. There was a dark-brown cross of hair on his stomach and he had scars on his legs she didn't remember. But none of his fingers had been cut off, he was undamaged and gorgeous despite his forty-three years. The skin on his throat, hands, forearms and feet was darker where the dust from the works had eaten its way in. His soft, thin hair was dark brown, thinning at the crown and temples, where it was curly and starting to go grey. His nose was narrow. She had never been able to pinpoint the colour of his eyes. They were brown or amber, and shifted with the light. She knew he had once had other soft places, too, and probably still did. His eyelashes were fine as the web in a quill pen, his lips were thin and had felt childlike against her neck. That she remembered. When she saw his hand lying on the bedcover, the top of her hand so intensely recalled the palm of his that she felt her hand move involuntarily from the window frame to cover her mouth.

She could not disown this old familiarity. She even recognized his sex. It had a large round tip that had always made it difficult for him to penetrate her. She had used that fact to her advantage in those days when she didn't want him inside her. She had been afraid of getting pregnant.

He made a sudden movement. It was only to reach for his trousers, which were on the pile of clothing at the foot of the bed, but it made her realize that at any moment he might raise his eyes and see her face staring at him through the window pane. She turned her head and continued along the wall to the arbour. When she looked over towards the Cosmopolitan, she thought she saw Berta Göhlin's face at the upstairs window and decided to walk in amongst the apple trees and home through the yard behind the brewery if she could cut through the hedge. She could always say she was going to buy a keg of porter if she met anyone. Her heart was pounding and her mouth was dry. It still said STRICKE on the café window when she ran off.

I just do a bit of baking at night, she thought. I'm not a member of anything and Berta Göhlin is nothing but a widow with a café.

One evening when Tora was walking to the bakery along the rutted road, wet with rain, she ran into Ebon. She didn't see him coming because she was looking down feeling shivery and chilled and angry about having to work four nights out of the week's seven instead of sleeping.

'Good evening to you, Tora,' he said, stopping in front of her. She realized he was asking how she and her boys were but afterwards she couldn't recall how she had answered. Not until she was inside the Cosmopolitan and had started measuring flour for her dough did the tension ease. She went right into the darkest corner of the bakery over by the big cabinet where the china was kept and where nobody could see her from the window. She sat there for so long with her face in her hands Berta Göhlin must have noticed things were unusually quiet and come downstairs to see if she was all right. Tora responded bluntly.

'I got the curse,' she said, which was also true. 'Just when I was going to start baking.'

So Berta went up to her apartment, brought down a bottle of cognac, and made her a cup of coffee. Afterwards she felt a little better. But her back ached all night, though she didn't really start bleeding until morning. By that point she was just tired and her belly felt tender. While she was making gruel for the boys she boiled herself some water and poured it into a litre bottle she wrapped in a thick towel. She fell asleep with it between her legs and it made her nice and warm all the way up to her belly and groin, and she knew the worst was over for this time.

On Saturday evening she didn't have to bake. She heated water and began by bathing the slippery bodies of the boys in her zinc tub. When they were done she hung the rope between the painted blue cupboard and the damper on the tile stove and hung a sheet across it. Then she washed herself behind the sheet, taking her time. She had to heat up a little more water to pour in, because the bath water from the boys had cooled. When she was done she asked Dagmar to come and sit with them without saying where she was going. As soon as the boys were asleep she left.

As she walked down Hovlunda Road the crickets were chirping in the gardens. It was evening and it would soon be night. She was sure Ebon would be standing in the window of the upholstery shop watching her approach and that he'd step out into the street as he had done the last time. But it was dark in there. Maybe he was sitting with idle hands resting on the table top, not wanting to waste paraffin oil. The moon rose and every leaf, every blade of grass was lit up and reflected the light. She was tingling with anticipation.

She heard the door of the upholstery shop open, and footsteps on the gravel. She saw Ebon's white collar from a distance, long before any other part of him became visible. When he turned into the road he lifted his hat in her direction.

'Out for a walk?' he asked. 'Well. It's a lovely evening.'

After which he nodded and vanished, striding quickly in the direction of Chapel Street. Tora walked on for a while, as slowly as she could, until his footsteps were no longer audible. Then she started to run towards home. But she realized she wouldn't be able to go to sleep even if she went to bed, and besides she didn't want Dagmar to see her face. So she passed 60 Hovlunda Road and headed out towards the meadows. The heavy dew of late summer wet her skirt hem. There would soon be night frost, when the air turned bitter and the grass stiffened and yellowed. Just as well, just as well, she tried to tell herself with every step she took.

By the third week there was no more flour to be had. Tora couldn't bake for her own stall at the market and was told she wasn't needed at the Cosmopolitan either. She went to Lefvander's and asked for a word with the merchant himself. Old man Lefvander had died, and Valfrid Johansson married his widow. He talked to her from behind the desk that had once been Lefvander's, and invited her to be seated on the brown artificial leather divan. He was in uniform. Well, there were plenty of uniforms around these days. Valfrid was now Assistant Fire Chief and was on his way to a drill. He had braided trim on his sleeves in a pattern as complex as her old rattan carpet beater.

'There's no flour to be had for love or money,' he said, looking her straight in the eye with a sorrowful gaze. She almost had the feeling he thought it was her fault. He kept sighing and shifting around on his chair, but his problem was a colicky stomach that sent gas bubbles shooting through his system and bloated his stomach though he was otherwise flat as a side of dried stockfish.

'Now you see where it was all leading,' he said. 'The mills are at a standstill.'

She said nothing. So he explained to her that the foundation of any society was morals. And now there was no longer any semblance of morals. At that point his stomach let out a fierce rumble and he glared so hard at Tora that for once she looked away.

'Crudeness and dissolution,' said Valfrid. 'Now we see where it was all leading.'

'Oh, I'm not so sure,' said Tora, wanting to lighten up the conversation but not knowing what to say.

'You know very well that among the better classes there was some sympathy with the plight of the workers. You can't deny it.'

'I really don't know,' said Tora. 'I'm not denying anything. I just came by to ask about the flour.'

'Sacrifices have been made in order to placate the sense of dissatisfaction and improve conditions. But now the workers have shown their real faces. The faces of predators. Whatever morals there were are in dissolution, Tora.'

After this he warned her solemnly against his brother Ebon. Astonished and upset she realized that somebody must have seen her speaking to Ebon on the street, maybe even seen when she stood outside the window of the upholstery shop looking in.

'I don't neeed to ask anyone's permission,' she said, sounding far more plucky than she felt. Her knees nearly buckled under her on the way home and she had the feeling people were staring at her everywhere, a sensation she'd been spared now for many years.

When the grain mills began to grind again and Lefvander's started getting shipments of flour she took up her baking. The upholstery shop was rented out, and was dark and empty at night. Tora tried not to look when she passed by. Actually, it didn't matter. She knew he was in Norrköping.

Just as well. Just as well. In the end Eriksson left too. He said he'd send Frida money as soon as he could. But it probably wouldn't be easy. When she saw Frida and the children she couldn't help thinking that Ebon's strike had resulted in nothing but trouble.

It's Saturday night and Frida's gone back down to her place. Tora is asleep in her front room, which smells of sleeping children and cold stove ashes. Suddenly, though, she wakes up. Has she been sleeping a whole hour or more? Somebody's out in the hallway whistling. Her whole body is suddenly prepared for it to be him. She sees and hears him and feels the taste of him before she can put up her defences.

But the footsteps pass. They're quick and light. Her body is still throbbing and she doesn't know whether it was all just a dream. Time and again that winter it happens, she dreams about him. But it hurts. She feels as if she has been torn away from his presence when she wakes up, and she puts her arms around herself wanting to slip her hand between her legs to ease the hollow pain.

The footsteps vanish down the stairs and she hears no more whistling. She realizes he hasn't been there at all. He's in Norrköping and she knows nothing about his life.

A suit of clothes was made for Fredrik Otter. The tailor whose shop was on Highway Road had come by a roll of grey-green English tweed and made a jacket, waistcoat and trousers for the young man. But it was dear. Fredrik was to travel to Gothenburg with his mother and show his relations there his school marks. She wanted to be able to send him to the co-educational intermediate school. Schoolmaster Nordkvist had said the lad had a good head and she figured that if his grandmother and uncles got a peek at the lad who was, after all, F.A. Otter's son, and at his marks, they might offer to pay for his books or his tuition, which would come to seventy kronor a term. That was more than she paid for her market stall.

But the war got in the way. Nordkvist cut a long poem out of the newspapers and gave his cleverest boys a verse each to learn by heart. Fredrik's was:

The fire from machine guns whizzes by me —
Shouts of victory, cries of agony.
And through the lines across the trenches
Move the Emperor's troops, strong as iron wrenches.
Strongholds fall and armies flee,
Our banner flies for all to see.
German soldiers conquer all
Whether they stand, or to the Lord fall.

But that didn't stop him from being on the side of the entente in the afternoons after school and shooting Germans from the outbuilding roofs the moment they raised their heads, or from chasing them up to the park by Heavenside Spring.

The trip to Gothenburg never materialised, not to mention that the war broke out just when Tora had signed the contract to take over the Cosmopolitan Café from Berta Göhlin. She was to pay two thousand kronor for the business and the furniture and fittings. To make the first payment on the signing of the contract she borrowed five hundred kronor from Valfrid Johansson, who became her supplier.

They made the trip the next July instead, but by then everything had changed. Fredrik had shot up incredibly during the winter — never mind what people said about children only growing in the summer! He was tall and heavy-set and could barely get into the suit, which had been put away for a whole year so he wouldn't spoil it. His marks were no longer anything to boast about, both because he had been lazy and because he had got himself on Nordkvist's bad side one day when Nordkvist had ridiculed him in the woodworking lesson. The schoolmaster had taken the knife-stand he was making and that was coming out crooked, lifted it over his head and shouted in his sharp Närke dialect:

'Take a look at this fellas! Otter's knife stand!'

Fredrik had torn the stand out of Nordkvist's hand, because he was taller than the schoolmaster by now, and pale with fury at the nostrils and the corners of his mouth, he had thrown it to the floor at the Schoolmaster's feet.

In Gothenburg his uncles inquired if he was interested in pursuing his studies. Fredrik's skin was pimply and his voice was changing and out of control. Fredrik answered that he hoped to be taken on at the works as soon as possible. They took the train back home and Tora tried not to think about what this journey had cost: the tickets, the suit, a new coat for her, meals on the trains. They had given them a red wooden sledge with an embroidered cushion that had been F.A.'s when he was a child.

There was a heat wave on. They said not a word to one another until after Hallsberg, but Tora found herself staring at the boy for whom she had had knee-length trousers made a year ago, with plenty of room at the waist and a buckle at the back. Now he filled out the whole suit so the seam between the buttocks was straining and his big bony knees were sticking out and kept bumping her in the narrow space between the seats.

'Pull in your legs!' she hissed.

He had his sports club tie pin on, and when his eldest uncle noticed it he shook his head, saying that sports was a boil on the back of society and ought to be lanced. Fredrik was so shy that he barely spoke when he was spoken to and didn't dare look people in the eyes. His sex was bulging in his trousers.

'Sit up like a gentleman,' she said. By the time they got to Oxtorp he had had enough and went out to stand by the windows. Or so she thought. What he actually did was get out and walk the rest of the way into town. Tora would have to lug everything home herself. She understood that he was afraid all the other young men would laugh at him if he walked through the town in the summer heat in a too-tight suit of nubbly wool carrying a red wooden sledge with embroidery and tassels.

Adam had come to the station to meet their train, and was standing under the clock with a lollypop in his mouth when the train pulled in. All she had to do was look at him to realize whom she should have taken along to Gothenburg. His hair was cut so short it felt like brush bristles when she drew her hand through it. But he had a shapely head. His nose was aquiline, his eyelids rounded — he was the image of F.A. He would have placed his hand in his grandmother's if she had asked, let himself be kissed, said thank you for the sledge, found the right turn of phrase. He was a prince in disguise standing there on the platform in his torn shirt with coal dust between his toes. But his marks were never as good as Fredrik's had been before he dropped the knife stand on Schoolmaster Nordkvist's bunions.

She had learned that poverty is as heavy and implacable as the stones in the ground. And wealth is beyond your wildest dreams. Its spires and turrets stretch so high an ordinary person can barely catch sight of it as she shuffles by. But it doesn't bother ordinary people much either, unless they have a jealous streak, as soldier Lans used to say before he passed on.

Frida's brother Valentin said she had a defective picture of the world. Tora didn't say anything back, just gave Frida a look. Konrad still carried books home and read them. They included *The Mystery of the Universe* and *A Study of Development*, *Revisionism* and *The Social Revolution*, and a book that scared Frida in a serious way and for which she held Valentin responsible the next time he came round: *The Diary of a Seducer*. But he leafed through and made her and Tora read bits here and there and they had to admit there was nothing in it that might do Konrad any harm, just stuff no one could possibly understand.

'Read it yourselves,' said Valentin. 'In fact, you really should. I'd give anything to see you sit down with a book some time.'

'Right,' said Tora.

'Truth is you've got a lot to learn, too, Tora Otter!'

She turned her back on him and started wiping Frida's kitchen table. She could boil her sheets, mix a twenty-five litre bread dough and bake the loaves that same night, set up the loom, prepare the weft, wind and thread the heddles of an eight-harness loom, or even a twelve at a pinch. But now she was expected to learn the names of stars and countries and men who had written books that would change the world. However, the world wasn't about to change! She'd been around long enough to know that.

Konrad said a lot of things were going to change over time no matter what she thought and that the era of transformations had already begun. They'd be around to see more amazing things than ordinary women who read books. Love was going to be free, he said. To his mother. Frida had to turn away and smile when he stood there in the middle of the kitchen floor and said that.

Love had always been free, said Tora bitterly. What cost was the consequences.

'But nowadays there's contums!'

She slapped him hard then. Konrad's cheek slowly turned deep red, because Frida could still deliver a good whack. That was how far things had gone – a young man could stand there and say things like that to his mother!

They took a little look through his things when he'd gone and in the drawer beside the kitchen settee. But they didn't find anything suspicious, no bottles, nothing. Just a little dirty laundry and books. *Inhabited Worlds. A Moment of Eternity. From Science to Utopia.*

'And he thinks he's going to be a baker,' said Tora.

Tora was moving. Having taken over the Cosmopolitan, she couldn't stay on at number 60 Hovlunda Road. It was too far away. Both she and Frida pretended that was the reason. But things were uneasy between them when everything was packed and ready the last evening and only the beds were untouched.

Tora's room had a stove, a solid little Näfvekvarn in the niche for the tile stove. The room had been empty but for that when she moved in. She had bought the wooden blue-painted cupboard herself. On the open shelf she had kept her zinc tub and cutting board and above the tile stove a coffee roaster, an iron and two copper saucepans. The walls were papered with two different patterns, rolls of wallpaper left over from when they did up Göhlins. She had covered a damp spot with a picture of an angel resting her head in one hand. She had both a bed and a settee and a kitchen table with a crocheted cloth she removed at mealtimes. She had used a piece of gathered fabric on a drawstring to skirt the washing up table, where there was a pail and a tub. Her black dress and her suit jacket were hanging in the corner with a sheet over them, as far as possible from the tile stove, and the rest of their clothes were in the dresser. In the top drawer she kept what little she had after her husband, a few photos and ornaments.

She had been so frugal she had only bought the few things they had; she hadn't even taken a two-room flat in the building when she had had the chance. First she wanted some money in the bank, enough so she knew she could stay solvent.

She had lived in the village for so long she had seen how the people who hovered between the stones on the ground and the turrets and spires above whirled like the snowflakes in Fredrik's paperweight. If you didn't stay solvent you would crash irretrievably. Now she had purchased a Chesterfield sofa, an extra bed and two washbasins, chairs and a few other things. Big changes were about to take place and they had been planned long and thoroughly. She was renting a two-bedroom flat with a kitchen and a sitting room and she planned to let both the bedrooms, furnished. She didn't intend to give up her stall at the market, either. She had it all figured out, how each of her enterprises would support the other when necessary.

She had been secretive as usual but now that she was moving she explained the whole thing to Frida. She took a paper bag and wrote it all down, when the payments on the café would fall due, the income she counted on from the market and the rented rooms, and then she wet the tip of the aniline pen and wrote how much she had to take in at the café to make all the ends to meet. To Frida, these figures were completely meaningless. Buying sugar and flour in huge sacks from Lefvander's — well, she usually found herself scraping the splinters at the bottom of her flour canister by the end of the week.

'True, there are ups and downs on the path of life,' said Tora.

But that wasn't so. She could see in Frida's expression that poverty is as heavy and implacable as the stones on the ground. And she herself was tired and confused. Surrounded by everything she owned packed in boxes. Her waffle iron was wrapped in newspaper so as not to blacken the cutting board; its handle protruded like a warning finger. It was beginning to feel like one of those nights when your mouth is dry and your body aches but you just can't sleep no matter what position you lie in.

'You'll be all right too, you'll see,' she said to Frida. 'You're muddling through.' And it was true that the worst seemed to be over. She remembered the late winter of 1910 when Frida had had to pawn her sewing machine. That was cutting off the branch you were sitting on if ever anyone had. Without the extra earnings she brought in from making shirts, she wouldn't manage. At least spring had arrived and it was warm out by the time her little girl was born. Frida christened her Ingrid, the same as the princess born in March that year.

The next winter there seemed to be no way out. Eriksson hadn't come back, nor had he sent much money. They didn't know if he was drinking or what the matter was. Far, far into the autumn Frida sat warming up milk for the baby in her tin ladle right over the lamp flame because she had no wood. That was when Tora realized that she would have to work something out, and before winter really set in in earnest, Tora's brother Rickard out by the Ridge had taken Ingrid under his wing. He'd returned from America with his family.

Ingrid came home in spring and didn't have to be sent out as a foster child again that year. But late the next winter things were desperate again, and Stella and Rickard took her back for two months to put some meat on her bones. Then Frida was hired as a washerwoman for the laundry at the corner of Store Street and Hovlunda Road, which was the best thing that could have happened to her. Dagmar was at home looking after Ingrid. Her back problems still prevented her from having any other work than taking in shirts. In a way Tora thought that was fortunate. Otherwise she would soon have moved out on her own. They left home earlier and earlier nowadays. Frida was lucky to still have Konrad at home, leaving his pay packet on the kitchen table. He preferred reading books to running around, and it was best for everyone that she let him have his way.

She talked and talked until her mouth went dry and Frida nodded in agreement but looked a bit quizzical. What it sounded like to her was that Tora suddenly needed to balance all her books and settle her accounts before she left. It was as if she were going on a much longer journey than just riding down Hovlunda Road to Store Street and then a couple of houses up near the printers'.

Tora didn't sleep a wink. In the morning the cart came rolling noisily down the empty street. The stableman hadn't sent Kalle Bira who drove her to the market on Saturdays, but Trotter, the driver who always did the night soil run. That hurt. She took it as a personal affront from the stableman. Konrad helped him to carry the heaviest things. Fredrik and Adam flew like shuttles in a loom with all the movables, and she took the fragile things herself.

The cart was packed so early Fredrik and Adam hadn't left for school yet. They sat at the back of the cart, their legs dangling, holding the potted plants to keep them from breaking against one another or falling off. Tora started walking behind, but as the cart was pulling out she suddenly shouted:

'Sweet Jesus, I forgot the basement!'

So the cart backed up again. The horse didn't like being made to walk backwards and was foaming green at the mouth. This was a bad omen, going back now, a really bad omen. But it had to be done. She had her big table and all her bread baking things down in the basement. How could she almost have left behind the things she needed most?

This time Fredrik and Trotter had to carry the heavy things because Konrad had left for work. He worked at Anker's now. Frida had left for the laundry, too, taking her by the hand and saying farewell as she passed. Tora had snarled:

'What's wrong with you? I'm not exactly moving to Timbuktu.'

She sounded angrier than she felt. No, the morning hadn't begun very well. When they were finally done she was so tired after her sleepless night and all the carrying she thought her knees would buckle under her. She climbed up alongside Trotter, not bothering about how awful he smelled. He looked pleased with himself, and swished the reins against the huge buttocks of the horse. The gravel clattered under the wheels and they were off. This time the load was heavier, and the horse showed it. His back strained under the harness.

'Well, here we go,' said Trotter. 'A two-bedroom flat on Store Street and the café as well. That's what I call coming up in the world.'

'It's nothing but debts!'

'Oh, right. That's what they always say. Nothing but debts and responsibilities. Debts and responsibilities.' His wide, knotted whip-end played across the horse's back. It was a sunny summer morning and as they passed Carlsborg the mist rose like a light haze over the short grass. She didn't say another word to him. Sitting there early in the mornings transporting barrels of human excrement when no one else was awake seemed to have made a philosopher of him. The cart bounced along the bumpy road and she shouted out to the boys at the back to hold on tight to her potted plants. Then she felt the tears rising in her eyes. Maybc it was the pollen from the blossoming bushes. She always had trouble in early June. She wiped her eyes and hoped no-one would notice.

'That's right, you always leave something behind,' said Trotter. 'Something of yourself, I mean.'

'Every single thing I own and care about is in this cart,' Tora answered curtly.

'I do hope you're wrong,' he replied.

He was a sign painter named Eliasson, but people called him the Cock. Nearly every shop sign in town was his creation, the most famous being the sheaf on the glass door of the Agricultural Society's offices. You could distinguish every single grain of wheat, and they were golden.

Tora had arranged with him to come and repaint the words Cosmopolitan Café on the black glass along on either side of the café door. The gold letters had started to crack and peel on the inside. He never came. He wasn't a man who be counted on to keep his word; his services were so sought after he could do more or less as he pleased. Six weeks passed, and the gold curled up and fell down behind the glass. Tora was raging but controlled her anger because she knew the Cock was easily offended. She took out a long wooden bar left over from when the carpenter put up the curtain rods in the window.

So one morning when the men walked by on their way to Wärnström's workshop they noticed a long rod extending out over the door. No sign appeared on the rod, and nothing more happened except that the pigeons took to sitting there cleaning their robust chests and dirtying her steps, and it surprised people that Tora Otter let them go on doing so. When the rod had been up for a while, people started asking Tora what it was for, and she answered:

'I thought I'd put out a perch for the Cock.'

'What would he want with a perch?' people wondered.

'I guess he'd need something to settle on, if he should happen to fly by here one day.'

This reached the Cock, of course, and he was flattered. Yes, it was just his style! Something extra, a little spice. He scaled the wall of Jonsson's Menswear and changed it to Jonsson and Sons the day he heard that, and was just about to fold up his ladder and take his brushes straight to the Cosmopolitan. But then his imagination started to spin.

He waited until Saturday evening, and turned up in all his finery. He had a suit of English worsted and a soft hat and he rang the bell and stood in the open doorway smiling, hat in hand, until Tora came out of the kitchen and found him there. He tossed his hat on to the hook.

'Top o'the evening,' he said.

She went and stood behind her ornate marble-topped wooden counter, and there they stood, staring at one another. She wanted her lettering redone, but he had drawn his conclusions too fast, and assumed she was inviting him to court her, walk out with her, marry her and get three meals a day out of her and his socks darned. She let him go on believing it until the letters were gold-leafed again. Then she asked him how much it would be.

'Nothing, for you Tora,' he smiled, brushing his soft hat with his hand.

That was when Tora informed him that there was nothing at all between them but an unpaid bill, and the people sitting out in the café listening thought she might have broken it to him a little more gently, or at least with a sense of humour. The Cock's face went black. Afterwards he said he hadn't cared a bit, on the contrary in fact because she was as lifeless as a mangling rod in bed and never thought about anything but her café. Not to mention the fact that she mixed roasted rye in her coffee so it tasted worse than ape sweat and he, for one, intended to have his coffee at Anker's in future.

It was true that her mind was almost always busy with the café, and she did have to mix rye in the coffee because there was a crisis on. When the war broke out and men were called up, everyone took out all the money they had in the bank, the merchants were drowning in orders and prices skyrocketed. People stocked up on as many things as their credit would stretch to and Tora, who was new in the business, would have got nothing at all if she hadn't had Valfrid Johansson and her wholesaler in Eskilstuna from whom she had been buying sugar, fruit flavourings and agar-agar for her sweets business for a couple of years.

For the first few weeks the café was silent as the grave. The church bells rang and rang to remind the men to enlist, and Wärnström's closed down. But the panic gradually subsided and people started saying there would be more work than ever at the workshops. Others, however, preached gloom and doom and there were rumours about Alexander Lindh having overextended his credit in the difficult times before the war started and losing his export business to American competition. The general consensus, though, was that he was a small but strong man who would land on his feet — telephones were ringing and telegrams being sent. During the first few months he hardly left the office, night and day. Then one morning he complained of a sudden splitting headache and only managed to get to his desk and sit down before he collapsed on to the desktop, unconscious. He died before they could get him to the hospital.

He was buried one Saturday morning in August, the church heavy with the scent of roses and carnations. The workshops closed for the funeral. His coffin lay in the grave in the churchyard under two hundred and twenty-two wreaths, one of which came from the poorhouse and another from Wärnström's.

But in a house by the railroad crossing on Highway Road an old woman sat in a black satin dress, her legs far too swollen to carry her. She sat looking at the hanging birch that was so big and so heavy that she no longer had a view of the street and thus no longer anything to pass the time looking at. She could see a huge stone, the top of which was already covered with yellow leaves. She found the stillness of the August day, the wormy cabbage in the garden and the rotting brown apples oppressive.

There was not so much as a puff of wind to move the deep purple, white and lilac bands covered with last wishes that lay over the body in the coffin out there in the churchyard. The next day she read every detail of the description of the funeral in the newspaper, and the words of the pastor, which were printed inside a black border. She looked up the hymn numbers in her hymnal and read each verse through to see if she found them appropriate. The obituary spoke of his courage and his Swedish entrepreneurial spirit and his unfailing interest in the working classes, but not of his dry warm hands and his quick footsteps. She remembered those things.

Tora kept the Cosmopolitan open after the service, thinking that it would be an important day for the café. She didn't even go along to the cemetery, because she wanted to be there behind her counter, and she had stayed up doing extra baking the night before. She was counting on people's need to spend time together afterwards, mulling over the funeral and bringing the day to a dignified conclusion. She anticipated that this day would be a turning point for her, when the better-off people would finally find their way to the Cosmopolitan. She had a hectic morning. All the glasses had to be shined (she planned to serve water with the coffee like they did in the nicer places), and she didn't want any flies hovering over the sugar bowls.

But they didn't come. Just the regulars, a couple of painters on their dinner break, the schoolgirls from the co-educational in black coats for the funeral. After them the café went silent again.

She often stood with her hands on her hips in the café doorway. What was wrong with her place? She had round marble-topped tables, paintings of glimmering lakes and elves and fairies dancing, red velvet curtains. Her best piece was a full-length mirror with an ornate gilded frame. Although it looked like wood, a corner damaged in transport long ago revealed that it was plaster. The Cock had bettered the gold.

In the shop, the display window was backed by a short velvet curtain on a rod. There were cake plates and platters of pastries on tiers covered with lilac satin. Not a fly, not a leaf of tobacco. Not a spittoon in sight. A galoshes stand, an umbrella stand, a wooden cupboard for glassware that would not have been out of place in the temple in Jerusalem. Nickel-plated trays and portraits of royalty. Everything had remained virtually unchanged since 1894 when Berta Göhlin and her husband had collected it all in Norrköping and Stockholm, and it was all kept up with silver polish and furniture wax, and the floors were smooth as old leather gloves from twenty years of soap and elbow grease.

So why did the more elegant ladies go to Anker's after their shopping? Why didn't they come into the Cosmopolitan and sit there planning their collections and their stockpiling? Personally, she found Anker's shabbier, and there was only one room, all the way inside, where you could sit and get away from the market people. It puzzled her.

Then one day after a suffrage demonstration in the schoolyard of the co-educational, a group of freezing-cold women came down to the Cosmopolitan because it was closest. That was a lucky day, because after that they continued to come, even started holding their meetings there, and asked Tora to keep their table pennant there and put it out when they were coming. She would stand in the doorway with her hands under her apron and listen to Magnhild Lundberg, who had once been the Headmistress at the school, lecture on the national pension scheme and Fröken Levin recite Viktor Rydberg's poem 'The Flying Dutchman'.

With that exception, most of her café customers were young men who sat there for hours, careful not to drink up the last of what was in their glasses or cups. They sat pouring over their books, or working two by two on pads of graph paper, erasing so often that the tables and floor were covered with shreds of eraser by the time they left. These were the boys from the vocational school. They had been in the merchant marine for a year or two or worked in the forests to save up enough money for the three-semester course. She should have switched to weaker bulbs so they couldn't sit there and study, but that wasn't her way. Their rented rooms were cold, what with the fuel shortage. How could there be too little firewood? Tora couldn't understand it. It was less puzzling that there was also a paraffin shortage, as Kaiser Wilhelm probably needed it to fire his canons with. Fredrik thought he'd die laughing when she said that. But what was so funny? He just needed to flaunt what he knew and ridicule her for her ignorance.

The boys came back in the evenings to see if there were any girls around. They were bolder then: one bottle of fizzy lemonade, eight glasses and a box of matches, please! And hurry it up, we don't have all the time in the world. She couldn't keep from laughing. But if she caught one of them with a flask in his inner pocket he was out on his backside in no time. And she was tired of their filling the rooms with the smoke from Luckys and Camels that took up residence in her curtains, and their leafing through her magazines until they fell apart.

In the days when she came in to bake for Berta Göhlin, the

gilded mirror, the curtains and the marble tables had looked to her like security itself. Now, however, she sometimes thought they were nothing but a pile of rubbish gathering dust and for which she had placed herself deeply in debt.

In order to make ends meet she had to buy on credit and get everything as cheaply as possible: flour, sugar, coffee, the lot. The price of food rose and it got harder and harder to get hold of staple items. Valfrid stayed faithful to her, and she had her wholesaler in Eskilstuna, too. But she handled him differently.

She would travel to Eskilstuna in Ebba Julin's fox fur collar, a black plumed hat and brand new galoshes — a tad too tight so they creased and rubbed at the ankles. She would allow herself to be taken to the hotel for a meal. Mellberg, from Eskilstuna Flavourings, was over sixty and probably thought of her, at thirty-eight, as a spring chicken. By the time they got to the coffee and arrack his eyes had glazed over. That was when she placed her orders. In her home town Tora would never have been caught dead behaving like this, but now she was in Eskilstuna, and quite good at the game.

When it was time to catch the evening train home things got a little sticky and she would simply have to come back to his place for coffee the next time she was in town. Absolutely!

So just to be on the safe side the next time she took Linnea Holm along. Linnea was one of her young waitresses, from Örebro. Tora paid for her ticket and settled her in at a tea room. When evening came around and she and the wholesaler were on their way to his house for coffee, and he had taken her by the arm so she wouldn't stumble on the cobblestones, Linnea was standing guard as she had been instructed at a certain street corner. What a surprise! What are you doing here? No, I never expected to see you, either. When are you going back? Which meant that she also had to take the evening train home with Linnea to protect her good name. Of course Mellberg would understand.

One Sunday evening late that autumn she came again, left Linnea at the tea room and met the wholesaler, who had a certain gleam in his eye. She wished she had brought somebody other than Linnea along. Repeating the same manoeuvre wasn't exactly creative. But scheming was actually as uncomfortable to her as fox collars and thin pumps.

He invited her to his place for dinner. All right, she said. Well, she was no baby and could do as she pleased. When they left the hotel, where they had just had some wine and he had taken Tora's orders, he walked her quickly and by another route than she had expected. They went around the other side of the park and way off between the trees she caught a glimpse of her rear guard.

'Oh my goodness, there's Linnea Holm,' said Tora.

'Lucky she didn't see you,' said the wholesaler, giving her arm a little hug.

She said she hoped he hadn't gone to a great deal of trouble with the meal, and he assured her he had a housekeeper, which made her feel somewhat less uneasy.

The housekeeper had set the table, and prepared a copious meal of herring au gratin, cold poached eel and little meatballs. The table was laid with white china with a gilt edge and a white linen tablecloth, immaculately starched and mangled. Bottles glistened on the sideboard. But there was no housekeeper in sight.

'Evening off,' declared the wholesaler. 'Chapel.'

He winked at her. He was heavy and his paunch swelled under his waistcoat. His hair was thick and hardly even greying although he was nearly sixty.

'You obviously have good help,' said Tora, looking around. Not a scrap of lint or piece of thread to be seen, and the meal was well-made. They didn't seem to notice the butter shortage here. The meatballs were swimming in browned butter.

'She's religious, though,' said Mellberg. 'That's the only trouble.'

He proposed a toast in Tora's honour. Toast followed upon toast and he kept refilling their glasses, jenever in the shot glasses and porter in the beer mugs, hers mixed with fizzy lemonade. She felt it beginning to go to her head and realized that she would have to be careful. After the meal she offered to help him clear up before she left, but he put an end to that idea by planting her firmly on the divan.

'You sit still there while I start the coffee,' he said.

'But we can't just leave everything!'

'She'll deal with it,' he said, not so much as glancing at the messy table, the half-empty glasses and the crumpled napkins. Still, Tora was embarrassed despite the fact that she realized it was hardly likely that the housekeeper had the slightest idea who she was. When he had poured their coffee he sat down beside her, and the sofa springs creaked under their combined weight. He lay his arm across the back of the sofa behind her neck, and their conversation deteriorated. Tora kept staring at a huge oil painting of cows tramping their way slowly down to a lake shore. He leaned closer and closer while she leaned the other direction, thinking it would give him a stiff neck. He didn't complain, however. Just kept blinking his eyes at her and pursing his lips. She couldn't help thinking it was unbecoming to such a good-looking man. By this time they were all the way out to the arm of the sofa, the point of no return. She was trapped and pressed slowly into the edge while he put his arm around her and began brushing her face with his lips. But when he tried to fondle her breasts she straightened up and got moving so fast he couldn't keep up, and the coffee table tipped on two legs. The cups danced in their saucers, and brown rings appeared around them.

She was overcome with disgust so quickly she didn't even know where it came from. Could a mouth, the smell of aquavit coming out of it and of food be so distasteful simply because it was unfamiliar? He had a strong hand with a white cuff and a black signet ring on his little finger that felt inconceivable on her breast. She was so confused she couldn't really think straight, but she gave him a piece of her mind. She liked letting him know one or two of the things that made her sick about him, that felt good. He had no reason to think that she was a loose woman, not her! They had a business relationship, and if now he intended to start taking advantage of the discounts and the sugar he gave her — and God only knew where he had got his hands on sugar when people didn't even have a spoonful for their porridge — then he'd just have to try it with somebody else instead. But before she left she was going to clear the table. She would never leave a place in such disarray.

She didn't even look at him but thought he must be quite put in his place because he trotted right behind her — he'd even removed his suit jacket — while she carried the plate of meatballs and the bowl of potatoes into the kitchen. She found her way to the larder, a wooden door into something that was more like an old-fashioned storeroom. There was food enough in there to make anyone feel ashamed. In times like these! He wasn't, however, entirely browbeaten, because the next thing she knew he was grinning at her and gulping a ginger pear right out of the jar. Holding it by the stem he put the whole thing into his mouth at once. Ugh! Tora looked the other way. Quick as could be he was there with his arms around her, moving his hot, damp mouth towards hers. Then, strong with jenever, virtue and fury, she lifted the bowl of potatoes over her head and brought it down on his. It broke, and the potatoes rained down over him. He tottered slightly from the hard blow she had dealt. Then he stood, legs wide apart with his back to the door, and said:

'Don't you ever do that again.'

He took her by the arm, twisted it and pushed her ahead of him out of the larder, through the kitchen and the dining room to the bedroom door. It was hot in there. The grating on the tile stove was closed, the embers glowing behind.

'I don't belong in here,' said Tora.

'Oh yes you do.'

The bed was turned down. There were linen sheets with a wide lace edge and two pillows side by side.

'Don't,' she said when he reached for her and kicked off his shoes at the same time. She tried to get through the doorway past him, but he was after her. He may have been heavy, but he was still agile. He pulled her down onto the rug out in the vestibule, which was as far as she got. She became aware of a cast-iron umbrella stand near her head, and was relieved she hadn't fallen right onto it. A moose head hung above her.

He locked her arms and began prying her knees apart with his strong legs. She no longer spoke, but tried to throw him off her by pressing her heels to the floor and thrusting her torso. She was unable to budge him though, and her stomach began to ache, as did her back from all the resistance. He took one of his hands off her arms to tear at his fly and her skirts, which enabled her to free her own hands, and they flew to his face. When she was about to claw at his eyes, however, she hesitated for a moment, in fear. That gave him the opportunity he needed to grab her wrists again and press her arms back over her head. It hurt, hurt, hurt. She could have screamed, wanted to, but didn't want to give him the satisfaction of so much as a sound. Now that he was bent over her, she wanted

110

to bite his face, or to get her knee into his belly or, better yet, his crotch. He would be outraged, but she didn't care, she intended to kick the moron off her if it was the last thing she did.

It was horrid, his weight, his wide-open mouth, his rough skin pressing down on her cheek and his hard knees working at her thighs to wedge them apart. If she could only get at his eyes again she wouldn't waver. She scratched him when he shifted his grip from her wrists to her upper arms. By the time he got her arms to the floor he had long red scratches on his cheeks, and he swore at her.

She lay tense under him and he pressed her down but was hardly moving and she felt the minutes pass and his exhaustion, he was sick of it all now, but he had no intention of giving up. Maybe it wasn't even lust from his side any more, but just raw hate, like hers. So they lay still, and now and then he made a sudden effort to get between her legs. He shifted his grip on her arms or wrists and she had to grit her teeth so as not to scream. She felt his heart pounding and wished he would have a stroke. His jugular vein throbbed, but she couldn't get at it with her teeth, and the sweat was running down his forehead into her eyes, stinging so she had to close them tight.

Just lie still. I'm still, too. When I inhale you exhale. My thighs are just as strong as yours and I have nails, teeth, muscles and hard bones in my body. You can't humiliate me. You'll have to beat me to a pulp.

She caught sight of her hat, which had fallen from the shelf above the mirror, and the black top of her hat pin gleamed in the dusky vestibule. So she lay there tense, waiting for him to lash out again, and when he did and his back was arched for an instant to give his legs more clout, she focused all her remaining strength in one single heave. He tumbled off her, still gripping her arm with one hand, but she got at her hatpin and came up to crouching. She was pointing it at his crotch. He halted his forward lurch and let go of her arm.

'You devil,' he said. 'You damned she-devil. Are you out of your mind?'

She couldn't get past him to the door so she just stayed perfectly still as he rose. She had to see where he was going.

He didn't dare come too close, but manoeuvred her into the sitting room and went at her, so she countered with the pin and he screamed. She didn't know whether it was from fright or whether she had really stabbed him, but it made him keep his distance. She, however, was trapped between the divan and the sideboard and couldn't move. He poured himself a cognac, a whole seltzer glass full. She stood, trapped, with her hatpin at the ready, monitoring his every move.

Suddenly he plopped down on the sofa without uttering a word, his eyes heavy. Then he shut them, clearly no longer afraid she would fly at him, at any rate. He just lay there, his huge head on a black satin pillow with a painted swan.

She knew he was drunk, but not what to expect. She was reeling with exhaustion. Her upper arms, recently numb, now began to ache, and she dared to rub one. But she kept her hatpin extended straight out in front of her, not sure whether he was squinting at her from under his eyelids. He exhaled heavily through his nose, regularly and slowly.

She listened to the clock ticking and dared to lean against the sideboard. 'What if I faint?' she thought, followed by 'He's asleep'. And he was. She was nearly sure. His chin had dropped and a thin line of saliva ran down onto his collar. She walked silently across the floor, never taking her eyes off him. When she made it to the vestibule she first opened the door and left it ajar, then took her coat off the hook. But it was all right. She even managed to get her hat and pumps and Ebba's fox collar. Silently, she shut the door behind her. The lock clicked, but there was not a sound from inside. She fastened her hat with the hatpin and started walking back, shoes in hand.

It was very late and dark. She walked fast, afraid she might meet someone. The night air was refreshing, and cooled her cheeks and her aching throat. She realized she would have bruises. When she got to the station it was closed and she had to sit on a bench outside and wait. The timetable was posted on a board; there was no train until four a.m.

The wind picked up and the street lamps outside the station house swayed on their cables. Now and then the gas level sank and there would be nothing but a red spark in the middle, around which the flame would rise a few minutes later. Tora's eyes got tired from staring at them, and she looked away.

She wasn't cold yet. Her arms and legs ached and under her coat, her body burned. She stared at the gobs of spit on the pavement, and the cobblestones, not worrying much about what to do if a tramp came along. She was too tired. Nothing more could possibly happen to her. Or at least nothing worse.

She hated herself for everything she had said and done with Mellberg before the moment he twisted her arm. She hated him, too. But the shame was the worst part. If she could have excised it from her body with a knife, she would have. Her head drooped and swayed like the street lamps, but she didn't dare doze off.

Once upon a time she would have gone home after this kind of awful incident and sobbed her shame and misery into a striped pillowcase. That was when she was Tora Lans. In those days she would walk the last bit home to the croft barefoot in the grass after

113

dancing on a Saturday night, to cool her aching feet. The chilly evening enclosed and comforted her, and the house was inhabited but asleep.

Her grandmother would wake up and stomp around. Ask her what had happened, of course, but not get a definite answer. She would have stayed up for a while, though, making a noise with the tripod and the kettle, been around her. Been.

You grow accustomed to not crying when there's no one to listen. It just leaves you with a headache and swollen eyes but nothing changes. So you learn to keep silent about yourself and your life.

You had eyes on you from behind net curtains and window panes. But nowadays she was both more careful and less frightened. She knew what they were up to.

They were sharp and could spy a damp spot on a skirt from a hundred metres away. They could catch the whiff of death, and of bedrooms. They recognized illness before anyone else and told one another. They kept an eagle eye on the cemetery. When relations returned from a journey and the begonia had died or there were elm leaves littering the gravesite, there would be words scratched with a stick in the wet sand: HERE LIES A FORGOTTEN MOTHER.

They were most merciful towards those whose lives ran on like the fulfilment of a prophecy, and who never went out bareheaded, not even down to the shop to buy a little coffee cream.

There are tribes — known as primitive — where the women's genitals are circumcised to keep them from experiencing pleasure. This prevents infidelity. In our world, though, both the brain and the genitals are circumcised. If you butcher the brain sufficiently and mess around with the other place just a little, the result is benign. You can be comforted for your slip-ups; she will cry over you just as she did when the Queen passed on, over the fact that children are starving in the world and over dogs who are force fed. But the women whose unbridled organs have been most thoroughly mutilated and tamed become sharp-sighted and merciless in the service of the order that mutilated them.

They see everyone. You rush though life with your hems coming down and your shoes badly soled, fumble with your crocheting, try to hide your book behind your sewing basket when you hear someone coming, fill the cookie jar with store-bought (and think they'll look home made!) and conceal your secrets in the bottom dresser drawer. But you can't fool them.

Tora Otter had eyes on her when her illegitimate, adopted-off son Erik Lans came asking for her at the market. That time they had her by the eyeteeth! Every single person saw her shoo him off. She hadn't given the poor lad so much as the time of day, oh no, not Tora Otter. She knew what she was doing, too. And they said she had told him to go away and never come back. She had boys of her own to think about and she didn't want people talking. That was how hard a woman's heart could grow once she went into business!

But Frida Eriksson and Ebba Julin kept telling people Tora had had a different reason for getting rid of him. From the very beginning she had promised his foster parents never to have anything to do with him again. And if Tora had made a promise, she kept it. Because she was like that, said Frida.

Tora herself said nothing. She might lie in bed remembering him, but no one knew it. His cap was too big, and brand new. His face was familiar although she hadn't seen him since he was new-born. Did they look alike? He had bushy eyebrows. Once she got out of bed and lit the lamp. She had to look in the mirror.

She had been terrified at the market square when she realized who he was. That couldn't be denied, but she wasn't about to tell anyone, not even Ebba and Frida. She swore to herself she wouldn't think about him, as it was to no avail. But now and then she would still wake up at night remembering that day at the market square. Things are different at night.

He had stood there in his spanking new hat. He was scared, that was obvious. And then he blurted out that he was on his way to Strängnäs for his secondary schooling. But he didn't know if he

116

wanted to, he said. The pastor had said he had a head for studies, he would have his room and board at another pastor's.

But what had he come to see her for? Well, he was afraid. He didn't know what it would be like in Strängnäs. She had hardly been listening when he said that, and afterwards she didn't understand what he'd meant.

'Good lad,' she said curtly. 'You've been a good lad and that's fine.'

She stuck a coin in his mitten and poured him a bag of sweets. But she had to be quick. There was one thing he had to understand. He must on no conditions come to see her here. Not at the market.

He just stared at her out of those light blue eyes under his bushy eyebrows. 'Not here,' she said. 'Come to my place this evening. Number 60 Hovlunda Road. Not before half past nine or ten, though. You have to understand. My boys are big now. I don't want people talking.'

He left. She felt exhausted, though it was only morning.

He didn't come that evening. It got to be ten, and then ten-thirty, and Tora was still sitting there listening for his footsteps. Then she thought she heard something out in the hallway, but it must not have been him. He'd probably had second thoughts. When it got very late she went down to the station. It was so cold her footsteps crunched, and there wasn't a soul anywhere on Store Street. She stopped on the steps leading down to the tracks, gazing down at the circles of lamplight. But there was no one at all waiting for the last train. It was cold, and the rails rang with the chill.

Nowadays she saw him every so often. He was tall and thin and wore a graduate's cap. He would sometimes come to the café in the company of an elderly pastor she didn't recognize. They didn't come frequently, once every couple of months or so. They obviously had some errand in town, and would have coffee at the Cosmopolitan when they were done. After a while she figured out that they probably came by train, and went out to the cemetery with some flowers.

Every time she saw them come in she would go into the kitchen of the café and stay there. She would let Linnea, who had no idea who the young man in the cap was, serve. But once they took her by surprise. They were already seated and had been served their coffee before Tora saw them. She was standing behind the counter making trays of biscuits. He saw her and nodded.

The old pastor slowly worked his overcoat and galoshes on with the young man's help. He had his stiff graduate's cap on his head. Then she heard him say: 'I'll be right along, there's someone here I'd like to have a word with.'

He crossed the floor quickly and comfortably, like a real grown man. Twenty, clean-shaven, with a tie pin.

'Hello,' he said, extending his hand.

She had never in her life felt such a total fool. He spoke, her ears were ringing with her rushing blood and she couldn't have heard more than half. But she did realize he thought she worked at the café.

'It's my place now,' she said. 'I'd very much like to treat you to something.'

'Thank you, but I've just had my coffee. It was excellent.'

What a lie. How easily the words poured out of his mouth.

'A drop of wine then,' she said.

She walked over to the cupboard and removed the madeira bottle and the crystal glasses she had never used, not even for the women teachers from the co-educational.

'Go in and sit down. I won't be a minute.'

She put some almond sweets on a high cut glass plate, gave one piece a pinch to make sure it was fresh and hadn't dried out. Then she changed her mind, shifted it all off and set a doily under. She felt as awkward as in a dream.

118

They said 'skål' as they lifted their glasses and she sat wishing someone would come in and see them so he would realize she was no longer worried that people might talk. At the same time, she knew that the people who were talkers would no longer recognize him.

'Congratulations on your graduation,' she said. Their eyes met for a split second over the rims of their glasses and then slipped and let go. That was the only sign of uncertainty she saw in him.

'What'll you be doing now?'

'I've been given the opportunity to study law,' he smiled.

'Heavens!' flew out of her before she had a chance to catch herself. She would have liked to go on and ask 'But whoever's going to pay?', although it would have sounded begrudging so she didn't. And he didn't let on. The old pastor he steered so gently by the arm? But wouldn't he rather have had him study theology?

'I guess so much schooling'll take some time,' she said, after which the conversation petered out and they both looked out the window, though there was nothing special to see. There was sun on the apple leaves in the garden on the other side of the street and on the tarpapered roof of the upholstery shop.

'I'll have to be going,' he said. 'The gentleman's waiting for me. Thanks ever so much.'

'It was really nothing,' said Tora. 'I hope the sweets weren't too hard.'

They shook hands again and he put his stiff hat back on.

'Well, I wish you the very best,' she said.

When he had left she stood there by the hat rack, hoping no one would come in for a while. Why hadn't she been able to get herself to say anything about the last time? I'm sorry. I'm sorry about what happened at the market. That I couldn't do anything for you that time. But you seem to have turned out well, anyway, haven't you?

And no one saw them, either. No one at all. But that was mainly

119

because people didn't exactly go out of their way to have coffee at the Cosmopolitan. Except for the youngest teacher, that is. Her name was Gerda Åkerlund and she had been a student at the co-educational once upon a time, and then gone on to teacher's seminary. On Thursdays the women's suffrage group had their meetings, and Gerda Åkerlund would come running down Hovlunda Road half an hour before the meeting with the record book under her arm in a thin oilcloth case. She would settle into a corner and write the minutes of the previous meeting at top speed, and Tora always wondered why she had to do it at the café.

Now that the war was on, they sewed during their meetings as well. Fröken Åkerlund would read aloud from a book called *The Status of Women in Sweden*, while the others made clothes for the needy. The war had made everything so difficult. They sat there in poor lamplight, and made more than eighty articles of clothing in the course of one winter. Once a woman from Stockholm came and held a speech entitled 'When the Fatherland calls', but that time Tora went out into the kitchen and busied herself with the coffee. Or whatever you wanted to call it. Some of the women drank tea made from dried cherry leaves, and she had to extend the butter for the sandwiches by mixing in some flour and milk paste. Sometimes everything felt so hopeless she just felt like taking what coffee beans she had left and making one pot of really good, strong coffee. She wanted to spread the last of the real butter on thick slices of sweet, white bread and serve it all to the sallow women who sat there sewing things out of old bits of woollen cloth turned inside out, to gather up all the newspapers with their stories of Belgian refugees and typhus and burnt down cities and make a fire in the stove with all of them, a really hot fire with whistling birch logs. But you can't do that. You drudge on and measure what you have and dilute and try not to apologize for the watered-down things you serve.

After a funeral, people would sometimes come to the Cosmopolitan, as it was near the cemetery. You just walked straight up Hovlunda Road and then continued out Vanstorp way a little. Families began to reserve the place for coffee and cakes after funerals. She decorated the cakes with ersatz cream and a black crucifix. This wasn't what she had originally had in mind. She was not a fundamentally melancholy person, but she was becoming one. She would do her figures, over and over again with an aniline pen on a paper bag, trying to make ends meet. And at the same time, Berta Göhlin sat upstairs imagining how Tora was lining her own pockets at her expense, that she had sold her the café for a song and Tora was now making a great profit. Berta counted every single person who walked in to the Cosmopolitan, but she had a tendency to count them a second time when they were leaving. Tora lay in bed at night, sometimes half the nights, reading and rereading the purchase deed to see if she could find some way to get her amortizations postponed. One morning Adam grabbed the deed from the chair next to her bed, and danced around on the lino singing the text:

'The Vendor transfers to the Purchaser her café, located at property number 219 Hovlunda Road, and all the relevant Furniture, China, Carpeting, Light Fixtures and other Fittings ...'

'The relevant Furniture,' Fredrik laughed, his voice cracking, and there were the two of them, spinning around the floor, Adam with the deed held over his head and Fredrik thrashing the air to get it. But Tora pulled it away from Adam, giving his ears a boxing.

'That café puts your bread and butter on the table young man. I wouldn't make fun of it if I were you.'

However, that wasn't strictly true. She was actually keeping the café running with her income from the market and her tenants.

121

The line moved forward at a snail's pace, the men stamping their feet. The snow creaked under their three hundred boots, and there was a little squeak every time someone knocked against the iron gate, which had not been closed properly and kept swinging on its hinges. The snow was blue in the pre-dawn light. Some men covered their scrofulous ears gently with their hands, but most of them had earmuffs or Russian hats pulled all the way down. They wore outdoor vests of thick corduroy, turtle-necks and other heavy sweaters, heavy Norwegian knits and cotton Lahmans, Jaeger wool and rabbit fur, and their bodies were stiff, frozen to the bone as they moved along down Chapel Street. Stamp, stamp and the queue turned in towards the foundry, thinning out at the doorway, where the guard let the men pass, one by one, in front of his window. One of the men who had made it inside where it was warm commented that it was so cold out there a man didn't dare take a piss.

Fredrik Otter was in the queue with his lunch box and the woollen mittens his mother had insisted he wear. She had finally let him go. On the day of his confirmation he had received a telegram from his relations in Gothenburg: 'Our heartfelt congratulations to Fredrik on this special day' with a border of gold crowns and red roses. But that was all. Nothing more was heard from them. In the end his mother folded the telegram into the Bible and said:

'I guess the time has come for you to queue up at Wärnström's.'

But it wasn't that easy, jobs weren't growing on trees. So for a while he ran errands for the café — chopped the wood, cut the kindling, got the newspapers, and carried sacks of flour from Lefvander's, after dark and down the back alleys so as not to be seen. He found this a time of terrible humiliations; once he even whipped egg whites for meringue. After some time there was an opening for him at Wärnström's, he was to be a bogie boy at the ironworks.

He had sandwiches with cold turnip mash in his lunchbox, and a workingman's overall, stiff and clean. When he was introduced to the manager he bowed from the waist almost instinctively, as his mother had taught him. Someone over by a wall in the dark workshop snorted, he couldn't see who.

Luckily Konrad's uncle Valentin was there, and Fredrik tagged after him the first day whenever he was at a loss. Valentin's hair was thinning but he had let his curly beard grow out, and had grown a moustache to conceal the scar from his cleft lip.

'Oh, so you're not afraid your lungs'll rot,' he said. 'Or you'll get rheumatism. You've set your heart on being a foundry man.'

Fredrik didn't contradict him. But he actually had no intention of becoming a foundry man; what he wanted was a job in the workshop. To begin with he got to cart around two-wheeled bogies full of sand, sift it, and roll the moulds out to dry. The black, trampled-down snow out in the yard made his clog bottoms slippery, and he was afraid the moulds would fall off his barrow and break. The foundry was an old one-storey building with a blackened beam ceiling. It reeked of coal and slag in there, the coal dust smoked and he was soon black inside and out, even his nostrils. The new factory building with the workshop was across the yard. That was where he wanted to work. It was a concrete building four stories high and inside there were lifts and water closets. He considered the men who disappeared behind the door

123

of the workshop in the mornings when the queue divided as belonging to a different, higher species of humanity than the blackened foundry men. And he was the single least significant individual in that latter category. There were experienced foundry men who couldn't stay home for a day because if they did there would be no one to tap the furnace. But all he did was push bogies around and sweep up around the moulds, and gather up the waste pieces for scrapping, and felt proud the day they started allowing him to coat the dies with coal dust. It would be a few more weeks before he got to be a mould boy or to fettle castings.

He wheeled the cast pieces for engine blocks into the workshop and once he got in and away from the heat of the foundry and the icy winds of the yard he would push his barrow slowly, looking around. The furnaces roared twenty-four hours a day in here, and the wheels turned, the belts ran from the minute they were turned on each morning until dark fell. Fredrik did his errands as slowly as possible, staring at the shiny blue lathe dust swirling out of the piece being turned and at the drill that ate its way down into the steel as if it were soft cheese.

His gaze followed the route of the taut belts to the wheels up under the roof that drove them, thinking about what would happen if one of those flat, hissing leather serpents grabbed him by the shirttails and pulled him up with it, his shoulder being crushed by the wheel, or his leg or his hand. He stared at the pieces of steel waiting to be turned and at the drill, realizing that they would react to human flesh and steel exactly the same way.

The machines didn't distinguish. They flattened skin and sheet metal identically, crushing bones and teeth. But the most amazing thing, the one thing Fredrik couldn't accept, was that human flesh was so robust and so strong-willed. If you spoil a piece you're turning, you toss it on the scrap heap. It will have to be melted down in the furnace and cast again in a new mould. But human flesh heals.

So there were men walking around down there at the smithy and in the workshops with mutilated stumps, because the machines had chopped off bits of them. The flesh had healed and grown in around them and wrinkled up. A hand that had been crushed healed gnarled around fragments of bone, nails pushed up from the scars, and cartilage grew around shards. He felt frightened when he saw them, these stumps and tangled scars and thought he'd prefer to be melted down like scrap metal in the smelter than to have a body that insisted on healing over the things that shamed it.

He turned away when he saw them, preferring to look at the sanders and the mills, at the shapers and the lathes and the new drills manned by lads not much older than himself. In the din he enquired as to the name of every machine, and usually got an answer. If not, it was only because they were in a rush. Nobody up here was unfriendly towards him, though each man sat like a king over his own machine. He thought of the man who ran the automated turret lathe as the emperor himself.

In his opinion, this was the most excellent of machines. It worked independently, as if its heavy mass contained a brain. No twisting and turning when the tools were to be changed. The mount of the turret lathe held a full set of tools, and they dropped into place one by one, all in accordance with the setting. He could have stood there forever if he hadn't been afraid of the foreman and if the foundry men hadn't been waiting for him to come round with his barrow.

Down there he was more frightened. The first day one of the other bogie boys asked him when he was going to bring his breaking-in bottle, and after that he was constantly worried about it. He had heard stories about what they did to boys who didn't live up to all the breaking in rituals: rolled them in coal dust and gravel until their clothes were ruined and they were bleeding, threatened to cut off their dicks with a knife and then greased them black with lubricating oil, dipped them in ice-cold water. But all that happened was that one of the guys grabbed him by the neck and pushed his head down.

'Bow! I've heard you're good at that,' he said.

Fredrik was glad he was just as tall and broad as his opponent. He never got told to bow again.

He couldn't get hold of a breaking-in bottle, as he had no money and would never have dared to take that much out of his pay packet, which his mother counted. Drink was rationed now, and very dear. A foundry man who started some time after him somehow managed to bring two litres and a piece of knackwurst, but the aquavit was quite yellow. They forced him and the other lads to have a drink so they could laugh at them when they started babbling. Fredrik went silent as the grave, terrified the home brew would leave him blind.

And the fear took hold of him, the chill blew through his clothes, the heat went to his face, the din deafened him, the oil and soot crept under his cuticles to stay, the loads stretched his muscles and ligaments and then he was no longer frightened and no longer new. He fettled castings and another lad came along and pushed the bogies. When they stood holding the sieve to sift sand now, it was Fredrik who told the new boy to be careful not to drop the moulds, not to heat up his dinner before the foundry men, and not to take any scrap metal home with him.

In the beginning he was so tired he would fall asleep on the kitchen settee before supper and when he woke up he just wanted his meal and to get into bed. His mother would have to push him in the direction of the water she had heated up for him to wash in.

But he got used to it. Nowadays he didn't feel tired at all on Saturdays. He could smell it was Saturday the minute he got up: newly ironed shirts and floors scrubbed with soft soap. He heard the cork pop out of a bottle of beer at the neighbours', his mother's tenants were singing and practicing their dance steps. Well, it was only Franzon singing, he could hear that. No doubt he was trying to teach the other fellow to dance the one-step.

He was at home alone, thank goodness, and he had a pot of water heating on the stove. His mother had left his supper in a frying pan. There were fried rutabagas and two slices of liver, but he only ate the root vegetables as he suspected the liver was horse. She got creative when times were hard.

He added a couple of logs to the fire and let his work clothes fall to the floor. The mirror was hung high above the sink and he lifted it down and put it against the wall so that he could see a little more than his face now he was alone. He pulled in his stomach muscles, noting that his belly looked flat and square. His arms were thin but beginning to fill out. Valentin had felt them today, saying: 'You're getting there!' His torso was white and nearly clean, and the blonde hairs on his body stood out in the cold kitchen as his skin went prickly. Otherwise, though, his complexion was smooth and his body muscular, not as bony and ugly as it had been a year ago. And he had real curly hair down below now, no girlish wisps just getting longer and longer. Look at that! So he whistled as he poured the water into the basin and added some cold from the pail. They had a drain now, but no running water. He hummed: 'my combination, my new suit dear, for confirmation, I'll be wearing it right here!' his hands frothy with soap from the jar. He left it on to do its job for a while, as he rotated slowly in front of the mirror, trying to see himself from behind.

He didn't like it when his mother stood next to him with towels while he washed. She inspected him so closely he was embarrassed. He sort of felt he owed it to her not to change. He tried to turn the pages of the paper on the kitchen table without getting them soapy, but of course it couldn't be done. He managed to see that they were putting on 'My Sweet Pea' at the theatre and that you weren't supposed to tear off your sugar coupons.

He heard footsteps and voices from the tenants' rooms. Saturday sounds, sort of lighter and brighter. That Franzon fellow wouldn't let up on Westin until he had taught him to dance. Hop left, hop right and one, two, three! Slide together, slide together, swing! What the hell kind of a dance was that anyway? Nobody could learn it. So they gave up and Franzon opened the window. What was the point of that when it was so cold out? Mamma had told them to keep the windows and doors shut whenever possible, because wood was outrageously expensive. A cord of mixed alder wood and birch cost thirty kronor. Still, Fredrik opened the kitchen window to see what Franzon was doing. That was it, he was opening a tin of anchovies out there and the brine sprayed high as a fountain. Then he pulled it in and Fredrik heard the clinking of bottles. What a fellow that Franzon was, he sure knew how to live it up. He had a dance band though he didn't play very well himself. That didn't stop him from being the concertmaster just the same! During the week he earned his keep in the office of Electricity Installation. They had two women working there as well!

His water was cold now, he'd have to add some hot, holding the pot carefully with his soapy hands. As usual, he started by washing his hands and brushing his fingernails. The water grew black and oily and there was nothing for it but to pour it down the drain. So he took a new basinful, as hot as he could stand it. He was being wasteful, but it was only Saturday once a week, and then it stayed

Saturday all day long! He'd better be careful with mamma's soap though. She was no pleasure to listen to if her soap was grey when she wanted to have a wash in the evening. He scrubbed his face and neck, spitting and puffing so hard the wooden panelling got spotted with dirt, washing the insides of his ears with his little finger and grimacing into the mirror. He blew his nose to get the soot out of his nostrils, and then went on to his body. But at this time of year when he wore lots of layers at work he was pretty clean.

Finally he moved the basin onto the floor with a newspaper under it – he didn't forget it this time – and washed his feet by placing them in the basin and sitting there for ages curling and extending his toes before he brushed them with soap. The soot had crept through his stockings and up over his ankles, incredible. Now the water was cold and black and he poured it down the sink. His mother called that sink a blessing, and she was right about that. He remembered the pail they had had under the washing table at 60 Hovlunda Road. What splashing. And the clumps of spit floating there after they brushed their teeth, and the tufts of hair – it still made him nauseous to think of it. Fredrik had one weakness, but he hoped he'd outgrow it – his stomach was easily upset.

He was cold, and put a couple of logs in the stove before he began to dry himself. His buttocks were rough, but that was just as well. A year ago his skin had been as smooth as a girl's. His prick, however, had shrivelled up from being wet and cold. It looked awful and he had to try to smooth it out and see that no harm was done. 'Your thingamabob,' his mother said. Still! Put on your long johns so mister thingamabob won't catch cold. Good Lord, what didn't a person have to put up with? One of these days he was going to put a stop to it.

He took a corner of the towel to clean his nose. Not until he looked and saw how black the towel was did he remember that he wasn't allowed to. He couldn't recall what she had told him to use instead. He used his pocket-knife to dig out the dirt from under his nails, but he couldn't get rid of it all. It was permanent; there it would stay as long as he lived. He curled his fingers and examined his fingernails. Short and wide, like on his mother's side. Adam's fingers were long and thin, and if he could just stop biting his nails they would arch out. When he got rich, very rich, and could do whatever he liked with his money, he'd buy a signet ring. A black bloodstone like Franzon's, or even bigger.

There were clean long johns on the settee for him, but he sneaked stealthily over to the dresser and found a pair of undershorts in cotton weave instead, good, mangled ones with flat covered buttons. His legs wouldn't be cold, not on a Saturday anyway. He could hear the clinking of glasses from Franzon's room, they were drinking to someone's health. Oh, a person deserves a little ... nope. His mother might come.

He hung the mirror back on its nail and water-combed his hair, parting it on the left. He had a cowlick on top of his head, that stuck right up. Once he'd tried to get rid of it by cutting the hair on that spot clear down to his scalp. He wouldn't make that mistake again.

He was starting to get facial hair, no doubt about it. Long, soft strands above his top lip, more of them for every day that passed. What if he shaved them off? Would they grow in thicker? The question was what to use. Maybe Franzon's razor? He and Westin had gone out now and their rooms were quiet. Fredrik tiptoed in. The recently abandoned room smelled warm and secretive. He could discern anchovies, aquavit and hair tonic. They'd forgotten to shut the damper, of course. His mother should've seen that. If anybody came he'd just say he'd gone in to close it.

There was a blue bottle of hair tonic on the windowsill. Maybe he'd try it on his cowlick. Naah, it wouldn't help a bit. He couldn't resist opening the top dresser drawer, carefully so as not to mess anything up. There they were: the shaving brush made of soft badger bristles in two different colours, his almond-scented shaving soap, his razor with its yellow bone handle and brass rivets. He ran his index finger over it. It was probably very sharp. The leather strap was hanging alongside the mirror. If your father was alive you got whipped with a strap like that, but in this house his mother's hard hands governed their interpersonal relations. He'd never been whipped, but he'd had little slaps that smarted, his arm pinched and his ears duly boxed.

You needed hot water to shave. And the razor did look sharp. The coppersmith over Vanstorp way had cut his throat with one. But Anker's confectioner had used cyanide. Konrad had told him that it was the same as bitter almond oil. Just one swallow and you went straight to meet your maker.

There was something underneath. The corner of a magazine. No, just a flyer. Oh! A sepia photo, soft flesh, thighs, cloth, folds, wavy hair. He kept booklets of nudes here, anybody could have guessed. Slowly he eased the folder out, trying to remember just what order everything was in. A box, a green box. What was in there? He could hardly swallow, his throat was pounding and constricted and he suddenly felt as if he needed to spend a penny, though he really didn't.

'What the hell is this? You tell me that! Say something!'

He slammed the drawer shut when he heard that voice, knowing everything must be getting tumbled around in there. He rushed out, his hand in front of his undershorts where they were protruding behind the stiff cotton weave.

'Get a whiff of it!' As he came to his senses he realized that the voice was coming from downstairs, from the Olssons' place, he must be shouting out on his balcony. Now there was a woman's voice involved as well, swearing she had no idea. Fredrik sat on the chair, holding his feet up from the icy cold lino as he put on his socks. The shouting and squabbling continued from down below. He began to get the picture: old man Olsson had a hatful of anchovy brine but seemed not to have realized yet that it had come from upstairs. His clothes had been put out for an airing after a lodge meeting and his wife hat set his hat upside down.

'My hat? You needed to air my hat? You must be daft! And what the hell did you have to pour anchovy brine in it for? Smell it! Don't tell me that's not anchovy brine! What else could it possibly be? Don't try and make me believe the cat pissed in this thing.'

Fredrik dressed quickly to get out before they started looking up and wondering. He'd better leave this to his mother to deal with, she was a tougher nut. His newly ironed shirt had an iron burn on it, but it was on the tail you tucked into your trousers, so who cared? His mamma was good in her way, but the truth was she was often in too much of a hurry. He pulled his knotted tie over his head and put his football club tie pin in place. Then jacket, trousers and belt, which he pulled a notch tighter than the week before. These days you couldn't put on weight if you tried.

His shoes were already brushed, he'd done them on Friday evening. It was an entire ceremony, because he followed his father's rituals. His mother had told him all about the shoes, how he had brushed and buffed them. Now he put on his overcoat and his cap, and his rounded, shiny shoes clattered down the steps the very moment before the Olssons' door flew open.

'How about a walk through the city?' people asked one another nowadays. 'Let's do the city for a couple of hours.'

Of course the houses and wooden fences were the same as

they'd always been, there were the same piles of snow yellow with dogs' urine that had been there before the first of the year, and the lumberyard hadn't moved either, it was still right in the middle of town. But on New Year's Eve a podium had been put up in the marketplace with flags and banners, evergreen branches and garlands of lights. Everybody who had two legs to walk on had turned out that cold night to hear the officials of their city sing one another's praises, priding themselves on their bravery, their spirit of initiative, their wisdom and their foresightfulness, as they had been doing for nearly thirty-five years. Lodestars and lighthouses had beamed down upon them, the paths to the future been paved before them, the Good Lord, His Majesty and the dear departed merchant had all been present in some invisible sense. Afterwards there had been a banquet, and although no one ever told him what had been served, Fredrik would have been bet his life it had not been fried horse liver. And from that day forward their community had joined the sisterhood of cities. So now he could go into the city if he pleased.

In the city he'd go to the café, of course, but most of the time he wasn't able to just sit there and be in peace like most people because his mum almost always needed something doing. He didn't dare go out dancing because he didn't know how. It seemed so horribly complicated knowing what to do with your feet, and to do it and make it look easy and look the girl right in the eyes and maybe chat as well. About what?

Konrad Eriksson often took him along to the Community Centre when there was folk dancing. That was a little different. You'd trot around the floor and the songs made it pretty clear what to do, and you never had to ask a girl, either. Suddenly there would just be one in front of you and you were supposed to take her by the hand and then swing her by the arm or lock elbows and take a few steps forward or backward while you sang about skipping to my lou, lou lou. He never sang along though. Mostly the girls did the singing.

After the folk dancing came the real program, which usually included Konrad. But when the readings and speeches were over, the coffee cups empty and the choir finished singing, the difficult part began. That was when the band started playing, usually Franzon's dance band, and the floorboards sagged under the weight of the dancers. The light bulbs hanging from the ceiling swayed precariously, the paper garlands drooped in the heat so the dancers' heads kept bumping them. Konrad never danced with the girls, but his uncle Valentin was often seen on the dance floor. He was an ace waltzer, his heel taps scraping as he swept backwards across the floor, his brow glistening. Fredrik's palms went all sweaty, he knew that it would be ladies' choice quite soon. He rolled his hankie around in his hands until it was nothing but a damp sausage. Then he shifted towards the door, stumbling out just as the leader of the band announced that now all the charming ladies out there would have their golden opportunity.

Mostly, though, when he had time off he would go to Hovlunda Road, all the way down to number 60, striding along with his hands deep in his coat pockets. Adam had gone back the very week they had moved to feed the hedgehog, afraid it would die of starvation otherwise. Then he found some tame squirrels on Store Street and forgot all about Hovlunda Road. But Fredrik often went down there. Occasionally his mother would send along a bag of something, but usually he'd drop in empty-handed just to get to spend some time with Konrad who would be reading on the kitchen settee. Above his head there were postcards tacked to the wall. Photos of Marx and Lasalle, as well as of Oljelund, Höglund and Hedén, the three who'd been charged with high treason. Every time he got a new postcard he'd show the message side to Fredrik. They all came from Norrköping and were written in Ebon Johansson's brusque, impatient hand.

Konrad didn't have a father either. Eriksson was dead. Passed on, his mother had said, her mouth reduced to a tight little line when he asked at home. At the café he heard Eriksson had been drunk and walked into a tram. But their not having fathers wasn't exactly a similarity between them, because Konrad was grown up. Though he was a very strange adult. He didn't grab Fredrik by the front of his trousers and ask whether the young cock would soon be crowing. He didn't say: 'Just prattle on. I can hear your common sense isn't stopping you.'

What he did was to listen. He didn't send him out to get booze and Matanza cigars, didn't ask if he wanted to arm wrestle or pinkie finger wrestle and then suddenly give way with a laugh so Fredrik fell on his face. He never asked Fredrik if he'd dare put his hand under the big sledge hammer, and didn't mention his whiskers the minute he walked in through the door.

He'd just sit there under his postcards, reading lots of books and believing in the revolution. But he said it was an extremely slow movement in the oceans of history, a wave rolling them slowly but surely towards the shore. What was happening in Russia now was just a whitecap, a roller, and a froth of sea foam on top.

One day he said the revolution was a light illuminating more and more people and making them visible. Fredrik thought he understood that one. They gained dignity when the light fell on them, he said, when they'd had no human value before. No one had counted but the wealthy, the upper class and the intelligentsia. Now an ordinary worker counted too, at least if he took his job seriously. There would soon be as many Social Democrats as right-wingers in the city council. Nowadays people had to admit that a good worker was worth just as much as a person of good birth, didn't they?

'No,' said Konrad. 'We're not fighting this battle so the merchants will acknowledge our human value'.

He went on to say that Trotter, who picked up the night soil early in the morning before anybody else was up, was the only true revolutionary in this city. But that was going too far! Trotter who wasn't organized in any movement, who wasn't part of the struggle at all. If Trotter was a revolutionary then he, Fredrik Otter, was a chimpanzee!

Every single individual, according to Konrad, who attributed some human value to himself without trampling down others to attain it, was a revolutionary.

And if it was mostly about not trampling, Fredrik guessed Konrad was a pretty good revolutionary himself. He went to Anker's and kneaded his dough but wasn't the least bit interested in how it became bread. He gave his pay packet to his mamma and borrowed books from Ebon Johansson, who sent them from Norrköping.

They sat across the table from one another, he and Konrad. Frida had cleared away the plates but not wiped the table. There were potato skins on it, and that was something Fredrik didn't understand. He was remembering F.A. Otter, who had been his own father, and what he would have thought about potato skins on the table. He had to imagine they weren't there because they spoiled his picture of Konrad.

He sat there reading. Above his head were the lines Frida hung laundry on. They were full of knots, and strung every which way. Ingrid walked up and down the kitchen wheeling a rag doll carriage David had made for her, with big wooden spools as wheels. She had a doll she called Lena-Malunta. Fredrik had never in his life seen anything so filthy, so absolutely permeated with dirt as that doll's face. From the beginning it had been made of a bit of cloth from an old vest. He wished she would at least not kiss it, but she insisted. She kissed it hard time and again saying: 'Oh my little sweetie, my dear, my own Lena-Malunta.'

She had a knitted dog too, and she called him Muffelutten and kissed him as well and took him for walks on a bit of rope. Those two, Konrad and Ingrid, were often at home alone together, which meant Konrad couldn't go out because Ingrid couldn't be left by herself. But it didn't seem to bother him, and he often held her on his lap and to Fredrik's secret aversion she would kiss him with the same lips she'd just been kissing her dirty doll with, especially if he'd done something she'd asked him to do. He'd broken off the long bones from the spine of a dried stockfish, scraped them out, and abra cadabra she'd had a tiny coffee service for her dolly. Fredrik never dared to do anything she asked him to out of fear she'd be kissing him next.

He didn't understand everything Konrad said, but he'd begun to realize that his opinions weren't exactly the same as those of most of the speakers at the Community Centre. His uncle Valentin was less subtle. He'd grabbed Fredrik outside the pay office and instructed him to pay up his union dues, and that settled that.

The poverty at Konrad's frightened him, but he didn't try to understand why they were poor. All he knew was that it was a balancing act, with poverty down below the tightrope, and if you fell you were finished. But you wouldn't fall if you worked hard and put on clean socks on Saturday, didn't put your potato skins on the table, tried not to use bad words too often, not to jack off all the time and not to be too socialistic and agitated.

And Konrad didn't make any of those mistakes, either, on the surface. He said quite calmly that now they'd put up machine guns on the roof of the Royal Palace in Stockholm.

'Why ever?' asked Fredrik in surprise. 'Is the war coming here after all?'

'No, but there are hunger riots. The women are raiding the milk shops and the butchers.'

'And are they gonna shoot them?'

He didn't answer. He was sharpening matches to serve as pieces on the fox and geese board, and putting them into the holes.

'They're right to do it,' he finally said. 'Those women who're plundering the shops. You know who's eating the food the poor ought to have. And the rich are scared now, after the revolution in Russia. That's why they've put up those machine guns on the Royal Palace.'

Then they played. Konrad was the fox and won an easy victory. He jumped goose after goose, it was a real massacre. Then he turned the board around and played the geese for a while just to show Fredrik that the geese, of whom there were so many, could corner the fox and starve him out. But that game took longer.

Fredrik had a picture of the German engineer and inventor Werner von Siemens on the wall above his bed. He himself spent his days in the dim foundry preparing for the moment when his first invention would come to him. He had often read about the light that flares up in the brain of an inventor, of things saying click, of sudden flashes. He had some vague idea of what would happen. He wasn't so childish as to imagine that automatic revolver lathes and complete locomotives rushed forward and took their place as visions in the mind of the inventor.

Fredrik thought technology would liberate mankind, and found it difficult to feel strongly about Konrad's revolution, particularly as it appeared not to take technology into account at all. Not even rapid-fire canons with recoil brakes sketched out on graph paper on the kitchen paper interested Konrad, and Fredrik thought that they might at least be of some use. No, his revolution appeared to be fuelled by bodies and words.

But the human being is a machine with poor mechanical effect and, above all, extremely costly to operate. He had read this in the same magazine in which he had found the picture of Siemens. During a normal, uninterrupted ten-hour working day a human being generated approximately one-fifteenth of one horsepower. And Konrad said that human beings slaved like animals in workshops and mines. What they slaved like was one-fifteenth of a horse to be exact. Fredrik tried to explain to him that a human being was not especially efficient, and this was the only time Konrad made fun of him. Still, he knew he was right, his own body knew it! The nutrition he consumed was inadequately transformed into effective results. It was required for maintenance. He was growing.

He was growing so fast the sleeves of his shirts seemed to be crawling up his arms and he was constantly hungry, hungry and nauseous, because his mother was really creative when times were hard, with horse liver and boiled cod's head with big, slimy, melancholy eyes. But there was a limit to what he was willing to eat. Sometimes a few wrong words were enough to make him lose his appetite. She'd made headcheese from the less noble parts of a pig. Adam, who'd queued for the meat, said that that particular pig must have had a head both front and back. That made Fredrik suspicious, and he poked at the wobbly slices with bits of allspice and bay leaves he had on his plate, but he didn't eat any more.

At the café there was piano music with the surrogate coffee and biscuits made with pea meal, in order to keep the boys who went to the vocational school from going elsewhere. She'd bought a used piano from the auctioneer and persuaded Franzon, her lodger, to come down and play in the evenings.

One February afternoon the revolution did seem to have arrived. A group of women gathered on the square and paraded all the way down Store Street so the mud sprayed. The one at the front of the line was carrying a placard. 'BREAD', the slogan read, 'OUR LITTLE ONES ARE HUNGRY': They walked all the way to the vocational school, standing outside the door and shouting to the headmaster to come out and speak with them. After a while faces appeared at the classroom windows but the students, who usually paced the schoolyard smoking on their breaks, didn't come out. The women shouted in chorus:

'Down with the vocational school. Go home!'

The word spread through town about the bread march on the schoolyard, and by sunset on that February day the schoolyard was full of spectators. The women stood crowded close together stamping their feet in the cold and shouting 'Go home, go home!' incessantly. The lights went on in the classrooms, revealing blackboards with numbers on, and light fixtures hanging from the ceiling on cords. The men who were the students at the school stood at the windows, but the minute they opened so much as a crack, one of the women in the schoolyard would call out:

'Get out of here! You're eating our children's food.'

No one had seen the headmaster, but when it was nearly dark and not a single one of the almost one thousand students at the school had come out, a rumour began to circulate that he was on his way down. The school caretaker shuttled back and forth, reporting on the situation both inside and out. A few minutes later there was the clattering of chairs and of heavy boots on the stairs and the doors opened and there was the headmaster in his black hat and overcoat, with his starched white collar. His face was red and agitated in the light from the doorway. Behind him on the main stairway were the students, some of whom wore whittling knives hanging from their belts: the students at the vocational school came from all over the country, plus some Finns and one Russian. People said the Russian was so kind he was a real softy, though, and only interested in playing chess.

'Ladies and citizens!' the headmaster began.

'Get out of here,' shouted the women.

'I can understand, in these difficult times, that all you want is what is best for your little ones...'

'Get out of here, the whole pack of you. What do we need you here for?'

'Are our children to go hungry because adult men are sitting in the classrooms?

'What's wrong with you? Don't you want work?'

'But let us begin,' said the headmaster, 'by eliminating one fundamental misunderstanding.'

'We'll see to it they eliminate you, too!'

Now the headmaster was offended and shouted to his students, asking if they were going to let themselves be driven off? There was a roar from the stairwell, where the acoustics were as powerful as in a bathroom. Then he slammed the door and that was the last they saw of him. The caretaker locked it.

Fredrik heard about the uprising and rushed over as soon as they finished for the evening at the foundry. By that time, though, most people had left: the students had departed through the back door, and the spectators were ambling along Store Street under the gas streetlights. Some of the women were still around, and their poster was there to be read, but Fredrik wasn't very impressed with this insurrection. He heard them saying their feet were cold and that they needed to get home and put on the rutabagas to boil.

This war was nothing but shit. To begin with it had been exciting, the church bells had rung from morning to evening when the reserves were mobilized. General von Emmerich had been victorious and the newspaper had published a portrait of him as the subjugator of Liège. Putte Lundholm's brother, who lived in Stockholm and served in the Göta Guard had come home in a new uniform to say farewell to his mother. He had three stripes on his sleeve now and a dog tag and was going to be sent out to Värmdö where it was likely he would meet his death. But now it was 1917 and he was still alive and came home now and then and was still nothing but a petty officer. Now there were shortages of everything, even potatoes, and people were taking sick. Was everything always so trite and pathetic? Why didn't anything big ever happen?

T owards spring, when Anker's was no longer able to get hold of any flour for baking, Konrad lost his job.

'What'll you do now?' asked Fredrik.

'Write my thesis.'

He was sitting there as usual under the knotted laundry lines that criss-crossed over his head. For the first time in his company, Fredrik felt impatient.

'In order to gain access to the renowned faculty of philosophy at the University of Hovlunda Road I shall write my thesis on the bedbug. The announcement will be posted on the door to the woodshed in the yard. I'm about to start the chapter on the bedbug and love life.'

'Wonder if you could get work at the foundry?' said Fredrik, scanning Konrad's white baker's hands and his thin, willowy body.

'Not the love life of the bedbug, which I leave to the scientists. But the bedbug and human love life. Imagine that the four legs on Romeo and Juliet's bed stand in four anchovy tins full of paraffin oil. Night falls, there is a scratching sound behind the wallpaper. Romeo is whispering as, one by one, the flat little creatures that are the most steadfast companion of mankind, drop from the ceiling. Scratch, scratch. Juliet, who has pale, sensitive skin and sweet blood, tosses and turns. She's itching. Things are starting to creep around in the bedclothes. They're dropping in hoards from the ceiling, no longer timid. Romeo sits up in bed, clawing at his skin. Welts are swelling up and they bleed when he scratches, but he can't stop himself now. All higher emotion has vanished, all

143

shyness and shame. There are rustling, scratching sounds under the bedclothes. The bedbugs of the world are uniting!'

'Shush!' says Fredrik.

'Next chapter. The bedbug and human dignity.'

'Want to come along to Oxtorp? I'm going to collect two stewing chickens somebody's promised mum. One of them's yours.'

They made their way up to Oxtorp in the heavy slush. It was ten kilometres. The farmer gave them the hens he'd slaughtered, their necks askew and legs tied together. They took the train home, settling into the empty first-class compartment. Konrad undid the hens, setting them neatly in separate plush armchairs, their broken necks drooping against the backrests. They were pale and their eyes looked tired. He held forth to them all the way home, and just as if they had been alive they were too haughty to answer him. No conductor came in to check their tickets until they were passing the switch into town, at which time, although there was no point in making them clear out, he still did.

By the time summer arrived Konrad Eriksson was as thin as a razor and his back was bent. He walked around looking as if his stomach ached, which it did. He said it was the bitter dandelion root coffee that upset it.

He took Fredrik along out to Rosenholm to fish. That wasn't bad. The sky vaulted blue and Fredrik lay on the bottom of the old rowboat puffing on Lucky Strikes. Now and then he had to wring out and restuff the rag that was damming up a leak, or his back would get wet. They could just make out the little manor house at Rosenholm behind the alders and they could hear someone raking the gravelled path.

The miller had lent Konrad some fishing nets and they put them out on Saturday evening and were going to take them up early the next morning. Sunday morning was a difficult time to get Fredrik out of bed, however. When they finally got out there most of the little bream had died in the nets, which were in shallow water that heated up early. But the tenches were still alive and had to be killed and gutted right away, or the meat would taste of blood. In the end, fish turned their stomachs. Their hands were full of bits of bloody innards and fish scales, and heavy streams of dark blood flowed from the tench heads. The sun dried the sides of the greenish-black, thick-skinned fish to leather and the skin of the bream to scaly sets of armour where the flies searched for cracks. They left the pile of fish at the bottom of the boat and went and lay down in the grass, staring straight up at the empty sky and having a smoke to settle their rumbling stomachs. They could hear the sound of cards slapping against the nearby jetty where somef young people were lying around playing rummy.

Dragonflies with long trailing feelers swayed on the tips of the reeds. They lifted up behind, as if they were ready to mate; their bodies looked humped. But they shimmered as they flew and Fredrik tried to keep his eyes on them, but lost them almost at once. It smelled marshy. He didn't want to look down at the water where a leech was working away at a snail he was consuming and sandworms curled in the sludge of the lake bed.

'Have you seen the sea?' Fredrik asked Konrad.

'Mmm, at Oxelösund.'

'Is it as incredible as they say?'

'It's clean.'

Fredrik lay there trying to imagine a huge body of water without leeches or worms, a body of water as pure and as bitter as eau de vie, a sea stretching all the way to Estonia.

'My pappa couldn't live without the sea,' he said.

'No.'

'Do you remember your pappa?'

Konrad laughed awkwardly.

'Of course I remember my pappa. He took butter in his coffee.'

Eriksson had been one of those people for whom things just didn't work out. That's what Fredrik's mamma said. After the strike he was out of a job and then he apparently started hitting the bottle. He had had several accidents in Norrköping. It almost looked as if he was tempting fate, like some people who go out and play around with their Remingtons in the woodshed or with a rope in the attic, though nothing ever comes of it. He ended up under a tram. No one spoke ill of him and he hadn't been a really heavy drinker, at least not before the strike. But he had no gumption, his mamma had said.

'He really did take butter if we had any,' Konrad said. 'A whole spoonful. He'd put it in his coffee and then let it melt into beads and circles at the top of the cup. Then he'd drink it up. It was real coffee in those days, though. Do you even remember real coffee?'

'No.'

'Real coffee's like the armhole of a mulatto woman – brown and hot and soft and aromatic. You drink it with a slice of rye bread covered in butter – or else...'

'What's this?'

'Damn,' said Konrad. 'Must've been the mulatto that brought them over.'

'We're eating,' he said amicably to the heads sticking up over the reeds.

'Eating what?'

'Slices of rye bread spread with lard.'

There were three young men and a girl with mosquito-bitten legs under a far-too-short skirt. One of them was still holding the

deck of cards in the hand with which he pushed aside the reeds.
Fredrik felt confident because he was with Konrad who, although
he was skinny, was at least grown up.

'White, really soft drippings with little pieces of onion and
apple in it,' he said 'I usually dice a slice of cold pork in as well.'

'The hell you do,' said the tallest card-player. 'You've got no
food.'

'No, just a few kinds of hot meats,' said Konrad. 'Little
meatballs and herring with onions and sausage and rollmops.'

'What kind of shit are you talking?' asked the tallest, heaviest
one.

' 'Scuse me. How about potato pancakes instead? But we have
to admit that they're leftovers. We usually hold them in the palms
of our hands and spread butter on them. But I s'pose you insist on
ham?'

'If I had a potato pancake I think I could get it down with
nothing on it.'

They crouched in the grass. Fredrik thought to himself, I
wonder what kind of a girl would be out here with them? Such
bitten legs. And look how she's sitting. You can see all the way up
her crack. Incredible! Konrad's something, himself, just prattling
on like that and waving his hands. So white and soft from bread
dough – they might think he's never done a decent day's work and
then they'll beat up on us.

'Toast drippings is something you do eat, though?'

'That's when you fry bread in pork fat,' the girl said.

'Mustn't forget to add a splash of milk. And serve it with bacon.'

'My old man used to dip bacon in his coffee.'

'But that had to be American bacon, I guess? Oh, you lovely,
fatty bitter-salty Chicago bacon, what could make you taste better
than a steaming hot cup of Java?'

Konrad stopped at nothing. He lay on his back in the grass with his arms under his head looking up at the bright blue sky, and began a description of black pudding.

'You can tell by the way it wobbles whether a black pudding's been properly simmered. The shake and the smell. Then there's the cream sauce. Thick and smooth. Add a dab of butter – it never hurts and you might be the lucky one to get it in your spoon. But here I am, lying here talking and forgetting the most important thing of all!'

'What'd that be?'

'The pork sausage,' Konrad almost whispered. 'Virtually the king of the table – hail sausage! You're smooth and well-filled and slippery – and just think of your little knotted ends and the string. We have to be careful here, 'cause you know sausage skins are fragile and these ones are stuffed with all kinds of goodies, with the best pork and lard and a little fine potato flour, all ground 'til it's pink and liquidized, pink as a piglet. Prick it with a little stick, pat it on its pink little bottom and slide it carefully into the broth. Allspice. Bay leaves. A bit of onion.'

The girl had her sunburned paws on her knees. But she was sitting in just the same way as before. Fredrik tried not to look.

'Now it's simmering oh so gently and little pearls of fat are rising to the surface and bursting. Oh me oh my. Meanwhile we're boiling the potatoes. Ones we've peeled first, of course. They need to get done fast. A little salt. Keep an eye on that sausage. Put an extra ring under the pot, so it doesn't boil too hard. When the potatoes are soft – use a birch twig from the whisk to check – pour off the water. Meanwhile I'm turning the sausage – there's not much broth there. We don't want that sausage drowning in water, 'cause some of the good stuff oozes out and we want that for the sauce. Goodness, don't forget to put the mustard on the table. Now we take the masher and mash the potatoes. Right, that's it. Don't leave a single lump. There's nothing so awful as sitting with a plate of mashed potatoes in front of you and finding a nasty, almost raw bit in your mouth. No, soft and airy. Beat lots of air in. And add an egg yolk!'

'You're kidding!' said the girl.

'I'm not. That's what you need. No stinginess here. Just keep beating. Nutmeg's good in mashed potatoes, but that might be a little over the top. Pass the cutting board. And the knife. Thanks a lot. Now I lift the sausage out. Bother, it broke.'

They held their breath.

'Never mind. It's in place now and I lean the cutting board at an angle to get all the liquid into the saucepan. Look, it's changed colour, almost red now, curling right up as I slice it, the skin rolling back like stockings.'

They were gaping as they listened, and Fredrik forgot to keep track of how the girl was sitting. It was as if the very pores on their skin had opened up, and their eyes were burning from not blinking. But who cared? Konrad's white hands were waving as he described slicing the sausage. Their eyes were glued to those hands.

'Oh well,' he said. 'All good things must come to an end. And sausages have two ends! Hungry?' It was all too sudden, he should've brought them back to reality more gradually. Fast, altogether too fast, they hit bottom with a bang as if they were hitting the tin bottom of an empty milk pail. And there they sat.

Their stomachs were clenching up tight and they were swallowing their saliva. Konrad got up with a little laugh at them. Fredrik thought he'd behaved stupidly. He was too nonchalant and turned his back on them as he walked over to the boat, and suddenly something hard hit him right between the shoulder blades, knocking the wind out of him. When he turned around he was smiling but with a foolish sort of grin. He couldn't tell who'd done it, all three had their hands in their pockets and the girl was still sitting in the grass.

'Come on,' said Fredrik, hopping into the bobbing rowboat.

One of them gave Konrad a rough shove and a sock in the upper arm, after which he fell into the boat, stepped right on a tench and lost his balance. Fredrik got the oars up but couldn't row through the reeds by the shore. He lifted one out of the oarlock and pushed off against the bottom. Two of the boys were wading out into the mud to get at Konrad. Fredrik kept poling for all he was worth, thinking he'd bang them on the head with the oar if worst came to worst. But why was Konrad just sitting there still looking surprised?

'You're a right idiot! Come here and we'll tell you a story.'

'We'll cement your big trap shut.'

But now the boat was free and Fredrik was rowing as hard as he could, splashing with the oars. All around them pondweed and handfuls of mud were landing with loud splashes, they were getting wet. Of the four kids on the beach the girl was doing most of the throwing but she didn't have a very good pitching arm.

'What got into them?' Konrad wondered when they were out of reach. He tried to lie down on the bottom of the boat to catch his breath, but it was all wet, and the tenches and small bream were afloat.

They rowed to the mill to return the nets and then walked the home on the big road into town with their fish in a pail. Fredrik didn't talk much. He didn't at all like the fact that the boys down there had gone after Konrad, who was a grown man. Something had changed, and he didn't want that.

He was at 60 Hovlunda Road on the Saturday afternoon Konrad came home asking where Ingrid was. Fredrik knew she wasn't down in the yard playing in the rain. She had been sent away into

150

foster care again, but this time with a family who lived in the houses for the railway workers. His own mother was the one who'd delivered her there. Frida hadn't the heart. Fredrik couldn't understand why Frida told Konrad so abruptly, almost as if she were blaming him. And then there was the awful part from which Fredrik would have liked to be able to look away but couldn't. Konrad's face went all stiff and he gave Frida a terrible dressing down. When she reacted by saying that they just couldn't have Ingrid at home any longer, he pushed her up against the stove. Fredrik stood watching though he didn't want to, he saw Frida bump the iron rail that ran around the wood-burning stove, he heard her hip joint hit it. It must've hurt, she put both hands to her hip and sucked in her bottom lip.

'I had no choice,' she said.

Konrad rushed to the window and stood with his back to her saying they took everything, wasn't it bad enough that they ate up their food, and did they have to take the children as well?

'Go on home, Fredrik,' said Frida.

Konrad grasped the curtain and pulled it to the floor, rod and all, and Frida looked like she was about to burst into tears, but she didn't.

'I'm going over there!' he shouted.

'Oh no you're not. When you've settled down you'll see we had no other choice. The child needs to eat. And there's nought here. You don't have a regular job any more.'

Konrad began to cry and said it was all his fault. Now Fredrik wanted to leave but he couldn't get around the kitchen table and over to the door with Konrad standing there crying. Then he noticed that Ingrid's old doll was lying there on the floor along with her knitted dog, and he gathered them up and said he could at least take them round.

'No,' said Frida.

'But she'll need them!' Konrad wept.

Frida took them and wrapped them in newspaper and told Fredrik he could take them.

'Their name's Ek,' she said. 'He's an engineer and they live in the railway housing. Say we sent you.'

He took the hastily-wrapped parcel and slunk past Konrad and out the door. At first he thought he'd never be able to go back. His next thought was that it had been like a bad dream. The next day they wouldn't even remember that Konrad had been crying. He hoped the awful dog and doll wouldn't protrude from the parcel as he walked across the city. How strange it was that Konrad was so attached to Ingrid, who was so little. Odd that he didn't just think of her as a problem. Which she was.

He knocked on the door of the family named Ek and a woman in slippers and a big, clean apron with a frilled bib opened it. He stared at her and held out the dog and doll.

'What's that?' she asked.

'Ingrid Eriksson's toys,' he said. 'They sent me.'

'Oh,' she said. 'Fine. Thank you.'

But as he was leaving, he saw her stuff the parcel in the hallway wood bin and he was certain that by evening it would have been consumed by the kitchen stove. Personally, he thought it was just as well.

L et's have a look at what happened in March 1918 the evening Tora Otter and Frida Eriksson went into the city to see 'Der Graf von Luxemburg' at the Casino Theatre.

They hung their coats on hooks under the painted brown shelves in the lobby but didn't remove their hats. They kept their sweaters on, too, as it was cold. They'd bought their tickets in advance from the tobacconist and Tora had a bag of mixed sweets in her handbag. They went inside, nodding to everyone they knew, right and left, and looking at the painted white seat numbers on the brown benches. They sat down and Frida stared straight ahead at the curtain. Tora kept looking around for acquaintances and telling Frida who was there. Then the orchestra came out and took their seats below the stage, pulling their chairs and music stands about noisily, after which the horn began to bray noisily and the clarinet to play scales up and down.

When the auditorium was full, the ceiling lights were dimmed and the conductor entered, moving into the spotlight that was already shining on the curtain. He was wearing tails and a soft shirt, and he had the same absent expression on his face as the musicians. The curtain didn't rise right away, they played some music first, and quite a long piece at that. People began to chat, but Palmquist the watchmaker shushed them.

When the curtain finally started to move it got about halfway and then came to a halt, after which the stage hands started tugging at it. Then it rose up and vanished. There was a cold gust of unheated wind and the smell of old clothes and then it was blindingly bright and full of people holding tall slender glasses lifted overhead as they began to sing. 'A festival! A happy ball, we greet you all! Tra la la la!'

Tora whispered to Frida that they should've hung on to their coats as well. More bursts of cold air kept blowing off the stage in their direction, but the actors and dancers had such rosy cheeks you couldn't tell whether they were cold. 'All day, all night, our feast's a lovely sight,' they sang.

The man playing the Duke of Luxemburg wore a black coat with a little cape at the shoulders. He jumped up onto a table singing and all the others stood around him with their glasses raised. 'My forebear was the Luxembourg of which the tale does tell,' he sang. He went on about what it was like to be poor, and how you could still go through life laughing and singing. He really looked like he knew what he was talking about, because he was thin as a reed and had blue circles under his eyes. 'Fa la la lee, life's good to me.' Well, it can't be all that much fun to travel around with the set and trunks full of costumes and maybe not get home again before Christmas.

The skinny fellow was to marry the girl called Angèle, but only as a favour to an old man with a glass eye and white gaiters. They'd be divorced right away after the wedding. Neither Tora nor Frida could understand what the point of making things so complicated was, but then it was the interval and they were out in the lobby chatting with the other watchmaker, the one who didn't put on airs like Palmquist, and he explained it was so she could become Duchess. It was the only way for her to be able to marry the old man with the tufted, grey hair. But what did she see in that old lobster who was all red in the face? Ebba was in the audience, too, and you couldn't help wondering what she was thinking. She held her brewer tightly by the arm and had her fox fur collar on indoors. Which wasn't a bad idea when it was so damn cold. Tora told Werner Karlsson who was the caretaker and yard tender at the Casino that he'd lit the boiler too late. But he put the blame on the municipal heating authorities.

They got married with a screen between them because the old man said they mustn't see one another. 'Laaaave is what I've never known,' she sang. 'It's left me thus far all alone. Oh, laaaave.' But she had a nasty gleam in her eye. They liked the other woman better, whose name was Juliette. She was chubby and robust and when she sang, she sounded like a clucking hen. 'I may be hungry, the weather may be cold, but I stay cheerful even when my purse has nought to hold. We'll vanquish the world with a lot of good cheer (cluck cluck), and we'll only live as long as we're here!'

Which was as true as could be. Mind you, she was a little heavy-set and the floorboards creaked under her. They sagged, too, and that miserly Malmén probably wouldn't do a thing about it until the whole operetta company fell right through when the stage collapsed. Frida couldn't keep her eyes open and Tora elbowed her gently and fed her sweets to perk her up.

'Are they married yet?' Frida asked.

'Uh huh, and now they're going to meet, but not recognize one another.'

But in the end they fell head over heels in love. Each time they rushed into one another's arms the chandeliers shook. Sometimes when the music went soft you could hear people coughing and blowing their noses. 'Love, you are the spice of life! And sweet as a toffee, too. Love, you are my everything, nothing else will do.' Tora gave Frida another bonbon and they both winked.

At the next interval Krantz the watchmaker walked up to them again, in the company of Ivan Roos, stock manager at the ironmonger's. They treated the women to lemonade.

'Should've been champagne, of course,' said Ivan Roos, raising his glass. But that just inspired the watchmaker to remark that what they were seeing on stage was a deceptive picture of life.

'Oh,' said Tora. 'Don't spoil it for me.'

People were pretty quiet in the lobby, and the caretaker went around telling those who were lighting up that they'd have to go outside, despite the fact that no one would have been happier than Malmén to see the theatre burn down so he could collect on his insurance.

They found the last act a bit long, and Frida dozed off several times. But now they were having a waltz up on stage and oh how lovey-dovey and dancy-fancy it all was. He was trying to look handsome and athletic, but it should've been Kalle Barkling instead. This one was so thin. They never did get divorced, of course, but you suspected that from the very beginning. Just as they were dancing a final waltz the last row of seats in the auditorium tipped over backwards. The boys sitting there were pretty fed up with the whole thing, and overturned it on purpose. For one instant everything was still, but shortly the cast went on dancing and singing as if nothing had happened. When the boys righted the row it scraped against the floor, and voices and suppressed laughter could be heard. They'd probably had a bit too much to drink, but such was the way of the world.

The curtain went down and the orchestra went silent. In the blink of an eye they'd put away their bows and mouthpieces. There was applause from the audience, and the curtain went up again, got stuck, was pulled loose, and all the actors came back out curtseying and bowing. The audience went on applauding until the curtain got stuck in the closed position, and that was that.

Slowly they headed home, with Frida's mouth pinched tight with embarrassment because the watchmaker and Ivan Roos were walking on either side of them. As they were walking down the steps to the market square the watchmaker asked whether they wouldn't all like to come in to his place for a drink before splitting up. At first Frida said no thank you, very firmly indeed. But when Tora had squeezed her arm a few times and said they'd be happy to, she went along after all. They said they'd not be taking off their coats or sitting down, and they didn't. Krantz lit the lamps; they could smell that a bachelor lived there, and he poured them each a glass of wine. The minute they'd all said 'skål' and taken a sip, the women began to button their coats up again. But the watchmaker set his empty glass on the sideboard and did something then that surprised them and which they'd never forget. Never once had they ever heard from anyone that Krantz the watchmaker could be funny. He set one foot in front of the other, bent his knees slightly, opened his chubby hands in front of himself and sang:

> There was a little butterfly
> Perched on a red rosebud
> lamenting of his misery
> his longing and his love.

> Shyly lisped the rosebud red:
> 'In my boudoir, do make your bed!
> Buzz, buzz, buzz, abuzzy buzz buzz
> Buzzy buzzy buzz!'

When he got to the buzzy buzz part he stamped his foot as if he were dancing, and held his hands out from his body. He repeated the refrain, bowed his head and was done.

When they had thanked him they stepped back out into the cold street and went their separate ways. Frida would trudge back to her place, and Tora to hers. She lived close by the watchmaker. But she crossed the courtyard slowly, more slowly than usual, thinking about the fact that she was over forty years old and had thought she knew most of what there was to know about life and about what might happen. But never in her wildest imagination had she pictured watchmaker Krantz singing like that.

She started thinking about love. Not that she was in love with the watchmaker, heavens to mercy no, nor with Ivan Roos for that matter. But love.

How little it is. It requires nothing, not even someone at your side. Just being together and happy. Yes, it feeds on intimacy, shining with the gentle sheen of a buttercup.

And that was the end of the evening when she and Frida Eriksson went to the Casino Theatre. She went inside and although she didn't give it another thought she didn't forget it, either.

Algot Dahlgren, the railwayman, was a little predator. Gustaf Krupp von Bohlen and Alexander Lindh may have been sabre-toothed tigers and man-eating sharks, but Dahlgren was certainly a mongoose. He was the one who built the laundry shed. A stream ran across his property, he built a dam and put in a washing tub with a roof over it. Then he charged people to do their washing. This was monopoly capitalism. He didn't shut down his enterprise until the water in Trash Moat was so polluted with the domestic sewage from the nearby households that people's laundry came out brown. That is, when the housewives refused to send their washing. He just sat there brooding, which didn't make him a true empire builder. And he did have his pension from the railway.

People in the community then managed their washing as best they could until the laundry at the corner of Store Street and Hovlunda Road went up, at the initiative of chief railway engineer Johan Sterkell. He had no money to invest, nor did he intend to turn a profit on the laundry. His idea was quite simply to give the washerwomen a decent place to work and the housewives somewhere to get their laundry done. Sterkell was preoccupied with what is often known as the general good. He didn't even want to be reimbursed for the hours that turned into days and then months and years of his life spent at meetings of councils and boards. Nor was any reimbursement forthcoming. So what was he after? Esteem?

Well, he had nothing against a little esteem. But above all he

159

wanted people to do what he said and think he was right. He appreciated traditional expressions of gratitude. But he would have been embarrassed if he'd had to be immortalized as a bust in that spot known as 'Mulle's grave' after the deceased dog of a long-ago stationmaster, with an inscription on the base reading: 'ENERGY, INDUSTRY, GENIUS'. What he wanted most of all was to be able to walk through his community and see it growing and know that its water was clean.

He was a morning person, didn't like to lie around in bed with his night thoughts slithering around the empty bowl of sleep. When he awoke at five o'clock he would get up and make his coffee himself. In summer he took his morning constitutional at that early hour. He preferred to walk the streets alone, while the windows were still blindered and shut and the gardens lay dewy. The mist rising from the roof of the stationhouse was rainbow-coloured, sparrows bathed in the thin layer of dust in the yard, freeing themselves from lice. All the evil forces were asleep in murky rooms, and all the good ones as well. Soon enough there would be late-night meetings and endless compromising, dry palates and burning eyes. At this hour he could imagine himself the absolute ruler, and he was ambulatory.

He heard the willow warbler singing in the honeysuckle on the veranda of the stationmaster's house. There were rustling noises coming from inside, and if he stood really still he could discern a bright, kohl-rimmed eye. Now was the time he could allow his fears to rise and subside again, the time his thoughts might stumble and fall, get lost and find their way back, and often discover something he had never noticed before. These thoughts were always on the subject of road maintenance, housing construction and waste management. He both noticed and ignored the way the hose tower on the fire station turned red and glistened in the sunrise on the side that was always in shadow, and the squirrels chasing one another in the lime-trees in the park outside the courthouse.

He often arrived out at Wärnström's around the time the workingmen assembled before the gates, and he would walk slowly along the other side of the road, listening to their voices and occasionally glimpsing their faces. When the gatekeeper opened for them he would often turn back and sometimes he would stop and watch them being let in, and scrutinize the factory area. But he never went inside, any more than had the family members of the workers who brought them their packed dinners and bottles of milk in Wärnström's day. When Swedish Motor took over the plant the gates were closed, and after that they remained shut and guarded.

The new laundry establishment was a red, two-storey brick building with arches patterned into the bricklaying over the tall windows. Clouds of steam rose from the smokestacks, escaped from the vents and poured through the open windows. There was the smell of lye all the way out to the street. In the winter, the window sills near the warm, pleasant steam were crowded with pigeons and crows.

Sterkell had no money to build with, so when he put up the laundry shed he joined forces with Mangusson the master builder, and with Alexander Lindh. In 1906 they bought a new steam boiler and reorganized their project into a joint stock company. Since then shareholdings large and small had changed hands on many occasions, although the ownership had basically circulated within the group of propertied gentlemen and investors who actually comprised the community. Their portfolios included not only profit-making enterprises but also companies that were being kept alive out of due consideration for the general good and, to some extent, social prestige.

161

In 1918, when the city took over the laundry, Carl Wärnström, the factory owner, and Holger Iversen-Lindh, the engineer, sold most of their shares. But the director of the electricity utility also had a shareholding, and there were a number of smaller shareholders, including Valfrid Johansson, the merchant. You might wonder why on earth he wanted shares in a laundry that would never turn a profit. The answer is that nowadays he belonged to the circle of people who, to use the words of the dear departed merchant Lindh himself, shouldered the social responsibilities of the community. Sometimes Valfrid found this shouldering a costly business. But at the end of the day it was of his own free choice, and that reinforced his confidence in this show of solidarity. Mind you, he was pleased as punch the day his shares were sold and he found he had not suffered a great loss.

There is no overestimating the virtues of that laundry. It was both an attractive and eminently useful construction. It smelt good and, even from its humble beginnings, provided a living for five workers. Eleven at its peak. It produced clean laundry for the entire community, was an inexpensive place to have your washing done and even cheaper if you did it yourself. The enormous steam boiler puffed steadily away and would have gone right on puffing today had it been required to do so.

It was operated by a machinist named Evert Berg. He had a deep, lovely singing voice and an enormous diaphragm in which it resonated. It rang out loud and clear within these walls, and the washerwomen scrubbed to the sounds of 'A String has Broken', which he was rehearsing to sing at funerals. He was a tall, fair man with short hair covering his rosy scalp, and the singing and the steam boiler had also made him a happy man. The women had coffee with him each day and he never had to bring himself any cake.

The building smelt good from sudsy water and clean linens. Sheets clapped, the mangle clanked, the steam hissed and clogs clattered along the wet wooden slats. The scrubbing boards resounded in the basin room and the women's voices chirped like birds above the din. There was fury when a clean sheet hit the floor as it was being stretched, quarrels echoed when someone was missing a pillowcase, and there were harangues over the bins when people's laundry had got mixed up in the tubs. There were conjectures based on soiled garments, spotted sheets were smuggled aside in the soaking tubs, but there was laughter every day as well. The washerwomen handled the hot lye calmly and helped one another rub out stubborn stains and redo tablecloths that had slipped crooked on the mangling rods. The skin on their hands swelled and developed fungus infections, the muscles in their arms were strong and their legs were criss-crossed with blue clusters of varicose veins. They were clean and their cheeks rose, they wore yellow oilcloth aprons over white housedresses. There were also baths where two female attendants handled the bodies, doing so matter-of-factly and firmly but not without tenderness. They had steam boxes to put the men in, and wooden benches to rub them down on. Families arrived with their clean underwear in bags and baskets, and bathed in tubs every second or third week. Afterwards they went back out into the cold winter weather, their skin rosy with the heat and itching under their stockings.

Railway engineer Sterkell had his idea about the laundry building early one morning as he was walking though the little park below the ridge, listening to Heavenside Spring running beneath the stones. He both heard it and ignored it, as his thoughts were preoccupied as usual with community affairs. Later other men had ideas about shutting women in below the ground in cellars with concrete floors, alone with machines that intimidated them.

Even later they would shut them into kitchens with appliances with built-in obsolescence, and fabric that stank of sweat after only one day's wear, and these women had to send their linens to huge establishments where they were washed harshly in strong detergents and mangled on hot mangling irons until they lost their sheen, where they were folded mechanically and came out smelling mildewed. The brains that produced these ideas may have been sharper than engineer Sterkell's, but they didn't produce them in the morning.

Now there'd be no more scratching your behind, no more coffee, no more taking a treacle sandwich to the privy, or fighting with the boys or gulping down your food standing at the kitchen sink so you could run out and play. Imagine beef stew, for instance, or rump roast. You can't exactly eat things like that standing at the sink.

'Well, sweetheart,' said the other washerwomen. 'Aren't you the lucky one? My, my, my. You'll appreciate it one day yourself. Such fine people!'

Frida didn't say a word, though, because she didn't like Ingrid's coming round the laundry and standing by the wall looking on.

The first thought Ingrid had when she moved into the railway housing was that now she would find herself surrounded by the Scabs. They lived in the railway housing and fought with the Baker Kids on the other side. Their leader was Reinhold, known as the Flop. He was head of the gang. Once, Edvin Anker had slung a dead rat he'd tied to a piece of rope at him and hit him. The Flop was going to kill Edvin when he got hold of him, and he'd do it with a crowbar. Every day he got reports as to Edvin's movements. Meanwhile they tied Big Lasse to the flagpole out by the Good Templars' and left him there all night. He got a fever.

She sat inside for the first few days. She sat there thinking about the others, sitting on the outbuilding roof playing cards, setting fires under the lumber piled in the yard. If she went out they'd tie her up. She didn't dare say anything to the Eks; and they'd never believe her anyway. They had no idea.

She, however, had known how things were since her very first day at school. There was nobody else from Hovlunda Road to go with, and Ingrid had had to walk down the steps of the house all alone with her schoolbag, with the Scabs standing there behind the station master's house waiting to scare her. Ingrid took everything seriously. There are people who do. As there was no help to be had and she did not expect to be spared, she turned around. She armed herself with a grey stone, put it in her school satchel, and as she walked back down the steps she felt its weight. In good time, she began swinging the satchel by its shoulder strap. It twirled heavily, in a wide arc. The Flop was standing by the kiosk. He laughed when he saw her looking so plucky as he moved in her direction to give her a scare. Of course he expected her satchel to be empty, and was extremely surprised when its weight hit his arm. Had it hit him in the head it would have killed him, though neither he nor Ingrid knew it.

'That's one helluva kid there,' he said, still laughing at her as she sped around the corner of the Lindhs' house, heading uphill along King's Road at a sprint.

The Baker Kids heard about it and from then on she was one of them. There were only three girls in the gang, they had rough hands and scarred knees. Every afternoon the Baker Kids lit paper and twigs underneath the piles of boards at the lumberyard, sat there around the brief, bright flames until the heat had dispersed, stamped them out and climbed back up from underneath the pile. No one knew very much about their lives, and their songs were never written down.

But now she no longer belonged. She was living in one of the railway workers' houses and when she finally had to go outside nothing happened. The Scabs no more noticed her than they noticed the little girls playing outside with their dolls and chipped coffee cups. She'd been given a new pinafore and had started wearing

166

stockings in her shoes even though it was summer. Were they afraid of Ek, the locomotive engineer? She had no idea. Sometimes she felt like she had begun to dissolve, or that she had lost her voice as sometimes happens in dreams when you want to shout out and your heart is bursting with terror.

So she walked across to the south side in her pretty pinafore and sat outside the smithy watching Edvin and Sune Anker feed the ram cigar stubs and lumps of chewing tobacco people had spit onto the street. They nodded to her but didn't speak. She felt like doing something to make them pay attention to her, to make them say: 'That's one helluva kid there'.

She was tempted to jump the ram or throw bits of coal at him to annoy him. But she didn't dare get her clothes dirty.

Just then Tora Otter came walking down the street with a jumper pulled over her dress and very dusty shoes. Her pale eyes looked at Ingrid and she said: 'Heavens, look at those huge frills on your pinafore. They look like wings.'

This infuriated Ingrid to speechlessness. Edvin and Sune rolled somersaults, as they always did when they were pretending to be doubled up with laughter. After that they called her 'Angel'. And every time she met one of the Baker Kids at the marketplace they would gesticulate in her direction as they did to all silly girls. They'd put their hands on their knees and turn their behinds towards her pretending to pass air.

So, now she was supposed to play with girls, and not go climbing hills or filching unripe fruit from trees, and she was supposed to call Ingeborg Ek 'Mamma'. She didn't call her anything at all.

Behind the huge garden in back of the Lindhs' house there was a foundation. Long ago there had been a croft there. Nowadays it wasn't much more than a big rubbish dump. Greyish bones protruded from the grass, along with pieces of glass and gaping boots. The girls played house within the confines of what had once been the croft, and they cleaned and cleaned, but the weeds just grew stubbornly back up out of the hillside. The place was permeated with a strange combination of terror and tenderness. Every morning when they arrived at this pretend home, with pieces of broken brick to demarcate the rooms, they had to poke away the slugs that had crept into their pots and pans and left them streaky.

From the beginning Ingrid had no desire to join in, nor did the others let her. Gradually, however, they realized she wasn't scared to remove the slugs with her fingers. After that they started sending her to pick the flowers they called 'coffee', the big leaves of which could be found growing in the rubbish dump if you hunted hard enough. At this time of year the plants were still small and green; it was too early to pluck off the brown seeds.

'Never mind,' they said. 'It can be spinach.'

'Are you the one they call Angel?' a girl asked. Ingrid didn't answer, but felt everybody staring at her.

They played families, but no one wanted to be father. When the boys passed by they would kick over their tins full of coffee beans and water, or pretend to be drunkards, reeling so the coffee cups spilled out into the grass. They'd have to tidy up after the men who'd had one too many. Uffe was the only one they could play with, since he was just five. He was fat but they could still carry him. They took turns using him as their baby. Some days he'd be bathed and put to bed up to ten times. When he was supposed to be ill they would get down between the elderflower bush and the wooden fence and take his temperature. Their hearts would pound in their throats.

'And what did you play today?' Ingeborg Ek would ask. When she heard they'd been playing families, she asked, 'With the boys?'

'No, just little Uffe.'

There were lots of things you didn't tell. Ingrid didn't say that she sometimes went home. She was not unhappy about being the Eks' foster child. She'd already been at Rickard and Stella Lans' over by the ridge. You got as much as you wanted to eat and mamma would visit. When you got some flesh they let you go back home.

In the beginning, the Eks didn't have all that much food themselves. Everybody suffered during a war, Ingeborg would say, sighing so deeply her chest heaved. But the war ended and things got better. She made brisket of beef and apple pie.

But her mother didn't visit. Ingrid asked several times the first week if it wouldn't soon be Sunday. And then Sunday came, the church bells rang loudly and the gravel walkway leading to the railway workers' housing was neatly raked. Ingrid sat at the window waiting for Frida to arrive with her hat on her head and a little bag of sweet buns from the Cosmopolitan. But she never came.

So Ingrid went there. Konrad was so happy he could hardly speak. He lifted her high above the washing lines and the lamp.

'My little Flia,' he said. 'My sweet little Flia.'

'What's got into you?' she asked. 'As soon as they fatten me up I'll be back.'

He didn't answer. The next Sunday Ingeborg Ek said she shouldn't go to Hovlunda Road.

'Why not?'

'You're going to be our little girl now. You'll like that, won't you?'

Her voice was shaky as always when something was wrong, so Ingrid realized it would be best not to tell when she went to Hovlunda Road in the future.

How well off she was now! It was warm at the Eks' house even in winter. When you went to bed you hung your clothes on the tile stove and they stayed warm all night and you could pull a warmed-up vest over your head in the morning. Yes, here you wore different undergarments at night and during the day. The day one was a little vest made of ribbed cotton weave with a ribbon at the top that kept coming undone and buttons down the back that never went missing. The buttons down the back showed that it wasn't the cheapest kind. Her knickers were light brown on the outside and white on the inside and had elastic at the ankles. At the bottom edge of the vest was a nice, new elastic band, not an old, drawn-out one. Her stockings were of a colour Ingeborg Ek called 'baishe'. And she had brown boots, and shoes with straps for Sundays, along with dresses of checked fabric and pinafores with great big frills.

On Sundays they'd go out walking, or take the train to their relations in Simonstorp, and then she had on a light-blue coat and hat. Her hat had a big brim at the front out from under which her little Angel face peeped. But her quick eyes and her ever-shut thin-lipped mouth were anything but angelic.

Engineer Ek and his family got to ride the trains for free, so they did quite a bit of travelling. They had relations in Flen, too, but that side of the family were non-Conformists. In town they knew a man with a shoe shop, a hairdresser and the head clerk at Melin's, the ironmongers. Engineer Ek was the most prominent citizen among them. Mind you, the shoe shop was beginning to do well, and the hairdresser's, too, but you never knew when times would be hard again. Then people are more inclined to go to the shoemaker than to buy new shoes, and to cut one another's hair at the kitchen table. But the trains never stop running, that's for sure.

Ingeborg Ek was one of the most industrious, most thorough people on earth. She had been cook at the Lindh home for four years time. She had harassed the kitchen maid, terrified the butcher, and never made a hollandaise sauce with fewer than ten yolks. Then she married Assar Ek who preferred boiled and mashed root vegetables with knuckle of ham to vol au vent. She had intended to work one or two evenings a week catering for dinner parties, but Assar Ek said:

'No wife of mine is going out to work. I am the breadwinner in this family.'

So she became a devoted housewife. She was most devoted of all at Christmas time, when she regularly wore herself out. But by the new year she was always resurrected, and she was her old self by Twelfth Night when relations came to visit day after day. Afterward there were pine needles on the rugs and cigar ash between the cushions of her sofa with its pedestal armrests. The Christmas tree was thrown out and it was time to clean, to scrape away candle wax and polish off the rings on the tabletops in the sitting room. The candle smoke had blackened the insulation between the window panes and dirtied the curtains. The doors on the tile stove had already lost their sheen, and the cutlery was tarnished from the lutefisk. Then the sewing machine would thunder and the loom would bang all the way until Lent, when she would bring in birch branches to force the leaves, and bake Mardi Gras buns to be eaten after a meal of brown beans. As soon as the first spring sun peeped forth, the windows had to be washed.

She had arranged for the washerwoman to come at the end of March, and when she arrived they did all the winter laundry, saving a bit of lye for the coloured things as well. The scrubbing boards clanged, and afterwards she was left alone with a mountain of clothes to iron. It took two to run the mangle. They would carry the baskets of clean wash to the mangling shed and back, and she spread the sheets on the wooden settee in the sitting room to finish drying. She sat down to pleat the pillowcase edging with a table knife, quite exhausted. But who cared? The linen cupboard was more sacred than virtue itself, and if she was ever concerned about the meaning of life, all she had to do to feel restored was to open those brown oak doors and gaze at the fragrant piles of clean linens and the fluttering pillowcase edging on the shelves.

She baked for Easter. In addition to coffee buns and cakes, there were jam wafers, sand biscuits, almond forms, vanilla crescents, meringues, dreams and brandy rings. Thank heavens the war was over and there were cream and butter again.

Then it was time for spring cleaning. She'd bring everything up from the basement and down from the attic, out of the closets and back in again, clean all the cupboards and shine all the prisms on the crystal chandelier, and give all the furniture cushions a good airing out. She rolled up the winter rugs, changed the curtains, polished the copper, removed the window insulation and cleaned the kitchen paint with a rag, swept the wooden walls, scouted out the cobwebs in the corners of the ceilings with a mop and a flannel, and polished the floors. There was the scent of Lux soap flakes and the sizzle of scouring powder, the lather from soft soap in the bucket and the bubbling of caustic soda in the drains.

The larks had returned long ago, the starlings had begun to quarrel about the nesting boxes on the outbuilding wall, and the wagtails were promenading between the puddles in the gravel yard where the spring sun was reflected, but she saw none of it. Star-of-Bethlehem protruded through the grass, breaking off when she lay out the big cowhide rug from the sitting room. But when the spring cleaning was done she went out and picked bouquets of blue anemones, cowslips and, later, lilies of the valley.

Yes, summer is a lovely time. For midsummer she washed the windows again and buffed all the white shoes, made meatballs and marinated herring. They made a trip to their relations in Oxelösund, and while the others swam in the sea she would sit on the cliff top in the sun crocheting lacy shelf edging for her cupboards.

When the first berries ripened she made jellyrolls and compotes. When the berry picking began in earnest she started to make jams and syrups so she'd have time to pickle the cucumbers and ginger the pears later on. The kitchen was steamy and sweaty, her hands were red and blue and her face shiny with steam. With every year that passed she found it more and more difficult to use up all the old preserves, from last year and the year before. There was too much to eat. Her arch enemy, green mould, spread silently in her dark food cellar, attacking the corks on her syrup bottles. Still, the new berries had to be picked – you couldn't just leave them to rot on the bushes or be gobbled up by the fieldfare thrushes. But why did there have to be so many gardens in the family? Her relations would arrive with laundry baskets full of apples she would slice and put in lemon water, and slice and core and slice. She made lots of applesauce – enough, she guessed, to cover the marketplace if she spread it out, but she didn't. She made compote from the best apples. That was for after Sunday dinners. But God save her if any relation of hers found a hard little sliver of seedpod from a core in their compote! Well, of course that depended on who got it. If it was Uncle Manne he might not notice.

'I do believe you've got a bit of core in your mouth,' said Aunt Hedvig. 'Don't let it go down your throat.'

'I don't mind,' said Uncle Manne, swallowing with the same diabolic grin he wore when swallowing a raspberry worm. 'Good for the digestion.'

After which he would hold forth on the intestines, punctuated with apologies from Ingeborg about not being able to imagine how it could have happened, until Aunt Hedvig said:

'Well, it really doesn't matter Ingeborg, dear. As long as it doesn't go down the wrong pipe. It's all right, honestly. We're just a bit fussy about what we eat, that's all.'

They finished, and when they'd said goodbye and thank you Ingeborg had a headache and had to take a powder, pull the shade and lie down. She spent a lot of time this way and once a month she'd spend a day in bed with the top of a pot warmed up and covering her stomach, her brow sticky. She'd ask engineer Ek to be quiet going in and out, but he often forgot, so she took to closing the bedroom door.

Then it was time for the lingonberries. She usually picked fifty litres. The new jam was light and luminous. Last year's was dark as clotted blood, and they'd eat like mad to empty the brown stoneware jars. Late in the season they had it for afters every single day: a bowlful with chunks of crispbread crumbled in and milk on top. But she still ended up having to buy some new jars.

After the lingonberries came the elk hunting season, when Uncle Elon from Strängsjö would arrive with elk meat in a hand basin and a stoneware crock. She cut it into pieces, scraped away the ligaments and dug out every chip of bone. Then she minced some of it to fry into meatballs, marinated some in milk for sauerbraten, first browned and then simmered. Then she would invite the family to dinner. Before which she had to wash the

174

windows again now that the frost had finally put an end to the flies.

Meanwhile, the laundry accumulated in sacks, smelly and yellowing. At last the washerwoman would arrive and soak it. Six months worth of underwear and slips and sheets, all of which would have to be mangled and ironed in good time before the fall cleaning began.

At autumn cleaning time, windows slammed and rug beaters pounded. Rug ends clapped in the frosty air, the caustic soda sizzled, the root brushes growled, and the beater flew over the sofa cushions. The winter rugs were rolled out once more and the windows insulated with miniature gardens of white moss, dried flowers and cotton, and taped shut for the winter. She shook the mothballs out of engineer Ek's winter overcoat and cossack hat, and things grew dark and calm and quiet after the noise and bustle of summer. The first snow arrived, falling light and airy on the branches of the trees and the gravel paths, towering up in small, delicately balanced crystal prisms. Oh, if only it had fallen a little earlier, if it had decided to be an early winter anyway, so they could have brushed the rugs with it.

But usually the first snow was nothing but a sight for sore eyes that lasted a day or two. The heavy fogs and hopeless rains of late autumn weren't over. Sometimes their shoes dragged in mud and gravel for a good part of December as well. Now she'd start to get the silver and copper out, covering the kitchen table with newspaper. The dance of the chamois polishing rags began, the pink polishing powder was mixed to a paste with water, and the paste turned black when you had been polishing for a while. After the polish you buffed with newsprint and the paste turned back into powder that was transformed to a film of dust in the air. She shined the pot tops that stood on the hearth mantle, the muffin tins and aspic forms, the pudding pans and the coffee pot, the little saucepan and the iron candleholders from Skultuna, as well as the brass mortar and pestle. All this had to be completed in good time before the Christmas cleaning, so she would have time to soak the lutefisk, bake the Christmas cookies and crullers, and stuff the sausage.

After this she would wipe and put new edging on the shelves, put up other curtains, lay new runners on the tables, and then it was time to marinate the herring and make the headcheese, soak the ham and bake the coffee cakes. After which she generally didn't remember a thing until she came to again when the ham had begun to look a bit the worse for wear, and all that was left in the jar from the marinated herring was bits of carrot and onion, by which point it was January.

January arrived with sun on white snow and the light shining mercilessly in through the windows showing that it was the time of year when there was candle wax on the runners, pine needles on the carpet, cigar ash on the sofa and rings on the tabletop from glasses.

They sat on the stairs leading up to the attic, because hardly anyone ever came up there. The light from the courtyard filtered in through a net curtain someone had nailed across the little window, and that had never been washed. They would sit there, talking as softly as they could and nudging one another, but only in a gentle, friendly way, waiting and listening to the sounds from the house down below. When, at last, they heard Konrad's whistle and his footsteps on the stairs, Ingrid would go down to the bottom step of the attic flight and stick out her head.

'Hello up there,' he'd call, listening upwards, but it was so quiet he couldn't be sure they were there. That was as it should be. He took the stairs slowly, two at a time, the grey wood creaking and screeching, to find the little group sitting by the attic door with their hands in their laps and their eyes gleaming.

'What're you doing here?' he'd ask, sounding surprised. 'Whatever does this mean? Are you waiting for somebody?'

They were perfectly silent, Maj-Lis suppressing giggles.

'Well, I won't disturb you, then,' he said with a special look, which was also part of the ritual, as he headed downstairs. Ingrid flew up and threw her arms around his neck and wrestled him down until, conquered, he would settle in on the stairs, sighing as if a terrible chore awaited him, like beating the rugs or tackling the greasy dinner dishes. The group that had been jumping around him, pulling at his jacket sat down in silence, their hands clasped around their knees. They sat down and he told stories.

This was what Ingrid remembered. That he told stories in spite of being grown up and how proud she was to have a brother who was both grown up and also told stories about trolls, about the squirrel in the box, about the one-eyed old man in the cellar with teeth as long and as yellow as macaroni, and about the wily young man who tricked the king and made him fall into the well.

They were the neighbourhood children. Maj-Lis and Greger, the policeman's twins, Gudrun, Pickpocket, and little Paul and Naemi, but not Birgit. She was a big girl now, who read Rydberg's *Singoalla* and knew the secrets of life (on the wedding night the groom sneaks in to the bride's room while she is asleep and sticks something soft and secret into her). There was the Chimney Sweep too, who had been dead as long as she could remember, but the others were alive. She always wanted to start by remembering how each of them looked, before she remembered Konrad's stories. How Greger's brown paws would be on his knees and how they were warm from the heat of the whole summer and smelled like burnt lichens on a boulder. She wanted to remember the streaks of dirt on Maj-Lis's neck and her very fair hair and eyebrows. Pickpocket's sweater his grandmother had knitted and Naemi's hat, a stiff beret of deep blue plush with a silk tassel so long it tickled her neck. She wore it every time she went to Flen to visit her aunt. Once they were sitting on the steps high up above all the flats and all the noise and the smell that hangs in the air after meals. Naemi was supposed to be going away but didn't, because they hid up by the attic door when her mother called and no one answered, and his story wasn't over.

Now they never sat on the stairs any more, not even when she came home, because almost everybody down in the yard was embarrassed when she came and just said hi and that was all. She went straight upstairs to Konrad. She thought it best to come when mamma was at the laundry because her mother had told her not to be toing and froing. She was living with the Eks now. It would soon be winter. They had a huge abyss ahead of them with no light, and a sky the colour of cabbage broth. Konrad was pleased to see her, didn't mention toing and froing and refreshed the coffee from the old grounds for the two of them. Then he would tell whatever story he was in the mood for, usually about trolls. But his stories were growing more and more stern and peculiar every time, much more than they'd been on the attic steps. Sometimes Ingrid, who almost never had trouble following, felt quite dizzy from all his words and from not understanding.

'Have you ever seen the trolls?' he asked. 'Trolls that dig around in the forest, grey ghostlike ones? Haven't you ever seen them, little Flia, those uneasy shadows that disappear under boulders and barn floors? They make your heart stop. But it all happens very fast, you never see them for long. Unless, of course, they happen to lose their balance or snag their worn sock on a root. If they turn around their faces are quite vacant, empty eyes, just one big gray blotch.'

'Tell me a real story,' she begged. 'Not stuff like that.'

'Once upon a time there was an old troll woman,' he began. 'It was a harsh winter in the forest and she needed food for her child. She dug in the ice and clawed at tree bark, but she never found enough for her child to get full on. The child looked hungry all the time and its teeth were like files from gnawing at everything in sight. It didn't take much to see that the kid would never make a very good troll, skinny and droopy, with terribly pale skin, like rhubarb that's under a bushel basket and striving constantly up towards the light but never finding it.'

He leaned back on the settee, speaking with his eyes shut; she didn't like that. She shook him by the shoulders, wanting him to look at her. He went on to tell her that a mother's love is not always

179

eternal and unchanging throughout the lifetime of a troll. Christian people, whose lives are very different, of course, who have plenty of fat and food and sleep and lethargy and peace and quiet, love their children so much it makes bells ring and your hair curl.

'But oh, no, not the trolls,' said Konrad. 'They suffer from lack of sleep and are always rushing around, coming and going in a way Christians would never have the energy for. And they have hate and heartache where there should be joy and birdsong.

But the trolls do feel shame, strange as it may sound. They are ashamed of their kids when they won't grow and get big, pointed ears, flat fat faces and chubby tails. They roll them in rags and hide them under boulders, which is why you should never turn over a stone in the woods. You might be stuck with a troll child. And no mother troll has ever been known to leave her child to die under a rock without a needle of ice puncturing an unhealing hole in her heart.'

'She wouldn't, she wouldn't,' Ingrid would scream, pounding so hard on his chest that he had to grab her by the wrists.

'No, not this mother troll. She had her father troll and together they made quite a sensible troll couple. It was just that this rough winter had made the mother lose her senses, and she wandered around with a vacant gaze. But the father troll was of sound mind and sometimes he would go to the village and settle in by a grinding stone and sharpen knives. He'd tie his tail back well and pretend to be a traveller, and he'd usually get away with it. So he'd make a little money and be able to bring back some sausage ends or rusks.

One day he was working under an open window where there was a strong scent of the fatty cooking smell he hated just as much as badgers or foxes. He heard two people talking, a man and a woman, loudly lamenting the fact that they had no children. Oh me oh my how sad and empty their lives were! No one to boss around and no one to feed and hug and punish and no one to fuss about or be fussed over by in their old age and no little grandchildren. 'What touching misery', the father troll thought, letting his grinding stone spin round and round on its own. 'I'd really like to help these unfortunate people.'

He went home to the forest and took a look at that child of his who resembled a stalk of rhubarb. She was pale yellow like a human child and her tail had atrophied right down so all he had to do was poke it a little for it to fall off like a dried-up umbilical cord. That made mother troll scream and shout, however, for she hadn't given up hope that it might recover.

Then the father troll went and sold his child to the people in the village who had been so unhappy to be childless. Face scrubbed, hair straightened with a stick, rags removed and abandoned on a fern leaf, the child was quite presentable and looked almost human. The human woman wept and her husband paid the troll a whole sack of money, for which he was so happy he practically skipped out through their cottage door. Back he went to the forest, and when he got to the bridge he just sat there holding his sack and sang:

> Ripple little stream
> This gold's a happy dream

Mother troll wept some as well, but then she had to get out and dig in the moss, branches and stones again scavenging for food for all her other kids.

Away in the village the troll child grew up with her human parents, became a Christian with her ears washed, and had to memorize poetry. Now you might have thought that her being a troll would eventually show, pointy heels and hair like nails and such strong hands that the human couple would be dreadfully ashamed of their ugly child, but far from it. What people have always said came true: love made her hair curl. The straight-as-nails troll hair curled right up, because there is no power in all the world like human love when it comes to shaping. It could turn a crowbar into an embroidery needle and make butterflies fly in straight lines instead of weaving across the meadows and the rivers. She grew round as a sunflower and pink as a pansy and soft as rising dough. She was a source of nothing but pleasure, and no sorrow at all to her human parents. They said it really makes no difference where a child comes from because love is all that matters.

And father troll would say to his children: 'Well, well, now our ugly kid's sitting in a human palace eating cream cakes for breakfast instead of gnawing a fern root,' And then he'd tell them how you baked cream cakes. He got one or two things upside down and backwards, but most of what he said was correct.

'You take lots of cream and sifted flour,' he said. 'and the cream's what's all the way up at the top of the udder, you know, so you have to empty the whole darn cow to get at it, and that takes some time.'

'But what about the milk?' his children asked. 'Do they just let it run down over their feet? Do they? Do they?'

'Oh, no,' said their father. 'They don't waste the milk. They feed it to the pigs.'

'How can human beings be so incredibly good to their pigs when they are so awfully horrid to trolls?' the children asked.

'They keep pigs to get lard and they need lard to grease their baking sheets when they make cream cakes,' said the old man. 'So they need them, that's all.'

'But what about the pork?' his children wailed.

'They don't waste that, either. They boil it up for the dogs, 'cause dogs are man's best friend and they bite trolls. You get sifted flour from shaking a sifter over a church steeple seven times on a Thursday night. You shake so hard there's nothing left but a little fine powder...'

'What about the coarse meal?'

The coarse meal is so pretty on Sundays in advent that people get tears in their eyes and spray sparkles in the coarse flour and light candles.

'How about the chaff?'

They spread the chaff under the cows and the cows give them cream and the pigs get the milk and the dogs get the pigs and the trolls get ...'

'Bit!' shouted the kids. They knew what they were supposed to do when they listened to stories, since somehow or other father troll had time for storytelling now and then in the summer when there were plenty of sorel greens growing in the woods, and long, lazy forest slugs they could just pick right off the leaves. But after some time the kids would get noisy and wild from listening. Their cheeks would be red and their eyes bright and they'd roar like monsters. He'd have to box their ears, give them a dressing-down and rough them up to settle them. After which he could lie down in the moss and have a nap.

Some people happened to be in the forest just then, and one sat right down on the belly of the troll, fanning himself with the fern and saying 'My, it's hot in the woods and heavens what a lot of mosquitoes there are here and how badly my shoes are rubbing'. So the father troll had to lie ever so still and not breathe so he wouldn't be discovered. But, truth be told, human beings' eyes are no better than their noses and it's something of an accomplishment to be noticed by them.

If a couple of trolls are standing in the moss breaking branches off a tree, people will often walk right past them. They will step right on their heads in the mire, they're so busy trying to cross without getting their shoes muddy. They'll skate on the lake for miles in March when the winds have blown all the snow off the ice, seldom looking down at the ice, where they might see the trolls' faces, and why should they?

In these ways, the troll child who got sold off was like the humans. She'd walk in the woods herself without hearing anyone shout as she passed or anyone whistle or swish or sing laments high up in the tops of the pine trees where the strong winds blow. All she'd hear was chopping axes and barking dogs, rifle shots and dead branches snapping. She was chubby and lively as a redpoll with its crimson crown and rosy breast. She hated the spiders and flies and larvae and mice she had dug so energetically to find as a child, and when she drank from the spring she noticed nothing.

The song thrush sat by her ear and trilled so sweetly and so wisely: 'Little sister, what do we know about the world, anyway? Let's join forces and solve all the riddles of life, one at a time. Or let's just play together, living on a seed and a lick of honey until the last cranberry in the very last marsh has frozen under the snow and we are silenced by the cold and the ashes from the great fire.' She didn't answer things like that, goodness only knew if she even heard it. She was in the woods to gather nuts, and that's what she did there, too.

Whenever she was there a whole gang of troll children trailed her, admiring and gazing at her without being seen by her. The blueberry bushes swished, the branches of the fir trees crackled, and there was a sound like fine scissors in the meadow grass. She had lots of brothers and sisters she knew nothing about, for mother troll had had more children. That's what mother troll was like and there was nothing to be done about it, she birthed babies between the stones and the branches wherever she happened to be. They had dirty faces and knobbly legs, of course, and couldn't understand how their sister could be so fair and so chubby. But their mother told them that it was all about love, as she poked out the very last seeds from a pine cone and gave them to them to eat. She was in a nice mood because it had been the kind of mild winter when the mother deer easily found food and their kids developed little tummies soon after they were born.

On midsummer's night the trolls went almost all the way up to the towns, as usual on this one night of the year. They'd look at the people who were dressed in white, with birch leaf decorations and aquavit to drink. They watched them beat one another up and slash one another with knives and be dead drunk and cheated on and scream in desperation and horror. The fiddlers' music enfolded the landscape in a veil and the wild chervil was in bloom and it was so lovely.

Their little sister sat at the edge of the forest on a blanket with another human being who was larger than she. For once she seemed to be listening to the forest sounds.

'What's that clicking sound?' she asked.

'It's nothing,' the human being replied.

'And what's that swishing noise?'

'Nothing but the wind.'

The girl leaned forward to hear better, holding the human being by the hand, possibly from fear.

'But what's crackling in there?'

'There's nothing crackling but the sound of crackling. That's all.'

And their little sister was satisfied with the human being's explanations and went home to bed. And nothing crackled in the woods, the blowing of the wind whistled softly and the swishing went on swishing.'

Now his voice was terribly soft and, yes, Konrad looked as if he was asleep again and Ingrid had to pound on his chest to make him open his eyes.

'What happened next?' she asked.

'That was the end.'

'That wasn't an end.'

'Yes it was.'

Then she begged him tell her another story. But he refused.

One day she came home. Though it wasn't home, said mamma. The snow had melted, there were pits in the cold sand that were perfect for shooting marbles, and hopscotch squares scratched into the gravel in front of the privy. Maj-Lis said hi, but just softly, and exchanged a look with Naemi. Greger didn't say anything. Konrad's bicycle wasn't in front of the door, but there were wet tracks on the cement leading down to the cellar. She couldn't understand why he would have taken his bicycle down there. The spring sky was blue, although there had been a little rain that afternoon. Beside which he seldom bothered to put his bike away.She went upstairs. Her mamma opened the door asking what she wanted but blocking the door the entire time.

'Where's Konrad?'

'Out. He rode into the city.'

There was a long silence, her mother blocked the door, her eyes perfectly vacant. At first Ingrid couldn't think at all, her mind was blank and almost at peace. Then everything came back to her and she asked:

'You mean he *walked* downtown, don't you?'

'No, he rode his bike. Now you go back to the Eks, they'll be upset with you otherwise. Remember how much they've given you. Promise me you won't be toing and froing any more. Do you promise?'

She went downstairs, taking one step at a time. Her mind was blank and her stomach ached and throbbed.

The bike tracks were still there. It takes a long time for bike tracks to dry, she thought, when the sun isn't on them. They had a snakeskin pattern, she knew very well that it was Konrad's. Only Konrad's bike made tracks like that.

They called her Angel, and apparently she was in heaven. God was a railway engineer who came home from long, tiring trips to other worlds. They'd serve him baked beans with bacon and light his lamps. While they ate, Ingeborg would tell him what they'd been doing, that they'd been to the market for herring, for instance. He would nod and eat and then take out his knife and sharpen the end of a match to clean his teeth with. Now and then he'd tell them that upon arrival at Hallsberg the lubricating horn of the right cylinder had gone cold. They didn't know how they were supposed to react. Should they ask why, or was it obvious? Should they say how awful, get all upset, or be surprised? Eventually he'd dispel their confusion by explaining that the holes in the oil filter had been clogged.

'My, my,' said Ingeborg.

Or he would say:

'A pipe in the smokestack on locomotive six-forty-eight sprang a leak. But we got it plugged up in Södertälje.'

'Lucky!' she replied.

But it had set them back forty minutes. Forty minutes! Did she have any idea what that meant? Ingeborg stared at the wall, letting her embroidery fall to her lap. No, she probably didn't really. Freight and passengers, long sets of train cars, important travellers, possibly royalty. The heavens and the earth trembled and all she could do was go to the market square for herring.

'Terrible repercussions,' engineer Ek mumbled, his gaze already fixed on the newspaper. 'Terrible repercussions.'

Sometimes he'd read them an obituary from the local paper, or a weather forecast. Skirts were climbing up the calves he'd say the paper said, and of course they'd noticed that. Once he read them a poem. It was in the paper and was written by somebody calling himself Black Mask. It was about a wife who had nothing to do because she had no children. Oh, Kalson, she cried, how dull and grey my life is. And she begged him to give her a little pet, at least a cat. Karlsson came home with a box and told her there was a monkey in it but it was so awfully wild that it would have to stay in the box until the next day. There was a hole for it to get air through, but she had to promise him not to peek. And she promised, but of course she couldn't resist. The minute he left for work she was down on the floor looking into the hole. When Karlsson got home he probably expected the baked beans to be on the table as usual.

> But, ah, his wife had swooned away
> And passed out on the floor
> She'd seen her own reflection there
> Need I say any more?

That gave engineer Ek a good laugh, a really good one. Ingrid made him explain the part about the mirror in the hole and the empty box time and again until she finally got tired of hearing it. That was the only time she ever heard him read a poem.

He read them that the workers' demonstrations had failed and said that the dissatisfied and unsuccessful were the ones who became the most furious socialists. A party of grumblers, he called them. None of their friends was particularly active in politics, nor were they religious. They were healthy, ordinary people, said Ingeborg, and she had reason to repeat it frequently. She would also say that healthy, ordinary people didn't have enemas except when they really needed them.

After he'd eaten came the good part. He'd set Ingrid on his lap and bounce her up and down until her teeth were rattling, or pat her behind in a way that sounded like cards being dealt on a card table. After that he'd lie on the sofa, and after a while the newspaper would be over his face, with the clock ticking, the rain running down the window pane, and Ingeborg's crocheting needle gleaming in the lamplight.

Most of the time, of course, he was on duty and they were alone.

'Eat up now,' Ingeborg would say. 'I made it specially for you.'

Ingrid would make a little pile of her mashed potatoes on the side of her plate and criss-cross it with her fork.

'Stop playing with your food,' said Ingeborg. 'Be a good girl and eat up now. You've told me yourself that you're here to get fattened up.'

She didn't say that any more, though. Hadn't for a long time. Now Ingrid cut the herring up into tiny pieces and shifted them around her plate with the tines of her fork. They went around and around, just like the boys who ice-skated in the hockey rink.

'Be a good girl now. Here, let me.'

The fork came at her, her mouth shut tight, and the tines hurt the thin skin on her lips. She turned her head. Afterwards she drank water, but never when Ingeborg was looking.

'Everyone needs to eat, you know. Just look at you.'

She looked down at her hand, thinking it looked like it always had. But Ingeborg was worried about her now, staring at her all the time, and whispering to Ek. Then one evening the strange thing happened. He took the plate and fork himself and sat down next to her.

'And now you're going to eat, young lady,' he said.

The fork came at her, she turned her head. He stank of lubricating oil and the nausea rolled up and lodged in her throat, threatening. He grasped the back of her neck. The fork poked at her lips and squeaked at her teeth, and he forced her jaws open.

'You eat now,' he said.

And the first bite went in.

'Right,' he said. 'That's fine.'

The second bite, and the third and the fourth. He was counting. When her plate was empty she sat looking at his back. He was removing his shirt. Ingeborg had heated water for him to wash in. His body was white as the finest lard but with a fine layer of black hairs, and he was getting goose bumps all over.

Suddenly she could see Konrad before her with his tan back and his vertebrae vanishing down below his wide black belt into the folds of his trousers. The next time Ek turned towards her she opened her mouth and let her dinner flood back down over her chin back onto her plate. Some ended up on the table. She had to open and shut her jaws a few times to get it all out from inside her cheeks.

At first he just stared. Then his hand flew across her cheek. Ingeborg was crying loudly.

'You just wait 'til tomorrow. That's all I can say.'

And he didn't say another word to her that evening. The next day he fed her again, this time seeing to it that she swallowed every bite. It lay like lead in her stomach. She sat feeling its weight, getting sleepy, unable to raise her head. She felt her mouth fill with saliva, and ten minutes later she'd vomited it all up into the sink. They both stared.

'Well, I never!' said Ek. Then he lay down with the newspaper and didn't speak to either of them.

The next day her head was buzzing, she felt weak but excited and she knew she'd won: he had never! Clogged oil filters and leaking pipes – but nothing like this! She realized now that she was really ill, and that having a sick child is worse than when the train from Gothenburg derails. That made her feel weak-kneed.

She had to stay in bed, and Ingeborg kept bursting into tears. The chair beside her bed filled up with glasses and cups, but she couldn't get anything down. There was chicken broth that congealed and developed a skin on it, cream of vegetable soup that went pink and stiff, and cocoa with whipped cream that had melted. She lay there thinking about nothing at all and imagining she could see places she'd never been. There were gardens, shiny and damp after the rain, with sun on every leaf. There were bright green trees with little white blossoms, and huge stands of spring flowers on the lawns. She knew this must be a different country and was surprised there were no people in the houses or the gardens. Not a soul in sight.

The doctor was coming. She could hear him in the vestibule and Ingeborg's anxious voice above the scraping sound of galoshes being removed.

'It stinks of death in here,' he said. Afterwards Ingeborg always said she'd swooned when she heard that. But Ingrid never heard her hit the floor. The doctor came in and held her wrist, probed her tummy with cold hands. His clothes reeked of smoke, and she was so sensitive to smells now that her stomach clenched and she gagged. He prescribed medicine called suppositories, and Ingeborg poked them up her behind. That evening she took some diluted berry syrup, and the next morning Ingeborg had beat an egg yolk into another glassful and she was able to keep it down.

Ladies came for coffee. They spoke in low, worried tones and she could hear that her illness was called stomach cramps. But her stomach didn't hurt. Before the ladies came Ingeborg aired out the room and sprayed it with eau de cologne. Ingrid was sleeping in Ek's bed nowadays so Ingeborg could keep an eye on her at night. He'd moved out to the kitchen settee.

Everything was unreal. It was somewhere between dream and reality. How could it be so nice to do nothing, to be nothing, just rocking gently in bed. The wet bike tracks were in some other world, no more real than the gardens and the rooms she visited. Everything that hurt was far away.

In the end Tora Otter came. She was the one who had arranged for Ingrid to live with the Eks. She sat down on the bed with her hat on, and she had closed the door.

'Are you homesick?' she asked.

Ingrid waited for Tora's face to dissolve, for unreality to carry her away. But she didn't move.

'I asked are you homesick?'

'No.'

'Are you sure about that?'

They both sat silently for some time. Tora's face was still there. Her lips were as thin as Ingrid's. Ingrid bit hers lightly and she could feel they weren't numb. It hurt a little when she bit.

'Do you want to go back home?' Tora asked, her light blue eyes unblinking.

'No. Never.'

'Don't you want to go back to Konrad?'

'I don't give a toss about Konrad.'

'What about mamma?'

She didn't answer.

'Say something,' Tora commanded.

'I don't give a toss about her either. I never want to go back there.'

Tora appeared to be thinking. Next to her head was a framed embroidered dog. When Ingrid sat up in bed the room spun, but she could see her own face reflected in the glass over the embroidery. It wasn't quite as real as Tora's, but more real than the dog's.

'All right,' said Tora. 'I'm leaving now. But this is such a shame. I'd planned to ask if you could come along to the market on Saturday, but never mind.'

'What for?'

'Well, I just need some help with the sweet stand. But I guess it's no good.'

'When?'

'Saturday.'

When Tora had left she ate some gruel.

She couldn't go to the square on Saturday. Her legs wouldn't really carry her and she couldn't go out yet. She was dizzy when the cold air hit her. But other than that there was nothing strange about anything. The dull morning light was itself and the trains switched tracks outside. She didn't want to go to Hovlunda Road. But the next Saturday she went to the square.

'Good,' said Tora Otter. 'I've been expecting you. Stand next to me here and I'll show you what to do.' She showed her the brass weights and the iron weights, the cash box with its different compartments and the scoop for the sweets. Children passed, looking at Ingrid. She weighed out sweets and was paid. Some of the children came and bought their sweets from her, but they didn't dare say anything to her except what they wanted to buy.

At the Eks' home in the railway housing she continued her semi-starvation. It took ever so little to turn her stomach. Then the mouthful she had would grow and grow, like cotton, but not go down. When the whole class was to be photographed in the schoolyard she had to stay at home because she was so thin. She knew Ingeborg was ashamed of her.

She got to buy the school picture even though she wasn't in it.

That evening Ingeborg had a look. She dried the dish water from her hands and held it and said it was quite good. Ingrid watched her face attentively. Then she put the photograph on the table and looked at it herself again, examining each and every one of them as they stood close together with the school wall behind them and gravel under their feet. There was no hole where she should have been. It was as if she had never existed. She took her pencil and put the point down between Göta and Hildur. But there was no space. Then she traced Göta's arm, which was also Hildur's sleeve. First she traced down and then a little harder up so the pencil left a deep rut. Then she drew several more lines, but mostly where Göta's elbow was and in the end there was a hole in the paper, a hole with the edges pressed down.

When Ingeborg saw what she had done she wasn't even furious. Her face just went all rigid and she said this was the last straw. She was going to speak with Assar. This made Ingrid realize that things were worse now than when Ingeborg was furious, and from that moment on she tried to displace her face and her voice. She only heard her from a long way away. Nothing that happened that evening had anything to do with her. She didn't get a thrashing. She could see that engineer Ek would have liked to give her a beating but didn't dare. His voice and his hands were also far away. I don't give a toss about them, she thought. She felt like saying that when Ingeborg started crying and asked how in the name of God she could do something like that. Hadn't they always been kind to her? Hadn't she been given everything she needed? I couldn't care less about that, she thought. But she didn't say it because that would just extend the argument for ever and ever and all she wanted was to go to bed. She wanted to be alone in her bed and lie there being nothing, feeling nothing, rocking gently.

Konrad had said that Ingeborg and Assar were going through

life with all their possessions chained to their ankles. They dragged their copper pots and their empire bed and their cuckoo clock around with them and so did their relations and the hairdresser and the ironmonger's assistant and the shoe shop owner with whom they played whist. And when they danced they had all those things chained to their ankles, which meant that they couldn't leap very high and couldn't swing their legs so easily either. When they made love, said Konrad, the grating on the tile stove rattled and the copper pots and the heavy flatiron and the family bible, too. And when they had to run for their lives they actually walked slowly and erectly because that was their only choice.

But she really didn't give a toss about Konrad. She wasn't even supposed to think about him. She'd sworn to herself. She'd stuck a pin into her finger and pressed out three drops of light red blood, one after the other, letting them drip into the hymnal onto the worst verse she knew, where the angel of death is hovering everywhere and crying out. That meant she would die if she thought about Konrad. If her teacher noticed the hymnal Ingrid planned to say she'd had a nosebleed.

She wouldn't die because she'd thought about all those things they had tied by ropes to their ankles. That didn't count as thinking, she'd just seen an image Konrad had made up. Now she could finally go to bed and be nothing. She could hear Ingeborg's sniffling and walking around but she wasn't bothered. Not at all.

Ingeborg Ek was desperate. Hadn't they been kind to the girl? Of course! But how did she thank them? She was thin and nervous, tight-lipped and irritable, ruined her things, fought with the boys and when she wasn't picking fights she was lying listlessly on her bed refusing to eat. She didn't seem to be homesick, either. Because nowadays they sometimes asked her.

'Aren't you homesick?'

'Nope.'

'For your mamma?'

She just shook her head.

What was more she was left-handed. You weren't allowed to write with your left hand at school so in the beginning she almost never wrote. When she tried, some force in her right hand drove the nib of the fountain pen deep into the paper, pushing and pulling. Suddenly the point would split, the two metal legs bending in either direction, after which the pen looked dumb and was of no use. Her teacher got angry, of course, but that didn't help. The same things happened the next time as well, the strength of her arm just bent it. And her upper arm was sort of buzzing. She tried to explain to her teacher.

'I get a cramp in my arm. It just buzzes up there.'

So she was allowed to try using her left.

It was equally difficult to teach her to crochet. Since she had to use her left hand Ingeborg couldn't just crochet one step ahead to show her how. Everything had to be turned around backwards. Finally she remembered that Tora Otter was left-handed, too, and she took her there.

Tora looked at the child sitting down in the corner by the counter of the café with a tight little skein of wick yarn filthy from hand sweat, with the crocheting needle in her left hand.

'You're strong,' she said.

She made her go and wash her hands. Then Tora cut off the yarn, threw the dirty yarn away, and they started all over again.

Every Tuesday a little man with hair in his ears and a worn briefcase under his arm stepped off the Norrköping train and went straight to the Lindhs'. Everyone knew he was Lilibeth Iversen-Lindh's voice teacher. If there was a window open you could hear him going 'mem, mem, mem' with a deep resonant voice which, when the wind was blowing the right direction, could be heard all the way down at the post office. She would sing, but not ordinary songs. You couldn't even tell what they were about, though they always sounded melancholy.

When the children of the staff and former staff of the Lindhs' were at the annual downstairs Christmas party in 1920, it happened to be a Tuesday. 'Mem, mem, mem' and 'mum, mum, mum' could be heard from upstairs. They were sitting around the kitchen table and had emptied their soft drinks and finished their sticky buns when the housemaid came down and said they were to come upstairs to hear Fru Iversen-Lindh sing.

She was sitting on a little chair close to the grand piano and each of them had to go up and shake hands with her. Ingrid felt what a thin hand she had. The music teacher was sitting at the piano, but he didn't take anyone by the hand, he just glared. They were told to take their seats on a long, curving sofa covered in light green velvet.

She sang two songs. Ingrid needed to have a pee all the time, she'd had so much to drink. The housemaid had left and they were all alone with the singer whose perfume filled the room and the teacher who sat in the matte ray of sun from the window so you could see the sheen on the sleeves of his suit coat. Ingrid looked out the window and could see people coming and going at the door and dogs peeing in the piles of snow. Evert, the constable's son, sat next to her scratching his legs, and you could hear every breath he took because he had adenoid problems.

Now Ingrid had to pee so badly she couldn't sit still on the sofa, but had to sway from side to side. The moment Fru Iversen-Lindh had finished she would say she had to go to the WC and ask where it was. It would be fun to have a look at their WC.

But the second song started so fast that there wasn't time after the first one to ask . Now Fru Iversen-Lindh sounded like she had a knife stuck in her and was suffering like a wounded beast, and it would have been impossible to interrupt her. But she couldn't hold it any longer. Ingrid slid off the sofa thinking she could find the WC without asking. Fru Iversen-Lindh had a tormented look. Evert, the constable's son was staring at her, breathing heavily through his open mouth.

And now the unfortunate thing happened: Ingrid took the wrong door and instead of coming out into the hall with the elk horns and umbrella stand, she walked right into the smaller dining room with lobsters and artichokes and crumbly French bread on the walls, English chairs with caned seats and a sideboard with a silver Russian samovar. She hurried through, as the dining room frightened her. She didn't really know what she was looking at or what it was for. Fast, fast she walked through the double doors, looking for the door to the WC. There was driven silver on the buffets, and her reflection made her look like a big lump with a little head and short legs and a tummy stretching out sideways. There was an odour of polish and wax in the rooms she hadn't noticed before. It was like walking into another country, the only thing she recognised from the city and the rooms she usually lived in was the dull light. It filtered in through the cracks in the stiff velvet curtains.

There were everlastings under glass domes and she couldn't understand how flowers could live under there, until she walked right up to them and could see they were artificial. She walked through the yellow sitting room where the furniture had curved legs and the green sitting room where the furniture legs were straight. At a great distance she could hear Fru Iversen-Lindh's educated babble, otherwise there was only silence, silence that seemed to resound from this furniture and these satin-papered walls. She was almost happy to hear the ticking of a clock with a glass cover. But the sound was more fragile than spiders' legs, her ear felt crude and her blood coursed thunderingly when she tried to listen to whether the little thing was working. She was about to wet her panties. She could already feel that a few drops had dampened them. A little later she felt better and she loped amongst the paintings that were smooth and shiny with brown oil paint and gleamed in the light from the windows. When she stepped a little to one side she saw a greenish head with unblinking eyes on a platter.

The singing voice and the piano chords grew more and more distant. No WC in sight, not so much as a little door in the wall. There were just big double doors leading to room after room. She was in the deceased merchant's study now. The air there was dry as dust and the furniture dark brown. On the desk was a bronze figure. She had to see what it was and she squeezed her legs together and waddled over. An eagle. He was sitting with his head raised high and the crown of his head was all shiny with wear. His eyes had a vacant look and he stared right past you. There was a hare in front of him. He was actually holding the hare down with one of his huge clawed feet. Its stomach had been torn open and was pouring out. She stared, somehow wishing she could keep herself from looking, and swallowed to get the saliva out of her mouth and settle her stomach.

This must be hell – an old lady screeching at the top of her lungs, decapitated heads and tortured animals as decorations. Konrad should see this. Then she remembered that it was the death penalty for thinking about Konrad and the nausea passed. She stumbled on, across high doorsills. Now she was sure she would be coming out into the hall but it was another sitting room, gentle grey-blue from the silky soft rugs on the floor. She mustn't. But every time she moved now it dripped. In one corner of the room there was a blue and white jug between the legs of a gilded table with a mirror. If she could just get over to the jug she could pee in it. But she knew she wasn't going to make it, it was too far.

Then she had the idea that if she just sat down she'd feel better and that would give her a respite so she'd be able to think of a way out. One step backward and she was on a sofa covered in grey-blue velveteen. Oh, that felt wonderful. And then she wet herself.

At the first surprised instant she just thought it was lovely. Her thighs were wet, the soft velveteen seats loose and warm, and she leaned back and let it run.

But soon it felt cold. When she stood up and turned around there was a big dark-blue stain on the sofa. Good Lord on your throne in heaven have pity on me, thought Ingrid Eriksson. Now I've done it. Now there'll be hell to pay. I'm really in for it.

And she was, but not right away. First she covered it with a throw pillow embroidered with little roses all over, tiny cross stitches called petit point, and then she ran back the same way she had come: past the eagle with the hare, the decapitated green head, the clock you could barely hear tick, the dining room with the odd smell, and then she was back in the music room where the audience was stiff from sitting still for so long and everybody was shifting and scratching their legs, where Fru Iversen-Lindh was singing 'Come sweet love' and the pianist was banging along. She took a seat near the door. The vocalist couldn't see her and when they were allowed to leave she edged out with a wet spot on her behind.

All afternoon she ran along fanning her dress. It dried, as did her stockings. But that evening she had to stuff her knickers down in the back corner of the woodbin. They were so thick they wouldn't dry.

After that the disaster ran its course with predictable regularity, as disasters do. Ingeborg Ek bumped into the Lindhs' housekeeper, who commented that the children Fru Iversen-Lindh invited round for a Christmas party every year were like animals, at least some of them, and that if it were up to her they had now had their last Christmas party. Some child had sneaked out into another room and urinated on a sofa when no one was watching. Ingeborg oohed and ahhed but with an innocent look on her face. The new firewood hadn't yet been delivered, and she hadn't yet cleaned out the wood box. That was the next day, and she found a pair of damp, odd-smelling knickers. Questions and answers. Until engineer Ek took down his razor strap from its hook next to the tray-holder in the kitchen and said don't lie. She confessed.

Ingeborg considered suicide or paying a visit to Fru Iversen-Lindh to tell the truth. There were tears, calamities (Ek's turnip and potato mash wasn't on the table when he came from work), attacks of nerves, and conversations behind closed doors, swollen eyes. All the time Ingrid tried to be nothing and to rock gently but she didn't succeed too well. She had trouble sleeping at night.

Ever since Ingeborg Ek's wedding day she had been waiting for the fortuitous event that would justify her spending her days wasting the housekeeping money and making life four times as expensive for engineer Ek as it had been when he was living with his old mother. But she menstruated monthly and felt as if she were letting him down. And the years passed.

It was more than odd that she never became pregnant. No one but Assar Ek had ever been inside her, and he was as healthy as a winter carrot. Never had she sat out on the damp ground and developed a chill and sticky discharges. Her body was broad and she had a big abdomen below her breasts. It looked as if there should be plenty of little children in there, arranged like ginger pears in a jar. But there just weren't.

She went to the doctor. He recommended she didn't try too hard, which just made things worse. Aunt Hedvig said:

'You're lucky you two. No one to think about but yourselves. No worries and you can go out whenever you please.'

That sent her home crying. She felt she was constantly bringing bouquets of asters and a fruitcake to pale mothers who lay there looking exalted, with a prune-like bundle in their arms. Or narcissi and a fruitcake, peonies and a fruitcake, because it happened in all seasons. Assar really extended himself, too. She celebrated her thirty-fifth birthday and the bundles had grown and started school. They looked so much like Viktor and Evert and had Aaron's nose and Harald's eyes. But there was no one in the whole world who had Assar's feet but himself.

He stopped extending himself and started feeling his age. Ingeborg turned forty and they started thinking about taking in foster children because they can get to be just like children of your own – because it's all about how you bring them up, you know. But one had ringworm and another had pitted tooth enamel and the third looked awfully much like the bicycle shop owner who drank (which was fair enough since he was the father). Then one day Tora Otter stopped by with Ingrid Eriksson, who had curly blonde hair. Tora had washed it in soft soap to be on the safe side before taking her around there the first time. So they ended up with Ingrid even though she was fairly old. Assar was no longer interested in screaming babies and she was more of an age with the cousins.

Ingeborg Ek didn't stop trying, though. On the contrary, the doctor had said everything might work out if they took a foster child. It got a lot of people on the right track and they often ended up having several children of their own later. Assar Ek was nearly fifty and no longer enjoyed the physical exertion. But Ingeborg was persistent and wasn't ashamed of it. She didn't pretend to be overwhelmed with passion, either, but quite simply said:

'Let's give it another whirl, Assar. All right?'

Assar turned away and pretended to be asleep but that didn't always help. And so he had to try again. This was no secret to Ingrid as the walls were thin in the railway housing and she was a light sleeper. She slept like a puppy with one ear perked, and she could always hear Assar and Ingeborg trying again. Once she even heard engineer Ek say:

'What the hell are you up to?'

But his voice sounded sleepy. Ingrid also wondered what Ingeborg was up to because it was silent as the grave and not until five or ten minutes later did she hear a long sliding sound and a tired sigh. Engineer Ek had been asleep for ages by then. Ingrid could hear him snoring.

All Ingeborg was doing was trying a method the shoe shop owner's wife had whispered in her ear. Afterwards you were supposed to put your legs straight up and your feet against the wall until you were sure it had taken. Her feet were deathly pale and her face was bright red but she endured, and Ek hardly noticed a thing, he was so sleepy afterwards. And it worked!

Oh, Lord! She was forty-four years old. At first she just thought it wasn't coming anymore. If she wasn't getting her monthly, she could no longer hope. She was all washed up as a woman and the hot flushes and sweaty nights would start, and as sure as the day she was born she would soon be having weeping spells. She was already doing quite a lot of crying and having to change her night-dress in the middle of the night. Then the morning sickness began. She still didn't suspect. Perhaps she believed that such a miracle in your body would make itself known kind of like when the current converter on the electric locomotive makes contact with the electricity line and there is a streak of blue lightning. Instead her body closed in around its doings and secrets and went on working methodically without her having the slightest idea of what was going on inside. Her breasts swelled and ached, she was tired in the evenings and had dark lines on her face. At some point one of her maternal aunts said:

'Ingeborg, dear, I do believe you had better go and see the doctor. You appear to be expecting.'

And she was! Miracle of miracles! Jubilation and tears of joy! Happiness beyond all bounds! She was carrying a little Assar inside! Engineer Ek would be immortalized. There would be a meaning to her own life. She would buy everything in blue. The child would have the best education. A pram would have to be purchased first thing. She would refuse the loan of the cousins' rattan pram. They had loved one another so deeply they had created a likeness of themselves inside her. There would be an Assar after Assar and an Assar after him for ever and ever amen. And, no, he wouldn't have to work on the railway if he didn't choose to. And Ingrid...

Well, Ingrid. It was true, of course: it wasn't really the same when they weren't your own. And you can't straighten a branch that's begun to grow crooked. They'd done their best, God only knew. Even asked her if she was homesick, wanting to go back to her mother's again. Yes, they'd told her right out that she could if she wanted to, they wouldn't prevent her.

But she wasn't easy to understand. Before you knew it you'd hear a catcall from behind the privies, and you'd know who it was. At least she was big enough now to help look after little Assar. Which wasn't a bad thing, as it's exhausting to have a baby when you're over forty. But she did spend most of her time at Tora Otter's café.

He'd been gone a whole year. Just don't wear your best clothes every day, she'd written. Nor your best underwear and who's doing your washing now I can't help but wonder there are so many things I wonder about sitting here.

He was working at a big crispbread factory in Stockholm. When he rolled the huge wheeled racks into the ovens it was nice and warm and he couldn't complain. He was living on High Hill Street on the southern holm of the city, and on winter nights he was cold as any animal. He couldn't get used to how cold it was when he left the factory. When he couldn't afford wood he ended up heating bricks on his gas fire to keep him warm at night. He was good looking and thin but he was lonely. When Saturday nights came around there was no girl to count his vertebrae under his shirt, which would have been nice. On weekday evenings he would go to a café at least, reading all the fine print of the agreement regarding the Third International. He felt that the days of deception and collapse were far in the past, and he was happy and optimistic.

Otherwise not much has changed, though lots of people are out of work and plenty have left including David, his mother wrote. The Lord only knew if she had written the letter herself, of course. He thought if she'd done the writing the letter would be as vacant as her face, completely blank. Maybe Tora Otter had written it for her, what do I know, Konrad thought.

Krantz the watchmaker lent us some money, so Dagmar's gone to Norrköping to learn Patterns and Dressmaking out there, gracious she's a good girl though her back's given her so much trouble.

Did she have any wishes? He tried to imagine himself back home at the kitchen table, looking into her eyes. Was it possible to surprise her? Was it even possible to frighten her any more? Well, it's damned easy to make her grateful, anyway, he thought. Next fall she'll be voting for the first time, well no she won't. She won't go to the polls because she doesn't know how to do it and would be so embarrassed if she made a mistake.

Now I work at the laundry and don't have to slave in other people's homes and be lower than the low and we are also very good friends at the laundry although of course we have our troubles who doesn't. And I do have Tora at the café and we've got to know the watchmaker and Ivan Roos as well if you remember him from the ironmonger's. There's nothing to it so don't go imagining. I'm an old woman as you know very well.

No, however hard he tried he couldn't recall her face. He could see her body, even the pattern in her dress fabric, but her face was nothing but a blank to him. Can she remember our faces any more, he wondered. Has she ever been able to see them? Our faces were mouths to feed of course, one kid after the next, mouths to feed inside her own body. But were they anything more?

Valfrid Johansson has built a house by the square, Wärnström's dead she wrote.

Incredible that he got away before he had become a piece of the furniture in her kitchen. Amazing that they were still walking their grey streets down there, that there was noise from the construction sites and the engine yard. That Ingrid was playing hopscotch somewhere, falling and scraping her knees. Sat sucking on them in the evenings.

I think about Ingrid every day.

Oh you do, do you? You think about Ingrid every day. Suddenly his hands took over and crumpled the paper and then smoothed it out again and started tearing it into pieces. When it was all ripped up and he could breathe again he took a little lukewarm coffee and drank it. Then he put the letter on the oilcloth and started puzzling the pieces back together, which took some time.

If I only dared I'd ask to have her back home again but she bears a grudge against us and in my foolishness I've turned her against you as well, I might as well tell you that. It's difficult to be a mother who has always had good intentions but not always done the right thing.

Oh, mum, you idiot! Frida! If he could only have written to her, or spoken with her. But our lips go stiff in one another's presence and our faces blank.

We've had a good spring. Dagmar left Norrköping with excellent marks and it's been good drying weather all spring. Tora Otter sends her regards and says you can phone the Café and let us know what your plans are if you don't want to write. All the very best from your mamma Frida.

What are your plans?

Ingeborg's boots were going a mile a minute, the brim of her hat flapping in the air. She was on her way to buy partridge, and she had Ingrid with her. She marched into Färman's cheese shop with neither hesitation nor humility, the doorbell ringing as she entered. Everyone in the shop turned to look at them. But Ingeborg didn't stand by the door waiting her turn. She went on into the next room where the shopkeeper had fowl and game, saying as if the other customers weren't even there:

'I'd like some poultry for Fru Iversen-Lindh!'

Färman was cutting into a huge round of Västerbotten cheese and said to his wife:

'Serve her please, Hilda!'

So Hilda Färman put down her cheese wire, wiped her hands on a burlap towel and trotted behind Ingeborg.

The Lindhs' cook had fallen ill with gallstones two days before a big dinner party with guests from Stockholm. So Little Assar was being looked after by a neighbour and Ingeborg was going to step in at the Lindhs'. Ingrid was with her at Färman's to help carry.

She had never been in the back room. It was cold in there and there was damp, reddish sawdust on the floor. The smell of death mingled with the odour of brown goat cheeses and with the pine boughs and huge sides of smoked salmon exuding shiny fat and with skin like gold displayed on the marble countertops. She saw dark meat with tufts of hair on it and thin, yellowish bits of bone. Färman sold both wild poultry and game. But she couldn't tell which animals they were and didn't dare to ask, as Ingeborg was a different person from the usual Ingeborg in here. She was going to do a dinner for the Iversen-Lindhs.

Now she tested pheasants' beaks with her index finger and wondered if they weren't dull the way old birds got, and Hilma Färman stammered explanations and assured her that they never sold old fowl here. Ingeborg didn't tell them right away that it was partridge she wanted, but let the shopkeeper's wife take down new pheasants from the wall where they were hanging by their tail feathers until rigor mortis set in and they fell down. She poked the abdomens of plucked birds with her index finger and nodded her satisfaction when they yielded to the touch. But their blue-black skin and the claws that had bent in and gone stiff made Ingrid gag. Did people have to eat things like that?

Now Hilda Färman was climbing a ladder to get at the partridges hanging two by two with pine boughs between their feet, assuring Ingeborg that they were young and fatty, you could tell by their big pointed feathers, old birds had rounded ones. When Ingrid walked around the room looking she noticed a hare on one of the marble slab countertops at the back. His coat didn't look like the tufts of hair and bits of fur left around the bones in the dark-coloured meat. It was soft and fluffy and you could see each individual hair if you looked closely and there were white spots standing out from the brown parts, a dense white cottony bottom she would have liked to touch with her finger if she'd dared. He was unlike the other animals with their closed eyes and slack necks. It had been a long time since they'd hopped from branch to branch or hopped across the fields. They'd been dead for days, were grossly altered and destroyed. But this hare was different. His eyelids rested so lightly over his eyes.

She hadn't realized how you changed when you were dead. She sneaked her hand out of her coat pocket and looked at it. It had blood in it, always flowing. If the blood flow stopped her hand would go stiff and you'd notice the dirt on it much more clearly. Then it would change colour and the skin would get cracks. It would never be the same again and if you rubbed it hard, as she was doing now, no red spots would flare up. It wouldn't even spring back if you slapped it.

She walked over to the hare for another look. A person could imagine he wasn't really dead. When she looked closely she thought his eyes were more open than before. There was a little blood around his nostrils. She grabbed Ingeborg by the hand.

'Look here,' she said. 'I don't think he's really dead.'

'Of course he is.'

They were inspecting the partridges two by two, poking at their claws and beaks. Ingeborg hardly looked up.

'Look at him, though!'

'Why must you always be like this? Settle down.'

So Ingrid walked over to the hare alone, she walked right up close to him and scrutinized the area around his muzzle. Blood was oozing out of the tiny cracks on the side, light red, slightly foamy. She could see a bubble grow bigger and bigger and then burst. So she pulled Ingeborg along with her to show her, and when she tried to turn away Ingrid pulled her arm hard. Hilda Färman was busy putting the partridges in a basket and didn't look.

Ingrid reached out, index finger and long finger tight together, and placed them and on the hare's chest, right by the foreleg where his fur was thin and white. There was heat coming off his skin. She looked up and Ingeborg tried to pull her away but she was no longer afraid and just stood there with her fingers against his chest. After a great deal of concentration she could feel his heart beating ever so weakly.

'He's not dead,' she whispered to Ingeborg.

'Come along now.'

'But he's not dead. Didn't you hear me?'

'Whatever. But we're done here now. Come along. We'll take our basket of fowl now and be off. We have a busy day ahead of us.'

She said these last words loud and clear so Hilda Färman would hear. But Ingrid held on to her hand, whispering that the hare was still alive.

'We're going home now, Ingrid. That's right. Don't worry about all that.'

'But he's still alive. It must hurt.'

'His senses are so dulled. That's what happens. They don't feel anything after a while. Come on, now,' Ingeborg whispered, pulling her along.

Then Ingrid's stomach started to heave. Hilda Färman looked up just in time to see her contorted face.

'What's the matter?' she asked.

'That hare's heart is still beating,' Ingrid said loudly.

Hilda went over and lifted him up with her red hands.

'Sweet Jesus,' she said. 'Something's not right here for sure. He hasn't been gutted, either.'

'We'll take him home,' said Ingrid, talking fast and feverishly. 'We'll take him home with us and put him in a box like they did with the squirrel so he can get better. Let's take him home!'

'What're you talking about?' Ingeborg asked. 'What squirrel? No, you stop that right now. Ugh! Do something, Fru Färman! I can't stand it. Never been able to stand the sight of blood.'

'What on earth can I do?' Fru Färman asked in resignation. 'Somebody must have shot him without killing him. I could never kill an animal.'

'Nor I,' said Ingeborg. 'You do something about this or I'm leaving right now.'

'I'll get my husband.'

He came in and when Ingrid saw him with his belt tight around his white shirt and his knife at his side she began to scream. Ingeborg ran over and shut the door to the cheese room and then tried to press Ingrid's face into her coat to suppress the noise.

'Do something fast!' she cried to Färman.

'Oh Jesus, he wasn't killed, just paralyzed,' he said. 'This kind of thing never happens. I just got him in, from the gamekeeper on the estate. He brought in so much game today I guess he didn't notice.'

Ingrid was struggling to free herself, and she watched Färman hold the hare up by his back legs and strike his head against the edge of the marble countertop. That broke his skull. Ingrid ran to the far end of the room where she vomited violently against the wall and then curled up with her back to them, wailing. Ingeborg was acutely embarrassed and didn't know where to look. Someone had opened the door to the cheese room and was looking in. Färman wiped his hands on a rag and his Hilma paced back and forth with the basket of partridges over her arm.

'Come along now,' said Ingeborg, trying to get Ingrid to her feet. 'Look at you Ingrid, your coat's full of sawdust.'

She dragged her towards the door, with Hilda Färman and the basket at her heels.

'You'll have to send them,' said Ingeborg, dragging Ingrid through the shop without looking up at the other customers who stood there staring at them, at Ingeborg's deathly pale face and Ingrid's sawdusty overcoat and her shoes, spotted with spew. Out on the street she was crying so loudly she was wailing again and Ingeborg was practically running with her and trying to appease her at the same time.

'Animals don't have feelings.'

'Oh yes they do!'

'But not like ours. He was all limp.'

That just made her scream more and when they finally got to the railway housing there was a face in every window and Ingeborg's cheeks were bright red and her eyes glazed. When they got inside she took Ingrid hard by the arm, shoved her into the bedroom and locked the door.

'Enough is enough,' she said. 'I've had it.'

Then she began to cry. On the other side of the door the little girl was weeping and screaming in wailing tears that had begun to derive their force from anger.

Everyone has some other poor soul to lord it over. A person who lords it over another, even when that other is only a child or a hare, has the power to deny the other's pain. When Little Assar cried Ingeborg was distraught because she loved him. Sometimes, however, his crying didn't worry her. Then she said he was screaming to give his lungs a workout, as all children needed to. At times like that Ingrid would pick him up and look deep into his eyes, and she could see that he was frightened.

She'd seen his first smile. It wobbled across his face, the corners of his mouth rose and he bubbled spit. He was a little cross-eyed. But he was smiling. And after that he did it over and over again. She showed Ingeborg. 'No, such small babies don't smile,' she said. 'It's just stomach gas.'

He didn't really start to smile until a couple of months later. Then even engineer Ek could poke him in the belly and get a reaction.

Ingrid stopped wailing. Her body was exhausted and her eyelids stung. Her whole face itched from the salty tears. She remembered that she was supposed to try to feel nothing, nothing but nothing, that she should just have rocked gently when she saw the hare and all those things happened. But she'd forgotten. It didn't matter.

She wasn't afraid any more. Ingeborg was one of those people who was unable to look into another person's face as if into a mirror. She didn't allow that. Here is a pain you must deny. Otherwise it might become yours.

Konrad was keeping himself awake on the night express from Malmö. He'd been there to speak on the religion question at a meeting the comrades down there had arranged, but he didn't really think he'd managed to do away with God. On the contrary, he had a strong feeling nobody'd heard a word he said. His voice was always soft. Now he was passing the time as the train drove through a landscape of semi-overgrown marshes, thin, low vegetation and reeds that had been under water only a few weeks ago and where most all there was to see was the grey and yellow tufted weeds from last season. He was on the lookout for a croft or a rail maintenance man's cottage he could identify. But the train just went on thundering deeper and deeper into the flat landscape of undergrowth and sparse fir trees where there was nothing to catch his eye. For a few moments at one point he imagined he was somewhere completely different. One swampy tract is very much like the next.

One moment he was uncertain, the next there was no question, for now the train was slowing down and the long line of carriages was passing the first sparse groups of buildings on the outskirts of the city. There were no houses or churches yet, because the approach from this direction was through a flat, low industrial area he knew like the palm of his hand. So he went into the sleeping compartment and lifted out his suitcase, quickly stuffing into it what he had removed, then disembarked. He'd made an impulsive decision to get off and visit the city although he was travelling at expense of the Party.

As he crossed the tracks in the cold morning air he noted that it wasn't even four o'clock. He raised his jacket collar, since he hadn't taken the time to put on his shirt once he'd decided to alight. He pounded on the locked waiting-room doors, thinking this felt perfectly normal. This was the place on earth where he would always feel bare-skinned. A dispatcher came out the side door, asking what he wanted, and he asked if he could leave his suitcase and inquired about departure times for trains to Stockholm. Leaving the station he had second thoughts. It was quite a cold spring dawn. There was no place to go in and get a hot cup of coffee and he had two hours to kill before he could resume his journey on the heated train to Stockholm. He'd have to keep moving.

There wasn't a soul on the streets, and although some new buildings had sprouted up since he'd left town he felt completely at home. He discovered that his familiarity with the city was in his backbone; his whole body knew how steep the incline up to the big railway bridge was, his legs already knew how far it was to the Co-op. This place had no such secrets from him. The light fell in a way he knew perfectly well and even felt safe with. When he thought about it he knew there could be no other place in the world where he could walk around at four in the morning thinking that the light fell in a safe, familiar way.

He thought the ugliness of this city had damaged his soul more than anything else, and he knew he'd grown up with an illusion: the world is a little, safe ugly place. It's not dangerous.

Actually, he wondered whether he'd ever really left this town. The world is a big, evil, horribly beautiful place. He knew that now. Sometimes he would find himself alone in a strange, windy city an early Sunday morning when he could do no productive work and had no company but his own. At times like that he would imagine he was back here. The buildings were grey, people and dogs had peed against the wooden fences and the sprawling trees were black. Yes, he was home again. This was now, this was always, and he would never get away.

Now he walked fast in the rather grey morning chill until he got to a private park with arborvitae bushes and red beech trees. He stood there for a while looking for the stone base of a crofter's cottage that had once been on the hillside. But there wasn't even a mound in the grass any more. He walked along a hedge, the cold dew soaking his shoes. Then he sneaked between two houses and their hedges – one a magnificent red brick building that belonged to a wealthy man and the other a two-storey stucco house with large panes of glass around the veranda. Dogs could be heard barking inside and he knew his steps in the mossy lawn had been noticed.

Now he was looking for something he thought was more important than the house he was born in: a big apple tree that had stood outside it. It hadn't been the Åkerö or Säfstaholm apples people tended to have around here, just a big wild apple tree that, although it was very old, produced bushels of sour little fuzzy grey apples.

In the old days he would lie looking out at it. In October when its leaves fell he could lie on his kitchen settee bed at night and gaze at the stars through its branches. The schoolmaster had said the earth wasn't as big as it seemed to them; it was nothing but a little apple in outer space.

This had given him a very clear picture of the structure of the universe. At night he might wake up and, if the sky was starry, imagine he was lying there looking at the tree of the universe. His arms and neck itched from bedbug-bites and his little sister was sniffling in her sleep next to him. The bed was toasty. The stars sat there on their pointed branches, every single little branch of the old tree had stars on it and the earth was nothing but a frozen apple that would only hang on until the next storm.

Lying like that looking at the tree on clear, desolate nights gave him a feeling somewhere between horror and security that he could neither explain nor recall. But it would wash over him unexpectedly and when it did he recognised it. Later in life he had read books about the cosmos. But his childish picture of the world and the heavens was strong enough to survive all the knowledge he'd acquired.

He pushed aside the thick, dried grass, but couldn't even find the stump of the big tree. He found that upsetting, and a little frightening. He wondered whether it had blown down or been removed.

Now he felt uncomfortable and would have liked to leave if there had been a way. But he decided to walk all the way up to the churchyard. He knew it was downhill to start with, then straight and flat between the houses, and finally it turned and continued gently uphill. It wasn't actually the churchyard up there, but a cemetery. The church, built much later, was on the other side of the tracks. But his father was buried in the cemetery.

It was an unmarked grave, so there wasn't much of a chance Konrad would find it, especially as he couldn't really remember what section it was in. He walked between the black trees that were starting to get little light-green buds and looked at the graves and noticed that the trees had grown since he was here last. He remembered that at the old country graveyard where people were buried before there was the cemetery, there was a headstone that read: A RAILWAY PASSENGER, DIED 1877. That made him think about having left his suitcase with the dispatcher and about how he wasn't carrying a wallet. But he didn't realise that almost anyone would have recognised Konrad Eriksson anyway, and he didn't feel at all secure.

There were lots of little rises with violets that had just bloomed, crocuses that had wilted, overbloomed spring squill and rosebushes that had been covered for the winter with pine branches that had lost their needles now. Lots of other graves were nothing but grassy mounds without so much as a headstone. Some had piles of dog excrement on them and he found that upsetting. He picked up a gnarled elm branch and pushed one little pile off one of the mounds before walking on. Behind the cemetery he could hear a train rush past and he ran to see which way it was going in case the dispatcher had misled him, but it was nothing but a freight train with rattling, empty wagons. Afterwards he was breathing very heavily and feeling slightly sick.

On his way back he passed between rows of houses where people were asleep with the curtains closed. He turned off the street onto a path that climbed the long gravel ridge with an occasional evergreen tree. The ground was very eroded here, and slippery with pine needles. Where the old roots jutted out they were worn down from trodding feet, and there was hardly any ground cover left at all. This steep ridge had been one of the places where he had played in his own childhood, and he knew that his own feet had contributed to the erosion of the soil. In the old days there had still been blueberry brush that had sprouted pale green buds at this very time of the year, and he missed them.

When he was a boy he had occasionally stolen things he wanted badly. Once he'd taken a classmate's pocket knife. Of course he couldn't use it without being discovered, so he'd buried it. He was standing on the very spot now. Yes, he was certain this was exactly the right tree and the right root. He'd stuck his arm deep under the protruding root of a fir tree in the sandy soil, with the pocket knife in his hand, and made a hole in there to put it in. He'd never been back to get it.

Although it was early morning with everyone else asleep and it was more than twenty years since he stole the knife he looked around surreptitiously before going down on his knees and inserting his hand under the root. He couldn't find anything there.

He dug out sand and sought deeper and deeper in, but it was empty. He dug so deeply the sand grew damp and cold under his fingers.

Since he was absolutely sure he'd found such a good hiding place that no one else could possibly have discovered the knife, he thought he must have looked in the wrong place. Not the wrong fir or the wrong root, but quite simply a different city. Although this was identical with the little community he'd grown up in it was still the wrong place. Of course he returned to reality as soon as he got back down to the road. There was the house the black-haired lady had lived in, the one who played the piano so you could hear her all the way out in the street, but whom you almost never saw.

Until now he had avoided thinking about the townspeople since all he felt was indifference towards most of them. When he thought of them as a whole, if there was any feeling at all inside him to be dug out from deep down and from very long ago, it might have been that he despised them. They'd given him an ugly nickname when he was growing up and he often thought of the people living in this city as the people who were unable to hate but who were good at inventing nicknames for others. But the black-haired lady who played the piano so you could hear it out on the street wasn't one of them. Still, he had no idea who she'd been.

At other places in this city, he thought, places as unfamiliar to me and as secretive as if they had been underground, there are other kinds of people. There are knowledgeable, imaginative people, people with strong feelings and will power. They've survived, somehow they have. I wanted to know their secrets. I wanted to get into the deepest depths of this rat-stinking hole of a city and see if their secrets were there. At the same time I wanted get away, I had to.

Now he turned the corner by her house and into the park at the bottom of the gravel ridge called Spring Park because there had once been an old spring here. He didn't know exactly where. The park was very dark because it faced north. The ridge descended steeply down to a little path that ran along it. It looked like a fairly large room, an amphitheatre with the dark side of the ridge running steeply down to the path. The fir trees were not alone here, the park was full of alders, because the ground was damp.

He didn't really like this park. The fact that it faced north made it so dark. The only plants that thrived here were ones that didn't crave sunshine. There were nothing but ordinary alders below the ridge, though by the brighter openings to the east and to the west where he'd entered there were some birches. The sallows had split when they were small. It was too shady for lilies of the valley here, there was nothing but the modest herb Paris and spindly blinks. These were dull herbs, and the people who walked through the park barely noticed them. The only colourful flowers he could remember seeing here were red campion with their thick, downy leaves.

Partway up the slope was a bandstand with a railing around it and benches inside. He knew there had been dancing here, but his own thoughts went mainly to thundering brass bands and burgundy banners hanging from the rails. As he recalled it they had all had burgundy banners: the Order of Good Templars, the Salvation Army and the labour movement. He even thought the Co-op movement had had burgundy banners to begin with. His own older sister had performed with the Pure Spring Lodge for Girls. That was a big day for the whole family and he remembered it well.

First his mother had plaited her hair when it was wet and the plaits had stayed in for three days. When they were undone it was all curly. She had worn a gold crown and held a globe in one hand. He had personally been sent to collect it at the schoolhouse in an old pram. Her other hand held the pole of the red satin flag with the emblem of another woman on it and the words 'National Templar Order' in gold. He could still recall how much his sister had resembled the woman on the flag, who was also holding a flag with the figure of yet another woman sketched on it.

His sister had been deeply committed to the lodge, arranged parties, managed the library and eventually been treasurer. She had voting rights in the lodge. His mother went to no meetings, neither those of the lodge nor those of the congregation of the non-Conformist church. He thought his father had probably not allowed it. Union meetings had frightened her. But he knew that now that his father was dead his mother had started coming to the park in the evenings to hear the Salvation Army band. He didn't think she was the least bit religious. She was one of those people who have only one life to live and that's it.

He didn't like thinking about his mother, and he seldom did. He couldn't recall her face, and wasn't sure if that was because it had once been so intimately a part of him or because when all was said and done it really was perfectly blank.

Some people are like the grass you walk on. Treading on them is the basis for your existence in life, and you don't like thinking about that. You'd have a very difficult time if you didn't stamp on their dignity, which is just as fragile as your own.

He hoped his mother had a secret life he knew nothing about, maybe when she got a bit older and sat here in the shady park listening to the music. At least it requires a little dignity to live even the humblest underground life. Did he dare call it that? He also knew that there were people who are lost, and dignity that can never be restored.

The place he was in now was older than the thundering, shrill brass bands, he knew that very well. This had not only been a morass and a ridge around which roads and houses had been built.

There had been earlier paths, the ground had been levelled by passers-by. Still, he had no idea of what had gone on here in earlier times. Women were afraid of being raped here on the dark paths, children ran through the park as fast as they could when they were alone. People had also done things in the distant past, but he could hardly imagine what. Had they come here to perform superstitious rites, to pull their children through hollow trees to ward off illness? He didn't know but he hoped no old dirty-fingered woman had pulled him through a hole in a tree when he was too young to remember. He wouldn't have liked that.

He preferred to think about the brass band and the heavy banners no wind ever stirred down here in the shadowy corners. People had moved from crofts, farms, and shanties to become station clerks and lumber yard hands, washerwomen, foundry men, waitresses and boiler men in this community and they had built up their own organizations. He liked thinking about his sister who had voting rights in the Pure Spring lodge. But beyond their energy, their strength, their sense of community and their strong moral fiber, there must also have been something awkward about them to begin with, something that belonged to the forest and the night, something deviant and illusive. A kind of dignity, he thought. Maybe goodness. He tried one word after the next, but like piety and goodness they were already labels for people in daylight and there were none left for the ewe and the lamb, for the hollow and the crown, the waves against the cliff, the dog's tongue, the rain, the grass and the warm hands.

He was afraid they were no more, those who had borne more than their share of things of the night and the forest. Early on they must have attended the union meetings and lodge picnics, stood in the Co-op with protest lists or collection boxes. But he didn't know where they'd gone.

Now he realized he was freezing cold, and he headed up the ridge thinking that he'd look round the other side and see if the sun was beginning to rise and could warm him. He frightened a big black woodpecker up out of a fir tree, and it took off between the trunks without a sound. The boundary between night and morning was not easy to determine in this park, because even during the day the birds were often silent. But the summer night was dissolving now. He was happy to be awake and see it happening, although he was as miserably cold as you can only be in the transition between dark and light.

Suddenly he heard a clear burst of laughter that was quickly suppressed, and low voices full of veiled happiness. He thought the noise was coming from a spot where the trees were denser and where a thick growth of alder and vegetation had sprung up, as if this particular spot were a very moist one. He also thought he heard a clinking sound and came to think of people with picnic baskets, bottles and cups. Although it was near Ascension Day, he still wondered who ever would come up with the idea of going to sit in the dark Spring Park with its northerly location to celebrate the sunrise. He knew perfectly well where people around here went if they wanted to listen to the birds, sing barbershop quartets or hymns, raise their glasses of aquavit in a toast, and spread a cloth on the grass for little sandwiches with sliced meatballs.

When he heard the voices in the distance a second time he could tell the laughter was that of girls, and he thought: 'I have to remember this: there are people who survived. God only knows how they did it, I am nowhere near sussing out their secret. But there are people over there laughing, it's morning and they're happy.'

He absolutely wanted to see what they were doing now that it was perfectly silent over there again, so he crossed the little alder wood, trying to move the branches aside without making any noise himself. Time and again he stopped to listen. Now and then he heard the voices; now they were whispering and sounded serious, almost solemn.

In the end he was so close that he could see there were four girls in their twenties climbing up a stony hillock. They were wearing coats and heavy walking shoes. One of them was carrying a silver soup ladle.

'So,' he thought, 'they're on a picnic. They've got a basket of food with them and are looking for a good spot to sit down. It's a cloudy morning and it's going to rain pretty soon. They've picked this place despite the fact that it looks north because they can be out of the wind here. But it will pick up soon, I can hear it in the treetops. There's nothing strange about that. A pretty feast, solemn and still a happy occasion. One of them is carrying a long rowan branch with light-green leaves at the top that look like bird's feet, one has Star-of-Bethlehem in her hair. They'll be spreading a towel on the grass any minute, taking out their coffee and maybe some thin pancakes with jam and honey.'

But all they were carrying was the long-handled ladle. They were not out for a breakfast picnic. Confused, he saw them balancing close together on the mound of stones that was as long as a dike and looked very out of place on the ridge side. Their backs were towards him and there was no way he could see what they were doing. The ladle rang out against a stone.

He was afraid they would notice him and be frightened, so he went back into the park and walked up towards the bandstand. He was standing there, close to the trunk of a fir tree when they left. They headed down the path towards the east and disappeared, chattering in low, happy voices.

He wanted to know their secret, but it was time for him to leave if he was going to catch the train. He ran back, noticing that he was now almost afraid of the sound of his own feet on the ground, which rang hollow and made his footsteps resonate loudly. In the spot on the mound where they had gathered he could find no trace of what they were doing, and not a stone was out of place. Not that they could have moved such heavy ones even if they'd wanted to.

A sound reached him. It was like very distant singing, like voices rippling harmoniously but with no regularity. It couldn't be a song, nor was it chatter. Then he realized it was coming from the stones, and he went closer. The music was coming from underneath the stones. He tried to peek between them and get a look, but below them there was another layer of gravel.

His common sense told him that to reveal the cause he could start lifting the stones, trying to shift the top ones, and that he probably could, because his body was stronger than the girls'. Or he could spend the few minutes he had left in the park just listening. He chose to sit down on the singing stones and listen, without thinking and without trying to draw conclusions from the murmuring, constantly returning gentle babble and humming beneath him.

Not until he was on the train again, out of breath from having run nearly all the way to the station, did he realise he had discovered Heavenside Spring.

At night the Cosmopolitan Café shut around the smell of cold tobacco smoke. The shop window was empty and the chairs were upside down on the tables. Just before five there was a rustling in the creepers at the back: Frida Eriksson groping in the drainpipe for the key. It was early September. Apples with slugs on their skin lay in the damp grass and the summer was thinning out almost imperceptibly, leaf by leaf. Yellow birch leaves already clung to Frida's shoes when she entered the bakery and took her apron down from behind the door where it was hanging on the hinge.

She got out the tin bucket, the long-handled mop and the rags, irritated that she was still expected to wash the floors with an old pair of knickers. They didn't absorb much. Tora Otter was a decent person in the main, but sometimes she would have terrible attacks of penny-wise. Frida wasn't going to say a word. She would just crochet a new floor cloth and leave it lying there on top of the bucket.

The stove and ovens were still warm. It was easy to get the fire going again, and after a while she added some more coal from the pail. The water in the back boiler was still hot enough to do the bakery floor with.

The bakery was narrow and cramped. There was a stool pushed in under the table, but no room for chairs. The girls had to rest their bottoms against the counters if they wanted to have coffee back there when there wasn't too much to do.

She dissolved a glob of soft green cleaning soap in the water. Nowadays there were all kinds of powdered cleaning agents, but she

229

was suspicious of them, and stuck to soft soap, without the scent of which she never thought anything was really clean. She dampened the broom a little before sweeping, so the dust wouldn't fly up onto the baking boards and into the clean tins Tora had set out. Most of the things were covered with tea towels. When she swept she leaned forward over the broom, almost crouching. She'd grown nearsighted and was worried about missing the bits of fluff in the corners.

Most of what was on the floor was cake crumbs and flour, and when she emptied the dustpan into the fire it flared up. Then she wound the knickers around the mop and dipped it in the bucket. They kept coming undone, the legs flapping against the linoleum. It wouldn't be long before the lino was so worn down in front of the table and stove that it cracked, and the water would start running through. She'd have to show Tora. There was surely no money for new lino, but they could patch it with the pieces left from when they laid the new floor in the back room. Damn cloth! Oh goodness, here was the baker already. Lucky the floor was done at least.

'Good morning,' Frida said kindly when she walked in, but without expecting an answer. She was young. Her cheeks were rosy from walking fast in the cold morning air, but she wasn't cheerful. She just nodded in Frida's direction, walked over and looked at the stove, put a hand into the oven.

'Not very hot yet.'

'All in good time. And how are you today?'

Frida was curious about her. Her name was Irma Karlsson and she was married to a sheet-metal worker with his own workshop, but she still went out to bake. There were no children. Something wasn't quite right about that plater, he didn't work like he should. He'd make promises and then not come through, although he wasn't a drinker.

'It's a nerve thing,' Ebba Julin had said. They were neighbours.

230

Well, to each his troubles, Frida thought. You're lucky as long as you're healthy, she'd say to herself. She dumped the dirty water out of her pails, replaced it and clanked on into the shop. The baker was dragging out flour sacks and starting to measure the flour while the milk was heating on the stove.

The waitresses always wiped down the tables and did the washing up before they left in the evenings, and turned the chairs up onto the tables. She only had to do the floors in the mornings, that was it. But she always brought a wiping cloth into the shop, too, because some evenings the girls were tired or couldn't see well enough in the lamplight, and Frida found rings on the tabletops. The shop was especially difficult to get right. There were three tables with blue-veined white tops of imitation marble. The countertop above the glass case was real marble, though. It was easy to chip the biscuit plates against it. The glass case and the tall cabinets behind it were the finest pieces of furniture at the Cosmopolitan, not counting the big mirror in the back room. The glass case had brown ornate wooden edging, and the back wall of the cabinets was a mirror that multiplied the number of glasses and jars of sweets inside. She never had to dust the wooden edging on the case. Tora said Ingrid did that every afternoon. She'd sit on her heels with a dust cloth wound to a tight point and poke away at the cracks.

She swept the floor, collecting up a little pile of gravel she had to carry out the back way since Tora had the front door key.

'Don't bring that dirt through here,' said the baker, who was kneading a huge batch of dough for sticky buns and didn't want any dust in it. This would be pleasanter if we two could chat, Frida thought. But we all have our problems.

Now she was mopping the floor with sweeping movements, although she didn't really feel mopping got it clean. She knew it would be better to scrub it on her hands and knees, but Tora had forbidden it. 'If you want to wear your body out, do it someplace else.' Dear heavens, it wasn't that hard. Just the getting up and down. Besides, this was the only place she still cleaned now that she had her job at the laundry.

The last thing she did was to hasp open one of the windows to let out the damp and the stagnant night air. A milk wagon passed along the street with a farmer at the reins, wearing a bowler hat and white collar. She felt like making a nasty comment about him, but the baker got there first, shouting 'Shut the door, will you? How do you expect my dough to rise in a cross-draft?'

In the back room the air was cold and smelly. She shut the door behind her and opened both velvet curtained windows as far as they'd go. The net curtains were old, yellow and brittle, and had to be handled with care. The floor was filthy with gravel and pipe ash and matches under the tables, and she swept it with rapid, angry strokes. Scraps of paper and dried leaves swirled up in the draught from the open windows. The men who were out of work spent the evenings in here turning the pages of the newspapers until they fell out, and playing chess. They'd made the back room their own as early as that first winter when there wasn't much work, which was not at all what Tora had had in mind. Still, she couldn't turn them out. Fredrik was one of them. Adam, however, had never gone to work at the foundry. He was now the projectionist at Bertil Franzon's cinema.

On the long wall on the street side the big mirror stood between the windows, angled slightly forward to fit between the floor and the ceiling. The frame had an endless number of little gilded plaster buds that blossomed at the top. Behind the top of the frame a pair of eyes peeped out. They belonged to Karl Marx. Ages ago the youth group had put portraits on the wall. Tora had instantly recognized Hinke Bergegren and stuck him in one of the cupboard drawers before he could upset enough people to deprive her of the last of her regular morning customers. She'd been less certain about the identity of the bearded man, however, and so he ended up above the mirror. Between the frame and the glass there were lots of photos and club information sheets. Still, there was plenty of mirror space left, enough to see the whole floor with the muddy-coloured lino patterned like a Persian rug, the brown tables and chairs, the cupboard with the chess board and pieces, decks of cards, men's and women's magazines and locked drawers where the club ledgers were kept.

Sometimes Frida would look in the mirror while she washed the floor and removed the bits of dust from around the legs of the chairs before she set them back down on the floor. She was small now. Her dresses were getting too big. Her legs were thin and her swollen, knobbly veins visible through her stockings. Even her shoes looked too big. Sometimes she would stand right in front of the huge mirror and stare at her own little reflection against the floor, thinking it looked as big as a battlefield after combat.

'Grandma, you're so tiny,' her oldest grandchildren would say. They, on the other hand, were sprouting right up.

'Well, nowadays the only growing I'm doing is downwards, like the cow's rump,' she would answer. 'Time's catching up with me.'

But it upset her that the old Sunday dresses she now worked in, with an apron over them, looked so big on her nobody would ever think they hadn't first belonged to someone else. Her hair was thinning out, too. The bun she wore in the back was just a tiny roll nowadays. If she was going out on a Sunday she would roll her hair into a low knot at the base of her neck and put a hair pad under it to puff it up. She couldn't curl it at all in the front any longer and had stopped trying. She'd part it in the middle and pull it straight back, but she had to be extremely gentle with the comb or whole tufts would come out.

When she got the job at the laundry she got herself a set of teeth.

'Now that I don't have to clean houses and be lower than the low,' she'd said to Tora. ' 'cause that's what it's like, I can tell you. You don't count a bit. Once upon a time the housekeeper at the Lindhs' used to call me 'Madame'. Nobody'd ever say that nowadays.'

'You wear them, Frida,' Tora told her. 'Wear them every day, to work, too. Now that you're ou tand about.'

In her apron pocket Frida had a rag that was a piece of an old sheet, and she wet it with some methylated spirits they kept in a bottle in the sideboard and polished the mirror carefully. She worked a little faster than necessary. There was something about that old café mirror. You'd be doing all your old chores and then suddenly your eye would be caught by an image you saw in it over your own shoulder. 'Here you are, part of the world,' the mirror said. 'This is what it looks like, that life of yours you hardly ever even think about.' Then it was suddenly as if even the old worn-out chairs in the back room looked different than usual, were charged with meaning against the light brown wall. People often sat in the café looking in the mirror, looking past their own reflections, at the sideboard and the chairs and the hat rack by the door as if they'd never seen those things before.

Seven years ago when Tora bought the café, she'd had the back room redone with wallpaper that had cost a pretty penny. It had little bunches of roses and gilded lyres running all the way down to the floor, and from the beginning the background had been beige. Normally she was a rational, practical woman, and she should have chosen a less expensive wallpaper. But this was the one she wanted, she'd seen it in a room one time, she said, and she knew it was durable. That was her only justification. Now the background colour had deepened, the roses were mocha and the gilding on the lyres shone heavy, looking strangely elegant in the otherwise shabby room. Perhaps she'd made the right choice anyway. But of course in time it cracked and hung from the wall, and now and then she'd mix up some paste in a coffee cup and stick it back up.

Frida set the last chair on the floor and began to gather her cleaning things together. Now Tora could be heard at the street door, her key in the lock, and the clock rang loudly, its steel spring clanging against the works.

'Whatever's happening, is Frida at her airing again? What about the dough, Irma? Is it rising? It's so cold in here a person would shit ice. Leave it to Frida!'

Frida shut the two windows in the back room and brought the bucket and broom and mop out noisily.

'If you don't air a place out it gets all musty,' she said.

'And good morning to you, too,' Tora answered. 'If you insist on airing you can't expect Irma to bake anything but flatbread. Well, we deserve a drop of coffee now, girls. I'll just feed the fire first. Well, what's this? The girls forgot to dump out the ashes last night even though I reminded them. You can't leave anything to anybody else.'

'Let it be,' said the baker.' I don't want the air full of ash around my dough. And you'll have to have your coffee out there. It's crowded enough in here as it is.'

Frida and Tora exchanged meaningful glances. It was the same every morning. She would set her coffee cup on the shelf above the stove, and she only wanted black coffee, nothing to eat. Tora and Frida never ate anything in the mornings before going to the Cosmopolitan, however. So Tora would grind a handful of beans in the mill, and make a little pot of coffee just for the two of them, as it was too early to start the coffee for the clients. Then she'd reach a

235

hand in under the towels on the countertop, take out two fresh white rolls and spread them thick with butter. Sometimes the rolls were still so hot the butter melted. They'd sit at one of the little white tables in the shop. The sun shone on the apple trees in the upholsterer's widow's garden across the street and sometimes Tora wished she could sit in the widow's sunny kitchen on a morning like this and get all warmed up.

'My blood's thinning,' she said. 'Get cold the minute I sit down.'

'Get cold from airing the place out too much, too,' said Tora. 'Have some hot coffee.'

Out on the street bicycle chains squeaked and pedals rattled. The first fellows to head for the workshops in the mornings were always the older family men. Their metal lunchboxes were tied to their carriers and bounced when they hit the potholes the rain had dug in the street. After them there were crowds of younger men, sometimes four and five abreast. Last were the late arrivals, mostly with no lunchboxes but with dreadfully noisy chains and bouncing tyres. You couldn't get away with coming ten minutes late any more, like in old Wärnström's day.

Today there was unemployment and mostly only the older men still had jobs. The street settled down again fast. Frida and Tora had their second cups, sucking on sugar cubes and examining every single man that passed. Just a couple of years back Tora would never have indulged in this luxury. She'd always had her coffee on her feet and always found something to keep her hands doubly occupied as she ate her roll. Now they sat still. Frida's eyes wandered over the floor and the newly-wiped tabletops. Suddenly she shoved her cup away and got up.

'What now?'

'Thought I saw some fuzz.'

She was near-sighted and was starting to worry she didn't see whether the corners were really clean.

'Getting on, I'm getting on,' she said. 'Not much good work left in me.'

'Nonsense,' said Tora.

Frida was born in 1863. That was the year the number of out-of-wedlock children in the parish doubled, the year after the western branch of the railway was completed and the men who laid track, the ones they called the 'clay pigeons', moved on. Her mother had been known as Embankment Britta. She'd sold aquavit to the rail men by the barrel, aquavit and food. That was nearly sixty years back. Occasionally she was tempted to say to Tora, 'Your mother and I were classmates. We were the same age and would have done our catechism together.' But Tora's mother didn't live to be confirmed.

There were things you didn't bring up. If you tried, Tora's face would go stiff and her eyes glaze over. You didn't mention her mother, or the death of F.A. Otter, or the boy who'd grown up in Stegsjö. And perhaps that was just as well, Frida thought. The past was the past and it was no use wasting your breath on it. But sometimes Frida would feel an incomprehensible desire to talk about the old days anyway. She might snort and say:

'Can you imagine me having walked arm in arm with Valfrid Johansson? It was on the way to a union meeting.'

'Well, he was red once upon a time, but it didn't take long to turn him black,' Tora replied.

'I even held hands with him, you know,' Frida said. Those times were so real and alive to her. Tora, though, didn't like the old stuff. She threw things away if she could afford something new. Rugs and wooden bowls and jugs from the croft where she'd grown up got tossed out. Nor did she like to talk about the days when the village had been nothing more than a bunch of derelict buildings around the station and roads deep in mud. With one exception, that is.

Sometimes she would reminisce a little about the days when she was restaurateur Winther's cashier at the Railway Hotel. Prima donnas, opera singers, bards and princes had had meals there and passed so close by her that she could smell the scent of their clothing. She might see a picture in the paper and say: 'I saw him at the hotel once when he was young.' They'd had bone china and silver-plated serving plates and cutlery. At the auction after Winther's death she'd bought a silver-plated table service with salt and pepper shakers, crystal oil and vinegar jars and a creamer. She still had it in the glass cabinet behind the counter. She often polished and filled it, though it served no other function than to remind her of the grand Hotel de Winther.

Sadly, the Cosmopolitan was a dilapidated, middle-aged café with curtains discoloured from smoke, and chipped cups. There was never really much of a crowd except in the evenings, and one single waitress was more than enough nowadays. But for some people it was an institution, even a kind of solace, and they didn't stop coming.

Tora hadn't imagined it would be like this. She had hoped to run a lady's tea room, where the housewives would go when they had been to Ölander's to try on new shoes or to Elfvenberg's textiles to look at fabric. She, too, was somewhat the worse for wear. Her chin and cheeks had thickened and her hair was now nearly brown although it had been perfectly blonde in the days when she had been Winther's cashier and worn it with a fringe and corkscrew curls at the temples. She let her chin jut out too. It had become a bad habit.

She still bought every issue of the *Ladies' Home Journal* and put it out on one of the tables in the shop. She'd given up on the thought of ever attracting the very best or even the second-best housewives, but she sometimes still thought it wouldn't be impossible for the girls who were studying at the home economics seminary to come in for a cup of coffee. Especially if the *Ladies' Home Journal* was just lying there waiting to be read free of charge, and they could study the details of stuffing a head of cabbage and then serving it so it looked whole again. Though she guessed they learned all that stuff at the seminary, actually.

'I'd better be off to the laundry now,' said Frida. 'I saw Evert pass by a few minutes ago.'

She put on her black braided straw hat, pulling the elastic band around the bun at the nape of her neck even though she was only going across the street to the laundry. As she left, Tora handed her a bag of sticky buns for the washerwomen's morning coffee.

The odour of ripe fruit and decay on Hovlunda Road seemed to have evaporated with the dew. There was the sweet smell of malt from the brewery, fresh bread from the Cosmopolitan and clouds of steam and the odour of lye puffed out of the vents at the laundry. The delivery carts rattled along Store Street and here came Fredrik Otter, cycling along with the café's big milk canister strapped to his carrier and the smaller cream canister swinging from the handlebars. It was quite a feat. He had to sit twisted a quarter-turn to hold the back canister in place. He wouldn't be caught dead pulling a cart through the city streets.

Berta Göhlin saw him through the upstairs window and shook her head over his still being out of work. In the bakery, dough and the rolling pin slapped against the bread board. Tora was shaping loaves alongside Irma Karlsson, and she rolled harder. The baker-woman thought, 'She's slamming all the air right out of that bread,' but she didn't dare say it. The community was entering its most energetic phase of the day. There were the wide-awake sounds of pounding, hissing, slamming, banging and whining. Still three hours to go before the morning coffee break. Birds could only be heard in the most secluded gardens, birds and the first chords on a piano.

'Where's Adam?' Tora asked Fredrik.

'Sleeping.'

She didn't answer, but her mouth went tight. He made his living. Still, she was more worried about him than she was about Fredrik, who spent the whole of these Indian summer days down by the beach café playing cards with the other unemployed men. Their otherwise pale bodies were tan after a long idle summer, the black lines around their nails were beginning to dissolve from so much time in the water. Some of them were wasting away from a diet of coffee and rolls.

Adam slept all morning, since he worked nights at the cinema, the dance hall and the local theater. Was that really work, though? He went about in his Sunday best seven days a week, in a shirt with a collar and tie. Brought money home and put it on the kitchen table; she just wished he wouldn't do it when Fredrik was around, who didn't even have enough for a coffee at the beach if she didn't give in to him. She would have preferred him to spend his days at the Cosmopolitan, but he wanted to do his chores early and then be off. He found it embarrassing standing there chopping wood for the tile stoves. Yes, he was out of work, but it was an illness he didn't want showing. He didn't agree with her that running errands and chopping wood was work. Work was only one thing: the foundry.

At eight Irma Karlsson really did stop for coffee, coming out into the shop, but only because she had to: at eight every morning the confectioner came for two hours to ice the Cosmopolitan's cakes and glaze the almond biscuits. He changed into his uniform in the bakery, and Tora and Irma always went out into the shop while he dressed.

'The ladies may enter,' he finally declared in his sonorous voice, by which time Tora was irritated speechless by the endless amount of time it took him to get into his checked trousers, his white shirt, the apron to cover his huge paunch, and of course his hat. But there he was, pale and floury in full attire, cutting a sheet of wafer dough, because he thought he'd begin by making some cream layers.

The minute the bell in the shop rang Tora went out and started bagging white rolls, puzzling as she did so over how she was going to get rid of that idler out there who just dirtied her utensils and demanded constant attention as if he were still at the peak of his career at Anker's café. Now he was a pensioner. He'd have to give up this little extra job, too. She hardly sold any fancy pastries nowadays. Soon she'd have to give him the sack, but she didn't know how she could do it. She was afraid he might crumble, like a meringue that got sat on. She listened to the dragging of his floury, slippered feet and to his bishop's voice, at the same time painfully aware of Irma's compact silence back there, too.

It was nearly nine, the baker undid her apron and said a curt good day, reminding them that the last sheet of sweet crescents was still in the oven. Outside, Tekla and Linnea were just coming across the street. The younger woman was tall and elegant, she turned heads. Tekla was the same age as Tora, forty-four, and was wearing an old crushed hat on her head. The two of them had been waitresses together at the old Railway Hotel once upon a time. Now she did the washing up, made the coffee and sliced bread and cakes at Tora's café. Linnea was the waitress.

The local lawmonger was almost always the first customer of the day. He was a man with short legs and an overstuffed briefcase, who set his bowler hat upside down on the sideboard in the back room. Then he would settle into the leather armchair and order a pot of coffee and two crescents. After a while, his clients would begin to arrive. He represented people in court, wasn't as picky as

241

the lawyers, and would even accept clients who had used a rat trap to catch pheasants, or taken revenge on their neighbours by burying a dead moose outside their kitchen window. Tora had been stuck with him ever since the time he went bankrupt and she bought his old leather armchair at the public auction. It drew him back. It smelled of his cigars and was stained from his sweaty back.

But Tora had wanted her café to be for women. Girls, young ladies, housewives. The well-to-do, if possible. At one point the switchboard operators got it into their heads that they'd have their coffee at the Cosmopolitan. They'd sometimes have their men friends in tow. And then suddenly the women up and vanished, rising like swallows, making the air swish. Gone.

Their gentleman friends stayed around for a while, but she didn't really want men customers. They make the place all smoky, there's something drab and dull about men. The housewives who've been out shopping peer in only to see two farmers and the lawmonger in the back room, if they can see anything at all through the thick, yellow smoke in there. They turn heel, of course.

So what can you do? Well, you certainly can't turn the solicitor out. You ask yourself how it happened that a place once as neat and bright as any other tea room gets taken over by men with shabby briefcases, schoolboys, the unemployed, girls sitting by the net curtains weeping, thinking they can't be seen from the street, people who've been to simple funerals, chess players, and travelling salesmen in soap and belts to ward off electromagnetic fields. Is it something in the air or the walls? Is the Cosmopolitan too dark?

She'd kept three of the little white tables and had them out in the shop where the boys weren't allowed to smoke their pipes; in fact she didn't let them sit there at all. At half past ten every morning Magnhild Lundberg from the co-educational intermediate school would come in and sit at one of them. She and little Gerda Åkerlund from the women's suffrage society were the last ones to abandon the Cosmopolitan. The society had been dissolved, it was no longer needed. The record books had been removed from the buffet drawer and the little flag from the sideboard. Tora couldn't honestly say she was glad their aim had been achieved. She missed them, and not just because they were customers. She seldom had time to go to the cinema or a lecture. She'd stood in the doorway with one hand on her hip and her nickel-plated tray under her arm and heard the whole of *Gösta Berling's Saga*.

It was also here that Franzon, who arranged cinema showings, organised dances and managed the local theater group, walked in one April evening when Gerda Åkerlund was sitting with her fair curly head of hair bent over the *Ladies' Home Journal*. Linnea Holm had once speculated as to what would have happened if Gerda hadn't looked up at that very moment, but had simply finished her page and then asked for her bill while Franzon walked past her into the back room, ordering half a pot of coffee.

So he came in, with his brown eyes and his soft leather gloves, light-grey overshoes and a rhinestone pin in his tie. Gerda and he looked into one another's eyes and that was when it happened, Tekla and Linnea were certain they'd witnessed it. Gerda was a teacher at the co-educational intermediate school and an extremely bashful, mild-mannered soul. Now she was transformed. Franzon had started playing on the piano in the back room. The felt coverings on the little hammers had long ago been worn away; the clanking sound was like the hammers hitting the springs under an iron bed. In an annoyed, arrogant tone of voice, Gerda asked Linnea to go in there and see to it the racket stopped. Tekla and Linnea looked at one another in shock. Fröken Åkerlund irritable and condescending! When the sounds from the old piano went on clinking and clanking, Gerda went into the back room herself and requested him kindly to cease hammering on that untuned instrument. From that moment on it was plain sailing. Not all at once or the first evening, but within six months it was all wrapped up. It began with his giving her free tickets to the cinema, which she proudly distributed among her pupils, and it ended with the two of them going to Stockholm together and returning home – Gerda a dove who'd been dragging her wings in the dirty street, a rose with a wad of snuff at its heart.

What no one else knew was that late one April evening shortly after their first encounter at the Cosmopolitan he had bumped into her in Spring Park. Gerda was extremely tired and quite upset after a long teachers' meeting. Nor did anyone else know what he said to her, but that was the moment when Gerda realized that the world was not just one big co-educational school where Magnhild Lundberg should be in charge but where, unfortunately, Headmaster Ossian Jansson held the reins instead. She became curious about his world, one she found peculiar, well, God forgive her, even a little inane, with dance bands and flickering cinema screens. But she was shocked to learn that in his world an IOU that had fallen due was pale green gravity. After this the haughty solemnity of the co-educational struck her as something of a parody. Sometimes she found herself standing in the auditorium singing along with that morning's hymn but with her mind full of worry about Franzon and his IOU. A person she hardly knew! Once, when he had overcome a financial obstacle, he asked if he might treat her to a glass of port wine at the Cosmopolitan. Tora just stood there in the doorway looking like the Angel of Death personified, and Linnea had to tell her what they had ordered three times before she served them. Gerda got a warning from the school's Headmaster, but the blood was pounding in her ears so all she heard was: 'Fröken Åkerlund the calling of a teacher gathered rumours of course not listen but immediately parents most seriously take to heart.' And the only part of this she could really make anything of was 'most seriously take to heart', as she was a serious person. Yes, it's a tragedy when a serious person drinks port wine and plays *à quatre mains* on an untuned café piano.

Her father was a minister of the church, her mother had died when she was a child. He was as strict as Jehovah and wore undergarments that complied strictly with the Jaeger health system. Gerda had been brought up on cold showers, and had learned to make sacrifices. Still, at some point when she was still a child, her wise heart must have seen through the man of the cloth and realized, although the heart does not realize things rationally but just embraces understanding and slowly expands around it, that Jehovah was a child who needed her. He swam outdoors even in winter and slept with the window open, ate raw onion, and it would have been easy to believe in his immortality if he hadn't had a stroke. He was bedridden for a long time, then able to sit up for six months and prattle while Gerda, who'd recently graduated from the seminary, looked after him. Then he had his second stroke, and it was the death of him. Gerda wept, was consoled by kind people, and arranged his funeral. She was the beneficiary of his estate, gave away some of his books, sold furniture and one evening sat and realized she was relieved. But of course she told no-one. She just grew even more severe.

What can be said about Gerda's kind of solemnity was that it was rooted deep inside her. On the outside she was rosy-cheeked and quite peppy, laughed readily at almost nothing at all, and took her youngest students tobogganing on the hill running down to the gates to Little Heavenside.

Franzon was a Paganini of the art of love, who pared his strings down so they'd be sure to break on stage, and then finished the piece on the single remaining one, lit fireworks on stage and performed in the clouds of smoke. Gerda, of course, was his adoring, uninitiated audience. She was twenty-six years old and had never kissed except Jehovah's forehead and the tops of the heads of her youngest pupils.

Next comes the story of what happened when Franzon's balls cramped up. Well, he treated her to port wine and went on to tell her about his unfortunate childhood. He took her for walks in Spring Park and spoke of the fire burning inside him, the fire of ambition.

'Oh, *I* got all kinds of encouragement,' Gerda said thoughtfully. 'Not least from Fröken Lundberg, Magnhild Lundberg who was my schoolteacher before we became colleagues. There was a time when I was convinced something great would become of me. I'm afraid I was rather childish. Now I believe it's preferable to try to be something *good*.'

Franzon, who intended to be rich, kissed her. When he'd finished kissing her he took her face between his hands, looked deep into her eyes and said:

'Gerda, you've been deceiving me.'

'Deceiving? Would I deceive you?'

'Yes.'

After which he went silent. She had to beg and beseech. Please, he really must tell her how she could ever have deceived him. All right then, Gerda hadn't been telling the truth when she said she'd never before been kissed. Good grief! How could he imagine that? It was perfectly true. Didn't he see: she was completely incapable of lying to him? At which point Franzon's voice thickened, he kissed her anew, an even wetter kiss, even more heavenly, and then he whispered into her hot little ear:

'But Gerda, don't you see? You couldn't possibly kiss like that if you hadn't been kissed before? You couldn't!'

After which he kissed her again and whispered into her other ear, now in an ever so muted voice. 'I see, I see. So it is possible. Oh, Gerda, Gerda!'

She was astonished. Never could she have believed there was anything special about her in that department, she'd hardly ever even given such things a thought. In which case she supposed it must be possible to have a natural talent for loving. 'That's right,' said Franzon. 'And you mustn't be ashamed of it, Gerda. It's a beautiful gift.'

This was when what became known as their 'traffic' began. And no end was put to it until Tora, who was always at the café all

247

evening, heard about it and evicted Franzon with immediate effect. She'd already packed his bags and she gave him such a booming piece of her mind that the water glass on top of the carafe began to quiver. He found her vulgar, in fact he always had. He left with no regrets. The room was dark and faced the courtyard. The only ornament in it was a painting of misty elves dancing on a meadow, and the lino needed replacing.

But the damage was already done. They were consenting adults, as Franzon quite rightly pointed out to Gerda. He was thirty-two and she twenty-six. They made their own livings and forced their views on no-one. They should have the right to see one another in peace and quiet and not have to freeze on wet benches in Spring Park or broil in the tiny room where the film projector rolled. Gerda was neither prudish nor insipid. So she, a grown-up, self-sufficient, responsible and thinking human being (she told herself) crossed the dark courtyard to number 9 Store Street, stopping behind the corner of the building with a pounding heart when she heard footsteps outside, and continuing up the stairs when they didn't turn in to the yard. Franzon wound up his gramophone, lit the little lamp with its beaded fringe shade and poured some port wine.

'Just a thimbleful,' said Gerda.

'You're not at a sewing circle,' he said. 'You're here to talk to me and to give me your advice. Shall I sell my shares in United Margarine? Shall I take out a promissory note and buy a new projector? What about *The Girl from Marsh Croft*? Do you think it'll keep the audiences coming for another week? How much does it cost to advertise? Oh, Gerda, I need you. I need the wise counsel of a grown woman. Talk to me.'

And Gerda, who had been at school for almost all her life, discovered as she sat there on his unsteady ottoman with its rust coloured upholstery and its huge cushions with crocheted covers, that life had gone on living all the time she'd been conjugating French verbs. She learned that the difference between United Margarine and Swedish Packaging could mean the difference between doubled prosperity and rack and ruin, that you could buy film projectors even if you had no cash if you just had a rectangular document, that if women wept Franzon made money, while if their decency was offended and they boycotted him he made none.

'Women are powerful,' he told her. 'Powerful and strong. Tell me how women think. Advise me.'

So Gerda went to see *The Girl from Marsh Croft* and told him to let it run another week because it was a serious, thought-provoking and very beautiful film, and she went to see *First Mate Ljung's New Flames* and told him to put it back in the brown box and pull the cord tight around it and send it right back to Stockholm. And Franzon sent back *The Girl* and held onto the *First Mate*, and made a lot of money.

He often fingered the lamp, an old-fashioned paraffin one. He liked the yellow light, he said, and Gerda also found it difficult to accept electric lighting, except when she had composition notebooks to correct. But it was a smoky, difficult lamp in every way. He had to turn down the wick. And the little room with the dancing elves got darker and felt warmer and they were adults who made their own livings and embraced and kissed and there was nothing wrong with that, as Franzon so rightly put it.

But it couldn't go on forever. Suddenly they would reach a point where Gerda realized things were getting out of hand and she must pull herself together. One moment it was heavenly and she could breathe, and she was hot in places she didn't want to think about and she had to gulp and gulp.

'All right,' she'd say. 'Time to come to our senses.'

And she almost felt like she used to feel when she tried to distract Jehovah from the winter swims he insisted on so unreservedly although he was over seventy. But one evening she waited too long, and when she tried to distract Franzon he was no longer willing to be distracted. He changed: his hands were rough, his legs were strong, and his breathing sounded like he'd been running. Gerda just had to get up and push him away. She turned her back and arranged the buttons on her blouse and then she turned up the lamp.

When she turned round again Franzon was in the most peculiar state. He was doubled over on the ottoman, holding tightly to one of the cushions with the crocheted covers and he was puffing audibly, nearly moaning. That made Gerda smile, thinking of Jehovah and all his little ways, and she raised Franzon's chin with her index finger to look him in the eye and joke with him a little. But he wasn't amenable. He had changed. His upper lip was beaded with perspiration and his face was ashen. It was very clear he was in terrible pain and he asked her in a muffled voice to please leave him by himself for a few minutes.

It took a while until he could converse again, during which time Gerda thought she might die of anguish. She didn't understand what was going on and thought he might be having heart problems and that she'd killed him with her tricks, the ones she was so naturally artful at performing according to Franzon, although she didn't know it herself. But he didn't die. She begged him for God's sake to tell her what had happened. At first he said he couldn't possibly, it couldn't be spoken. But after a while he decided Gerda was a mature woman. She had a right to know what had transpired between them.

When a man and a woman were together and cared for one another, their embraces were a striving for union, were they not?

Gerda was a grown woman and knew about that, there was no need to hem and haw. No, there was no need for hemming and hawing between them about anything. All right! Well, the fact was that man was created different from women. She did realize that, said Gerda, and Franzon had to turn his head away for a moment and lay his face in the pillow. She wondered if he was in agony again. But whatever it was passed, and he went on to tell her that the body of the man prepared for this union in a way that the body of a woman did not. This was not something he could control or consciously affect. And if, despite those bodily preparations, there was no union, if there was some sudden disturbance, then what she had just seen happen was the natural result. The man would suffer pain.

Gerda went perfectly silent. She wanted to turn her head, lower her eyes. But she forced herself to be courageous, look right at him. Was his suffering extreme?

'Yes,' said Franzon, sounding like an ancient Icelander who had suffered to see his hand chopped off but had gone on tightening his bow with the stump. At that moment Gerda decided never to hurt him again.

They sat at some distance apart, him on the sofa, her in the rattan armchair. They exchanged kisses and she gave him a motherly hug when she left. Another evening, though, they got carried away again, and before Gerda could pull herself together they were right back there. This time, however, she was no longer like an innocent, unknowing girl. She had known what might happen, she had tempted him into preparations beyond his control and now he would soon be bursting with pain and his face would go grey and damp with perspiration. Instead of pushing him away she lay down on the ottoman cushions and undid the waistband on her skirt he had been pulling at for so long.

'Come,' she said.

'Oh, my dear sweet Gerda,' said Franzon. 'Are you certain this is what you want?'

'Yes,' Gerda replied solemnly, for she had learned to take the consequences of her behavior.

Then came the summer of the infamous journey to Stockholm and Magnhild Lundberg's battle against the delegation of parents' representatives and Headmaster Ossian Jansson. It was about to be won when Gerda admitted to Magnhild that she had done exactly what people were saying about her behind her back and that she had no intention at all of refraining from Franzon's company in the future because she loved him. Her eyes were feverish. Her teaching contract expired and was not renewed for the next autumn but Headmaster Jansson agreed to give her a positive testimonial, even regarding conduct. Magnhild believed she would be able to help her get a position in Skara. Gerda said:

'I'm not moving. He needs me here.'

Even Franzon tried to persuade her, saying he didn't wish to be egotistical. At the end of the summer she moved into the room he'd once rented from Fru Otter at 9 Store Street, with permission to put the piano she'd brought from her childhood home in the sitting room. In August she began giving piano lessons.

'Don't do this to yourself,' said Magnhild, sensing how it might end.

'I've got to make my living.'

Gerda was no longer feverish, she was determined.

'Live on your little nest egg for a while and think about how you might put your life in order.'

'My capital's been invested.'

'By Franzon?'

Gerda nodded.

'He's good at these things,' she said. Magnhild didn't doubt it, and pleaded stubbornly with her to try to withdraw her nest egg.

'You don't start touching money you've made a long-term commitment with. That's how you lose it. I wouldn't have gotten the position in Skara in any case. The rumours about my way of life had preceded my testimonial down there. Besides, this is where I want to be.'

'This is the one place on earth you shouldn't be right now,' Magnhild signed. 'Do try to get your money back.'

'Forgive me, Magnhild,' said Gerda, 'but you've spent your entire life in a schoolhouse and cannot possibly know a thing about the stock market. In society today...'

'Oh, hush,' said Magnhild Lundberg. 'But whatever you do, don't marry him. I'm sorry to be so harsh with you.'

But there was no question of marriage. They weren't living in marrying times. Very few young people could afford a wedding in these days of unemployment, and Gerda knew it. Moreover, Franzon's business success resided in the very fact that he needed no more than a suit brush, some decent hair tonic and his wallet in his inside pocket.

He and Gerda did, however, become engaged. She told him her situation had become extremely precarious and he was astonished and somewhat shaken, for those were powerful words coming from Gerda, who was a girl with a true scouting spirit. He did not inquire into the details of what she had been through in the women's common room or the corner shop but took her for a brisk walk through Spring Park (as it was a chilly, windy evening) and placed a ring on her ring finger. They were at the very spot where he had first kissed her. It was a thin silver band with marquisettes surrounding a pointed oval bloodstone and he didn't make up anything about its having been his mother's, he just gave it to her. He'd bought it in an antique shop in

253

Stockholm. Afterwards they had a fine meal, filet of beef topped with crabmeat and asparagus and served with béarnaise sauce, at the Hotel de Winther, and Gerda asked if she might have a copy of the menu as a memento. She felt bashful, because she wasn't accustomed to dining out.

Three pupils signed up for her piano lessons and she thought: I suppose things will improve, others will follow. I'm engaged now and I'm sure everything will settle down. I haven't done anything wrong and people aren't really cruel at heart, just thoughtless and curious. Three pupils a week wasn't much of a living, in fact it was none at all. But Tora Otter gave her a respite on the rent and her dinners on credit, which Gerda found a bit awkward since she knew Tora detested Franzon as much as bedbugs and rats. The worst part was not knowing how to fill her time, so she began taking walks. In the mornings she'd walk up the ridge all the way to the gates to Little Heavenside and then home along the road. So as not to go mad with loneliness she would go to the Cosmopolitan for cocoa after her walks.

The three lads she gave piano lessons to were not at all like her pupils at the co-educational, but she tried to treat them the same way. The one called Sture who came on Monday afternoons would go right over to the piano, sit down, put his fingers on keys, and start playing 'Ring the bells, ring' with no hesitation and no thought.

'But Sture, it starts on C,' she would say. To her dismay she found that his hands reminded her of jellied pigs' feet. They were short and white and fat and he held his fingers close together. She was very upset because she'd always thought she liked children.

'What's the name of this note?' she would ask him kindly, playing a low C.

'Q,' said Sture.

She stared at him in amazement, thinking she noted a malicious gleam in his eye, but determined to put it down to ignorance.

254

'No, C,' she said. 'Now let's try playing together for a while, you and me. Put your hands right here, just like me.'

And they tried. After a while she noticed that her voice was growing shrill and she heard herself starting to sound like her own first piano teacher, who had marked the beat with a knitting needle she also scratched her scalp with. She had always started by asking when she arrived if Gerda's papa was at home, and Gerda was so innocent she didn't realize this German lady with dandruff hoped to become her stepmother.

'Start on C, now,' she said. And Sture's pigs' feet hit two notes in both the treble and the bass.

Listening to her own voice now, she realized that she'd never been very pedagogical. She had loved the co-educational intermediate school and been loved there, and that was that. Now the girls passed her with their eyes lowered, and although the boys raised their caps to her, they didn't meet her eyes.

At the shop people said she'd come downstairs one morning looking pale, and with her wrists bandaged. That wasn't true.

She stood on Tora Otter's balcony and listened to what people were saying about her down in the courtyard. It made her need to go inside and sit down. She stared at the insides of her wrists, seeing the pattern of veins under her skin, which was extremely pale just there. If she bent back her wrists the skin went taut and she could see her veins very clearly.

Some people are evil.

That was a forbidden thought. Unhappy perhaps, and ignorant. But in the evenings when she lay in bed she had to let go, and she dreamt about people with pigs' hooves instead of hands, who sniffled and grunted way down there where she was sinking.

How can evil people know our thoughts before we ourselves do? What do they want from us?

B etween twelve and one the Cosmopolitan was so quiet you could hear the buzz of the flies in the ceiling fixture. Tekla stood at the window watching the girls from the co-educational intermediate school turn into Store Street instead of coming in for cakes as they once had. Now they went to Anker's. She was glad Tora was in her flat frying herring for Fröken Åkerlund and Adam so she didn't have to see it. She imagined they'd been forbidden from entering the Cosmopolitan after the business about Franzon and their schoolmistress.

She was in the bakery taking almond biscuits out of a tin when she heard the shop bell ring. When she went out there was a man holding the door open and looking around, and the spring on the bell had sprung, so it had stopped ringing. She could tell from his shiny thick cardboard carrying case with its bicycle straps dragging along the floor that he was a peddler. That frightened her and her fear made a barrier between them, forcing his gaze to start wandering from cupboard to shelf until her eyes obediently indicated to him that the little black enamel cash box was right under the counter at her waistline. She had been instructed that at times like this she should shout out into the kitchen just as if Linnea were there and not at the cobbler's having a pair of shoes soled:

'Just a minute, I've got a customer out here!'

But she didn't. The peddler saw her fear and was prepared to fulfil her every expectation instantly.

An elderly couple dressed in black came through the door just then, however, and as if a weight had been tossed into the pan on one side of a scale, Tekla's spirits rose, the peddler's fell, and she asked him what he wanted. He asked whether the café had a problem with rats and Tekla, who had no instructions for such a case, answered honestly that they had their hands full keeping the rats out. The couple, who had sat down at one of the white tables in the shop and were dressed in full mourning, looked at one another and the woman shook her head under her veil. In that case, said the peddler, he could ease their worries. He had something in his case that was the very best answer when there were no men in the house. Or were there men in this house, perhaps? But Tekla wasn't all that stupid, she kept her mouth shut. The peddler said that whatever the situation might be, he had the only right rat trap for use by women, a rat trap that was guaranteed not to make mush of the rat. Because no woman wants to empty traps with crushed rats in them – isn't that so? And the old woman behind the mourning veil shuddered audibly and her husband tried knocking his stick against the table to attract Tekla's attention and place his order. But he was so timid his knocking just sounded more like a little tit pecking at the putty around the window, and Tekla didn't take her eyes off the peddler.

'We aren't having any,' she said.

This was a perfectly unambiguous message, and he got it, but he said he could offer them a look anyway, no purchase required. His traps were a revolution in combating rats that she couldn't afford to miss seeing. Because the problem was that traditional traps made mush of rats and trap-cages were just as bad because they didn't kill them and then you had to, and wasn't it so that no woman wanted to have to do that? Right, what he had here was the only trap guaranteed to neatly and tidily do away with a rat in a fashion even the most sensitive female could tolerate: strangulation.

If she just took a look at this little wire noose she'd see that the rat had to stick its neck inside to get at the piece of pork rind in this little metal box. So it would put in its neck and start to pull out the lure, which was attached to this little hook that was fastened to the wire. So the rat tightened the noose around its own neck as it were and the moment of truth arrived when the rat sensed something was amiss and pulled. That was when it broke its own neck, you might say! Thereforeit was a trap that violated all previously know principles of rat trapping, in that the rat was killed by its own fear, which made it a sophisticated form of suicide, actually.

At that point the old couple dressed in black walked out of the Cosmopolitan, leaning heavily, arm in arm. Tora, who had just entered from the street, passed them on the steps and when she came inside and saw that there were neither cups nor plates on the table she asked:

'They left?'

And Tekla nodded mutely.

'Why on earth?'

At which point Tekla and the peddler looked at one another for an instant, after which she said:

'I dunno.'

'Good grief Evald, what are you doing here?' Tora wondered. 'Haven't seen you for ages. Are you in work?'

'Yes, I'm selling a construction used to combat undesirable rodents for a sheet metal worker at number 43 on the High Street,' the peddler said.

'Oh, you mean Nils the rattrap man? Heavens! How far away have you been, then?'

'Way up north.'

'Well, you do get to see the world, you boys. Would you like a coffee?'

'Yes, I thought I'd empty a pot of Java before doing like the dew,' said Evald.

'What?'

'You know, evaporating!'

'What kind of a cake to go with it?'

'Just a plain bun, thanks.'

But she went out into the bakery and buttered two slices of rye bread anyway, making sandwiches with jellied veal and pickled beets.

'Don't charge him for this,' she said to Tekla, 'it's not from behind the counter. But let him pay for his coffee.'

'Would you care for a demonstration of the modern rat trap?' asked Evald. 'The only rat trap for women's use.'

'No, we'll have none of that in here, please. But I wish you the best of luck on your continued travels. Moving on again?'

'Yes, it's nearly autumn when I do like the swallows and wing my way south,' said Evald. 'Now I've replenished my stocks.'

And he ate, said thank you and was on his way, as he'd been taught on his wanderings: easy come, easy go Romany. Then he tied his cardboard suitcase to his carrier and cycled out Vanstorp way until he reached the cottage by Spring Park, where he turned into the Norrköping Road.

There was Konrad Eriksson with a thin girl dressed in black by his side and if you looked closely you could see he wasn't just holding her by the arm, his fingers were also intertwined with hers. Tora, Linnea and a little boy who had come in to buy two öre's worth of broken biscuits just stood there gaping at them.

'Well, good day to you,' said Konrad. 'I'm back.'

He'd brushed his suit carefully before returning home. Now he disentangled his braided fingers and his elbow from the skinny girl's and gave her a little push forward.

'I have the pleasure of introducing Agnes, my betrothed.'

Tora and Linnea looked at one another and then at the girl who really was wearing a ring but looked as if her hands were freezing.

'Good grief,' said Tora. 'How did you get off work in mid-week?'

Things were very quiet for a moment.

'Betrothed?' was the next line, after which the girl in the black dress looked ready to burst into tears and Linnea cleared her throat.

'I'm sure you'd like some coffee,' she said.

So there was coffee, and the thin little thing stirred and stirred the contents of her cup while Tora asked questions and Konrad answered and she had soon squeezed it out of him that he was unemployed and so was the girl. But she hadn't been laid off, she'd just up and resigned her position.

'Quit your job? In times like these?'

Yes, she'd quit to be with him, with Konrad, her betrothed. They were going to be married, of course. Did he really think anybody was getting married these days? When they had nothing to live on? Well, they'd have to live in any case, whether or not they were married made no difference, so why not get married? At that point Tora and Linnea looked at one another again, after which Tora shut the door to the bakery, looked Konrad right in the eye and asked him, so softly it almost came out as a hiss:

'Does she have to?'

At that, Agnes dissolved in tears, and Konrad walked around the table and put his arm around her and told Tora to watch her mouth. He wasn't a child any longer, he was twenty-seven years old and Agnes twenty-one. Then followed a short summary of the thin woman's life history while Tora had the cup of coffee she now felt she needed, with her eyes on the door in case there were customers. The story contained an elderly father who, until as recently as a fortnight ago, had been a glazier at a window shop in Stockholm. Agnes herself had worked at Herman Meeth's, where she was known as Agnes in satin, and lived in a boarding house for young working women where they were three to a room and many more to the common kitchen. She'd shared with Svea in perfume and Lisen in gloves, and no men were allowed in the rooms. At ten every evening Fröken Zahr, the owner, would go through the rooms saying 'Good night, girls'. She would take the gas canister from the kitchen into her own room so none of the girls would be able to make coffee or do herself in. At six each morning she was back with 'Good morning, girls' and the gas canister. The pay had been poor at Meeth's but they taught you. And she'd abandoned that job? Yes, she had. To come back with Konrad.

'Well, sweet Jesus,' said Tora. 'You poor things. Did you imagine there'd be work to be had here? What got into your heads?'

'It'll be easier for Agnes to find work here than for me to in Stockholm,' Konrad answered, and Tora went dead silent because she needed to figure out what kind of logic that was.

'She can work for a family,' he said.

'Pardon my asking,' Tora said with unusual tact. 'But is Agnes in mourning?'

Indeed she was. Her father the glazier had recently passed on. She was forty kronor in debt for the funeral clothes, according to Konrad. Not at Meeth's, she couldn't afford to shop there. And another sixty at St. Göran's Hospital from two years back when she'd had the Spanish flu. It had been a hundred and eighty to start with, and in the end they docked it from her salary, at five kronor a month, every month.

'What did you have to tell them that for?' Agnes asked when Tora went out to help a customer.

'That's all that was left. Now she knows every single thing, which is just as well because she never lets up until she's dug every morsel of information out of you.'

'Are we going to see your mother after this?' Agnes asked.

'Yes, but she's not likely to ask questions. Tora's the worst. Though she's sure to help us, too.' Then he was afraid he might be promising too much, that he'd let himself get carried away because he was back at the old Cosmopolitan. There were, in fact, no miracles here, and the same laws applied here as out in the town and behind closed doors and at work places. Tora Otter was certainly a pretty decent person but she couldn't perform the impossible.

She was worn out, and worried because the café wasn't turning a profit, but at least the place was still open, people had somewhere to go and sit where they knew there wouldn't be someone instantaneously standing there to take your order. You could settle into a corner and sit there for five or ten minutes listening to the slamming of baking sheets and the voices from the bakery out back. Nothing actually happened. You went to the old, familiar place, saw the old, familiar people, leafed through a magazine. At least what happened here wasn't happening secretly. Take, for instance, Gerda Åkerlund who'd come in one evening and wept instead of staying at home and taking a razor to her wrists. Even Agnes, who had been so intimidated the first time she was here, got used to it. She even dared to walk around, test the leather armchair, walk over to the big mirror and look at the photos of the club members that were between the glass and the frame.

It was the football team with Fredrik as goalkeeper. He was at the very back with his cap on, but he was so tall that there was no missing him, arms crossed over his chest. There was another photograph when he was at a masquerade party of Franzon's, dressed as a tile stove. All you had to see was the feet to know it was him. If you looked very closely you could see a second pair of feet in the tile stove as well. The masquerade party had been a lot of fun, and Tora had spent a great deal of time staring at that picture. But what kind of conclusions can you draw from a pair of feet? All she could tell was that they were black shoes with not very high heels and ankle straps. Adam was out at the far right in the photo all wrapped up and with a black beard glued right to his face. He looked dark and savage and was supposed to be a Bedouin. Well, he looked born to be in costume, while Fredrik looked like a big, gentle horse no matter what he put on. There was a post card Ebba Julin had sent her from Berlin when the man with the painting business took her there and bought her a fur coat. Their Swedish currency had bought them a whole suitcase of German notes. Incredible, but you had to take the opportunity while it lasted, Ebba had written.

Agnes looked a little less cold when they had been alone in the brown room for a while, and she sat back down across from

263

Konrad, stretching her hands out to him across the table. They sat there holding hands. She was as fair as he was, and had short hair. Tekla peeked in through the door every now and then and Tora, who was behind the counter, also had to peek at them every so often. Agnes wouldn't look too bad if she got a little meat on her bones. But what good was she? How could anyone dare to recommend her to a family? Did she know how to scrub a floor clean or roll out a batch of sticky buns? Agnes in satin?

At half past three Ingrid arrived. She always came straight from school nowadays and dropped her schoolbag down on one of the white tables. Tora said: 'Don't leave that there.'

Then she gave her a cup of cocoa and two plain buns. She climbed up onto quite a tall stool by the counter that was actually a little stepladder they used to clean the windows. Tora didn't tell her anything, but she kept looking into the room where Konrad was sitting with his back to the shop. She saw his back stiffen right up when Ingrid's voice resounded in the café.

'What's wrong?' Agnes asked.

He shook his head. But she pestered him for a while, her eyes wide with concern. So he finally whispered that the girl out in the shop was his sister.

'Why don't you say hello to her then?'

'She doesn't want to see me,' he answered. 'She hates me enough to choke on it.'

Agnes looked horrified at this, and so he said softly:

'You don't need to worry about her, though. She's a tough kid.'

He poured the last of the coffee in the pot out for them. It was almost cold and he had to stir for a long time to make the sugar cube dissolve, after which he stirred for a while more and Agnes could see him looking furtively in the big mirror. She knew he must be able to see the reflection of the girl in the shop from where he was sitting.

'I think I'll tell you a story,' he said.

'If you like,' she said uncertainly.

'I think I'll do that. I think I'll tell you all about Little Land.'

'Have you finished your cocoa?' they could hear Tora asking Ingrid, but there was no answer. 'Oh, you've let it get skin. Don't you want it?'

'Would you like a story?' Konrad asked, and the café was perfectly silent.

'Little Land is in Big Land,' he said. 'It's nestled inside like a nut in its shell or a bright red spot in a pigeon's egg.'

The bell on the door rang and voices were heard. Tora sold them a couple of slices of cake and they finally paid her a few coins and went back out through the door again. Konrad, who had been sitting all the time with his hands around his coffee cup and his back bowed, straightened up and said:

'There are little tiny streets leading to little houses where people are sitting having their cabbage soup with little spoons. There's a little chapel with such tiny bells that when they ring in the holidays they sound like jingle bells on horses and there's a grey sky above all of Little Land, covering it like a cap and making all the noise soft and close.'

When he stopped, the only sounds were Tora and Linnea's distant voices and the regular grinding of a coffee mill.

'In Little Land, where the horse droppings are no bigger than tapioca pearls, the farmers had ploughed their fields for hundreds of years. But then a little railway came, and booms went up and down and tiny trains puffed and little factories appeared. And there was a little social democracy and tiny tiny foremen who shook their fists and wore little bowler hats. When the big country had its

265

general strike Little Land had its own little strike but the little trains kept puffing of course and no damage was done.

Then came the war and the big famine made little tummies ache. The big workers shook their fists and said the revolution was coming and got hit over their heads.

In Little Land nobody mentioned revolution, because their misery was so minor. Then unemployment hit Big Land, and people's misery grew and was relentless. Yes, at the basis of all the progress in the big country was invariable misery. It was the foundation stone on which all the rest was built.

But there was very little unemployment in Little Land and the unemployed were ever so small and submissive. They sat around the cafés talking in their little language. And they said everything would soon be all right again since their land was so little. And so they just sat there looking at their misery and saying: 'Just look at our little misery, it's so small and so submissive.'

He went quiet.

'What happened then?' Agnes asked.

'That was all.'

'Was that all there was?'

'Yes, that was the end.'

'But that wasn't much of a ...'

Konrad put his finger to his lips.

'We'd better be going,' he said.

And they heard footsteps scurrying across the lino and then Ingrid was there in the doorway behind them. Konrad didn't turn around.

'That can't be the story!' she screamed straight at the mirror. He raised his head slowly and looked into the reflection of her little face, slightly skewed.

'That wasn't much of an ending!'

She was sniffling and shouting and suddenly she turned on her heel and slammed the door shut so you could hear the glasses in the shop cupboard rattle, and then the bell above the door jangled and rang as she ran out of the Cosmopolitan. They saw her turn into Store Street without her schoolbag, she'd left it behind, and with the belt on her brown coat flying behind her.

'Good grief!' said Agnes.

'We'd better be going,' said Konrad, happily. 'I'll have to come in tomorrow again. That's all there is to it.'

And he laced his fingers through those of his fiancée again after shaking hands with Tora and saying thank you when she said the coffee was on her, and Tora and Linnea watched them through the window as they walked down the street. Tekla came out as well, shaking her head. Agnes looked like a thin, black thread alongside tall Konrad.

'I'd be surprised if she had as much as half a litre of blood in her,' said Tora.

Two of the telephone operators walked by in light stockings and pretty short skirts, without even glancing in the bakery window. When they'd passed, Tora said: '"Lucky me", as Gustava said about the kiss she didn't get', but with no real conviction.

'Oh, God, here comes Herr Fusspot', said Linnea, running a cloth quickly over one of the tabletops, but the only reason she was surprised was that she'd lost track of the time, what with Konrad having brought his fiancée in.

Herr Fusspot came in every day at four, and had been doing so as long as Tora had had the café. He'd been Lindh the wholesaler's office clerk in the old days when the firm was small, and he was an extremely solitary person with pedantic habits. He had always looked like a young boy, had never grown whiskers or become heavy-set. He still wore a starched collar and cuffs and was so incorrigibly punctual that he stopped on the steps outside the café and checked his pocket watch before going inside.

He wasn't ageing like a normal person, just withering slowly away. His rosy boyish cheeks had grown grey and dry as parchment. Early on, he had always taken a table in the back room where he could sit looking at himself in the mirror. He never spent time with anyone else, but in the mirror he at least got to see a second little fusspot. When the boys from the vocational school took over the back room and smoked him out, Tora gave him one of the white tables in the shop, and every now and then he looked at his reflection in the glass on the cupboard door.

No sooner had Herr Fusspot finished his cocoa and wiped his dry yellow upper lip with his rice paper napkin when Magnhild Lundberg came in, asking for Fröken Åkerlund. She had been to 9 Store Street three times looking for her, and she had an urgent matter to see her about. Did anyone know if this was the time of day she took her walks?

Half an hour later she was back again. Although she was as elegant as ever standing there in the doorway, you could sense she had been scouring the streets all afternoon. Gerda was nowhere to be found. In the end they were both so keyed up that Magnhild Lundberg came over to the counter and placed her hand over Tora's, a strange feeling, and said softly:

'I think I've arranged a position for Fröken Åkerlund.'

'Do sit down and have a cup of coffee,' said Tora. 'Rest your weary bones. The minute Fredrik comes in I'll send him out to look for her.'

'I've got to be going right away, we're having a teachers' meeting this evening. When Fröken Åkerlund comes in, please just ask her to telephone Baroness Fogel at Sjögesta.'

'My heavens,' said Tora.

At which point Magnhild Lundberg became completely unable to go on holding in the news she had been longing to tell all afternoon, so she modulated her resounding voice to something resembling a whisper, and told Tora that the Baroness was looking for a travelling companion and reader for her old brother Jacob who was going to Switzerland for his lungs. But when she had left Tora stood at the counter for quite some time, getting used to the thought that things had gone so far that they were all supposed to be grateful that Gerda Åkerlund was going to have the opportunity to sit at a sanatorium reading to an old Baron who would spit into a bag.

She heard the factory whistle at Swedish Motor and after a while the men passed by on their bicycles in one direction, passing the ones who were out of work going in the other, on their way home from the café at the beach at Lake Hällsjön. They had hung their wet bathing trunks over the handlebars to dry, and they snapped in the wind as the bikers raced along. She imagined the water was starting to get cold despite the lovely late summer weather, but she also knew that at least Fredrik would rather be blue with cold than to show his unemployed face in town during working hours.

The first of the evening guests to appear was Valentin, and she wondered whether he was making himself proper meals at home since he always came in so early. He lived alone and his favorite dinner was a thick slice of Chicago bacon he'd fry and dip in his coffee. He spent his evenings at the café, because he liked being among the young people. He still had a heavy black beard to conceal his hare lip. He'd turn the pages of the local paper slowly, white smoke rings emerging from his pipe and floating up towards the ceiling.

'Want your coffee right away?'

'No hurry.'

She walked back and forth and up and down in circles around him waiting for Fredrik, but it got to be six and then six thirty and in the end Adam came in alone.

269

'Where's Fredrik?'

'Home changing.'

'Why should that take forever? Could you tell if Fröken Åkerlund had been in? In that case I need you to get on your bike and take a spin along Heavenside Lane and around the pond, back by the country road and if you see her tell her to get herself over here fast as lightning.'

'I'm off to the cinema.'

'There's time first. Tell her it's important. But that it's not about Franzon,' she added.

He grumbled as he got Fredrik's old bike out, strapped his trousers to his ankles and swore softly about ruining his suit.

The men who were out of work had started dropping in, and the pipe smoke thickened. Tora could hear the chess timers ticking as she passed through the shop and out the door to peer down the street. Then Franzon came in. He had a resolute look on his face, and Tora was afraid he'd heard the news about Fröken Åkerlund. But he just asked for Adam. She hissed back that he didn't start work for half an hour yet and there was no rush. Besides which he could run the projector himself if it came to that. He had a cup of coffee standing at the counter and told her to put it on his running account. She had heard that he went around bragging that as a matter of principle he never paid any bills until he had no choice in the matter. She didn't feel she could put the squeeze on him because of Adam, and after all he did settle his account once a week: he was a working man.

She stood there watching Franzon drink his coffee, thinking that of all the bloody men she knew he was the very worst and it was beyond belief that, serpent that he was, he had once sat at her kitchen table pouring himself milk from her pitcher and eating crispbread with cold fried herring on it late in the evenings after a performance at the cinema or a night with the dance band. And I even thought he was good for a laugh, she thought.

Twilight fell, the street grew quiet and the café noisier. Adam returned without having found Gerda Åkerlund anywhere and Tora went cold with worry but didn't mention it to him. A little later she caught him in the kitchen with the raspberry essence to his lips, and her hands shot out so hard at his ears he nearly dropped the bottle.

'Have you no sense of shame at all, young man?'

'Good grief, it's only to freshen my breath, mum! A fellow might meet a girl…'

'You can't fool me, I know it's the alcohol you're after. You get out of here now, and leave my essences alone, do you hear?'

Then Fredrik came in wearing a striped shirt with a white collar, his tie neatly knotted and his hair parted, exuding the scent of Vitalis.

'Has Fröken Åkerlund come in yet?' asked Tora.

He shook his head. Tora felt slightly sick by now. She'd been planning to have a coffee, but she couldn't get it down.

'Had supper?'

'Cold herring and fried some potatoes.'

'Where are you off to, then? Isn't it night school tonight?'

'Pictures,' he replied brusquely.

'And for that you needed to get all done up?'

He didn't reply, and when he'd left she looked at the photo from the masquerade party on the mirror in the back room. She stared at the feet in the black shoes with the ankle straps for a long time. There was a second photo as well, of him sitting in his German night class with the teacher and the ten other students, but they were all men. They were sitting under dim light bulbs suspended from way up on the ceiling, pencils to paper. He was clever, especially in maths, but he wasn't bad at German, either.

She looked through the pictures from the amateur drama group and the outings, but she couldn't find a girl who might have been the one in those black shoes in any of them. She was so preoccupied she stopped hearing the din around her and the racket of the piano. She didn't even notice the watchmaker was there until she walked back out into the shop. The lamp hadn't been lit out there, she'd forgotten, and he was sitting waiting in the dusky room.

'I've had one helluva day,' she replied to his slightly convoluted question. 'I've had to tell the confectioner I don't need him any more. And he pretended not to understand. Not to mention that Konrad Eriksson's lost his job in Stockholm and come back with a fiancée in tow. Adam's up to something and Fredrik's started running around. People've been in and out all day, but just look how much of my baked goods are still unsold! Soon I'll have to give the baker her notice as well – I'm selling so little I could perfectly well do the baking myself.'

'That's it,' said the watchmaker. 'Here we stand as life goes on all around us. Everything that happens in the moment seems so important, as if it would have implications for thousands and thousands of years.'

'I just don't know how she'll manage, though. I don't think her plater's well enough to work. But I have to make a decision.'

'And it will, too,' said the watchmaker.

'Will what?'

'Have implications,' he answered.

But she didn't tell him how worried she was about Gerda Åkerlund. She kept that to herself until very late when Magnhild Lundberg turned up outside the window, a big, tired face in the dark night. Tora just shook her head without the watchmaker noticing, and Fröken Lundberg walked right back down the steps.

Magnhild Lundberg went straight from there to the Casino Theater on the other side of the tracks, and asked to see Franzon. But the cinema projectionist – who was Adam Otter – told her he was at the Community Center, where the new cinema was opening. Magnhild made the long trek back again and by the time she was outside the Community Center she was very tired. The beer hall was at one end of the large brick building and the theater at the other. Now she could see it had a new sign on it, CORONA. She couldn't be bothered to look at the poster, and walked right by the little queue of people who all appeared to her to be small and weary and worn, straight up to the box office, where she asked to see Franzon.

'He's upstairs,' the cashier said. 'But I think he's got his hands full just now. Sounded like the lighting wasn't quite in order.'

'Kindly fetch him,' said Magnhild and after a split second's hesitation the cashier left her little booth, and there was total silence in the queue behind Magnhild. It struck her that she couldn't stand here in front of all these people and ask where Gerda was. So she followed the girl up the stairs, a steep flight that turned. On the wall were pictures of actors she'd never heard of.

Franzon approached her through the door to the cinema, pulling his blazer on. She caught a glimpse of the black satin back of his waistcoat as he turned around and shouted something to an electrician on a ladder, and she noticed he was wearing elastic sleeve garters.

'Where's Gerda?' she asked. She didn't realize until afterwards that she should have said 'Fröken Åkerlund', and it annoyed her that she hadn't thought about it.

'Right here,' Franzon replied.

'Let me speak with her.'

'Not just now,' he said, with a quick, somewhat impatient smile. 'We're about to begin. We've got an opening night on our hands.'

He'd finally got his blazer on right. It disturbed her to think of him spending time with Gerda in his shirtsleeves with garters.

'I'll go in then,' she said.

'But of course,' said Franzon. 'Just mention my name at the box office, and there'll be a good seat for you. Enjoy the show.'

As far as she could hear, there was no sarcasm in his voice. He was frazzled but perfectly polite. She went down to the box office, knowing this time that she should go to the end of the line. She felt odd standing there looking at the people in front of her, because they still seemed very short. She decided it had to do with their bearing, that this was the result of unsatisfactory physical education programmes in compulsory school. She read on the poster that the film was called *Madonna in a Pullman*. She had not been to the moving pictures since the phenomenon was quite new, and to her the cinema was watching people's trousers fall down, or seeing men dressed in bowler hats and undershorts fall into the water. It was also shots of heroines with painted lips rolling their eyes in horror as their chests heaved and fell at a wild pace. She had found it absurd. Gerda had tried to get her to come along to *Herr Arne's Hoard*, which she had said was an exceptionally moving and dramatic film. Magnhild hadn't gone.

When it was her turn at the box office she was given a ticket Franzon had organized for her and the cashier insisted that it was on the house. Magnhild didn't like that. She couldn't see Gerda

274

anywhere in the cinema, but she did see that Fru Linell, the seamstress, was in the audience with a young woman called Dagmar Eriksson who was slightly hunchbacked. The two of them tiptoed in as silently as mice in the hayloft at dusk. They sat down and stared straight ahead at the red velvet curtain with its gold and silver application of a leafy branch. Magnhild had to admit to herself that Franzon had done a nice job in decorating this crowded room up a steep flight of stairs. It looked expensively done up.

Now there was a banging and a shuffling from down below, a frightening sound she couldn't identify. But she was sitting with a good view of the staircase and soon, through the open door, she could see a wooden walking frame and a strong, twisted arm. The shuffling continued for a while until a head and a body pulled themselves up, and then struggled with the next step: walker, arm, body. One step at a time. The man was extremely disabled and Magnhild had never seen him before. Her first impulse was to get up and make herself useful, helping him up the stairs in a more dignified, less painful fashion. But she was quick to see she couldn't be of much use. A heavy man with paralyzed legs couldn't be carried.

After a great deal of banging and a slam every time the walker hit the floor he finally made it to his seat, and virtually collapsed into it. Magnhild breathed a sigh of relief and closed her eyes, but the sound of the walker continued for a little while as he worked it closely in by his seat, so that no one would trip over it. They'd obviously been waiting for him to get to his place, because now the lights were dimmed and the room grew silent but for the ticking, until someone coughed. She could hear light footsteps very clearly down there, and then the curtain parted with a swish. The piano began to play and soon the first pale shot flickered on the screen. There was a castle-like building against a sky of rushing clouds, with the words MADONNA IN A PULLMAN right across it all. The pianist was playing the *Moonlight Sonata*.

Magnhild was trying to be attentive in case Gerda came in at some point after it had begun, so she wasn't devoting much attention to the story. A young man was courting a young woman, they would meet in gazebos and groves near the castle, and the pianist alternated between *Whispering Birches* and *The Song of Hiawatha*. She recognized the pieces perfectly. Evidently the young woman's father was skeptical towards her beau, so they had to meet in secret. There was a strict housekeeper too, and the moment she appeared the music changed to *So oft ich meine Tabakspfeife*. She wondered how anyone had ever come up with the idea of playing just that, allowing at the same time that if you weren't familiar with Bach – and surely the audience wasn't – the theme was a pretty well-chosen representation of the strict but yet good-hearted person of the housekeeper.

Magnhild lost the story line again, until the girl's father mounted his horse. Now the music was *The Happy Peasant* and while it was utterly ridiculous she still couldn't help but wonder where the pianist had picked up this repertoire. She'd been expecting beer hall music. Now they were riding through the rough forest – *Der dreistige Reiter* – and then the horse bolted! The old man was hanging on to the mane for dear life, halfway out of the saddle, it couldn't end well – *Sturmgalopp*! Ah, the betrothed approached. How very courageous! Just look how the old man was hanging – perhaps his back was broken? The fiancé caught at and grabbed the horse by the harness. Relief, the father wasn't hurt after all. Amazing, really, what they could depict. How ever did they do it? There was no doubt that they had to be good equestrians. Magnhild had to remove her gloves, her hands had grown quite hot.

Now there was a scene by the hearth, with a game of cards. The young woman was pouring tea. And look, the young man was part of the family circle. He'd been accepted.

Now they were obviously departing on their honeymoon. Things happen fast and some parts of the story get skipped. Is it really possible that all these silent people sitting in the dark comprehend these astonishing contractions and lightning-fast shifts? It was all Magnhild could do to keep up, at any rate, and she had begun to wonder whether this art form wasn't above the heads of its admirers. In fact they looked like worshippers when she turned around and saw their upturned faces in the pale light from the screen. But they certainly looked far from confused or bewildered. They were following better than she was. That gave her a very strange feeling, one she hadn't had since she was a child, one she was unable to name.

Oh, the honeymoon was, of course, all sweetness and light, flowers and happines — train journeys, cruises, romance and gorgeous outfits. Apparently they were in Rome — and *Wien bleibt Wien* and the barcarole from the *Adventures of Hoffmann*, so they must be in Venice now. Yes, the music did explain a lot of things. Gold and silver. He was a very wealthy man. Why hadn't he told her? Well, of course he wanted her to love him for what he was first, the text on the screen even said so. My, how dreadfully naïve.

Still, it was nice that the girl made a good match. There was something fragile about her. Those black eyes, her long bangs. Was that really the way they were wearing their hair these days? It would have been interesting to see how it was cut at the back — ugh, people looked like they had brooms instead of hair when they cut it short at the back. But she wore fur collars in almost every scene, or lacy negligées.

Happiness, happiness. Magnhild almost missed the important

clue. The music brought her attention back. He started coming home late; almost every night, too. She lay there in the dark, which isn't actually very dark at all, worrying and waiting.

Suddenly Magnhild had the feeing Gerda was there, quite nearby. But where? She couldn't see any new faces, only the ones that had been there all the time, and above their heads the projector buzzed behind the little window, emitting a strong, bright ray of light. The ray expanded, growing into a wider and wider river until it hit the screen and was transformed into his tired, worried face where he stood, removing his tailcoat. Look, there he was in his shirtsleeves, if you don't mind. What intimate images. I hope it doesn't get any worse, Magnhild thought. Because here she sat, and had no choice but to stay to the finish. She'd be the laughingstock of the teaching staff if this got out.

It turned out he had gambling debts and he started bringing questionable types home. That was it, he was quite simply a gambler. Oh my Lord, the poor young thing, you couldn't help but feel sorry for her. And at the same time, she had her HOPES. Hopes? Yes, that was what it said, and he didn't seem to be evil through and through when he put his head in her lap and looked up into her eyes, happy in spite of everything. Oh, my, hopes. I dare say, thought Magnhild. What wouldn't they think of next? And then he promised her he'd never go near a casino again.

Completely idiotic ending, Magnhild thought. But as she was walking towards the exit, involuntarily squeezed in amongst all these soft-spoken people, she got her comeuppance when she realized she had only seen half the film. This seemed to be some kind of interval. But where were you supposed to spend it? On the street, with the reeling people who'd been thrown out of the beer hall? Probably.

Magnhild, however, intended to find Gerda now. She knew she

was there. Franzon had said so, and although he could very well have been making it up, Magnhild sensed Gerda's presence, unequivocally and strongly. Then she caught sight of the piano. It was all the way down by the stage. During the performance there had only been one little light, directed at the music. Now there was no one there.

She walked past all the rows of seats and down to the stage, and stood in front of the black piano that had sounded well-tuned and not the least bit clanking as she had imagined a cinema piano to be. Now she was alone in the room, which was warm with human breath and with the heat from the strong light of the projector. There was a whole pile of sheet music on top of the piano and she lifted up the first piece. The pianist had written her name on the cover in a strong, even hand.

'I didn't do well at all,' said Gerda. 'I'm quite ashamed of myself, I couldn't do it as I'd planned. There were several times I just couldn't keep up. Especially at the beginning. *Whispering Birches* and *Hiawatha* were such trivial choices – but I still kept getting lost.'

'You did splendidly,' said Franzon. 'Just the right effects. Sensitive. Powerful. Here's your coffee.'

She felt as if she was alone with him in all the world, and she perceived the odours of dust and newly-sawn lumber behind stage. Everything was so clear, so sharp.

'My hands are still trembling. Is there anyone out there who knows me?'

'Not a soul,' said Franzon. 'And no one can see you. Not that it matters.'

Cinema had gone literary as a drama form, he said. It was no longer vulgar spectacle, but rather literature, drama — and music! At the Rialto in Stockholm they had a fourteen-man orchestra for one opening. 'You can just relax and play, Gerda.'

She still wasn't as convinced as he was.

When she went back into the darkness she was almost more nervous than she had been during the first half. She sensed the presence of the audience in the hot room, their coughs and telegraphic whispers. But she couldn't see them. There were all kinds of difficult passages in the second act, lots of fast parts where she had to switch tempo. She pulled the string that lit the little yellow lamp, and at the very same moment the projector began to buzz and the first images burst onto the screen.

They had a baby now and were living in poverty in New York. He swore to her he'd stopped gambling, but before we knew it they were back in Nice again – new outfits, the baby in lace. Partying. Gerda wished she could have been all fourteen of the musicians at the Stockholm Rialto. Sparkling jewellery and women whose black eyes gleamed behind their fans. Alarm! The rubies are missing. Enter the police to the tune of Schubert's *Marche Militaire*.

They are running away – he's the one who stole the rubies, of course. They're aboard a train but he can't travel in the same Pullman as the child and herself, because the police are after him. She has to remain in the company of a loquacious woman whose mouth is in constant motion, like an onion-chopper. The police chase her husband along the roofs of the train carriages. Someone pulls the emergency brake, there are sparks from the wheels, and the whistle emits a heavy puff of vertical steam.

Is he dead? She doesn't know. Gerda plays the *Raindrop Prelude* as rain streams down the compartment window. The young woman can be seen looking out through the window as her husband is carried off on a stretcher. She's holding the baby in her arms.

It ends at the home of her father – clouds rushing across the sky over the castle, occasional glimpses of the moon. Gerda plays the *Moonlight Sonata*. She's left the baby in a basket on the doorstep, the old housekeeper finds it. *So oft ich meine Tabakspfeife.*

The father stumbles out in the rain, making his way to the old gazebo, its window panes gleaming in the moonlight. Gerda goes on pounding away at the *Moonlight Sonata*. Looking in through the window, he sees a small, pale hand dangling. There's a heavy black pistol below it.

Outside, the housekeeper picks up the baby and smiles. In the gazebo the father kneels alongside the corpse. As the last tones of the *Moonlight Sonata* fade, the castle vanishes into the clouds, which are about to consume the moon as well. Gerda lifts her fingers quickly from the keyboard and runs out of the room.

'Well done!' says Franzon. 'But you needn't be in such a rush. We won't raise the house lights until you've come out.'

'I didn't get the gunshot right. I'm sure I ruined the whole scene for them!'

'Oh Lord, no. There's not a dry eye.'

'Well, tomorrow I'll do better,' said Gerda. 'I'm sure I'll get the shot right tomorrow.'

'Magnhild Lundberg's waiting for you outside,' he answered.

A farmer in Närke hired a young girl to be his serving maid as soon as she had been confirmed. She was an orphan, and her name was Linnea Holm. When she was eighteen, she left the farm and went to Örebro to work for a cobbler's family. One Saturday she met the farmer at the market and asked him if he'd like to come around for a cup of coffee. She was proud of the home of the almost wealthy shoemaker, and wanted to show him the kitchen where she worked and the well-furnished rooms. They were alone.

She went to the police station the very same day to report his having raped her. The officers on duty took no pains to conceal their scorn for her plight. They asked: 'Did you make him another cup of coffee afterwards?'

'That's not how it was,' said Linnea Holm.

'You were a foolish girl to invite him in,' said the policeman.

'He was like a father to me,' she answered.

She showed them the bruises from his fists and they said:

'Angry cats get scratched back.'

No charges were pressed, but for some time her police report made his life a bit difficult. He had a wife and three children. Linnea got a job in a dinner café where people went out of their way to get a peek at her.

'She looks quite the know-it-all, that girl,' they said.

'Keep your hands off that one,' they said, too. 'She'll report you for rape afterwards.'

She had quite a stern face with regular features and black hair.

Some people thought she looked odd, that there was something different about her.

'But a hole's a hole,' they said.

She ended up working for Tora Otter at the Cosmopolitan, but it wasn't far to Örebro and after a couple of weeks everybody knew who she was and what had happened. It wasn't quite the same thing at the Cosmopolitan, though, since it wasn't a dinner café that served spirits. It wasn't a place where men who had had a few too many drinks sat around, but a place where half-grown young men came in after school or work. Although she undoubtedly satisfied all their hottest, most secret desires they hardly dared say a word to her of any but the most ordinary everyday kind.

The same evening Gerda Åkerlund played at the Corona Cinema for the first time, a man from Örebro came into the Cosmopolitan. He greeted Linnea as if they were old friends, but she just nodded curtly and asked what he'd like. While he had his coffee she walked around the other tables emptying the ashtrays, and he suddenly began, loud and clear, to narrate the old story about the girl who told the court: 'First he raped me and then we had coffee and then he raped me again.'

Everyone was quite embarrassed on account of Linnea's being in the room but most people laughed. The man turned out to be a real entertaining type, and he went on telling jokes and stories all evening, tales of sewing machine salesmen and wily crofters. And every time Linnea carried a tray into the room, he would shout:

'Have you heard this one, fellas?'

Then he'd start again on the story about the girl who is describing her rape in court and says, first he raped me and then we had coffee and then he raped me again. Lots of people were embarrassed but he was also so irresistibly funny and lewd you just had to laugh. He'd break off right in the middle of whatever anecdote he was recounting to tell that old familiar joke the minute Linnea appeared. The men were now so wound up they were laughing at him in spite of themselves, wondering how far he could go. The thought crossed one or two of their minds that they might interrupt but before they managed to figure out what to say he'd reached the punch line again. By this time it had boiled down to a short refrain: first he raped me and then we had coffee and then he raped me again. The men who were getting annoyed started leaving the café instead, and while they were settling their bills, Linnea was in the room with them for quite a while. The man held his whole harangue again then, letting his voice glide up into a feminine falsetto, which dissolved the youngest boys altogether. They were laughing so the tears were running down their cheeks, almost doubled up over the tabletops. Linnea looked rigid and inaccessible. She clearly had no intention of letting on she'd heard a thing.

The person who was most visibly upset by the tension and the peculiar atmosphere in the café seemed to be Tekla. She stayed back in the bakery, except for the occasional foray into the shop to fill up the trays. By the end she was meandering back and forth for no real reason, mumbling to herself as if she wanted to say something. Tora was busy in the bakery and extremely preoccupied with thoughts of Gerda Åkerlund. She hadn't noticed what was going on in the café at all. By the time Tekla had made up her mind to tell her, she'd sneaked away to Store Street to see whether Fröken Åkerlund had come back.

Now the man from Örebro and four young men were the only customers left in the café. His voice was beginning to sound a bit desolate, and their somewhat hollow laughter was less frequent. Finally they asked for their bills, and Linnea gave the bill last of all to the man she knew. He tried to give her quite a substantial tip, but

284

she refused all but the payment for his coffee when he started counting it out into her hand. His back pocket was chock full of coins, which he now lined up on the table. It took quite a while, and the boys were laughing nervously and making their way towards the door, because Tora Otter had come back; they'd seen her walk in and go into the kitchen.

'Lads, have you heard this one?' the man asked, reaching an arm around their shoulders. As they were opening the door and trying to get him out as well, Tekla heard him saying, for the last time, the words that had now lost all meaning. 'First he raped me and then we had coffee and then he raped me again,' he ranted. She leaned her weight on the counter, feeling faint. Linnea was in the back room clearing the tables, but she wouldn't touch the money he'd left.

Tekla walked into the room and gathered up all the coins, but once she had them in her hands she didn't know what to do with them. In the end she poured them into a pewter vase on top of the cupboard. It was a sports prize Fredrik Otter had won. The coins rattled down to the bottom of the vase, and Linnea looked at it.

'You just pay no attention to that man's words,' said Tekla abruptly, rushing over to her and taking her by the arm. Linnea was astonished to be touched. She reacted almost like a dog who gets stroked from behind, and for the first time all evening her eyes gleamed with hate. Tekla began to cry. She was an old woman and wept silently, wiping her tears with a bunched-up handkerchief before they could run down her cheeks.

'Oh, oh, oh,' she moaned softly.

'Hush,' said Linnea. 'I don't want Tora to hear.'

So together they cleared the last of the cups onto a tray, first pouring all the coffee dregs into a jug. Linnea took a rag and wiped all the cigarette stubs, ashes, matches and crumbled sugar cubes down into the jug as well. Tekla wiped the tabletops. She never stopped mumbling, sounding more and more defiant. After some time, she was speaking loud enough to be heard:

'You never did the wrong thing. You never did.'

Linnea looked right at her. It was the first time she let on that she had heard what was being said all evening except when Tekla had touched her and she had recoiled instinctively. Now she went back into the bakery and put on a pot of coffee for them. Tora had been counting the cash in the till, and Linnea asked her whether she'd like a cup as well. But she'd been drinking coffee off and on all day, and just shook her head and went on writing up the accounts in a brown marbelized ledger.

Linnea set cups on one of the tables in front of the mirror, and then she collapsed into the leather armchair, making the springs resonate long and loud. She took off her shoes and gently massaged her legs, from the ankles up the calves.

'Sometimes I've wondered whether you felt you did the wrong thing by reporting that man,' said Tekla, inhaling the coffee right out of her saucer without looking Linnea in the eye. 'I have. You needn't answer me, I think I know anyway. Since it didn't lead anywhere. He was never brought to trial or anything. I'm sure you've thought a lot about it. You've certainly had plenty of suffering for having reported him and I imagine you think you'd have been better off not to.'

Linnea just sat there stirring her coffee. Then she sighed deeply and almost looked like she was laughing. Tekla was a bit frightened by the look on her face.

'It hardly matters after all this time,' said Linnea.

'That's not true. You did a good thing by reporting him, I can tell you that.'

She couldn't look at Linnea as she went on.

286

'Although it's a long time ago now, when I waited tables at the railway restaurant there was a man who was so vile I wouldn't have touched him with a barge pole. But he had something in mind for me and when he didn't get it for the asking it's not hard to figure what he did. Well, I wouldn't have dared to report him or even cry on anybody's shoulder. Who would've believed me? I don't deny us girls used to have a bit of fun now and then. We'd run around with the railway crew and we were young and carefree of course. So who would've believed me? He didn't look any diffcrent than the other fellows, either. It was just that he was so vile. Still, I'll never forget it as long as I live. So you did the right thing in reporting him, in any case, I just want you to know. It's much worse to have to live with something all by yourself because you never forget it and afterwards you feel as if you're worth less than the air you breathe.'

'So what good do you think it's done me to report him, then?' Linnea asked roughly.

'I don't know,' said Tekla, and then she started to weep hard, overturning her cup as she leaned down on the tabletop. Linnea mopped up the spilt coffee carefully all around her arms and hands and patted her back, pleading with her to calm down, but it took a long time before the sobs stopped, for they were deep and painful.

'Look at me, foolish old woman,' she finally said, raising her head. She took the damp, bunched up handkerchief from her apron pocket and wiped her cheeks.

'That man from Örebro with all his talk just got me so hot and bothered,' she said.

'Well, he'll never be back,' said Linnea. 'He was in town looking for work, but he won't get a job here. Not that pile of shit.'

'Nobody wants him,' said Tekla. 'Old windbag. We'll never see him again.'

'Did you notice it was fresh coffee?'

'Was it?'

'You just weep and moan,' said Linnea. 'I make you a fresh pot of coffee and you never even notice.'

'You know what?' said Tekla. 'You should've spit in his coffee.'

'You're right, I should have. I even thought about it. But just think if it had ended up in somebody else's cup!'

'I honestly thought this day would never end,' said Tekla when she'd finished the washing up and hung the wet tea towels over the stove. She put on her little black hat, that had been battered about since long ago when it was once quite new, and now looked like somebody's old crushed bonnet.

'You really should get yourself a new one, you know,' said Linnea, elbowing her gently in the side. They both started to laugh.

'I do believe I'll do that,' said Tekla.

'What're you girls laughing at?' Tora asked from back in the bakery.

'Tekla's hat. She's going to get a new one.'

'You give me your old one, then, so I'll have something to shine up the stove with.'

They started laughing again. Then they said good night to Tora.

'Yes, good night girls. I'll soon be off myself.'

When she heard the door close behind them she felt lonely. She wondered why they'd been sitting in the back room having coffee all by themselves. Whenever she felt lonely she thought she must be mad. She was surrounded by people all day.

She was much calmer now that it was late. The last time she'd gone home she'd been able to tell from the light in the crack under Gerda Åkerlund's door that she was home. She wondered whether

Fredrik was back yet. Then she wondered once more why they'd shut themselves up in the back room and what they'd been talking about, old worn-out Tekla with her tired feet and young, stately Linnea with her black hair.

She shut the ledger. There wasn't much point in wondering how the café was doing, it was so complicated. The marketplace was another thing. There, she knew exactly how much she spent and how much she could make on it. The café's books had so many debits but only one source of credit: people who came in for coffee or to buy a bag of buns.

She shut the ledger. There wasn't much point in wondering how the café was doing, it was so complicated. The marketplace was another thing. There, she knew exactly how much she spent and how much she could make on it. The café's books had so many debits but only one source of credit: people who came in for coffee or to buy a bag of buns.

She put the brown ledger away where it belonged, in the cupboard next to the service from the Hotel de Winther and pub the cash box back under the counter. Then she walked through the rooms turning out the lights one by one, and the dark rooms went dark. From Hovlunda Road the vague grey light of a new street lamp shone in through the net curtains, and the window threw a black cross shadow across the floor. She turned the key in the lock on the front door twice around, and stood there for a few moments, looking out. But she could hear neither footsteps in the gravel nor voices.

The silence outside gave her the feeling that everything she could see outside the window was very far away, that the garden of the upholsterer's widow she could discern behind the street lamp was in a distant country. Suddenly she wished for a shower so the rain would patter on the tarpaper roof over there, showing her that it wasn't so far away after all. The next thought to come to mind was that the last hour, sitting there with the accounts, must have made her very tired. She would go home to bed. But first she'd have a piece of bread with cold herring on it and a glass of milk.

She put on her coat and hat in the dark kitchen, irritated as always over the fact that the light switch was in such a silly place, and that she couldn't turn out the light as she was walking out the door. Then she sniffed the air to be sure there would be no scent of ashes or of dirty dishrag when the baker arrived. The last thing she did before leaving the Cosmopolitan was to hide the key in the creepers above the rain pipe on the back porch.

Tora Otter sat chatting with Rickard and Stella Lans in the shade by the saddle maker's house as the yellow cream in the jug slowly developed skin. The coffee table was right up against the wall because the sun was so high there was very little shade. When Ingrid turned around to look at them they looked as if they were sleeping sitting upright. Fredrik and Jenny had gone off by themselves. She thought they must be in the house hugging and kissing in spite of the heat.

It was the second Sunday in July 1925, and Ingrid Eriksson walked alone through the village out by the ridge. The air was hot as bacon fat over the fields, and sizzling with the descant music of horseflies and blackflies. The sun reflected, gleaming off the windowpanes she passed. The houses were ranged along the country road, and she still knew who lived in most of them. If she walked right along the ditch at the edge of the road she could look into the closed rooms. Sticky yellow spirals covered with flies were hanging from the ceilings. Some flies were still struggling. On a settee under a window a man was lying with a newspaper over his face. He'd done about half the Sunday crossword with an aniline pen, which was foolish because he wouldn't be able to rub anything out. She was so close she could read the clues: 'What rings mean happiness?'

Jenny and Fredrik were engaged. Dagmar had said they weren't really cousins, as Rickard Lans was actually Tora's uncle, despite their being the same age. Once you were engaged it was all right to go off and be alone together, nobody said anything. If cousins got married their children might be deformed and end up in a home.

Here the road rose steeply up the edge of the ridge and then vanished down in the direction of the lake out by Moth Shack. It then led to the blacksmith's. She'd been there once when she was little, on a day as hot as this. He'd ordered something really costly from Rickard Lans, a harness of soft calfskin. But the measurements were peculiar, Rickard had said. He made it anyway. The smith said it was for an unruly calf. When he came to collect it Rickard had said it wasn't ready although she knew it was folded up on top of the cupboard. So she insisted on going along when Rickard finally decided to take it over there. 'I'll need to go in alone,' he said.

The smith wasn't at home. Had Rickard known? It was silent as the grave out in the yard and also in the barn where the blackflies only had one single newborn calf to torture. Rickard shouted 'Anybody home?' in through the open door but there was no reply. He told Ingrid to sit down and wait for him on the millstone down by the bridge while he went in. But she was quick to run round the back of the house and climb up on a bench to get a glimpse through the kitchen window. There were no white curtains like Stella Lans had and no windowsills, either. Flies were wading in the bottom of a coffee cup.

A woman was tied to an iron stake next to the stove with a home made rope halter. She was chewing and chewing at it. Her hair wasn't in a knot at the nape of her neck like other women's. Her hands moved back and forth between the pots on the stove and a worn tea towel.

Ingrid saw Rickard Lans' face when he stepped into the shadows, a pale grey splotch by the door. The woman spun around so she had her back to him. He tried to move around to her other side, but she just kept twisting and turning, and in the end she'd wound the rope all around herself. Rickard made his way backwards towards the door.

When he came out the calfskin harness was still under his arm. They walked down to the village, and Ingrid found it difficult to keep pace with him. Everyone in Roos' shop gathered around him when he phoned the asylum in Nyköping and told them to come and get the smith's wife. After a while the smith came too, from the tavern. When he heard they were coming to get her he said he wanted to keep her at home. 'She'll do for my needs,' he said.

The women who were kept at Saint Anna's in Nyköping had gone mad from unrequited love; the men there couldn't stop puzzling over God, or thought they must be the Emperor. When Ingrid was eight years old, her brother Konrad thought he was going mad. Personally, she never thought she would. She wondered how it felt for the smith's wife, being there with all those other women. She certainly hadn't been abandoned by her betrothed.

Once a madwoman had tried to stab saddle maker Löfgren with a set of stocking knitting needles. Luckily, one of his brace straps was broken, though, so he had a button suspended in the middle of his back. It had kept the knitting needles from piercing him. From that day on he always kept that button with him. It was a yellow one with four holes, and he kept it under the cover of his pocket watch.

'The needles knit, a button hit,' she rhymed, running up the step to the Good Templars' building. It was completely deserted, with a notice posted on the door saying that the next meeting would be 21 April. Those were the days. When she was little there was nothing she would not have done for a part in the plays Stella Lans arranged for the Templars. She'd collected bottles to make money on the deposits, and walked all the way out to Larsson's croft and back to borrow a cradle they needed for a prop. He'd had fourteen children, but the spa manager said it wasn't as bad as it sounded since he didn't have to pay for their schooling.

When she peered into the dusky room she could see the scenery that was in there now: weeping birches and a blue lake. When they'd put on 'Payday' they covered over the birches. The scene was in the home of a drinker. His wife sat by the cradle Ingrid had collected, looking at her baby. Three other people were sitting on the floor surrounded by bottles, but they hadn't let Ingrid play one of those parts, because they didn't think she'd be able to sit still.

A dog barked in the distance and there was the screech of wagon wheels on gravel. The whole place was so quiet she could hear the the swishing tail of the mare whisper to the muzzle of the foal. They were in the meadow behind the Bethania Chapel. A handsome walking stick was lying by the roadside. Somebody'd carved off the bark in a spiral pattern, and she forgot all about being a big girl now who'd been confirmed. She took up the walking stick and bashed the overbloomed wild chervil with it. There were bicycles outside the chapel that had fallen into a heap on top of one another. She played the spokes of the wheels with her walking stick, making a singing, clattering sound. Then she heard a buzzing, panting noise coming from the window that they'd opened despite the horseflies and gadflies. The organ started up and the singing began, one of the voices so high-pitched and carrying so well she could make out every single word:

> Shepherd's flock and friends of Zion
> Little brood now wandering back
> Towards the pearly gates of heaven
> Trudge along the thorny track.

Then Vera came. She appeared suddenly, in a cotton dress she'd just about outgrown, the kind most people had for everyday, and rubber soled shoes. That was how she'd been able to creep up so quietly Ingrid hadn't heard her coming.

'Remember me?' she asked.

She came from a croft on the other side of the ridge. She'd had plaits when she was smaller. Now she had short hair, cut off straight, with a long hairclip on one side. Ingrid didn't know what to say to her.

'Been confirmed yet?' Vera asked, and when Ingrid just nodded, she said:

'Not me. Next year.'

Dagmar had made a dress for Ingrid when she was confirmed, but she'd been ashamed of her hat. It was black oilcloth. Typical of Tora to buy a weird hat like that just because it was cheap. Ingeborg was probably supposed to buy her hat, really, but they never seemed to get themselves in order about who was to buy Ingrid's things or darn her stockings. Not mamma, anyway. Oilcloth hat. Lucky Vera didn't know.

> Children of Salem, parish of our Lord
> Little boat and mangy hoard
> Stranger in the world so wide
> Open to violence from all sides.

'Today is Mission Sunday,' said the parson. Behind the windows the adults were having prayer meetings, or napping or sitting gossiping about the advantages of putting in new double flooring. There were vases of dried flowers, paled by the sun, and outside there were peonies, buzzing with the insects that had drilled down to their cores. Betrothed couples found a quiet spot.

Jenny and Fredrik couldn't get married because they didn't have the money. Nobody did. They'd have to wait a while, the older people said. But Konrad and Agnes, they'd got married anyway.

Now they walked past the little houses where Ulla and Lotta had lived. They were so old the window panes had bubbles in them. They'd been the cleaning ladies at the baths. They had a little hand cart they pulled home behind them every evening, and they always had to shove and heave to get it over the doorsill. When they died, Ulla first and Lotta after, all the things they had collected in the hand cart and carried home from the baths during their long lives were gathered up and tossed into the ravine below the ridge. The schoolmaster had said it was an ice-age gorge.

Ingrid and Vera had run to the ravine with the daughters of shopkeeper Roos. To begin with they had just lain at the edge of the ravine looking, but later they'd climbed down and sifted through the stuff. There were artificial flowers, fans, broken heels, combs and ribbons. There were hundreds of medicine bottles with hardly anything in them. Rickard Lans had brought two men and filled the ravine.

Now they had walked all the way to the telephone operator's, with withered birches left from midsummer on the doorstep. There was no breeze at all. An anthill was buzzing, and the sharp, venomous smell pierced the air. When Ingrid swatted at a fly that had bit her on the arm, she saw it had left a little drop of blood. That was when she heard the sound of water running under the stones.

Konrad said that under the earth there was a landscape of water with rivers, bubbling brooks and lakes. It was like the surface of the earth and followed its rises and hollows but like the image in a mirror. Konrad said there were people whose lives were an inverse mirror image of everyone else's lives, and he claimed they had untested powers.

Now the path descended to the park surrounding the empty spa. It was cool down here under the trees, and the vegetation was sparse and pale. You could see brown earth between the roots of the trees. In the flower beds around the pavilions and gazebos thistly horse-tails had shot up, suffocating all other life. The door to the Geatish Spring meeting hall was ajar and the girls stepped inside, listening to the echoes of the dripping water. But Ingrid couldn't understand why the roof was dripping on a hot day like this. An iron scoop, almost too rusty to hold water, was hanging from a chain down into the brownish water that smelt of iron. Once upon a time this had been an elegant, high-class establishment, or at least intended to be one. She recalled herself and the Roos girls selling ginger biscuits in the park by the baths to women dressed in white who looked sidelong at one another and then fed the biscuits to their dogs.

'Thank you, sweetheart,' they had said.

There had been less well-to-do people in the simpler rooms and nearby boarding houses, and graceful women, with swaying buttocks and hands heavy with rings, hoping to be cured of secret ailments. These women would have been happy for someone to talk to and to kiss, but you had to keep your distance. The women who worked in the bathhouse had stories to tell about their bodies, both upper and lower, when they gossiped over coffee. But their own clean hands and swollen skin never caught any of these dangers, despite the fact that they touched them every day.

Vera was walking along kicking at the gravel and Ingrid didn't really know what to talk about. Finally Vera asked:

'Are you going into domestic service now you've been confirmed?'

She wasn't really sure. It was summer now and so hot. She didn't really have the energy to talk about it.

'I'm going as soon as I've done my catechism. I've got a brother in Stockholm,' said Vera.

'You do?'

'He's a soldier in the Göta Guard.'

After that Vera really didn't know what to say, either. She'd blown her trump card now that she'd produced her brother, the royal guard.

'I've got a brother who's married,' said Ingrid. 'They live above the Casino Theater and run the boxing ring for a man called Franzon who owns the building. They're gonna have a table-tennis room and a billiards salon as well.'

Konrad had a one-bedroom flat but they rented out the bedroom to the office of the Communist Party though she didn't tell that to Vera who was standing there poking the toe of her canvas shoe in the gravel. They heard voices from the road and spotted flashes of red and yellow between the trees. Then they saw it was the Roos sisters walking along, with a little girl between them. A little while later all five of them were walking side by side along the road down towards the spa restaurant. When they passed the Geatish Spring's Lodge again they turned back and walked the same stretch once more so as to stay in the shade under the trees. The shopkeeper's daughters were wearing their folk costumes and were very hot in the red woollen skirts that went all the way down to their ankles, with hand-knitted green stockings under.

The Roos sisters were two peas in a pod. They were sturdy young women under their folk costumes, the skirts of which fell pleated from just below the bosom, where they were clipped to embroidered gold satin vests. The shopkeeper didn't want his daughters following the fashion and cutting their hair short. The younger sister had thick, blonde hair with a whole system of plaits and ringlets hanging around her ears and down her neck.

'Were those your confirmation shoes?' one of the sisters asked, and Ingrid felt like saying no but didn't dare. They'd been bought with room to grow in, and the tip of the toe folded with her every step. They didn't talk very much. The sisters busied themselves with the younger girl, who was visiting them from Stockholm. They made sure her white straw hat with the anchor on the brim was straight, and pulled on the satin bands when they started to curl.

'There's Anna,' one of them said. 'She's waiting around for Ivar but he's sitting with Father in the study. Shall we tell her?'

She was, of course, avoiding them. There was nothing strange about that, if she was waiting for her fiancé.

Valborg Roos tried to catch up with her, and was soon breathless from exertion. Her red wool skirt was snapping around her legs.

'He's with Father,' she called, at which Anna turned around. When they got to the telephone operator's, she could see for herself. Roos the shopkeeper was walking out of the house with Ivar behind him. They'd removed their suit coats and were in waistcoats and shirtsleeves. The dead birches rattled when they passed. A serving girl with a tray walked behind them. Glasses were clanking against one another, and they vanished into the arbour.

'I suppose they'll be there for a while,' said Valborg. 'Too bad for you, hanging around waiting.'

'I'm not,' said Anna. 'I'm simply out for a stroll.'

She was all dressed up, in shiny silk stockings that made her legs look at bit fatter than they were. They all looked at her legs and at the silver chain around her neck, her wristwatch and her ring, gifts from her betrothed. He'd been made a sales representative and was doing quite well, mostly sewing machines but parts for crystal radio receivers as well.

'What will you do once you've been confirmed?' Anna asked. She was twisting her ring, and Gunhild Roos couldn't take her eyes off it.

'Time will tell,' said Valborg.

'The minute I'm confirmed I'm going into service,' said Vera. 'In Stockholm.'

'How can you even imagine anybody there'd want you in their service?' Valborg said, after which she whispered something in her sister's ear and they giggled. Ingrid guessed it was about the way Vera's dress smelled of the cowshed. Not very strongly, but still. She was afraid they were going to ask her what she planned to do after confirmation. She couldn't imagine a time after this summer. It was perfectly empty.

'Papa wants us to have an education,' said Valborg Roos.

There was money for them to become nurses or sewing teachers if they wished. They had done the embroidery on their gold satin vests and the handkerchiefs of their folk costumes themselves. But it was silly to train for a profession when you were only going to get married in the end. They didn't want to say that when Anna was listening, though. She was eighteen and had never had to go to work in a family. She had stayed at home until Ivar came along and now she was just waiting. She didn't really seem to be present, and Ingrid thought she probably just wished that she and Ivar could go off by themselves for a while. Despite the heat. At which point Fanny, the little girl from Stockholm, said what everybody was thinking. Though she turned it round backwards.

'I'm not ever getting married, not ever!'

'Oh, you're only twelve.'

Valborg Roos put her hands on her shoulders and then straightened her hat.

'Why wouldn't you want to get married?' she asked. But Fanny wouldn't answer.

'There's plenty of time for you to change your mind. You don't want to end up an old maid, do you?'

Well, no, but she didn't want to get married, either. 'Cause of you-know-what. They looked at Anna but she was just staring straight ahead, appearing lethargic in the heat.

'You-know-what?'

'Yes, *you* know *what*!'

'And what do *you* know about all that?' asked Valborg, as both she and her sister looked at Anna once more and tried to suppress their giggles. But Fanny who was from Stockholm and only twelve years old just babbled on about what she used to think happened to people once they were married when she was little. The pastor said or did something that made the seeds start to grow. The Roos sisters had to hold tightly onto one another and cover their mouths with their hankies.

'But what about people who didn't get married?' asked Vera. 'The ones who had babies anyway? What did you think they did?'

'Aw, they got 'em for their sinful ways.'

Now, however, she knew for certain that the pastor had nothing at all to do with you-know-what. No, she was never getting married in all her life! The Roos sisters were ever so red in the face and pretending to cough.

'Though maybe the woman doesn't even notice,' said Fanny. 'Maybe it's like being put to sleep.'

Flies were crawling up Anna's silk stockings. She swatted at them and got an ugly blood stain on the silk. She sat on the steps of one the pavilions and rubbed at her stocking with a rolled-up hankie she wetted by spitting on it. Everyone but Fanny watched.

'Do you know what the man does?' she asked.

'Asch,' said Vera. 'Nothing to get all riled up about. It's just what the animals do. You've seen them, haven't you?'

Her blush went all the way down her neck, and Anna looked away. Ingrid got a sudden mental image of a pointed, dripping dog penis and felt quite squeamish. She tried to rub the picture out of her mind, but didn't succeed. It came back and she felt like she was going to throw up. Valborg Roos grabbed Vera by the upper arm and said:

'What on earth are you saying. Do you even know?'

'What's wrong?' asked Vera.

'Are you saying people are like animals?'

'No, that's not what I meant. But in a way it's the same thing.'

Valborg slapped her.

'Oh, so people are like animals, are they? Do they do it like the animals? You take that back!'

And Fanny started to cry.

'Now she's crying! You hear that, you disgusting creature? You made her cry!'

'You take it all back right now,' said Gunhild.

Vera's hand was to her cheek. Gunhild grabbed her arm, prying her hand from her cheek, and slapped her again.

'Give me that walking stick,' said Valborg, taking Ingrid's striped stick. She was doing her best not to see that pointy, dripping thing on a dog in her mind's eye, and she covered her face with her hands. Out of the hot air around her rose the sound of footsteps stumbling and of pushing on the gravel and Anna's voice:

'Girls! Remember, you've been confirmed now. What on earth are you doing?'

When Ingrid looked up she saw that Anna had turned around and was walking back towards the village. Fanny was sobbing loudly and running after her. The Roos sisters were rushing down the hillside towards the spa restaurant with Vera in front of them. It was steep and she lost her balance. When they caught up with her they each took her by one arm and started puling her towards the building, and Gunhild kicked her in the back of the knees every time she tried to pull away. Ingrid crouched and slid down the grassy slope. By the time she got down to the gravel they were already inside. The veranda door was wide open, hanging crooked on its hinges. Every sound from inside could easily be heard because so many window panes were missing.

'Right, so people are just like animals, you say? Well, you look like a cow, anyway. Ugh, do you smell her stench?'

'I'll bet between her legs she looks just like a cow,' said Valborg.

Ingrid tiptoed from one piece of slate to the next. The grass and moss were prising them up out of the gravel bed. Willow herb was pushing its way up between the tiles on the veranda. When she was stepping inside her foot got stuck between two rotten boards. She couldn't get it out. 'I'm stuck,' she thought. 'I'll never get my foot out, I'll never get out of here.' She heard something hit the dining room floor, heard Gunhild shout:

'Oh, so you bite, do you? You'd better watch out we don't shove this stick up you!'

Ingrid had to cover her eyes. She couldn't keep the picture out of her mind, she'd never seen anything so repulsive. Dog's cock, they said. Who ever thought up such disgusting words? How can you get away from words like that? They're just there. She wanted to scream and strike out, and the foot that was stuck between the boards ached. She pushed it further down to exacerbate the pain.

'Look!' shouted Valborg. 'Look, I say! She looks like a cow down there. Just as I thought.'

Ingrid did not raise her head, but she couldn't help picturing the opening on a cow, filthy with dung, hills and dales all runny.

'Look!' Ingrid looked up. Valborg was straddling Vera's chest,

Gunhild was holding her legs out with her strong arms. Vera didn't look like a cow down there.

'Let her go,' Ingrid said softly. Then she started to angle her foot loose. Gunhild straightened up and brushed the dust off her red woollen skirt. Her face was glossy.

'Cow!' spat Valborg, getting up. They passed Ingrid on the way out, their plaits pinned so tightly to the napes of their necks that they were still in place. Vera had sat up and pulled her skirt down, and now she was scooting towards the wall, her knickers in her hand. When she got to the door she stood up and stumbled out through it and into the innards of the building. Ingrid could hear her crying.

The big, grey dining room floor was empty. On the walls there were murals depicting the Geatish Spring, Vallmsta church, and the manor house. She could hear the footsteps of the Roos sisters in the gravel outside as they headed back to the village. They were walking slowly and it was definitely very hot out there where they waddled along in their red skirts and green aprons.

When Ingrid called Vera she got no answer. It was very quiet and after some time she heard a door on the other side of the spa restaurant slam shut and she was alone.

The table at the Lindh household was set for dinner every day with an oval mirror centerpiece on the large dining table, silver vegetable platters, lace doilies and decorative place-plates underneath the service. Why on earth? No one in the kitchen knew the answer, except possibly that their mistress was out of her mind.

The menu was the one they had settled on that morning: spinach soup with hard-boiled eggs, beef patties with onions, pudding with fruit sauce. After due consideration Fru Iversen-Lindh put the silver candelabra on the table. It would have held its own at a wake. Ingrid was told to put out the glasses on the sideboard. From the right, there were etched seltzer glasses, sherry glasses with an octagonal foot, green Rhine wine glasses, red wine cupolas, and Madeira glasses. The seltzer glasses were to be offered round with mineral water just before the vegetable course was served. Vegetable course?

'Yes, we absolutely have to have one.'

'You never ordered it,' said the cook.

'Don't be such a stickler, Alma. Use your imagination!'

'You never ordered it,' Alma said stubbornly.

So she opened a tin of cold beans and poured some vinaigrette over them. The kitchen staff thought it looked dull, but in France it was known as *hors d'oeuvres*.

'Don't be so obstinate! And let's see a smile, too, it never hurts. We do our chores with a cheery disposition, don't we Ingrid?'

You weren't supposed to answer. Seltzer, sherry, white wine

305

glasses. No, no, my dear, start from the right. The Madeira glasses with the pudding. That's right. Then they decided to remove the seltzer glasses. Alma was unable to make either a puff pastry or a canapé at a moment's notice. She refused to scrape out rusks. Oh, well. Alma was set in her ways.

We fold the napkins simply, just a three-fold accordion. Then the silver chest was unlocked. The heavy silver cutlery was to be counted before Ingrid put it on a tray and the chest was locked again. Ingrid hadn't been in service there long, but she was already familiar with the ritual. She was to assist in the kitchen, and later learn the duties of a housemaid if she proved right for the job. Since she had no more than compulsory schooling, wasn't a kind-hearted soul, came neither from Småland nor from Norrland and not from a better family either, was not particularly clever, reliable, well-trained, quick, cheerful, dependable or responsible, she hadn't counted on getting a position with a family at all. Every time she walked into the blue parlour with her dusters in her hand she thought, if Fru Iversen-Lindh knew she had wet herself on this sofa she would never be here now.

She counted out the silver using the old names the merchant had once given them: soupspoon, fish knife …

'Fish knife?'

'Oh, yes, we'll have to have a fish course. So we can use the fish knives.'

That was the last straw. Honestly. Alma's swollen face was virtually expressionless, which was equivalent to a tantrum, the moment Fru Iversen-Lindh had left the kitchen.

'A little cold fish pâté? The problem is there are no bones in fish pâté.'

'Quite,' said Alma in a quivering tone of voice that implied that if anyone pulled out so much as a splinter of a bone from her fish pâté she would be prepared to pack up the contents of her dresser into her trunk and depart immediately. In the end they decided that two cold marinated herring per person would do for the fish course, and Fru Iversen-Lindh, who had demanded to be called Madame Counsel for the last six months, took her leave.

'Don't just stand there,' said Alma to Ingrid. 'Get those onions chopped. Learn to use every minute. This is no time to stand there daydreaming about the pictures or about fellows.'

'She's to lay the table with me,' said the chief housemaid whose name was Tyra, so Ingrid went up to the dining room with the fingerbowls and asked Madame Consul with a perfectly straight face whether they were to be put on the tables after the pudding.

'No, after the vegetable course. That's right. Keep a cheery disposition my dear! It's ever so important to be good-spirited about your work. Pride in a job well done, you know, Ingrid. Patrik, what are you doing with that cap on in the house?'

Her son was sixteen. He had come down into the little dining room in a sports cap with the ear flaps down, his pyjama trousers falling down, his dressing gown and a scarf around his neck. He had bad breath, swollen eyes and a hoarse voice. The tennis club had had its end of season banquet and ball the night before.

'I've got a cold,' he said. 'I think it's gone to my ears. Better safe than sorry.'

His mother told him to go upstairs and dress for dinner, which would be served in the grand dining room.

'For practice.'

He thundered up the stairs and Fru Iversen-Lindh said that Ingrid should take the opportunity today to learn how a large dinner party was served, since her employer had arranged this dress rehearsal in dinner etiquette for her children's sake. And there must be no hitches at all in the planning!

'A dinner party,' Madame said, 'is a battlefield, though fortunately a bloodless one, and a successful dinner is an honourable victory for the hostess.'

She found herself in such fine humour that she was telling the shocked, staring maids in the black wool dresses with frilly aprons and hair bands in their hair what a colonel from Stockholm had once said at a dinner party. It was at the home of a former court physician whose wife's name was Victoria.

'When it was time to give the speech thanking the hostess for the meal he raised his glass and said one single word: 'Victoria'.'

She looked at them. They said not a word and moved not a muscle.

'Victoria!'

'Ah,' said Tyra.

'Which means victory! In Latin. And that was her name, too. Do you see?'

'Oh yes,' Tyra assured her, and Ingrid looked aside. There were times when she dared not look the consul's wife in the eyes.

The Iversen-Lindhs' had had nothing but a daughter for eleven years, after which Lillibeth had surprised them all by giving birth to a son. During the war they also took in an Austrian refugee child as a playmate for their son. Wolfgang Altmeyer was still living in their home and was two years Patrik's senior. Their daughter had died and her two girls, Elisabeth and Caroline, were their grandmother's wards. They were seven and nine years old. Madame Iversen-Lindh now gathered all four of them in the sitting room where they waited for the man of the house who was almost always late for weekday dinners, and while they were waiting she addressed the subject of punctuality. Patrik was still wearing his sports cap with the ear flaps down but had put on a blazer and trousers. He had a thick scarf wound around his neck, making it impossible to see whether he was actually wearing a collar and tie. Wolfgang was perfectly proper, as usual, and the part in his hair was straight as an arrow, his scalp pale beneath his shock of black hair. He listened attentively but, as usual, the look in his eye made Lilibeth a bit uneasy. The little girls were playing with their dolls.

When at last the man of the house arrived and understood what was afoot, he said it was a good idea, a very good idea indeed. They'd have to learn sooner or later, they were like apes. Like apes! Yes, as a matter of fact. They ate like apes, and shouted like apes.

Now they filed into the dining room with the host and his dinner partner at the head of the procession, the hostess and her dinner partner bringing up the rear. Patrik was to be his mother's partner because he was the one who would profit most from being the guest of honour. Wolfgang forced a smile in acknowledgement. Patrik's pyjama trousers were now beginning to show. He had kept them on under his dress trousers and the waistband was loose. The hostess pretended not to notice and smiled at him, at the little girls, at the walls and the mirrors as they passed.

'Don't let an awkward silence develop now, Patrik. Wolfgang! What does one say?'

Wolfgang smiled but did not reply.

'Patrik! What if the conversation dries up as we begin to walk towards the dining room? Remember that the distance from the parlour to the dining room may be long. What do we talk about?'

'I've no idea. The stock market?'

'Absolutely not! Wolfgang? A suggestion?'

'Perhaps the paintings.'

'Excellent. Let us hear it, Patrik.'

'Let Wolfie talk about the pictures if it amuses him.'

They passed the greenish Dutchman whose head had been

chopped off and placed on a highly realistic silver platter. Wolfgang Altmeyer mentioned the names Harten-Troef and Dubourg as he had a fantastic memory, and Madame Iversen-Lindh was pleased that everything had begun to go so smoothly and laughed in a high-pitched voice. However, Holger Iversen-Lindh had brought the newspaper in with him, and she signalled to him by raising her eyebrows as they sat down and he laid it on the table alongside his plate. He started reading the stock quotations anyway, though, pointing out that it was the children who needed to learn etiquette, not himself.

The meal began noisily. Caroline detested eggs and they had to fish hers out of her soup. The newspaper was a thorn in Madame Iversen-Lindh's flesh for as long as it remained on the table. Patrik accused Wolfgang of having borrowed his argyle golf socks and left them damp and under the bed. The hostess thought a toast was in order. She had had her fiftieth birthday, as had her husband. They were of an age when the gums have begun to retreat irreversibly, leaving the necks of the teeth exposed. Thus a smile from a person of that age reveals so much more tooth than it used to. This was true for both the Iversen-Lindhs, but Holger didn't smile very often, being a man. The consul's wife even smiled at Tyra as she tried to fish the slippery hard-boiled egg halves out of the spinach soup without landing them on the tablecloth, because in her view the face of the perfect hostess ought to be shrouded in placid, unruffled pleasantness irrespective of whether the serving staff stumbled into the room, broke a leg, or dropped the veal roast on the doorsill.

When Ingrid brought in the fingerbowls Holger Iversen-Lindh remarked that it was improper to put them out after the vegetable course. They were actually meant to be used after the fruit.

'After the vegetable course,' Lilibeth Iversen-Lindh insisted with implacable hostess firmness and well-exposed teeth.

'Possibly, if it were asparagus! Or architokes.'

'Tichokes, my dear Holger. Not chitokes. The hostess proposes a toast to Wolfgang. Wolfgang!'

'Gnädige Frau!'

Wolfgang knew she liked him to use a little German. And Patrik to use his English.

'The point is it's wrong,' said Iversen-Lindh. 'They're meant to be used after the fruit.'

'If they were used during the fruit course, it would be to rinse the fruit in,' said his wife with a smile that had grown increasingly long-suffering and would soon be distraught.

'Rinse the fruit! Rinse the *fruit!*' shouted the Counsel of Andorra and the Knight of the Vasa Order. 'Is the fruit in a *home* to be rinsed at table? Perhaps at a restaurant. But never at a private home!'

Now he was laughing, in Madame Iversen-Lindh's opinion in a way only suitable for gentlemen's dinners, and she signalled to him with her eyebrows again.

'That's tantamount to assuming they hadn't rinsed the fruit downstairs! What a fine compliment to the hostess that would be!'

'My, my now,' said Madame. 'You may, in fact, not know everything about everything my dear Holger. And Norwegian customs may be somewhat different.'

This was truly the deathblow, and the attentive Wolfgang Altmeyer was astonished to find her dealing it out so early. Ordinarily, too, Holger Iversen-Lindh would have bled to death like a harpooned whale at the dinner table with this reminder of his Norwegian descent. That was because her remark contained an implication, a gentle reminder that his mother had been a fishmonger who made whale-meat patties and boiled fish balls in the kitchen behind her shop. But Iversen-Lindh wasn't listening. He had been holding a trump card and was busy anticipating playing it.

'You may be aware that the water in finger bowls tends to be perfumed!'

Of course the long-suffering, sorrowful Madame Lindh did know it, but there was no need for him to shout.

'And can you rinse fruit in perfumed water? Can you? And then eat it? Would you like your grapes rinsed in whatever-the-hell it's called that you pat on your underarms and here, there and everywhere? Would you?'

'Holger!'

'Naturally not,' said the counsel with satisfaction. 'The water in finger bowls, perfumed or not, is for washing your fingers in. After the fruit.'

'Holger, dear,' said Madame Iversen-Lindh with perfect equanimity and a sarcastic smile. 'Perfumed finger-bowl water is bourgeois.'

This was not a logical comment, but it was enough to throw the counsel off course. He knew what she was implying.

'What in damnation do you mean by that?' he screamed at the top of his lungs. 'What the hell are you getting at?'

His wife's eyebrows were rising and falling like railway barriers, but it didn't help. He slapped his palm on the table top, and his Madeira glass hit the edge of the centerpiece mirror. In such circumstances, it becomes the hostess to stay calm and pleasant, and to remark lightly while signalling discreetly to the staff to come and clean up the shards of her family glassware:

'Wonderful! A broken glass – doesn't that mean there's going to be a wedding?'

But Fru Iversen-Lindh had reached her limit. Her chin shot up and she screamed for the succor of the good Lord.

Tyra came in and swept up the shards of glass with the silver crumb brush. Ingrid gathered them in a napkin, Fru Iversen-Lindh cut her middle finger and the little girls were weeping loudly. Patrik asked if he could be excused as he had a sore throat, and the counsel shouted, as red in the face as a newly-cut whale steak. Wolfgang Altmeyer sat silently with his head cocked.

The dinner party was dissolved. Tyra took the girls by the hand and led them to the nursery where they were given their semolina pudding with fruit sauce. Leaning on Wolfgang's arm, Fru Iversen-Lindh made her way back to her own room, and the counsel withdrew to his study. In the kitchen, Alma made coffee for the staff.

Counsel Iversen-Lindh and his wife were frightened. He was not afraid of lifting his glass to the right height, or of beginning his speech of thanks before his hostess had placed her napkin on the table. He didn't give a damn about things like that. But he was afraid of losing money.

In the old wholesaler's days the money had flowed in. He'd been there to see it happen, admired the old man and learned a great deal. But most of what he had learned was of no use in the world after the war. He had travelled to Russia in the middle of the Great War to try to save the Russian assets of the firm from the Bolshevik revolution, and returned with suitcases full of bank notes that were soon worth no more than the paper they were written on. At that point he recalled that his father-in-law had not been positively disposed to doing business with Russia, and he wished he had had the same disposition.

The old man had filled the house with empire and rococo furniture, with coin and medal collections, English bone china, and more or less obscure Dutch painters, Dresden figurines, old weapons, leather-bound French classics, and cartfuls of pewter and silver. Most of it came from provincial manor houses.

There was a world to which not even the old man had gained entry, and from which he had very few possessions in his collection: the huge mansions belonging to the nobility and the estates of the landed gentry. Their wealth rested on land ownership, and Lilibeth thought of them as changeless as the mountains and the orbit of the sun, although she was wrong about that, as he had begun to understand after the war. However, what was true was that all this wealth was acquired long long ago and in the absence of any resistance to speak of. The old wholesaler had laid the foundation of an extremely large fortune, and he had begun it in aspen timber, a far less solid foundation than being landed. He had done this during a period when resistance was developing and men were beginning to organize. People who had had no other value than as human manpower, power which, although it may have had the ability to distinguish one thing from another and the ability to differentiate, as opposed to the horse, the steam engine and the combustion engine, was still no more than potential power, dependent on intelligent leadership and on patronage and empathy – these were the very people who now wished to determine the price per hour of their own labour, and even to refuse charity. A force had emerged, frightening as a combustion engine running at high speed, or a steam boiler that had been fired to the bursting point. It had been most alarming during the war years. Now the ministers of the caretaker Social Democratic government had proved rather powerless willing to let off steam from the boiler, a little at a time. These little bursts of steam were annoying, but not directly ominous. Deep down, human beings react not by thinking but by protecting the unborn child, their fear. Deep down, too, he knew his days were numbered, or if not his at least Patrik's.

His wife was frightened of her staff. No, she was not afraid in any way people noticed, she hardly even noticed herself. She still treated her staff with the gentle oversight she had learned from the etiquette columns of the *Ladies' Home Journal* and which was an echo from the huge estates where British self-control reigned. Her pleasantness was the ultimate insult, her unchanging kindness a humiliation to someone not regarded as a human being but a piece of the furniture. There was no use letting a piece of furniture upset you, hardly any point in feeling angry. But in her fear she sometimes lost control and treated her staff as if they were human beings, giving them earfuls, shouting at them, and having attacks of hysteria that ended in bed where Tyra would give her two grammes of bromine according to the counsel's instructions. She would also hold her hand until the convulsions passed. At moments like that they were close, and Tyra no longer felt contempt for her, but empathy. She was exhausted with screaming, tired as a baby.

But new days dawned and things returned to normal. The staff were unwilling to learn. They looked indifferent and she thought they had cold eyes. The new girl, whose name was Ingrid, stared at her, seldom smiled and answered only in monosyllables. Her foster mother, Ingeborg, had been the old wholesaler's cook, and Lilibeth recalled her with warmth and pleasure. Such faces had given her a sense of security. They were alert, grateful. They might have their own ways but they were – honest. Yes, that was the word.

When Holger Iversen-Lindh and his wife were frightened they withdrew to their bedroom, where they stabbed one another in the heart with barbed daggers. They would begin by bringing up table manners and accusations about bourgeois behaviour. They would end by bringing up their honeymoon.

When they were newly betrothed they had had the opportunity to travel around on a study visit to various manor houses in foundry towns where old merchant Lindh had done business and made friends and acquaintances. Lilibeth was given an education in running a household and being a hostess, including lessons in English self-control and how to plan dinner parties. They had, of course, had a chaperon with them – Lilibeth's music mistress, ten years her senior.

They were married at the end of the summer. The bride wore a white raw silk negligee with handmade lace. She had removed her hairpieces and powdered her cheeks with rice powder. When the bridegroom lay down, first next to her and then on top of her, and prepared to take out the instrument, the sight of which had struck terror in her, and which he, too, had imagined as red, swollen and hairy, he turned out to be impotent. He had an altogether mild-mannered rosy little penis that he was quick to hide back under his night-shirt.

Unfortunately, he had been under the influence of a fair amount of champagne, sherry, burgundy, claret, port wine and cognac. With sweat running down his neck and his scalp so hot his black hair was curling, he began to confess that he was unworthy of her. Yes, in the face of all this elegant white fabric with its lace from Vadstena he felt he must tell her that during their betrothal study tour, after having spent the evenings hugging and kissing his fiancée in the manor parks, he had spent his nights in the bed of her music mistress. But now nothing would ever stand between them again. He desired to confess and be absolved because, if the truth be told, he had been miserable all summer. But now he was miserable no more! If only she would just forgive him.

Lilibeth had a shock to her nerves and spent the autumn ill in bed. To begin with the matter hadn't been mentioned again. He had coerced her into bed with him a few times and then given up. Now they had been married for twenty-eight years, but the wounds in Lilibeth's heart were as fresh as ever, owing to the fact that they were regularly torn back open. It had begun during the war and the starvation riots because they were so frightened they were unable to bear their fear alone. They spent hours in the bedroom with its white furniture, hours of stabbing, silence, tears, violent shouting and, finally, hard blows as his wife, stiff as a ramrod in bed, boxed her own ears with both hands.

Soon enough they began to confuse the exhaustion that ensued when she was finally able to remove her hands from her burning face with reconciliation, and these scenes of reconcilement became the passion of their middle age, fuelled by bromine and cognac. They were deeply unhappy people, as anyone who had an errand in the dim halls of their house at night could hear, the halls where pewter beer steins and silver wine chalices shone dully, and the screams of Fru Iversen-Lindh echoed from the bedroom, distant as the screeching of huge birds on a deserted beach.

Tyra looked after the lady of the house. She helped her to dress and prepare for large dinner parties. This always began with one gramme of bromine and alternately hot and cold footbaths. Madame had a permanently waved coiffure that lasted for six months, but still had to be rolled and combed. Then she would sit for ten to fifteen minutes under a towel hood with her face over a bowl of hot water, after which Tyra carefully pinched her blackheads with her fingertips wrapped in cotton, and hydrated her face with lanolin cream. When she was powdered, Lilibeth Iversen-Lindh had a long, close gaze in the mirror to see whether her skin looked coarse under the rosy powder. She asked Tyra, and Tyra said she thought she looked fine.

'Are you sure?'

'Of course. You look as young as ever, Madame.'

She should say Madame Counsel, but at moments like this she wasn't corrected. Lilibeth would pinch the skin at her throat between her thumb and index finger. She would hold it a while and then let go, looking in the mirror to check whether it sprung quickly back. It stayed wrinkled, though, not resuming its shape. She asked Tyra to get her jewellery box and searched it for a necklace with a large pendant.

Tyra mixed egg yolks with almond oil and rose water and a few grams of tincture of benzoine from the pharmacy so Madame's arms would be pale and smooth. She spent a night with her arms wrapped in this mixture before every decisive campaign in the war of entertaining, and in the morning her arms were washed clean and creamed with Paulis' lily milk. Still, nowadays she preferred evening dresses with chiffon sleeves.

Tyra had her hands so full looking after her mistress that Ingrid had to do most of the cleaning herself. Twice a month someone came in to do the heavy work. But every morning she had to make the beds, air out and dust the bedrooms and whatever sitting rooms had been used the evening before, usually the library and the billiard room. After this she cleared away the breakfast things from the little dining room, but she didn't have to do the washing up, the girl in the kitchen did that. What she did have to do, though, was to dust the dining room and sweep away the crumbs. Now and then the woman of the house would tour the rooms with a watering can and a little pair of scissors, but most mornings she stayed in her bedroom or her study, where there was a telephone. Then Ingrid would water the potted palms and the window plants. If they had greenfly, the leaves were supposed to be sprayed. She never bothered to look. Occasionally she would find cigar stubs in the pots, and poke them down into the soil, wondering whether the plants would die.

Every day she was supposed to scrub her way through the house following an established plan in accordance with which she was to begin the month by polishing the pewter objects in the downstairs hall and shining the mahogany in the first and second smoking rooms, going on to use the different polishing cloths for silver, hardwood, and crystal in the empire sitting rooms and Gustavian dressing rooms, dining rooms and studies until, by the end of the month, she was in the bedrooms, where her round was completed by shining the bedside lamps and the mirrors above her mistress' dressing tables, her mirror and brush set, and the holders for her combs and powders.

She was to lay the table for lunch and clean up the dining room afterwards, serve at Madame's afternoon tea parties, lay the table for dinner, serve, carry in the coffee and after-dinner drinks, turn down the bedspreads and bring down the shoes that needed to be cleaned. She did not have to brush and air clothing from the closets of the counsel and his wife or wash Madame's blouses and iron them. Those were Tyra's jobs. However, it fell to her lot to remove the stains from Patrik and Wolfgang's trousers and ties, and launder their socks. By this time she was extremely familiar with the odour of young men. Her working day lasted from seven in the morning until ten in the evening unless there was a dinner party in which case it lasted until one or two o'clock and ended with her helping the guests on with their galoshes and overcoats, defending herself against bottom pinching and breast fondling, emptying the ashtrays and airing out the rooms. She was paid thirty-five kronor a month, and her first month's pay had to be spent on the black woollen dress and starched white apron she had to wear. She had only owned blue dresses and ordinary white pinafores before.

She couldn't seem to get used to the big, dark house with its nocturnal shouting and its rows of shiny objects to polish. To her the place was hell on earth, and she had no intention of staying very long. But in the early days she wasn't personally upset by her misfortune at having ended up in this house. She was tired, of course, but firmly convinced that this peculiar rubbing and polishing

319

of objects placed in rows would soon be over. She just didn't know how it would end. When she walked along the halls staring at oil paintings and silver objects, she felt as if she were in a funeral home. Tyra appeared to believe that money and valuables were part of some infinite fortune hidden somewhere in human existence and that it was just a matter of finding the treasure and digging it up. She herself felt as if she were walking the halls of the morgue; the Lindh residence smelled terrible. It reeked of death and exploitation.

She didn't particularly care for the rest of the staff. The housekeeper was their immediate superior, and Ingrid should have found her intimidating but didn't. Perhaps this was because she didn't mind if she lost her job; in fact she more or less expected to. Or perhaps it was because she wore something that looked like a bathing cap, with an insignia in front, to show she was a graduate of the Home Economics Seminary in Uppsala. Alma was bad-tempered, Tyra burst into tears at the drop of a hat, and the kitchen maid was terrified of both cook and housekeeper. When the Counsel's wife made her occasional trips down to the kitchen they usually sent the kitchen maid out into the back passage to shine copper and peel vegetables, because her apron was so dirty.

There was a chauffeur who drove the two cars and wore leather gaiters. He never spoke to her. Patrik was pimply and looked crude. Ingrid was older than he was and could stare him down. The Austrian was more difficult. He was hard. His body did not know the word shame, and he had a gleam in his brown eyes. She was careful never to be left alone with him. The Counsel didn't know she existed.

There were times when the Counsel's wife was exhausted and spent her days in bed, which meant a lot of running up and down with trays. In the end she had to have her lungs examined and then spent a month in a sanatorium. Ingrid wondered why she felt no sympathy whatsoever for the woman. Tyra was a nicer person than herself. She sometimes felt sorry for her.

In secret, they used to listen to their employer's wife's crystal radio receiver, taking turns putting on the headphones and hearing music from almost all over Europe except Stockholm, which was hard to get where they lived. She hadn't taken the radio with her; she was probably too ill to use it. Tyra's eyes brimmed with tears at first when she realized that, but both she and Ingrid really looked forward to being able to listen to the radio as much as they pleased. It didn't work, though. They turned all the knobs and set all the dials. In the end they showed it to the chauffeur, who explained that somebody had removed a small but vital part. He told them the name, but they didn't recognize the word.

'She begrudged us listening,' said Ingrid.

'Oh, she was probably so ill she just broke that bit,' said Tyra.

'You're a kind-hearted soul, Tyra,' said Ingrid.

She wondered what she herself would be like if she stayed here much longer.

Fru Iversen-Lindh returned and there were new dinner parties. A famous actor was coming. They'd seen him in the pictures. When he got out of the Daimler he looked just as they'd expected him to. It all felt like a dream at first, but soon they were touching him, or at least his overcoat, with the soft fur collar he'd worn turned up although it was the middle of the summer. They wondered if he was ill. He had deep blue rings under his eyes.

He had been invited out to Rosenholm, the little manor house the Counsel had purchased from Winther, the restaurateur. He was going to study his lines for a new role, and rest and recuperate in the country. But there was also to be a big dinner party, and the Counsel's wife spent the afternoons in bed with slices of cucumber over her eyes and egg paste on her neck. The dining room was decorated to resemble a Tyrolean tavern. It was, however, a disaster. The guests were supposed to float gracefully and leisurely around the little lake in boats, with bonfires and music along the shore, just as in Winther's day. They hadn't counted on the mosquitoes though. Most of the guests squeezed into the gazebo where the refreshment tables were. The worst part was the actor himself. He may have been famous but he was also taciturn. He sat through the entire dinner party looking gloomy and pensive, answering distractedly when he was spoken to. Afterwards he said he needed to study his lines instead of joining in the boating.

Fru Iversen-Lindh hadn't taken this need to work seriously, but he walked around all day carrying the script in a blue folder with a National Monuments emblem on it. He ruined his white shoes by walking too close to the shore while reading. Tyra and Ingrid tried to clean and buff them up and returned them to him, awkwardly mumbling their apologies. The girls were nearly hysterically timid. Tyra hadn't even wanted to go in to his rooms, but Ingrid refused to do it alone.

He was extremely kind and extraordinarily tired. He gave them five kronor to share between them and he asked whether they'd seen him in any of his films. After a while they found themselves standing there conversing. He never tried to pinch Ingrid's bottom or fondle her breasts when she came back with his milk and brandy. He just smiled and said. 'Thank you my dear, and do remember me.'

'Thank you my dear, and do remember me,' Ingrid had to repeat down in the kitchen. They stayed up until two. The party was a failure and their mistress needed cold compresses and bromine. But for the first time they felt a sense of community downstairs, and stayed up later than they needed to, reheating coffee for themselves.

'Thank you my dear, and do remember me.'

Just like that. And sort of sadly. Nor had he tried any pinching or hugging, as Ingrid emphasized. It was beautiful, it was almost like at the pictures, and they would remember his eyes with their dark rings and his fur collar turned up in the month of July. Yes, they would remember. He could be sure of that. The next day the chauffeur told them Mr. Great was only interested in young lads, which explained why he hadn't tried any pinching. But they didn't believe him, and Alma threw him out of her kitchen because she was going to bake.

After every non-victoria dinner party they would be ordered to clean. Fru Iversen-Lindh lay with throbbing eyes and temples. Walking around the big house in broad daylight watching the dust whirl in the rays of sun gave her severe anxiety. When the great, silent man had left and they had all moved back to the Lindh mansion in town, she ordered a thorough cleaning without hiring anyone extra to come in and help with the heavy bits. The red and green parlours were to be cleaned, every piece of fabric removed and brushed, beaten and aired. After that the floors were to be washed and waxed and the windows cleaned.

'There really isn't a hope we'll get it all done in time,' Ingrid said to Tyra.

'Well, we'll just have to try.'

'We haven't had an afternoon off since I started here. One free afternoon a week, I was told. How many have you had in all your time here?'

'Well,' said Tyra. 'We get gifts, like when she's been in Stockholm. We can't start fussing now. They've had so many dinners lately.'

When the Iversen-Lindhs had returned from Stockholm the last time, the entire staff had been standing outside on the steps to greet them. Gifts had been distributed. Ingrid had been given a flowered cardigan of worsted yarn.

They started by cleaning the red parlour, and Tyra vanished out into the yard with rugs and scatter cushions. Ingrid was to wash the floor, but she accidentally poured out much too much water. She was just standing there, with a vacant look in her eyes, swishing the water around with a mop, when the counsel's wife came in. She screamed. Ingrid, too, had realized the floor would be ruined, but she'd been incapable of doing anything but staring at it and swishing the mop around in it. Tyra came running and started wiping it up, wringing out cloths, and wiping up more.

Later, Fru Iversen-Lindh asked if she could have a word with Ingrid. They spoke for a quarter of an hour. In the end Ingrid's employer put her hand to her heart and, with disconsolate composure, asked Ingrid to come along down to the kitchen with her so they could hear what the others had to say. She said that, in fact, she was firmly convinced that her staff trusted her and placed their confidence in her. Ingrid was inclined to agree, but said nothing.

They lined up along one wall, as if they had been told to, and the Counsel's wife stood at the door to the serving room, leaning against the desk in which the housekeeper kept the accounts. She told them that Ingrid, who was the youngest of them all, who had no previous experience of domestic service and who, that morning, had nearly ruined the irreplaceable painted floor in the red parlour had brought up the subject of working hours, time off, and pay with her. She had, however, said nothing about loyalty or a feeling of belonging at one's place of work, and for this reason Fru Iversen- Lindh was afraid Ingrid's presence at their workplace was destroying their sense of satisfaction in a job well done.

'Do we not share a sense of satisfaction in a job well done?' she asked across the kitchen, with its musty odour and steam from the hot water heater. No one answered.

'I want you to speak perfectly openly,' she said, gently but a bit sadly. 'Have I taken unfair advantage of you, have you not had the time off you deserve? Ingrid is a very young girl, but I still believe she has a right to have her questions answered.'

Alma gazed at the Bolinder stove and the copper moulds on the mantle. She bit her lower lip, sucking it in audibly.

'Tyra!' That was an order.

'Well,' said Tyra, 'I really don't know. Time off, well, I can't actually say we've had any ... but of course you've had any number of dinner parties. So how could we?'

'What about your sense of satisfaction?' asked Fru Iversen-Lindh. 'Haven't we shared a sense of satisfaction in a job well done?'

At that, Tyra was silent. Then she helped Fru Iversen-Lindh up the stairs to her room, and went to the Counsel's study to fetch him. He was extremely annoyed, but when he realized the gravity of the attack of nerves his wife had suffered, he sent for the doctor first and then for Ingrid. She, however, had already packed her trunk and given her name and address to the housekeeper. She did this so no one could accuse her of having stolen any of the things she'd polished.

They crossed the stony surface of the terrace carefully, the old woman first with Ingrid behind her, carrying her towels and her bathing robe. In a drawstring cloth bag hanging from her wrist she had a pumice stone and a bar of Florodol soap in a glass box with a silver lid. The grass was still dewy, and the old woman raised her skirt. she At the shore she stepped very cautiously because it consisted of nothing but mud baked around the stems of decomposed reeds. The jetty sagged under them, and almost unconsciously Ingrid saw to it that the distance between them grew a little as they stepped up onto it.

A morning breeze rose, rocking the water lilies by the bathhouse. She saw black insects moving among the reeds. After a few minutes the reflections of the little ripples on the bathhouse walls disappeared. She sat down and looked at the wall as she had been told to, while the old woman undressed. The odour of rotting wood and the sweet aroma of water lilies and the sunny lake surrounded her.

Now the old woman was going to step into the water, and Ingrid took up her post by the ladder. At the same moment, she was asked to avert her eyes, in the pleasantest of voices, and she always did. The first few times she had peeked at the old woman's pale back. From behind, she was extremely thin. She might have little rolls of fat above her belly, but Ingrid had never looked. She had brought four children into the world, three of whom were still alive. One was a riding master, one an attaché, and one the wife of a wealthy landowner. Her three children lived in Malmö, Brussels and Herefordshire, and they did not permit her to bathe unaccompanied.

The steps of the ladder down into the not perfectly clear water were slippery with algae. She bathed every morning from Ascension to the first of September. The older kitchen staff said that she had once suffered summer tummy upset from bad strawberries she hadn't let them throw away. That day she hadn't bathed.

Before she had quite finished dressing again, Ingrid glimpsed her naked foot. Every part of her body that was not normally visible filled Ingrid with compassion and shame. Her foot was tiny. In fact, she had never seen such a small foot on an adult woman. It was as pale as her back. From the dry skin and the small but yellowing and thickened nails it was clear the foot was an elderly one.

The water was filmy with soap when they left. Ingrid looked back at the water lilies again and would have liked to say that at a distance they were very beautiful but when you looked down into their white crowns you could see both brown rot and little insects. She said nothing. She wasn't in the habit of speaking to the old woman unless she was spoken to, unless it was a matter of bringing her a message or asking what she required. The old woman, on the other hand, often spoke to Ingrid quite unreservedly.

After her dip, Ingrid helped her to put up her hair and tie her cap, which was actually nothing more than a flat little pancake on top of her head, made of a lace-covered bit of satin. The hair on the top of her head had begun to thin, you could see it if you were standing close to her when she removed the cap. She was a very short woman, so small she almost always chose to keep a certain distance from others. Otherwise she would have had to look up at them.

Ingrid didn't make the old woman's bed now, only opened the windows and took her chamber pot to empty it. When she carried it down the stairs she covered it with paper. There was no other way downstairs than the huge stairway leading to the main door, and you had to cross the entire hall to get access to the kitchen stairs. She was always supposed to stop and listen carefully halfway down the main stairs before she continued down with the pot. If any male individual had entered and was standing in the foyer cap in hand, she was supposed to place the pot behind an urn in a niche and then go on down and ask him what it was he wanted. She could perfectly easily distinguish male footsteps from those of the old women in the kitchen.

Before she brought breakfast up, the old woman came down to the kitchen for a few moments of prayer with the servants. The first morning Ingrid found it unreal. By now she had ceased to think very much about it, and she always joined in singing the hymn. It was also Ingrid who passed her employer the Book, and the case containing her glasses.

'Here you are, ma'am,' said Ingrid.

'Thank you, Ingrid. Is the bookmark still there?'

It was.

Every day at Little Heavenside began this way during the light part of the year. In the winter the day began when the housemaid lit the fires in the tile stoves, but Ingrid had not yet spent a winter here.

During the prayers she sat looking at the floor in the servants' dining room. It consisted, like the whole downstairs floor, of large squares of stone with an imprint of ancient, fossilized crayfish tails. She sat looking at Nanna's feet. This old faithful servant looked after the hens and did the simplest work in the kitchen. The cook's name was Beda. Her feet were flat, too, and knobbly on the sides, but unlike Nanna she could still get them into a pair of shoes. Nanna shuffled around the stone floor in felt slippers all day long. When she rolled up her sleeves and hitched up her skirts to scrub the floor you could see there were things on her knees resembling huge white fungi. Her elbows also had crusty, swollen scabs, but not nearly as large.

There was a smell of dirty dishcloth. There was no door to close out to the kitchen; the servants' dining room was just a big alcove. The old woman's nose wrinkled as she read from the Gospel According to Paul. In a while she would go and find the source of the odour, and Beda would have to feel ashamed. It didn't matter that it was Nanna who had done the washing up and forgotten to hang the smelly dishcloth out, the responsibility was still Beda's. The coachman wasn't there. He often found excuses to stay away from the prayers. Mostly he would say that one of the horses seemed unwell. Their names were Castor and Diana, and their state of health was a frequent topic of conversation in the house.

After the hymn it was finally time to prepare the breakfast tray. Her Ladyship had had nothing but her linseed gruel when she woke up. That was to keep her stomach running smoothly. So before she went upstairs she had a bowel movement in her chamber pot, as there were no WCs at Little Heavenside. It was one of Nanna's duties to empty the pot and clean it out. Out of respect for Nanna's swollen feet and legs that made it difficult for her to climb the stairs, Her Ladyship spent a few moments on the chamber pot downstairs every morning before going up for breakfast.

After breakfast she busied herself with letter writing. She used stationary that cost five öre per sheet and that could be written on both back and front. She filled it with her microscopic handwriting and concluded with:

From Augusta Jaquette de Valiers
Née Fogel, Little Heavenside Manor

She had a large number of correspondents, the most important of whom were her children. She wrote to them twice a week, about the weather, about the health of the servants, and about her own, which required very little space. She also wrote that she thanked God for that. She always concluded her letters to her children with one or two spiritual reflections which they may or may not have read. She had no idea, since they never mentioned them in their replies. Every now and then she would offer Ingrid a little anecdote from the past relating to one of the objects she was dusting.

This was her main task at Little Heavenside, dusting and polishing the ancient objects, most of which were extremely beautiful. Hardly any of them had been acquired during Her Ladyship's lifetime. It was also the meaning of life for the two old women in the kitchen, for the coachman and for Ingrid if she chose, to care for the body of this ageing woman and to maintain the old objects by which she set such great store, though not always in proportion to their market value. If a fire should break out at Little Heavenside, she had instructed them to see to it, first and foremost, that her father's full-dress sword and his portrait be removed to safety.

Now and then she would also talk to Ingrid about the objects that surrounded them, the figurines in the glass cupboard, the clocks and the little tables, and for a short time after she had told a story, it was easy to believe that the objects had hearts that beat and living surfaces that groaned when they were scratched or hurt. Her stories were often very educational. They contained kings and prime ministers, as well as ministers of justice. She was often ironic and not at all respectful in her stories.

Ingrid learned other things as well. One of the first days she stood waiting with a pair of paper scissors while Her Ladyship pasted picture post cards into an album. She was slightly bored, and was using the scissors to clean her nails, which was enough to make the old woman ironic. Did Ingrid know what the Social Democrats had to say about religion? Of course she did, but she didn't dare to tell her.

'Well,' said Her Ladyship, 'they say religion is to be considered a private matter for each individual. I would beg to differ with them.'

She poked avidly, working the corners of the post cards under the flaps on the pages of the album. When Ingrid passed her the scissors, she refused to take them.

'As I said, I would beg to differ with them about that. But anything having to do with a manicure, on the other hand, should most definitely be considered a private matter for each individual.'

After which she instructed Ingrid to give the scissors a thorough cleaning.

She never said what the objects were worth in cash. There was an extremely beautiful china service with pink flowers and little gold leaves they were forbidden to wash down in the kitchen. It was used on the rare occasions when she had company. Ingrid had been washing it in a special little corner behind the writing room when the count from the estate came back there and extinguished a cigar in her dishwater. Then he took one of his own cigars out of his pocket and lit it instead. He said he was pleased to see her doing the washing up with such attention. Most people wouldn't dare use china of the kind Fru de Valiers had her table laid with. Although she didn't have the foggiest notion of a good cigar, he added. Ingrid felt indignant on her behalf because she realized he was implying that Her Ladyship was stingy, allowing her table to be laid with china that was worth a fortune, but serving cheap red wine and poor cigars. Perhaps she was a penny-pincher; there was no question that she was extremely frugal. She had simple habits, and very seldom spent time with other people, except her servants.

She gave them birthday presents. They were ancient, dug out from the camphor-scented depths of her dresser drawers. White things had yellowed, paper had cracked and plumes were broken. Ingrid had been given a jar of lip balm from a *pharmacie* in Lausanne for her birthday. It was rancid cocoa butter. Her Ladyship was extremely upset, and smelled the contents of the jar time and again. But she meant well, and her good intentions told her that the slightly pink paste was all right.

On ordinary days she had her dinner at four in the afternoon, with plenty of vegetables, and hardly any meat. She found it unpleasant when her bowel movements were dark, and she turned around every morning with a stiff upper lip and examined them. If she thought they looked too dark she would eat even less meat for the next few days. Her servants ate basically the same meals as herself, just larger helpings, with the exception of little omelettes, certain delicate pastries, and sweetbreads. At five in the afternoon she began to get ready for bed. Ingrid would remove the little lace cap from her head and brush her grey hair. She would fill the bidet with extremely cold water from the spring that she did not want heated. What she did want was a copper warming pan, filled with boiling water, inserted with a long handle between her sheets.

When they had said goodnight, Ingrid locked her into her bedroom and placed the key in a niche on the tile stove in the servants' room. There was a bell-rope in the bedroom so she could call them. Although she was terrified of being locked in her bedroom asleep if there should be a fire, she did not dare to sleep in an unlocked room.

Ingrid often found herself thinking of the key when she was out. Suddenly it would just appear in her mind. She would see it in her mind's eye, in the little niche on the tiled stove, with painted blue flowers on a vine.

It was quite a distance to town, and she was not allowed to be out after ten o'clock. Of course Her Ladyship was asleep, and unable to check on her, but no one voluntarily violated her instructions. Or at least not behind her back. So Ingrid didn't get into town very often. Instead she took cold walks along the lane and the lakeshore, and sometimes along the road, all the way to Rosenholm.

She didn't have to go walking on her own. At first a young man called Arnold would walk with her. They would kiss in the damp boathouse. Later there was Birger, who was her own age. As she couldn't think of anywhere else, she went to the boathouse with him as well. They spent a few evenings together, but then he seemed to think it was too far to cycle out to Little Heavenside. She didn't particularly miss him, but she was quite bored as all the old folk went to bed so early. In town there had been unemployment and inflation, strikes and disruptions on the labour market during the years Her Ladyship had been growing old, but none of this changed the old woman's life. Now and then she would be driven into town to make a few small but essential purchases, and on these occasions she would take Ingrid with her. Castor and Diana were thoroughly groomed, but extremely slow. The coachman was hunched, the carriage seats cracked, and the leather stained green with mould. Ingrid found it highly embarrassing if anyone she knew caught sight of them, especially boys.

The second spring she was there, she met Harald. He was twenty-three years old and was a technical illustrator at Swedish Motor. She just couldn't understand why he would want to go out with anyone so much younger than himself. She was afraid of appearing childish, at the same time as she detested putting on airs and pretending to know more than she did. Their conversation often died; she just stared at the ground and kept silent. His curiosity about her grew when he felt she was keeping quiet for no reason, and a field of tension arose between them, as if she had been a much older woman.

Both Birger and Arnold had found it a nuisance that she was living so far from town. They wanted to go to the pictures with her, or sit at the Cosmopolitan or Anker's. Harald, however, found it an advantage. He loved walking. She soon realized that what he loved more than walking was being alone with her. He preferred the

333

boathouse to the open meadows.

They became acquainted at the time of year when the snow was melting, her second spring at Little Heavenside. He rode her home from the cinema, her sitting in front of him on the handlebars, as his bicycle had no carrier. Just as they were passing the estate workers' huge potato cellar on Heavenside Lane, she felt his lips in her hair. It gave her the kind of jolt as if she had stuck a hairpin in an electric outlet. But it wasn't painful. For a long time afterwards she could call up the feeling just by remembering the event, although it gradually abated. When he kissed her it deepened again, and she often fell asleep thinking about it. Despite the fact that both Beda and Nanna snored, she felt as if she were alone on earth when she lay there, awake. 'Harald, Harald,' she would intone softly into her pillow, feeling the rough pillowcase grow moist and warm from her lips.

They would pick Star-of-Bethlehem together behind the stables. He wanted her to stop under the oaks with him and his lips would search for hers, and they were cold in the wind, very hard and damp, but his tongue was warm. In the evening when she lay thinking about it she felt almost overcome. He didn't talk to her very much any more. She put on a yellow voile dress Dagmar had made for her, but he didn't even notice.

He kept working at the elastic waistband on her knickers. Sometimes in the evenings lying under the yellow Swedish wool blanket with blue edging with which Her Ladyship supplied the servants she would rub the spot where the elastic would have stopped if she had her knickers on. She never thought about the next day or what she would do. But she realized that for every time they were together it was becoming more and more difficult to talk and laugh.

Harald had wavy, ash blonde hair that stood straight up in front, and a perfect profile. His nose was large and very straight. She admired his teeth, where she'd never seen a speck of food lodged, and the whites of his eyes were clear. She loved thinking about him. By now there was practically more pleasure in thinking about him than in being together, and when she sang love songs, it was Harald she had in mind. 'I'm in love, I'm in love,' resonated through her. She wrote 'Harald Simonsson, 31 Vanstorp Road' on a piece of paper, and 'Swedish Motor Corp.' and then she burned it up in the stove, which made Beda suspicious.

On Midsummer's Eve Her Ladyship asked Ingrid to make little wreaths of wildflowers with which to decorate the table out on the terrace where coffee would be served the next day. Harald came out to see her and she asked him to help her pick flowers that evening. The riding master and his family were arriving on the late evening train from Malmö, so she hadn't really been given the evening off. She didn't mind, because Harald would be coming out there anyway. He didn't like to go dancing. He knew Esperanto and how to play the guitar, but he couldn't dance.

They were picking crimson cranesbill in the grove above Rosenholm, and he pulled her down under him onto the ground and started kissing her, wet and hard. He was also trying to pull her knickers off. When he was perfectly still with his lips on her neck for a few seconds, she managed to slither out of his grip, which wasn't especially tight just then. She was on her feet in an instant, but so things wouldn't feel so strange she started joking with him, enticing him to chase her as soon as he got up. He was arranging his trousers, and had dead leaves in his hair. She ran off, carrying the bouquets of cranesbill and buttercups, but he was quicker than she, and more determined, and he soon caught up. Then she climbed over a wooden fence, holding the flowers high above her head, and her feet hurt when she landed. He followed, but got caught on a fence pole, and she could hear the sound of his trousers ripping.

The rip was from his pocket towards the buttocks, and then at a

335

right angle straight down. If he didn't hold on from behind, there was a huge, gaping flap. Even when he held the flap up, his white underpants showed. He only had one dress suit. At first she laughed, until she realized he was in a rage. He'd have to ride his bicycle into town in torn trousers.

The next time she saw him, the tear was ever so neatly repaired, but it was still clear his trousers had been ripped.

'We're going to the boathouse,' he said.

She refused.

'Come on now. You can't go on like this.'

'I promised Her Ladyship I'd be in at seven. She wants a cup of honey water for her cold.'

She was lying, which she otherwise never lowered herself to doing. She preferred silence. But she was upset now. The next time they just walked up and down Heavenside Lane and he said he'd have to be getting back into town because he had a letter to write to the Melbourne Esperanto Society. When he was getting his bicycle from alongside the stables they heard a window open in the Big House, and then the voice of the old woman, surprisingly loud.

'Ingrid!'

She answered at the second call.

'I'm off,' said Harald.

'Ingrid's friend!' Her Ladyship called down. 'Ingrid's friend, come up and introduce yourself.'

They couldn't see her. The apple trees were between them and the white stone house, which was only two storeys high. Could she have heard them? Or caught a glimpse of Ingrid's yellow voile dress?

'Tell her I'd gone,' said Harald.

She could hear the gravel crunching under his tyres as she walked back towards the house, and thought Her Ladyship might be able to hear it, too.

She was sitting in her bedroom with a book called *St. Paul's Epistle to the Romans*. Ingrid asked how she was feeling.

'Very well,' she answered. 'You needn't be the least bit worried about me, Ingrid. It's just that sometimes I have difficulties falling asleep.'

'He left,' said Ingrid. She couldn't get herself to tell Her Ladyship a lie.

'Oh,' said Her Ladyship. 'Well, perhaps another time. I think Ingrid's friend ought to come up and introduce himself.'

He's not my friend, thought Ingrid. He's not. I know nothing about him. It's been more than three months. All I know is what he looks like and how he feels.

'You may retire now, Ingrid,' said Her Ladyship. 'I'll not be needing anything more.'

'Good night, Your Ladyship.'

'Good night, Ingrid.'

'She worries about me,' she thought, when she'd gone to bed. The room felt hot and airless with Beda and Nanna's old bodies. No, he's not my friend.

She spent a lot of time thinking about him. In fact whole days in the old house could be filled with doing almost nothing but thinking about him as Nanna's felt slippers scuffled along the stone floors. In the evenings, lying in her bed stroking her skin with her fingertips where her knicker elastic had left a line, she felt as if she'd had a fever. She wanted dramatic things to happen. Someone in a car should drive up to Little Heavenside and signal to her to come in under the apple trees where they'd tell her she must go with them to the hospital where he was on his deathbed. Her grief would be so overwhelming she wouldn't know if she could bear it. She stopped at that point, not thinking about the rest of the story.

She also thought about Fredrik and Jenny who might be getting married soon now that he had a better job, and she wondered whether they had been in a bed together. She wondered, too, whether Fredrik was Jenny's friend, and she wasn't sure. Falling asleep, she thought about good friends, about one little puppy licking the fur of another with long, gentle strokes, cleaning it, and about Bedrik and Old Man Kling in the cottage out at Bog Field.

Bedrik had developed an illness that made him tremble and shake all the time and no one could understand what he was trying to say any more. Old Man Kling would bend down over him with his ear to his mouth so it went all wet and he shook, too, from the seizures that held Bedrik's body in their grip. In a while he knew what Bedrik was trying to say. Sometimes it was no more than 'good day', although it took such a long time.

'He's saying 'good day',' said Old Man Kling.

'Good day,' Ingrid would return.

Every Saturday morning she walked to Bog Field with two baskets from Her Ladyship. The cottage was no more than two large identical rooms, each with a stove. In the middle of the floor was a table covered in newspapers. There were beds and settees with trundle beds under them along the walls, a wood box and a china cupboard. There was a little stand with a zinc washing up tub. One of the rooms housed Bedrik and Kling and a man called Danielsson who'd been a driver in his day. The other housed four old women. The minute you opened the door you were struck by the stench of urine. The first time Ingrid was there to bring the baskets and a newspaper called 'Witness to Truth' she started to unpack the baskets and lay the newspaper-covered table, but she had to go outside and vomit into the nettles growing around the stone base of the cottage before she could finish.

There was barley soup made with pork stock. Her Ladyship sent them coffee but no snuff. Everyone who lived out at Bog Field had once been a faithful servant at Little Heavenside.

The women wanted to take her hands and thank her, and they asked if she would stay and tell them what had been happening up at the big house that week, and how the old lady's health had been.

The walk to Bog Field was too long for Her Ladyship to make it herself, but she did walk down the lane all the way to the gatekeeper's cottage. Twice a week a herring vendor named Lundberg would walk all the way out to Little Heavenside to sell fish from his handcart to the wives of the estate workers. He did it because his own father had worked on the estate. As a child he had got one arm caught in a thresher, and although it healed he was unable to straighten it at the elbow, and so it hung at an awkward angle. He couldn't get a job anywhere, so he bought herring by the crate and wheeled it around to sell from his cart.

One morning they met Lundberg in the lane. Ingrid was carrying a dark green umbrella, holding it above the old woman's head, as the weather wasn't the best.

'Like a little herring, ma'am?' he asked when he caught sight of them. It took a lot to disconcert Her Ladyship, but Ingrid watched her swallow and purse her thin lips, making an effort to speak, but unable to get anything out. Lundberg seemed to think she might find the herring too red about the gills, so he said: 'It's first-class herring, ma'am. Won't you have a couple of kilos?'

At which the old woman said very timidly but in a perfectly clear voice: 'Pardon me, but I am accustomed to being addressed as Her Ladyship.'

Lundberg just stood there, ready to scoop some herring into a newspaper packet.

'Well, all I can say is her Lady's never shipped anything good in my direction. What about some herring then?'

As they walked back along the lane, the old woman was slightly short of breath, but she couldn't help smiling every time she spoke to Ingrid. They passed the estate workers' housing on the hillside. The old woman no longer had any connection to the estate workers or the farmhands. The farm itself had been sold off, and the new owner leased out the land. Ingrid hoped to herself that none of the estate workers' wives would come outside with a bucket full of dishwater to throw away, and nod to Her Ladyship. They walked a bit faster than usual through the thin drizzle that was really no more than a fine mist.

The days were so quiet and so monotonous. Each morning Ingrid would unlock the bedroom door and the only thing she could hear inside was the ticking of the mantelpiece clock. She often felt anxious, wondering whether the old woman was already dead rather than asleep. She thought the bed of sculptured oak looked like a coffin and she was frightened of Her Ladyship.

Yes, I'm afraid, she thought. Nothing ever happens here, and when I first came she was a total stranger to me. She could just as well have been a stone of an interesting shape, or a bird I'd never seen before. She is a stone, or else she's dead. But inside me things are happening all the time. I've learned to think her thoughts and to know what she wants before she knows it herself. When did this begin? She'd never think my thoughts, even if we should be here for a thousand years.

The old woman was on her back, pale and still. Her thin white plait was lying along one shoulder. Her nose was sharp, protruding from between two heavy folds that were her cheeks. It was impossible to see whether the chest under the white cotton batiste of her nightgown was rising and falling.

How shall we recognize our enemies?

A strid and Leopold's wedding photo hung on the wall in Dagmar Eriksson's hallway. Frida, her mother, would stand staring at it whenever she came up. After a while she would sigh.

The princess' wedding dress was of calf-length white satin. There were two rows of fairly large scallops at the bottom. Her train was long, and ran along the floor like double cream, lightly whipped.

'That's white satin crêpe,' said Dagmar, and she was a seamstress so she ought to know. The veil was Brussels lace, of course. It was capped over her head and draped across her forehead in waves, encircled by a little wreath of orange blossom. Her bridal bouquet was lily of the valley.

'Forced blossoms, I s'pose,' said Frida. 'The wedding was in November, after all. Yes, time does fly. A whole year ago.'

Quite far back on her head there was a crown of myrtle, and you couldn't help but wonder whether Princess Astrid had grown the myrtle on her windowsill in the windows with the white curtains on Farrier Road, or if it was forced, too, in the big royal greenhouses, as they needed so much of it. She had white, very shiny stockings, but you couldn't see her shoes: the train was over them. You wondered why. White gloves, though you couldn't see much of them, either.

'They say Märtha has big hands. Wonder if Astrid does, too?'

'Not her,' said Frida. 'People do talk.'

'Well, I met a woman who had worked in a glove shop along

Cabinet Row and she told me Märtha'd been in last year to buy lace gloves. She wore a seven and three-quarters.'

'No! it couldn't possibly have been more than seven and a quarter.'

You could just imagine how her hand was searching for his under the army cap on his lap. He was looking at her from under his eyelids. Everybody said they were so much in love, that it was a marriage from the *heart*.

'He visited her at Fridhem any number of times. Though they said he was somebody else, then. It was all ever so hush-hush,' said Frida. 'But people recognized that curly head of his.'

'What a lot of bits and pieces the poor fellow had to keep track of! Gloves, cap and sabre.'

'I'll bet he's really happy she's his, now.'

The bridal gown was quite low-cut, and she was wearing a necklace that looked as if it was gold with little pearls.

'Can you believe someone like that gets the curse and goes to the privy just like us?' asked Dagmar. 'I can't.'

Frida was embarrassed to hear her talking like that. Girls talked so much rubbish nowadays. There was nothing they were ashamed to talk about, either. And still Dagmar was one of the more sensible girls. She'd been determined from the very outset to make a success of her dressmaking business, and that meant minding your tongue and not upsetting the ladies. She rented a small flat on the High Street upstairs from the Mission Bookshop and Persson the butcher. The flat looked out over the courtyard, but she had the same entrance as the tenants with shop fronts. The next was high, but a good location paid off. The ladies never wanted to walk very far, and if you wanted clients who paid well you couldn't live in a place where the neighbours were noisy and the stairwells smelled of cooking.

The kitchen might have had nicer fittings. Still, there was an old zinc counter with a water tap and a sink. The stove had a tendency to smoke, but Dagmar didn't light it so often. She had a paraffin oil heater and made coffee over a Primus stove. If you have fabrics and garments hanging all over you can't very well boil cabbage or pickling spices and vinegar to marinate herring in. Nor can you fry fish or potato cakes. Her usual dinner was a slice of cold headcheese from the butcher's, and in between she really only had time for coffee and sandwiches.

Her sewing machine was a brand new Singer with lots of accessories: a braiding foot and a gathering foot and a hemming attachment, amongst others. She'd bought it on hire purchase, but wasn't worried about affording the payments. She had lots of orders. But was her health strong, Frida wondered to herself? She'd had rickets as a child and it left her back quite bowed. She actually found it difficult to sit in the same position for long, and Frida had seen her ramble back and forth across the floor as she oversewed the seams on a garment.

Her hands were not rough, as she had never done anything but work with soft fabrics, but her fingers were sadly worn with pinpricks, and she tried to soften them with lotion. It wasn't nice for clients to have coarse, scratchy fingertips against their throats when she fitted necklines. She made sure to wash her hair regularly in Lux soap flakes, because she had to be so close to her customers when they were trying things, down on her knees pinning up hems. She knew, too, that it was important to wash under her arms, and she would never put a dress back on in the morning if she'd sat up late working in it and hadn't been able to air it in between. She had made up her mind that she would be the one to sew for the wealthy ladies of the town. She often thought about Tora Otter, who had failed to get them into the Cosmopolitan for their morning coffee, and who could never understand what kept them away. But Dagmar thought she had some idea of all the little things that go into making a place the kind the rich will consider.

Fredrik and Jenny were finally to be married, with the wedding to be held on Boxing Day at number 9 Store Street. They were all invited: Frida and Dagmar, Konrad and Agnes, and Ingrid, too, of course. Linnea Holm, Tekla and Ebba Julin would also be there, and one could certainly hope the brewer would have the good sense not to come, as he wasn't the one who was a friend of the family's. Tora didn't intend to buy more than a couple of bottles of wine, either. Naturally Fröken Åkerlund would be coming, and she had promised to play her piano, which Tora still had in her sitting room. Tora'd even invited Franzon, that serpent. Well, time does have to heal all wounds, and Fredrik and Adam had both insisted he be asked. At least he knew how to look smart, Franzon. And wealthy. He really was. Stella Lans was on her own now that Rickard had died, living in a tiny flat upstairs from Kranz the watchmaker. There was no way she could have the wedding in that little hole. Of course they'd asked Kranz, and Ivan Roos, too, so they wouldn't be so short of men. She was sure the watchmaker would have written a speech and a poem. He was pleased to have been invited.

But Frida couldn't imagine what to wear.

'We'll make you a dress,' said Dagmar.

Frida was having none of that.

'You've got your hands full as it is.'

True, there were lots of orders to finish before the Christmas party season, but Dagmar took her measurements anyway.

'You know there might be a frock someone doesn't collect,' she said. 'Something I can alter to fit you. I need to have your measurements just in case.'

She was thin. Dagmar had to measure her hips a second time. She didn't believe her eyes.

'Well, a person just gets older and wretcheder,' said Frida. 'And my shoulders are crooked, you know. You could never alter anything so it fit me. Beside which, the fabrics you sew are such elegant ones. Like these lovely Egyptian cotton prints.'

'That's crêpes marocain,' said Dagmar. 'For Eriksson's wife, from the furniture shop. It's going to flow from the hip and be fastened at the shoulder with a silk corsage.'

'So no one can tell she's had a breast removed?' asked Frida. 'She had a tumour, didn't she?'

But Dagmar didn't reply. She discovered a lot about disease and defects when she was fitting people, and about dirt and smells under duchesse and crêpes de chines. She had seen costly corsets of Jacquard satin that were never washed, lovely feminine attributes that were laced in or built up with padding, bruises and scars. When she negotiated payment she learned quite a bit about people's money problems, things no-one could've imagined. There were worried husbands who made their wives arrange a dinner party and sent them to the seamstress just to appear solvent, and she had once, in deepest secrecy, even copied a Vogue pattern to save face and calm the creditors. However, there was one thing she had already learned. Not to gossip. If she did, things would soon look dingier around her, and she would be sitting there with serge twill and alpaca instead of brocade and moiré.

'Now we'd better pick out some material for you,' said Dagmar once they were into December.

'Not on your life!'

'Oh yes we will. You can't wear that old brown rag Fröken Lundberg gave you, with the lace collar that's nothing but cotton. It's yellowing, too.'

345

'Well, there's nothing wrong with the cloth, anyway. The seams have been picked and turned since I got it.'

'Let's go,' said Dagmar.

Fröken Benedictsson, who had taken over Tyra Svensson's fabric shoppe had promised her a rebate on some material to thank her for having convinced the Öhrström sisters to give up Elfvenberg's Draper's and Knitwear for her. 'I owe you a discount,' she'd said, which meant nothing less than that Frida would get her material at a very good price.

Her fabric shop was one long, narrow room with a long counter, covered with scratches from the scissors and the brass-ended measuring rods. Behind the counter there were rolls of fabric reaching all the way to the ceiling. First there were the cotton goods at the very left, from the simplest at the bottom: twills and cotton sheeting and upholstery materials – she even kept cheesecloth in stock. Then came the shiny chintzes with their flowery patterns, the denim and corduroy that made the young fellows' trousers swish as they walked. There was muslin and batiste for night-dresses, and below them the pink and baby blue flowered flannels most people bought. There were various thicknesses of piqué for collars and trimmings, and then that voile all the young ladies were wearing. It was fine and light when they left for their evening dances, but it slapped unpleasantly around their legs by the time they came home at dawn.

Fröken Benedictsson didn't carry all that much linen, which was what Elfvenberg's specialized in, but of course she had linen for hankies and loosely-woven school linen as well as tea towel linen. Not many people still did their own weaving nowadays. In the winter the shelves of woollens were full to bursting, and there were huge rolls of English tweeds, homespuns, and dark blue cheviot on the counter as well. She showed them the nubbly wool bouclé on the shelf, that Fabiansson the stovemaker's wife had had a walking suit made from. Well, times had certainly changed. She supposed even heavyset craftsmen's wives went out walking, since they needed suits for it. Incidentally she'd had it made by a seamstress who'd never heard the expression 'tailor made'. The stovemaker's wife had looked like a big wobbly rice pudding waddling around in all that nubbly cloth, Dagmar thought, but as usual she kept her own counsel.

The shopkeeper held up camelhair wool for them. It was silky-soft to the touch.

'Just feel this quality,' she said.

'My, my, my, so dear,' said Frida, looking at the price tags that were stuck in the ends of the rolls. But Fröken Benedictsson pointed out that it was double width. Did they know that the new wife of Wessén at Swedish Motor had had some sports trousers made of camelhair? Trousers! That was right, with wide knickerbocker legs that finished with a broad strip below the knees and buttoned with covered buttons in the same fabric. However, she didn't have the slightest idea who had agreed to make that kind of thing.

The best rolls were all the way over by the window, and they were the thinnest, too, since silk-based fabrics take up very little space. Dagmar knew all their names: the stiff brocades that could make a heavyset housewife look like a walking sofa if they weren't cut right, chiffon that concealed rough arms, crêpes, failles and foulards. You could only sell organdy for little girls' pinafores nowadays. It was too stiff and rigid for the dresses that were in fashion. No one was wearing taffeta, either.

'But feel this one,' said Fröken Benedictsson. 'Just feel it!'

And it rustled under their fingers and it shone and shifted depending on how you touched it, because the weft was black and the warp was red. Shantung was also a bit heavy and stiff, and nowadays she sold it mostly for bolsters. Tulle was always very popular at graduation time, when many of the girls got invited to celebrations in Norrköping. But since Astrid's wedding everybody had lace trains. Well, mostly cotton lace, of course, that could later be used as a canopy for the baby's cradle, Fröken Benedictsson explained. But when you saw it reappear as kitchen curtains, it made you wonder how the marriage was faring.

These days nobody wanted a stiff, rigid fabric. No, the softest, shiniest velvet. And didn't feathers and fringes look nice with silk velvet? Quite a smart idea, really, if you wanted to make a skirt look longer, to add a fringe. Styles were just getting shorter and shorter. Which was terrible for people with big legs, said Fröken Benedictsson in a whisper, because a couple of other customers had come into the shop and she could only see the top halves of them over the counter. Of course there were plenty of women who had passed their prime before the war, and who still preferred long skirts. But you had to admit they looked peculiar on young women. Most people seemed to go along with the idea of wearing mole-grey stockings and shoes, as it was a more flexible colour than brown or black. And, as Mistinguette, the fashion editor, had written in her column, the contrast against the ground and the paving stones was minimized. But whatever you did, fat legs were still fat legs and there was really no hiding them, Fröken Benedictsson breathed. Frida thought she was talking an awful lot of rubbish, though she didn't say anything about it.

The supple georgettes that were so lovely, with sequinned appliqué, hanging so beautifully now that it was in fashion to let the fabric fall quite loosely and then sweep it to one side with a brooch. None of the young ladies wore corsets any more, everything was so loose and easy. Well, whatever your opinion, fashion was fashion, as Fröken Benedictsson said.

The shelf of printed fabric, mostly the Egyptian ones that were all the rage with their hieroglyphs and bird-eyed faces she dismissed with a little sigh that indicated they were the kind of thing a person had to keep in stock, but not really worth thinking about. That made Frida completely confused, because she liked some of the printed patterns, they weren't all hieroglyphs and besides they had prices she could at least imagine paying. No, said Dagmar and the shopkeeper, turning back to all the dearer woollen fabrics. They pinched and stroked, and crumpled and started holding whole rolls up to Frida with a couple of metres flowing down, draping the cloth over her shoulder.

'This one hangs nicely,' they said, and her face stared dully in the mirror over their heads. They were deliberating between burgundy, mauve and cyclamen. The worst part was that while they were talking a number of other housewives had come into the shop and although Fröken Bencdictsson did help one woman who wanted a little elastic and a card of clasps, she let all the others wait. They were just as patient as Frida would have been in their place, and they watched Dagmar holding fabrics up against her face. It was awful. What would they think? Probably that something had gone to her head. Finally she put her foot down and said enough was enough, she just couldn't afford this kind of cloth and they would have to settle on a printed one. Dagmar poked her in the ribs with an elbow to remind her of their discount, which couldn't be mentioned when others were listening. Fröken Benedictsson winked wildly for the same reason. Her face was powdered white and she had lost her eyelashes and eyebrows after a high fever. Instead, she had painted black arches above her eyes, and it was difficult for her to give anyone a conspiratorial look with those tremendously arched eyebrows.

Finally, when everyone seemed to have agreed on a cyclamen-coloured wool georgette, Frida simply had to come out with it and say that she would never be caught dead in red. The shop was hot and she had to sit down. The finishing sprays made the room stuffy, and all the lint in the air also made it difficult to breathe. Then Dagmar noticed Frida's hand clutching the corner of a grey-blue wool crêpe; her fingers had returned to it time and again. She had pinched and pulled, and pressed it in the palm of her hand several times, and it hadn't creased in the least.

'Is that the one you want?' asked Dagmar.

She was unable to do more than nod in agreement, nor could she even recall any longer what the price tag had said. But Fröken Benedictsson blinked and winked below her deep black eyebrows, and they took three times the length plus the sleeves. When they went behind the counter to choose the thread from the rack, Frida couldn't even get up. She had sunk down onto one of the high stools, and was sick of the whole business, didn't want a dress any more, but just to go home and to bed. The cash register rang noisily and it was all outrageously expensive, even with the discount.

Dagmar was off to a fitting for a client who was housebound, so she asked Frida to take the fabric with her for now and drop it off on her way home from the laundry the next day. Frida took it home to 60 Hovlunda Road and put it at the very back of the cupboard without removing the paper, as she was afraid the smell of dinner would get into it otherwise. She'd moved to the bed-sitter that had once been Tora Otter's, now that she was on her own. Not even Anna still lived at home. She had seen to it that the landlord fumigated the room and painted the wooden panels. It was greenish, and she had quite a nice place now that she no longer had to have washing lines hanging every which way, like when the children were small. The top of the dresser was tidy, with a lace doily and everlasting flowers and the photo of Eriksson on his confirmation day; it was the only picture of him she had. But she missed the children. The clock ticked so loudly; she'd never noticed it before.

That evening she took the packet of fabric out of the cupboard, undid the string and unwrapped it. It was nice and soft, the grey-blue colour so gentle. It reminded her of doves' breasts. And it didn't have a single crease. She held it up to her cheek, and it was smooth. At the same instant, she noticed the lovely, dense scent of the wool. It reminded her of the very first dress made of new, shop-bought material she had ever had. She was quite little, maybe seven or eight, and she had been ill. They said it was cholera. That was perfectly possible, because her mother sold sandwiches to the railway workers and travellers of lesser means, and moonshine when no one was looking. Lots of contagion and other strange things came in with the trains. She didn't actually recall having been ill, but she did remember her mother standing there in the grey light of dawn, running her fingers through Frida's hair. She was afraid it would fall out. It usually did when you'd had that kind of fever, she'd said. Every morning she ran her hands through Frida's hair, saying there were too many strands on the pillow.

'We'll cut it,' she said. 'Might as well. It's falling out anyway. Just as well to get some money for it while we can.'

Of course Frida didn't want her hair cut off. But she was too weary to protest and anyway she thought she was sure to wake up bald one morning. Now her hair went halfway down her back. It sounded coarse and heavy when her mother sent the scissors through it, not fragile as she'd expected. She sat stiff as a ramrod.

Her mother, whom people called Embankment Britta, sold Frida's hair to Fröken Linnman who made hair crafts. It turned out not to be long enough for a wig. She probably didn't get very much for it in the end, and afterwards she regretted her decision. Frida looked like an asylum child. Her mother got such a peculiar look in

351

her eyes when she saw Frida, and she often touched the back of her neck where the sharp, short hair was growing out and said:

'It'll grow back fast. You'll see, it'll come back thicker. Just you wait.'

But it took ages. Soon she was well enough to be out of bed, the fever had broken. She didn't want to go back to school, but she had no choice. She had to wear a knitted cap and the other children stared. They asked if they could peek under her cap like they looked at Valentin's cleft lip or stood in a circle staring at that dog down at the inn that had lost a leg.

After that she remembered her mother showing her a brand new piece of cloth. It was bright and flowery, in sharp aniline colours. Swedish cotton from Västergötland, maybe bought from some peddler at a market. It had a sharp, acrid smell. Then her mother made her a dress with a very wide, ruffled skirt that went all the way down to her ankles, and she used two thin bits of cane to create a crinoline. It was lovely. The big crinoline rolled like waves around her as she walked. She wasn't actually allowed to wear it when there was anyone around. She was the daughter of poor parents and the parish gave her mother money to buy them shoes and books for school. If anybody found out she had made a dress with a crinoline for Frida they would claim she didn't need parish assistance and just wasted it on aquavit and clothes.

She'd walked all the way down to the lake in her crinoline. The washerwomen working along the jetty did see her, it couldn't be helped. She went closer and closer. But she had no memory of their teasing her. They'd lifted and spun her around, shouting she looked beautiful. She still associated the scent of the lake and the sound of birds singing with fancy fabric and a sense of happiness. She also remembered her mother's hand at her neck, and her saying:

'It'll grow back fast. You'll see.'

352

Dagmar had begun looking for a pattern in her magazines, but that just upset Frida. They were so strange. She had been born in 1863 and wanted the waist to be where a person's body was narrowest. That's where waists had been in her day. She'd gone out dancing in a tight-waisted black skirt with an elastic belt, and a shiny black straw hat on her head. She'd been pretty then. But Dagmar just smiled kindly at her.

'Seriously,' she said. 'You're thin. You need a pattern with lots of fabric, gathered and with wide sleeves, something loose with a belt at the hips. And that's what's in fashion, too.'

'Over my dead body,' said Frida. 'That takes so much cloth.'

'Well, the fabric's already bought. Four and a half metres.'

'Oh dear, why didn't I keep a closer eye on you two? I got so tired in that shop.'

'We had to have four and a half metres because it's only eighty wide,' said Dagmar. 'Three times the length plus the sleeves. You wouldn't have been able to do anything about it.' Finally, they agreed on a model, but not one you would have recognized in the magazines since they'd made so many compromises. The next thing Dagmar did was to sketch it in pencil on the rough side of the paper from Tyra Svensson's shop. The unfortunate thing was that she wasn't very good at drawing. She needed good drawing skills in her line of business, but her sketches were hesitant and blurry, and she would pencil the lines over and over until the paper started to wear through. However, she was able to fill her drawings out with words.

The model for the grey-blue wool crêpe dress was: a perfectly smooth back with just a couple of little darts at the shoulders. The front would be taken in slightly at the top, and from there three pleats would run all the way down to the hem on either side. Tidy, pressed pleats. A fairly low waist – she shouldn't be silly! They just couldn't possibly make her a new dress that was completely out of fashion, she saw that, didn't she? A tie belt. Long, pretty wide sleeves gathered at the wrist to puff out over a band that was reasonably broad, almost like a little cuff. Dagmar would make a V-neck and a collar that was really just folded-back flaps. A white neckline insert, piqué with lace sewn over it.

'No, there's got to be a limit!' said Frida. 'Not another öre, and I mean it. I can't afford lace.'

'I've got some lace lying around. Lace and piqué remnants. I've been saving them just for this.'

'Oh, Dagmar, you're a good girl,' said Frida. 'A good girl.'

Dagmar began with the neck insert. She took a bit of piqué and lined it with a stiffish tulle. Then she would sit down in the evening sometimes, attaching the lace a little at a time. It was delicate and enjoyable work, soothing to nerves frayed by long palavers with her customers, and there was no hurry. The little stitches had to be done invisibly along the edge of the lace, and the lines had to be straight and close. The lace had a scalloped edge and a fan-shaped pattern. Sometimes she used to wish she could have concentrated on some straightforward and uncomplicated sort of needlework, whitework for instance. No puzzling, no altering for human bodies that seldom matched patterns. Just tiny, careful stitches, patience and an eye for regularity.

Later, she got out large, rustling paper patterns and began to alter them to Frida's measurements. Her big cupboard contained all sorts of patterns. She tied a strip of the fabric she had used to make up a dress around each one, to jog her memory. They were crumpled and folded from repeated use and she had to smooth them out carefully so she didn't get her measurements wrong. Frida wasn't there when she laid out the pattern pieces and it was just as well, for she would have been shocked by the amount of material it took.

She checked over the material before she pinned on the pattern pieces and found a little flaw in the fabric after all, which she marked with a pin so she could make sure it ended up in a pleat or a seam. She could have had something deducted for it in the shop if she had been more attentive. She ironed out a crease in the material and then laid it on her big table, pinned on the tissue paper and made a few adjustments so it was in line with the grain of the fabric. Then she did what she always did before she cut anything out, however much of a hurry she was in. She had a cup of coffee. It was a precaution. You needed to pause for thought before you took the scissors to the material. Once it was cut it was cut.

She sat drinking the thin brown coffee and looking down into the yard where the boys were hurrying from Anker's bakery with trays of bread covered with white paper. The bakers were shouting at them from the wooden building in the yard, the waitresses could be heard through the windows of the café kitchen. She had worked alone for so many years that she wondered whether she could cope with being with other people now. She was used to making decisions her own way. In the early years she had seen customers as superiors, rather like employers or controllers. But now she knew that it was mostly a question of how you handled them.

The scissors thundered against the table, cutting the fine blue-grey wool. She didn't cut out the front pieces until she had sewn the pleats. She had decided to make them twenty millimetres, so she measured them out on the fabric with a ruler and snipped notches along the edge. Then she laid the material right-side-up on the pressing board she always had up in the room. She folded the first pleat and fixed it to the board cover with pins. Then all she had to do was carry on accurately measuring, folding and pinning firmly. She dampened the pressing cloth and took the iron from the ring on top of the stove to test it first. There was a hissing as her wet finger brushed the surface of the iron. She did the pressing carefully, through the cloth, and then she held the iron down with the pressing clamp so the steam stayed in the material. When she had finished she had another little cup of coffee. The material would have to cool on the board in any case, if the pleats were to hold. She thought: I ought to think of my stomach and not drink any more coffee. But this is so weak. It can't do much harm.

When she had cut out the front sections, she took all the pieces for the right-hand side of the dress and basted them together, and then put everything away, wrapped up in the paper pattern for now, in case she needed to make any alterations. Frida came up for a fitting after she had finished at the laundry, and it was only then Dagmar remembered that she couldn't just duplicate the alterations on the other side, because one of Frida's shoulders was lower than the other. She basted the left-hand side together too while her mother waited, and then they tried it on.

'The colour's becoming,' said Dagmar, who had found ways to address people respectfully, without having to be too formal. But how thin her mother was! She had to take the dress in radically on both sides. Apart from that it really looked quite good. Except for the shoulder of course. This material was dreadful for showing up the lopsidedness, it followed her contours so closely. If only she had been able to make it in a looser style with more pleats, but Frida was stubborn. She'd have to build up the shoulder with padding, there was no alternative.

'Have you always had that?'

'No, the other shoulder started hurting. Strange, it was. This one went crooked though it was the other one that hurt.'

'But wasn't this the side you carried things on?'

Dagmar was right, of course. There had been endless buckets of water before the pipes had been put in.

'Well, we'll build it up with padding instead. It'll be fine, you'll see. It won't show a bit.'

Lopsided and crooked, distorted and askew, fat where it should be thin, bulging where it should be flat - that was the human body. A few were smooth and hourglass-shaped, slender, with nicely-shaped breasts and straight necks. They were your models when you were building up with padding and buckram, shaping with stays and tight-lacing, when you were shifting waists to make long bodies look short or lengthening them with stripes and pleats, making fat little calves vanish as if by magic with fringes and mole-grey shades. The ideal was a body as thin and straight as possible. The shoulders needed some breadth to carry the clothes, the bust should hardly show. Worst of all were wide hips and big bottoms, narrow shoulders and short bodies. That was the female figure at its most typical, and it was every woman's despair.

It so happened that Frida's dress got put aside for some days, but one evening Dagmar took it out and stitched the darts. She was a little unsure about the back. It might bulge. She had taken it in a bit drastically. Perhaps she should have cut down the whole back piece instead. It was difficult working with a body so crooked and so very thin, like sewing for a little bird's frame. Everything angular and bony would stick out and show.

She stitched the yoke and the shoulder seams. The machine thundered and the treadle rattled like a hawk's wings as it hovers. After each stage she pressed her work. There was always an acrid, slightly sweet smell in the room from singed pressing cloths and irons that had been left on the board too long, for her attention was always on the material. The wool crêpe was delicate, she noticed, even though it wasn't so very thin. The seam allowances were tending to show through, so she pressed the seams on a seam roll. Then she sewed the cuffs into the sleeves and stitched the sleeve seams. The sleeves were quite full at the wrist and the material hung nicely. She didn't gather the top of the sleeve with thread like a tailor, for she was a dressmaker and preferred to work with pins, lots and lots of pins which she put in at right angles to the seam line so she could sew over them. There were often pins in her mouth, or stuck into her blouse, and they tinkled against the dustpan when she was sweeping up bits of thread and scraps of material from the floor. She let the wide sleeve fall into small folds up at the shoulder. That would spirit away Frida's sharp shoulder line.

When she came up for a fitting, loose threads were dangling from the garment and she had to pin up the hem so they could get some idea of the final result. But it wasn't very good. Frida looked scrawny and the dress looked big. She stared shyly into the big mirror, probably not daring to say what she thought, for she said nothing at all. Dagmar went round her with a mouthful of pins and a bit of tailor's chalk for marking. She was staring with that concentrated yet vacant look she always had at fittings, which sometimes made the customer feel she was fading and the dress was suspended all on its own in front of the kneeling dressmaker.

The top of the sleeve was no good, too full. It would have to be taken in or cut down. The fabric puckered shapelessly across the shoulder blades, indicating the neckline was too high at the back, and the shoulders too sloping. Blast. The whole lot would need unpicking. She went on marking and Frida looked anxious about all the trouble she was causing.

The full sleeves gathered into cuffs were a mistake. The only things that were big about Frida were her hands and feet. They had grown swollen and gnarled. Now her hands seemed to protrude from the cuffs with no warning, drawing attention to themselves. The style made the wrists far too slender and the contrast was catastrophic.

The neck was cut too high at the front as well, but she could save that for the next fitting. There was something about the pleats too, something Frida felt uncomfortable with though Dagmar thought they looked fine. It clearly felt too loose. She had wanted a dress pulled in at the middle, with a fitted bodice and a definite waist. It was modern to have no waistline but she was looking unhappy and plucking at the loose pleats.

'Is it all right?' said Dagmar.

'Yes,' she said.

But when she came up to Dagmar's the next time, there was an anxious look in her eyes. Dagmar had sat up until long past midnight with the seam-picker and she had done all the alterations. It was an entirely different dress she brought out and carefully slipped over Frida's head, so she wouldn't prick herself if there were any pins left in the material. The fullness had gone from the top of the sleeves. She didn't look so very bony after all. It was more neat and proper this way. The cuffs had gone and the sleeves had been refashioned to be quite close-fitting and smooth. She showed her how they would be finished with an opening and covered buttons instead, the same buttons as down the front, of course, fastened through worked loops. She had already taken the buttons to be covered. But the best thing of all was that she had redone the pleats and sewn them over cords instead.

'Good heavens,' said Frida, 'How smart and well-finished it looks. It's too much! How can you spare the time when you've so much else on just now? I'll come and do your Christmas cleaning.'

But there was to be no cleaning until after Christmas at

Dagmar's. Once all the dresses were ready and the party season well underway, once they had fluttered off in their voiles and rustled down the stairs in their moiré, she would come up and help her sweep up the threads and scrub the floor. Then Dagmar would take a whole day off and lie and read. And then she would go out walking, far out towards Little Heavenside and breathe in the winter air free of lint and dust. But until Christmas there was no time for anything but pressing and stitching.

She cut the neckline of the dress while it was still on. Frida shuddered at the cold scissors against her skin. When Dagmar did a fitting for her, they were almost too close. It was easier with a stranger. She knew the smell of this body, so familiar.

It was the most intimate smell in the world for her, it had enclosed her at such an early stage that she had believed it was the world. That face alone, whose worn look she could sometimes detect in other faces, could hurt her if she merely looked at it. Let me be, she wanted to say. Take me in. Let me be.

When she sensed the familiar smell of Frida's body, it embarrassed her. It was too long ago. She recoiled from it more than she would have from the touch of a strange man.

Disaster. Fru Eriksson, the wife of the furniture shop proprietor, had discovered that she and the dentist's wife Fru Hagman had bought the same material. Fru Hagman was having hers made up in a similar style by another dressmaker. Fru Eriksson wanted Dagmar to try to get someone else to take the fabric. But the dress was already cut out and half-finished, so Dagmar refused. She was too tired to try to talk the lady round and her words happened to come out a little sharply. Before she knew it, Fru Eriksson went marching off with the pieces under her arm, and Dagmar had lost a customer.

That evening she was so tired she felt ill, and she had had too much coffee. She made herself a bit of semolina pudding, which was supposed to be soothing for the stomach. But when it was ready she felt sick and couldn't eat. She lay there dry-eyed and wide-awake, counting the days until Christmas. In a way it was just as well to have Fru Eriksson off her hands. As long as she didn't go saying nasty things about her, so she lost more customers.

She was so tired, yet wide awake and sleepless, so she got up and poured herself a glass of Fernet Branca, quite a large one at that. She didn't stand on ceremony either, just drank it straight down, and fell right back onto her pillow and tried again to lose consciousness.

Every now and then Konrad would buy her a bottle. She never drank spirits, but she did have a ration book. The lay nurse who had helped her the time she had an ear infection had taught her to drink Fernet Branca. Because it tasted of bitter herbs, Sister Frideborg regarded it as medicinal, and drank it herself with a clear conscience.

On Saturday evenings Dagmar would take the bottle out and pour herself a little glass. She'd sit at the kitchen table so as not to have to be surrounded by a roomful of half-finished dresses, the ironing board and pressing donkey, and her black Singer. In spring she opened the window and sat looking down into the courtyard, where the lilacs were blooming along the wooden fence.

Sometimes she would go out on a spring evening and pick Star-of-Bethlehem or wood anemones. She'd put a clean cloth on the table and set the flowers in a little jug, then pour herself a Fernet Branca. If she listened closely and patiently she could hear birds calling in the distance. She had a book from the Good Templars' library in front of her, and fingered its rough cover, which smelled just like the sulphur cream the librarian used. Dagmar read books she recommended. *The Tale of a Manor. The Charles Men.* Fröding's *Poems.* Occasionally something Konrad brought up. There was nothing she liked better than to sit at the kitchen table at dusk with her little glass and a book, postponing the moment when she'd have to light the lamp.

Although she never discussed it with anyone, sometimes she would reflect on her solitary existence. Professionally, she worked in the close proximity of other bodies. She touched them. But in her personal life the only other person she had ever been intimate with was Frida, and that was when she was very young. Even if she ransacked her memory she could never remember Frida having caressed her. Or had she just forgotten? Had she ever sat on her mother's lap? Had that thin, slightly wrinkled mouth ever sought her hairline, had her lips touched her throat to see if she had a temperature? Dagmar didn't know.

Many people had told her how fortunate she was to be a single woman and able to support herself. Although it wasn't easy going, she did have exclusive customers and a good reputation. She didn't have to put up with a drinker. Frida's old friend Ebba Julin had said that to her, straight out. And everyone knew Julin the brewer was an old swine. She no longer desired a man the way she had when she was younger. Beside which she would never have dared to expose her back to anyone's eyes.

When she was young she had spent a lot of time wondering whether any boy would ever care for her, and at one point she had decided to take a look at her back for herself. At home the only mirror was the little dark, spotted square over the dresser. One night when the war was on she'd gone in to the Cosmopolitan. She knew Tora kept the key in the creepers so Frida could get in in the mornings. She tiptoed into the back room and closed the draped velvet curtains. Then she turned on the light. She'd brought the mirror from home in her handbag. Now she undid the row of buttons down the front of her dress, pulled her vest over her head, and stood with her back to the big mirror and the little one in her hand. She stood looking at her back for the first time, and she was already twenty-one years old.

It was hunched. Even more hunched than she'd imagined. The vertebrae were outlined under her skin, and they made a bowed shape. One of her shoulder blades protruded. Her unnatural posture had made her hips crooked, too. She supposed that was what made her limp so. All right, she had a crooked back. It was narrow and fragile-looking. No one would ever care for her, or want to touch that back. That settled it. It was no great disappointment, she shed no tears. She'd known, really.

Sometimes she looked at children, wondering what it was like to give birth. She imagined it hurting so much she wouldn't be able to endure. She still remembered when Frida had Ingrid. It had gone on for hours, all day and all night, and in the end Dagmar had grabbed her coat to walk out. But Tora had taken hold of her and told her to heat up some water and see that there were clean sheets and towels. Frida's screams, she said, were nothing to be afraid of. And her moaning was just her way of getting air in her lungs. Didn't everyone groan over a hard job? So she wouldn't be going out, because she was needed and would have to stay at home. It might take a long time, and Tora would have to go to the marketplace. Dagmar remembered her face. There was a harsh, agitated look on it she would never forget. It was as if Tora begrudged her the option of avoiding all this. But Dagmar had never understood why.

All she knew about having children was what she remembered from Ingrid. Everything else was so blurred and long ago. But Ingrid. What joy had there been for mamma in all that pain, that exertion? None at all, as far as she could see. Just disappointment and a guilty conscience. Was there any point in having children? She didn't know.

All she remembered was how worn out Frida was when Ingrid was small, and that there had been so little to eat she'd become apathetic. The baby's bottom had been red with nappy rash, and she was always crying. Then Stella Lans over at the Ridge had taken her in and put some meat on her bones. When they'd been there to visit she had smelled good and been rounded and lovely to hold. But by that time there was already a barrier of guilt between Ingrid and Frida.

Worry, guilt and disillusionment – was that what having children was all about? And might there be a difference for people who were able to feed theirs? She didn't know.

She could see two images. One was mothers playing with their children and kissing them. She could see their joy in the chubby little bodies and healthy skin, their clear voices, soft hair and tiny feet taking quick stumbling steps. The folds at the nape of their necks, their straight toes, the spotless whites of their eyes. She saw mothers take pleasure in their fragility, as if they were children of glass, and yet touch them without fear.

The other picture she could see was of mothers who mistreated their children, boxed their ears, and beat them, mothers with harsh, stinging voices. She saw the war, the unending war. Do as I say or I'll teach you, Oh my God, child, what've you done now? You make my life a misery. The razor strap whined and the rod swished. Bruises, swelling, red eyes, dirty hands over faces. I can't take any more, do you hear, you'd better just be quiet when he gets home, what am I going to do with you, tell me that, will you?

But her strongest memory of all was the anxious expression and the guilty conscience that would show on her face when she thought no one was looking, just a look in the vicinity of her eyes. Was that what it was like to be a mother? Was that the mark of motherhood?

Frida's dress lay in the cupboard. Dagmar hadn't had a moment to devote to it before Christmas. There were frayed edges and loose threads hanging from it and if she had seen it she would have given up hope of being able to wear it on Boxing Day. But Dagmar knew that it would be a quick job if she could only spend a few uninterrupted hours on it. On the morning of Christmas Eve the last two ladies came to collect their evening dresses and one or two others dropped in bringing hand-dipped candles and biscuits. That afternoon she had to tidy up the worst of it after all, and Frida helped her. They talked about the waistline again, but Dagmar was tired and her tone grew sharp.

'And you ought to have your hair cut, you know. Everyone's doing it these days.'

'Over my dead body,' said Frida.

'Even Tora Otter's had it done. And it's nice having it short. What's the point of that little knob at the back there, anyway?'

'An old woman like me,' said Frida. 'I'm not having my hair cut for anyone.'

Then they went over to the Casino to Konrad and Agnes's for their lutefisk. But Dagmar had to go home and get to bed early, knowing she would soon be struck by the dreadful fatigue that always hit her right after Christmas. She knew she couldn't give way to it until the blue-grey dress was done.

She slept until ten in the morning. No one knocked on her door and it was dead silent out in the yard. Then she got up and cut out a lining for the bodice while she heated the coffeepot. She used some Jap-silk she had been keeping in a drawer. Frida's bony back would be less obvious if the bodice was lined. She basted it onto the material with tiny littlel stitches, barely catching the needle in the fabric so it wouldn't show. It was a good colour, a grey silk that matched perfectly. She had already chalked the hemline, and now she turned up the hem with a French seam and pressed it carefully so the turned edge would leave no impression on the material. She oversewed the linings onto the revers on the wrong side and hung the dress on a hanger to see if they pulled. Perhaps she should have interfaced it. But the pieces weren't so large, after the last fitting she had cut the revers into two shallow scallops, helping to emphasise their neatly rounded line. It worked well. They didn't flop. Stitching them down to the bodice of the dress would have been a sort of cheating she would never have countenanced. They had to be cut so that they lay as they should.

She made a binding from a new bias strip for the back of the neck, which they had had to alter again, and after that it was time for the sleeve ends. Just then Frida came up and was plainly a bit worried about how things were going. They ate together. She had brought some cold lutefisk Agnes had given her. But afterwards Dagmar turned her mother out, because it got on her nerves having her around when she was pressed for time, and her back ached. She was anxious not to let it show. As a break from the hand sewing she stitched the belt, and turned it with the help of a long, thin pair of scissors.

The worked loops on the sleeve ends would have been fun to do if she had been feeling a little brighter. She lay down on the bed fully-dressed for a while, but fell fast asleep and woke up in the small hours. There was no point getting up. Instead she set her alarm clock, and just after eight she started on the sleeve ends and now she could see what was missing. She sewed in a cord as she turned in the bottom edges. It matched the cording she had done on the pleats. It looked smart and well-finished and she was really pleased she had thought of it.

Then there were the ten little buttonholes down the front. She had insisted on those: no cheating with buttons just for decoration, even though the neck was so wide that Frida could easily pull the dress over her head. No, proper, worked buttonholes. So there she sat with the buttonhole silk. It was slow work. It was the sort of job that had to be allowed to take its time. The important thing was that all the stitches should lie straight and evenly-spaced, just touching each other but never getting crossed.

She neatened the side seams walking to and fro across the room. The needle plunged in and out, in and out, without her thinking about it. On the stroke of twelve Frida arrived, with a glazed look in her eyes and newly-washed hair. She had managed to borrow some long clips and had put them in at the front to make waves. Dagmar was doing the final pressing, very gently to preserve the fine texture of the material and not flatten it or make it shiny.

Now Frida undressed down to just her slip, feeling a little cold as she stood in the middle of the room. She had on her old black dress shoes because new ones were just too painful a process. It took forever before they were broken in and shaped to the bunions on the joints of her big toes. Dagmar shook out the dress and drew it carefully over her mother's head so as not to disturb the waves. It sat nicely on her shoulders, it hung well. Proper little worked loops for the belt to go through so there could be no more argument about where it should be.

Next she tied it for her, quite loosely, and Frida's hands fingered the ends. No doubt she would have liked to pull it tight the way they used to, but she didn't dare because Dagmar said: 'This is just how it should be.' Couldn't she see how nice it looked?

Loose and elegant, and then those ends cut on the diagonal.

'Yes, it's a beautiful piece of work altogether,' said Frida, and Dagmar guided her over to the mirror where she stood, small and thin, not knowing what to do with her big hands, since her handbag was over on the sewing machine. Her feet looked a little too large as well, beneath those frail legs. But her body was so wonderfully enfolded in the soft dress with its well-made pleats, corded and sewn into place. They lengthened the look, Dagmar said. Could she see that? And the shoulders weren't at all thin, no, just slender. Just think, you'd never notice her right shoulder! It was a miracle, nothing less, Frida thought. So elegant from beginning to end: the buttonholes, the sleeve ends and the neck insert with its even rows of lace, so invisibly stitched.

'Well, it turned out lovely,' she said. 'That it did.'

Then Dagmar noticed how the blue-grey wool brought out the colour in her eyes. She had never thought of her mother as having any particular eye colour before, but so it was. She had blue-grey eyes and her body was little and her hair was silky. Beneath the soft waves her face looked smaller than usual. When Frida saw herself in the big, full-length mirror she didn't say: 'I'm only getting older and wretcheder'. She said nothing, just looked a little embarrassed.

'Pity we haven't got a maid or two under us to deal with all this,' said Tora, gazing out over the sea of dirty dishes stacked this way and that all over the countertops and the table. That made them both laugh again, so hard Tora had to sit down for a minute while Ingrid filled the big pan they usually used to make sweets.

'There's a little Madeira left,' said Tora. 'We might as well have another glass.' Ingrid did an imitation of Franzon proposing a toast, his neck craned, his body slanting forward. Tora covered her mouth with her hand, but you could tell from her eyes she was laughing.

'Can you believe the parson took Franzon's galoshes?' said Ingrid.

'Of course he did – they were the nicest ones!'

'Are you calling him a thief?'

'Yes, but there's a different name for what he does, it's a kind of sickness. He can't help it. Madeira's really nice, isn't it? For drinking and for sauces.'

The windows were open, so there was a cross draught and the winter wind blew along the floor, conquering the apartment, metre by metre. It exchanged the air that had been poisoned by smoke from Franzon's cigars and the puffing of Fredrik's pipe, as well as the smoky candles she had put on the little table they'd used for an altar. It dissolved and chilled the smell from the oven where the roast had stood ready, the smell of the water the potatoes had been boiled in and the thick aroma of coffee that's been kept warm. She'd been stoking the tile stoves with wood all day and they were so hot she was afraid they might crack, but they'd still have to close the windows soon to keep the heat in.

Outside there was snow in the air, but it hadn't yet begun to fall. The stone angels under the gable of the roof looked down on the empty street, they hovered in the fog, their cheeks rinsed clean by the autumn and early winter rains. There were no more footsteps on Store Street. They'd all gone home. Fredrik had left with Jenny.

'Wasn't that a lovely fox fur Franzon had given Fröken Åkerlund?'

'Yes, he's starting to come up in the world.'

She fuelled the fire with some more wood, looking at the logs in astonishment, remembering that Fredrik had done the splitting. And now he was a married man. He wasn't sleeping in the next room.

Ingrid took a birch root whisk and scraped and rinsed the dinner plates under the cold water tap. She pushed the bits of food from the plates into the sink.

'The bride and groom are a little sticky,' she said, rinsing them under the tap as well. 'Have you got to return them to Anker's?'

'Not a chance,' said Tora. 'I paid enough for that cake!'

No, they didn't bake cakes at the Cosmopolitan any more. 'It's all downhill from here, Fru Otter,' her old confectioner would say when Tora bumped into him on the street. All downhill. To hell with him. Tora didn't miss him.

'Well, now they're married, anyway,' said Tora. 'And it's back to the grindstone for you tomorrow.'

'Nope.'

Did she have that much time off? Tora had to look at her. She had a funny look in her eye, and was glancing down, twirling a glass between her fingers. It wasn't time off, she said. She'd packed it in. Resigned! How could she hope for a better job?

'I think you'll regret it this time!'

Tora started piling up the rinsed plates, and putting the cutlery that had been run under the tap into a pot of water. She collected the bits of food from the bottom of the sink and added them to the pig swill, putting the pail outside the kitchen door so she wouldn't forget it later. She thought about Fredrik again, with a sort of amazement. He'd never had the stomach to wipe out the sink, never been able to touch the remains of other people's meals. And now he was married.

She scooped some hot water from the copper kettle, dissolved some soap flakes in it and swished up the bubbles. The water was so hot she could hardly put her hands in it. She put cold water in the rinsing pan and crocheted mats on the marble counters so they could drain the dishes there. She'd already laid an assortment of tea towels on the kitchen table: thin ones for the glasses and somewhat thicker ones for the tableware and cutlery. Ingrid would dry the pots and pans on burlap towelling.

'Just think of everything you can learn in a position like that,' she said.

'I've learned to dust,' Ingrid replied.

But surely she knew she was being unfair. Tora didn't need to tell her.

'I got to play on the spinet,' she said reflectively, as if she were really racking her brains. 'And I learned to serve. All kinds of things. She's kind to me. But that wasn't what I wanted to learn.'

'Go into service in a kitchen, then,' said Tora. 'And learn to bake.'

'According to Her Ladyship I ought to attend the home economics seminary. Wonder where she imagined I'd get the money? But that's not what I want to learn.'

'I see. So what do you want to learn, then?'

'Mathematics.'

'I beg your pardon?'

'I want to learn to figure.'

That silenced Tora for a few minutes.

'Oh,' she said. 'Well, that's useful I s'pose. If you're going to work

371

in a shop or have a firm of your own one day. Maybe you'll marry into business. You never know.'

'No, not that kind of figuring. I want to learn to figure things out.'

Tora didn't know what she meant.

'I suppose you're like Konrad,' she said. 'He's always had his head in a book.'

'No, not a bit like Konrad. He's always making things up and dreaming. I want to figure things out.'

'All right,' said Tora. 'A person wants all kinds of things. Let's get these dishes done, shall we?'

She hardly dared immerse more than a couple of glasses at a time for fear that they would knock into one another and break. She felt clumsy from the wine.

'I remember when I used to work for the Iversen-Lindhs,' said Ingrid. 'How Ståhl the engineer and Iversen-Lindh himself would sit in what used to be the merchant's study late at night figuring out how to get out of paying their income tax.'

'Well, well,' said Tora. 'So that's the kind of thing you want to be able to figure out! How to get out of paying your taxes!'

'Come on,' said Ingrid, and they both burst into giggles and Tora had to sit down and wipe her eyes with the corner of her apron.

'Such worries you have,' said Tora. 'Your income tax!'

Then she got back to the washing up, though, and turned quite serious. She said she knew as well as anyone what a heavy burden taxes were.

'You know what I do with my accounts from the marketplace?' she asked. 'I keep the books in that brown ledger. I write what I make in one column and what I spend in the other. But I don't really put down everything I make. I deduct a little. In case the taxman comes round and asks to see, you know. And I enter the real amounts at the back.'

'What do you mean?'

'The right figures. All you have to do is turn the ledger upside down and start reading from the end instead. That's where you can see my real income and expenses. Because I don't want to fool myself, of course. I want to know how I'm really doing. And don't you tell a soul!'

'But what if the tax man turns your ledger over?'

'He'd never have the brains,' said Tora.

Ingrid was drying the beer glasses they'd had their wine in. She held each one up to the kitchen light to see if there were streaks. She handed a couple of them back, because Tora was a quick dishwasher, sometimes a little too quick. The tea towel was soaking wet and starting to shed. She took a dry one and hung the used one over the stove. Now the dinner plates were slipping around, knocking the edges of the basin. They were easy to dry. The tea towel, part linen part cotton, slid efficiently round them, the plates with the green seagulls gleamed, and the piles on the sideboard were growing. It was nice to know they would soon be down to the coffee cups and serving platters. Then all that would be left would be the cutlery, and the pots and pans that had been soaking.

'These few drops of cream aren't worth saving,' said Ingrid, letting the cream jug glide into the washing up basin. 'It's been out for hours, too. What're you staring at?'

'We didn't have any cream for the coffee! That was what I'd forgotten to buy.'

'Yes, but I went over and borrowed a little from the Fällmans.'

'You borrowed some? How many times have I told you not to go borrowing?'

'I know.'

'Don't you listen when I talk to you?'

How she shouted. What a furious gleam she could get in her bright eyes. Getting a dressing-down from Tora could make anyone feel they were worth less than nothing. Ingrid usually turned away. At least part way. Closed it out. Let her voice thunder on.

But this time she couldn't. She suddenly realized what an affront this treatment was and always had been. She was worth less than nothing. Her face felt stiff, especially around her nostrils. She realized she had blanched. Her heart was pounding hard enough to burst right out of her chest. I can't take it any more. For a little coffee cream. I've had it. This is the last time.

'You never want to borrow anything, Tora,' she said softly but clearly. 'You wouldn't ever want to be in anybody's debt.'

She walked over to the sideboard with the cup that had been wrapped in her hands in the tea towel all the time, surprised to find she hadn't been grasping it so hard it had broken. She distinctly remembered having once crushed a glass just like that. The towel had got blood on it. Now she put the cup down very carefully.

'You think it's shameful to borrow, don't you? Not what fine folk do. You got that from those damn bourgeois housewives you've always admired so.'

'Me? … Admired? And don't you swear like that, either. You use more foul language than any girl I've ever known.'

'Right, and fine folk don't swear either, do they? Fine folk don't borrow – where do you think that comes from? Not Linnea or Frida anyway. There's nobody who runs in and out borrowing things as often as Frida does!'

'She can do as she pleases,' said Tora. 'But in my house nobody borrows things.'

'So you hold her in contempt for being a borrower, do you?'

'Contempt. You and your words. You're just like Konrad. You talk and talk.'

'That's it. And now we need to talk. Don't you think I've seen Frida, going in and out with a measuring cup, a cream jug or the coffee cup she borrows sugar in?'

'The least you can do is call her Mamma. And the least you could have done was say a single word to her when we spent the whole evening in the same room. And now you hush your tongue!'

'No I won't. Do you really think she needed sugar or split peas or whatever it was she was borrowing all the time? Do you think that's really what it's all about? You though, you don't need anybody. At least you don't think you do.'

'I certainly don't need to run around borrowing, in any case,' said Tora, turning her back.

'No, and you don't need to talk. You like it when other people borrow off you. But you don't want to owe anybody even as much as a nutshell, yourself. And everything about your life is so damn special and solemn and not to be mentioned. Nobody dares talk to you about your private life. That man who died – FA they say his name was. It's as if lightning would strike the roof if a person dared to mention his name. Don't say anything. Don't touch. Tora keeps herself to herself, she doesn't need to talk to a single soul about her life. But what do your insides look like, I wonder, when you've kept everything shut in for twenty years? Or more.'

Tora kept on with the dishes, her back turned, not saying a word though Ingrid gave her some openings.

'I don't think you've a soft spot left inside, either,' Ingrid said softly. 'I don't think it would cause you any pain if somebody talked to you about that FA fellow who died or your mother or the little boy you had to give up. There's nothing but rough scars. I don't think anything hurts. Never once have you turned to anyone else for comfort, pretending you'd come round to borrow a little cream for your coffee. You don't want to be given any help, you just want to offer it. People who help others just hover over the surface, do you know that?'

But Tora didn't answer at all. She'd stopped washing up and was just leaning over the basin, perfectly still. Her apron straps were crossed in the middle of her back, her head was bent forward, the short hair at her neckline standing straight up. Ingrid no longer dared look at her. She sat down at the table, hid her face in her hands and went on talking, but very softly now, aware there was no need to shout. Every word she said was being heard, and the back she could see across the room was unflinching.

'You don't know of any other way to be with people than when one of them is above and the other below.

You're all alone.

I don't know that I've ever seen such a damn lonely person as you. The others have borrowed a lot more than a little coffee cream now and then. They've lent each other their very best set of sheets to take to the pawnbroker's in a pinch. Borrowed sometimes, lent sometimes. Nobody's been under or over anybody else. Down there.

Down there.

That's how you see it. That's where you don't want to end up. That's where you're afraid to be. Just as scared as you are of contagion and of lice.

But it's worse where you are now.'

'You can just shut up,' said Tora. 'You'd talk yourself blue in the face. You're just like Konrad.'

'True, I've learned a few things from Konrad.'

'Well, you just go right on spouting off, then. But you can't deny you've needed me to arrange things for you. I'm the one who got you into domestic service.'

'I don't want to serve others.'

'My, my, listen to her! So what is it you do want? To marry into money? To win the pools?'

'I don't want to serve others!'

376

The washing up was almost done, and Tora ended up finishing on her own, putting the pots and pans away, wringing out the mats they'd laid the dishes on, hanging them up over the stove, along with the damp tea towels. Ingrid had curled up on the kitchen settee by the window, with her back turned and her arms wrapped tightly around her legs. She was thinking it had all come out wrong. It was so difficult to put into words. She should have spoken to Tora in a different way altogether, as she herself used to be talked to by Konrad. But she couldn't. If I could just explain it to you, he used to say. You forget when you walk around here, arranging things. But didn't you once know? We borrow everything from one another.

Everything. We borrow fire to light our way and to get warm. The very first night in a new place we slip shoes on our bare feet and run between the buildings, with nothing but a shawl over our shoulders, borrowing from one another.

We have to borrow water when our wells run low and then dry. Deep inside me there are strong springs. But I can only bring them to life by borrowing. You have to moisten the dried-up ground first. Then the water will seek its way up to join the damp. We each have everything. But we borrow it from one another. We did come here to live a life with one another, but how to say it? How to dare say such a thing?

It was snowing outside. The light over the entryway gleamed down on the gravel that was becoming spotted with snow. The flakes were large and light, and falling more and more densely, staring at them was dizzying.

'What will you do now?' asked Tora. Her back was still turned but now she sounded more conciliatory. 'Since you don't want to be in service any more? Will you join the factory workers? It'd be a pity your being all on your own in Norrköping. You're still so young, really.'

'Time will tell,' said Ingrid. She got up and pulled on her cardigan, starting to do up the buttons. Then she went over to the kitchen door and found her galoshes and put them on.

'I'll take the swill out when I go,' she said.

'You're not really leaving, are you?'

She just put on her knitted cap and scarf.

'You can't go walking in on the Eks at this hour! I'm sure they expect you'll be spending the night here.'

'Well, I'm going.'

But why was she in such a rush that she left with her coat over her arm? It was cold out in the hallway.

'Good night to you, then.'

'Good night,' said Tora. She would have liked to say more, but the door shut. Why didn't I tell her I've sold the Cosmopolitan? I should have told her. I should at least have told one person before it gets out and around anyway.

But it was very difficult to tell people that the café was too much for her nowadays. She couldn't go on. No matter how hard she worked she couldn't make any money at it, and sooner or later they would have been proven right. But she wished she'd told Ingrid. Still, she couldn't get herself to call down to her. She stood listening to Ingrid's footsteps all the way down the long wooden staircase. Then she heard the front door open, then the clinking of the pane of glass. Quite a while later she heard the lid of the waste bin slam shut, and she thought: maybe she'll come back up with the pail. In that case I'll tell her. But she didn't come.

It was perfectly silent. This isn't possible, she thought. She put her hands to her cold cheeks, allowing her fingertips to play over her lips, and it was like touching someone else's body.

What makes a person so tired? You just want to sleep. But then something starts fumbling about your eyelids, as if to force them open. It's night, and there's nothing odd about being alone at night. Even

378

people who sleep next to one another turn inwards. They turn towards their jumbled images and they are alone, no matter how tightly they embrace.

She went into her little room where her bed was made tight under the brown spread she was about to remove and fold. Suddenly she was afraid of her bed. So she went back out into the sitting room that was deep in the grey light from the street lamp. She lifted the candleholders and the bowl of Christmas roses off the drop-leaf table, and put away the cloth. The window'd been open too long. Everything she touched was cold.

FA Otter had bought the bowl she'd put out on the table that day. But she wasn't sure Fredrik knew it came from his father. She didn't have much that had been his. His tailcoat and his walking suit, of course. She'd saved them for the boys, because who would ever have guessed how fast they'd go out of style? But the fabric in the tailcoat was excellent, anyway. She supposed someday it could be remade. A pair of ruined shoes wrapped in newspaper. How foolish to save such things at the very back of the cupboard. A little sheet music with F.A. Otter written in the top right-hand corner in ink that had gone brown. Watch and ring, a pile of letters from his mother in Gothenburg. His copy of *The Tales of Ensign Ståhl*, and his collected works of Tegnér.

Well, it was no good to be thinking about all that in the middle of the night. Otter was dead. She tidied his grave every Monday morning. She never went to the cemetery at the weekends, there were altogether too many people. He'd liked pearl hyacinths, so she planted new bulbs every autumn. But now, in the cold room in the middle of the night, she suddenly wasn't sure pearl hyacinths actually were what he'd liked. They were nothing but words. Just think if she'd misheard what he'd said, or remembered wrong. What if he'd really liked snowdrops or crocuses? If so, he'd still had nothing but pearl hyacinths on his grave for nearly twenty-five years.

It was twenty-three years. Time flew. What was the point of grieving and not forgetting? What sense did it make? And what did a girl Ingrid's age know about anything? Or that wretched Konrad for that matter? At that age you just threw things away.

That was when, with no forewarning, as she stood there in the gloom with her hand on the tile stove that was just growing colder and colder, the memory of an early morning in the house on Chapel Street came back to her. FA Otter was dead. Adam was newly born. Although she'd already been up and around for three days, the bleeding wouldn't seem to let up. She sat up in bed one morning and felt a sudden rush of heavy bleeding. It came over her very fast, and she felt it running down her legs. She thought it would soon ease off, but it just kept flowing. She felt the warm blood just keep coming, felt it pulsing through her. She peeked under the counterpane, was horrified, and quickly pulled it back up.

'Fredrik,' she called out. 'Go down and get Auntie Lundholm.'

But he was too little. He just stood there in the kitchen door with a rusk in his hand looking bewildered and somehow wily. He honestly looked as if he were trying to fool her even though he was so small. His rusk was so wet it was disintegrating.

'Please go down and get her,' she said to Fredrik. 'Please! Do be a good boy. Mamma's not well.'

She tried to make her voice calm and cheerful, but it was too late. She'd already scared him. He went and hid under the kitchen table, she could see him in a sunbeam. Somehow she managed to get up and make her way to the bucket. She sank down over it, feeling its edges cutting into her thighs. The blood just kept running. My life's flowing right out of me, she thought.

She managed to reach the broom down from its hook and banged on the floor quite a few times, trying to get the attention of Emma downstairs. Fredrik started to cry loudly from under the table.

'Auntie Lundholm will be here any minute now,' she said. 'Everything's going to be all right.'

Then she rose to semi-standing and grabbed a towel, pulling it so hard she pulled the loop right off the hook. She stuffed it between her legs, trying to hold them tightly together. Both she and her son watched the towel go dark red. Finally Emma Lundholm came running.

She'd had to spend ten days in the hospital. Emma helped her with Fredrik and they let her keep the baby with her. For a long time after that she'd had to take the stairs very slowly, been afraid to lift a full bucket of water, and had to carry just a little at a time from the pump to the building. And when she woke up in the mornings it was all she could do to sit up in bed.

But at night a new kind of fear came creeping. She was afraid she was going to start crying about Otter's death. She was afraid if she started she'd never stop. She just mustn't. The air was cold outside her bed because she didn't bother to heat the place as much now that he was dead. She put more covers on the children instead. Then she just lay there rigid, waiting for the night to end so she could get up and work. She started baking at night, and that helped.

There wasn't a sound from Store Street. Nobody came back. Now her eyes felt gritty, her mouth had a bad taste, and her tongue felt rough. I suppose this'll be one of those sleepless nights, she thought. The kind you sometimes have when you've overdone it. It's not the end of the world. It was cold but she couldn't get herself up to light the fire. There was no one to complain, anyway. The kitchen settee was empty, as was the brown armchair underneath the picture of the elves dancing. Fredrik had taken his things.

She pottered, pulling down the window blinds, feeling the space around the potted plants to be sure they weren't in a draught from where the window tape had cracked. The big mirror from the Cosmopolitan gleamed in the light of the street lamp over there by the bay window where it was standing all on its own and where there was no blind. She'd had it brought up to the flat before she'd started showing the café to prospective buyers. She'd glanced in it during the marriage ceremony, and had seen the entire party and the soles of Jenny's brand new white shoes.

I'd imagined somebody'd at least ask me about the mirror, she thought. They could hardly have imagined she'd had the mirror carted all the way up to Store Street just to decorate the place for Fredrik's wedding, could they?

But nobody asked her. Nobody dared.

Not until now did she get a glimpse of herself in the glass of the mirror. She'd already put her teeth in a glass of water, so her mouth was sunken. Her hair was thin and cut short, a greyish-brown colour. She no longer plaited it at night. Once upon a time she'd had blonde hair and had curled her fringe, or at least wound it around her finger with a bit of spittle when she was in a hurry. The fluff at the nape of her neck had been fairest, and soft as a baby's. It felt like thinking about a different person, and she had to put her hand to her neck.

Now she went over to the bed in her little room and pulled her flannel nightgown up over her head. She stepped out of her bedroom slippers and kicked them aside, rolled down her stockings and finally pulled her camisole over her head, too. She had decided to go back into the sitting room and turn on the ceiling light again. She thought she'd stand in front of the mirror and examine her relentlessly ageing body bit by bit until she felt she knew it intimately again.

But when she got a glimpse of herself, a grey shadow, dark spots, her courage failed her. It was so late at night. She shut the door to the sitting room. She would do it, but not now. So she put her night things back on and crept down into bed, trying to lie perfectly still to keep warm. The retreat was beginning, and she realized it might be a long journey.